# Slow Comes the Dark
# Dark
# Volume 2
# Serendipity

Vic Broquard

Slow Comes the Dark Volume 2 Serendipity

First Edition
ISBN: 978-1-941415-66-5
Copyright ©2013, 2014 by Vic Broquard

This is a work of fiction. All characters, organizations, and events portrayed in this novel are products of the author's imagination and are used fictiously.

http://www.Broquard-ebooks.com
Broquard eBooks
103 Timberlane
East Peoria, IL 61611
author@Broquard-eBooks.com

Artwork by Crooked Willow Studios.

For Morgan and L. Ron Hubbard

# Table of Contents

# Chapter 1—A Case of Mistaken Identity

Life's a bitch, especially when you are a bitch. Sondra's motto was hand-painted onto the wall of her small, efficiency apartment above Blackwater's Bar and Grill, a sleazy pub in the Snake Town, that is, the slums, of West Port, the capital city and main spaceport of Virge-C, a decrepit planet in the outer rim of the spiral arm controlled by the Galactic Federation, which was run by the big corporations. Virge-C had only been brought into the federation some fifty years ago and then only because of its mineral resources, certainly not because of its inferior space fleet, most of which were rusting, lumbering hulks. The corporations promised vast new, shining, modern ships, but had been slow to deliver on their agreements.

The Snake Town got its name from its hordes of rundown buildings and derelict people, that section of the city of ten million where drugs, prostitution, and crime provided the taxable income for the city, whose officials allowed it to go unchecked since its taxes fed their coffers quite nicely. Against all odds, Ben Blackwater, twenty-three, had managed to turn an abandoned brick building into a pub of sorts, where drinks were cheap, as was the food. "It's a decent living," Ben told anyone who asked, especially Sondra, who lived in the tiny apartment above the main floor, next to Ben's quarters, which naturally occupied most of the second story of the rundown place.

Sondra Sofia Shelly was twenty-two. She and Ben were both orphans, their parents died in the Red Plague that struck during the Pelling Uprising some twenty years ago. At least, that's what they believed. Both were placed with the same foster family, the Rosenburgs, who treated them like human trash, all the while collecting the nice government welfare checks to be used to help raise the two, which of course the foster parents didn't use that way. Right away, Ben and Sondra began looking out for each other, since their foster parents never did. He considered Sondra to be his little sister; she, her

1

older brother, which is precisely what happened when he turned twenty-one. When he reached legal age, he was given his inheritance, a small amount, but sufficient for Ben to get a loan for this building and to make his pub. Sondra came with him and often helped by tending tables and cleaning up. The two were quite close, though not romantically involved. Neither thought of the other in that way, rather as siblings.

Sondra's schooling was marginal, though she excelled with anything having to do with electronics and the Internet. She took on odd jobs involving such matters, though she'd hardly classify herself as a spy or a private investigator. Her clients came via word of mouth from those for whom her discretion and services proved quite valuable. She at least made enough funds to support herself here in the Snake Town, which translates to a status of Extremely Poor, as far as the tax collectors were concerned. Still, she never had taken any welfare dole, as she called such handouts, and was proud that she hadn't. So was Ben for that matter.

She couldn't afford fancy the makeup or the nice clothing, dresses, and shoes of the other women who lived in West Port, the wealthier citizens of Virge-C. Neither could Ben. Both were very practical and frugal with their meager funds. Their drab outfits also announced to anyone who saw them that they were Snake Town residents, though Sondra also had one *dress up* outfit that would barely pass when she went into the city proper.

Staring at her motto on the wall while soaking in her bathtub, she whispered, "Yes, life's a bitch that's for sure." She was soaking and trying to work out whether to accept a new *job* offer. It certainly would pay well and for probably only a few minute's work. Still, it was illegal and that always meant trouble, particularly so since the target would be in the fancier part of the huge city that sprawled for many miles in this valley system, straddling the Boca River. Snake Town and the spaceport lay on the western side of the river and once was known as West Port, but with the development of the spaceport at the extreme western edge of the city some two hundred years ago, the two independent cities merged, though some said the wealthier East Port simply bought up all the property in West Port, dirt cheap or so went the rumors.

She'd soaked for nearly a half hour and the water was chilling. She'd not reached a decision yet and sighed, climbing out of her tub and grabbing a well-worn, blue cotton towel to dry off. A bit later, she looked into the cracked mirror above her small sink. *I could be attractive, if I wore the makeup real women wear,* she thought, rubbing her face here and there. The only vanity that she allowed herself was her hair. She'd not cut it since she was a little girl. Her light brown, thick hair fell in gentle waves to the small of her back. As she brushed it out, she smiled. "I do love my long hair," she whispered to her pinkish reflection. Taped to the top right side of the cracked mirror was an old photograph of her mother, who had very long, brown hair. Sondra had no memories of either of her parents, only this one, well-worn photograph that was given to her foster mother along with herself. Perhaps, that was the reason she'd never cut her hair and put up with the amount of care it required.

Mechanically, Sondra got dressed in her usual drab, grey blouse and pants, then slipped on her soft-soled shoes. Finally, tying her hair into a ponytail, she glanced at the only clock that she had that worked, in spite of its cracked face. Time to go. She headed down the stairs into the main pub area, spotted Ben, and headed behind the bar. "Closing time again?"

"Yes, slow night. Got ten tables to be cleaned and this mountain of dishes to do. Which do you want to do tonight, sis?" he asked in his rugged, bass voice.

Her mellow alto voice responded, "Whichever you don't want to do."

"Ah," he said wisely, "you must want to discuss something with me. You want my advice, eh? I'm up on your tricks little sister," he replied playfully, but from her flush, he knew he had guessed right.

"Yep. So what do you want me to do, big brother?" she taunted back. He pointed to the dishes, and she groaned but began to do them. "If you'd clean them when the customer is done, you'd not have so many to do at closing time."

Ben laughed. She'd told him that a thousand times.

"Too busy," he replied yet again. Besides, he was more interested in listening to all the chat going on when his usual customers were here drinking their sorrows down.

A half hour later, the two sat down with a mug of dark ale, the night's chores finished. "Okay, sis, what's up?" Ben asked, taking a sip of his ale, allowing its heady flavor to saturate his taste buds and his sense of smell.

"Got this job offer. Pays well, but," she began.

"It's always those darn but's, isn't it?" he jested.

Sondra flashed him a smile. *God, it's always those.* "Well, yes. It's illegal. He wants me to clone a phone—one of the Galactic Dynamic's big shots. It would be an on-the-street job, only take a brief few minutes. Pays well. Still," her voice trailed off.

"Simple enough for you, Miss Hot Shot, but you're right. It's illegal, and it's a CEO or such. They won't be forgiving if they catch you," Ben cautioned her.

"I know. I think I can do it without raising the man's suspicions. My client gave me his itinerary. I can follow him on the public streets. Still," she again fell silent.

"Well, if it pays well and you think you can do it safely, then what the hell. Do it. Those off-worlders are hardly trustworthy. Where are all those fancy spaceships we were promised? I think our leaders got took by the damned corporations. I heard they've bought up many older warehouses on the northeastern edge of the city. Why? God knows, but it sure isn't in our best interests," Ben rattled on. He hated the corporations, which seemed to be slowly consuming all of Virge-C, though the why eluded him.

"Okay. I'll do it," Sondra decided at last. "I'll case the location tomorrow and then do the job the day after. I guess I can always back out if I don't like the location."

"True, as long as you don't take his money up front, sis," Ben cautioned her, though he need not have. She always guarded her own rear—she had too and so did he. Life wasn't going to give them any breaks. It never had and probably never would.

Dressed in her most expensive dress, a light cotton, simple, blue one, but extremely plain, one that was barely acceptable on the streets of the wealthier West Port, Sondra set off to trace the route her mark would be taking tomorrow night, that is, if she accepted this new client's job. She headed east and soon reached West Side Boulevard, the main north-south street that paralleled the Boca River on this side, just as East Side Boulevard did on the other side of the river. Five great bridges spanned the wide river, joining these two wide boulevards, but Sondra didn't need to use them.

Although her mark was one of the corporation CEOs or higher up corporate men, for unknown reasons, the man wasn't going to be around the skyscrapers across the river and in the central square miles of the city. No, he would be walking along Plum Street, heading towards the Red Light District of northwestern Snake Town.

Sondra had heard that every spaceport had a red light district, usually very close to the port itself. The crew of these star-bound ships often made use of local prostitutes when they landed. While Sondra had never been inside a spaceship, she could imagine how terrible it must be to be so cooped up for months at a time. Shore leave must be the highlight of their entire year or so she imagined. In any event, West Port made a substantial income from this red light district, which formed the westernmost edge of Snake Town, abutting the large spaceport.

This early morning, Plum Street was a hive of activity, from taxis, to private cars, to trucks, to the fancy air shuttles that the corporations had brought to Virge-C, and to a myriad of pedestrians like herself. While most of those on foot were far better dressed than she was, at least she didn't attract any attention, which was her sole objective. She paused a moment at the corner of Plum Street and East Side Boulevard. To her right lay the Plum Street Bridge, while all around her large warehouses loomed. The smell of rotting fish permeated the air, along with foul pollution smells from the brackish Boca River itself, a river which was as rotten, derelict, and forlorn as Virge-C itself. Just across the bridge, the giant skyscrapers loomed tall, blocking much of the early morning's sunlight.

Sondra glanced at her map image on her cell phone. Her mark's proposed route began here. She assumed he must be coming from the metal and glass buildings, crossing the bridge here at this point. The line headed on down Plum Street, so she did so too, noting her surroundings carefully. If the path were correct, her mark would be walking some six blocks down the street. Mentally, she estimated she'd need to walk close to him for a block at most, so she had plenty of time to clone his phone that much was clear. Where to do it remained her biggest concern.

She decided the smartest approach would be for her to lie in wait for him at the corner of West Side Boulevard and Plum. A number of trash bins would provide decent cover while she watched the bridge, which was always illuminated with blue lights at night. Each of the five bridges used a different color at night, creating a rather interesting nighttime effect. Here, she could easily spot him and move out onto Plum right behind him, following along behind him for a block, before she'd turn left and south down the side street, the deed done. Sondra estimated it would take her an hour to get here and another hour to return to her apartment. Glancing at her cell, she decided to leave at ten tomorrow night, giving her plenty of time to get to her hiding place, well ahead of his theoretical arrival time of around midnight. Finally, she relaxed. The decision was made, and she headed for home.

"So are you taking the job?" Ben asked her as she entered the pub around eleven. The smell of fish and chips filled the air of the diner portion, preparations for the coming lunch crowd.

As she headed for the back stairs to her apartment to change clothes, she replied, "Yes, it seems simple enough, out in the open and in a reasonable part of town, by the Plum Street Bridge. I should be back in time to help you close up. Back in a minute. Gotta change." A few minutes later, she reappeared, now dressed in the familiar drab grey, cheap clothes most wore here in Snake Town, ready to help Ben with the lunch crowd that brought in nearly a third of his daily income. She'd spent a minute sending her client a secure text message that said merely, Accepted.

After supper, she again changed into her *best* dress. Then, she carefully placed two of her special phones into her handbag, but only after verifying they were fully charged and ready for work. One press of a button and the cloning process would commence. Why two phones? She never took any chances. She had one chance to clone this mark's phone. If something went wrong, she had a backup. Besides, she was slightly curious about just who this mark was and why her client was paying such a large amount for such a simple task. *Hell, anyone could clone a phone. It doesn't take brains to do that, merely proximity.* If she wasn't so desperate for funds, she might have paid more attention to the tiny red flags that had previously bothered her about accepting this job.

Promptly at ten, she slipped out of the pub and headed off on her long walk to the bridge area. The night was cool, and she wore a hoodie jacket over her dress, the hood pulled up over her head. In the dark, she looked like any other derelict walking the dark streets of Snake Town. That meant she was safe. Had she been wearing only her dress or even worse, some fine, elegant clothing, she'd be a prey to some thieves within a couple of blocks. Her hoodie announced to all she was a resident. No one robbed or mugged Snake Town locals. That was the unwritten rule everyone here followed. Besides, robbing a local yielded one nothing of monetary value. This was Snake Town after all.

Within a few blocks, she left the heart of the derelict section of town, her position reflected in the sudden appearance of well-lighted streets. At this hour, she would be quite safe and continued on her way to the junction and the bridge. Around eleven, she slipped in behind the trash bins, taking up a position where she could see everyone walking across the Plum Street Bridge. The number of pedestrians had literally vanished during the last half hour of her walk here. The streets were mostly deserted late at night. She waited patiently.

As the midnight hour approached, she spotted her mark coming across the bridge, walking briskly. Wearing a fine, black business suit, complete with shiny, black leather shoes, which must have cost him a fortune, the man seemed wholly out of place. Still, she timed her ambling walk perfectly, falling in step with him, though some ten feet behind him. Her hand slipped into her bag, pressing the two buttons. Her soft-soled shoes made almost no sound as she walked behind him. The mark took no notice of her. She was obviously only a woman. From her poor clothing, she'd be passed off as someone's servant woman, at least here in this wealthier section of the city.

Time seemed to slow down for Sondra, who kept pace with her mark, still ten feet behind him. At any moment, he might get wise to what she was doing. He could turn around and confront her, or worse. Anything could go wrong. Scarcely daring to breathe, she continued walking, though slowly the distance between them growing, a step at a time. The man had a wide gait, far bigger than hers. Yet, she dare not trot, for that would give her away in an instant.

As the end of the block approached, she felt first one and then the other phone in her bag vibrate slightly, the signal the clone operation had finished. As the side street approached, she veered to her left as planned. Nothing could ever have prepared her for what she suddenly saw coming towards her from the side street!

She saw herself walking towards her! The woman was carrying a cell phone in her right hand, obviously texting as she walked along. She wore an expensive dress, perhaps satin from the way it reflected the streetlights, but unlike herself, she wore flats that announced her presence as she approached the corner. She looked up and stared at Sondra, just as Sondra stared in total disbelief back at her. The stranger had the same light brown hair, wavy and extremely long, flowing behind her as she walked. She had identical light blue eyes. The only difference between the two women was the clothes they wore!

That revelatory glance was but only a second. From behind her, Sondra heard her mark call out, "The hell you are!" Ping! A muffled gunshot rang out! Sondra involuntarily turned partially and saw that her mark had pulled out a small caliber gun, complete with a silencer on it, which was why the gunshot sounded so faint. From the corner of her eyes, she saw this strange woman slowly falling down, her cell phone dropping onto the ground. Everything seemed to move excruciatingly slowly, as though time itself was dying. *Am I dying? What is going on? Why shoot her? Did he miss me? Who is she?*

Ping! A second shot fired. The woman's cell phone, now lying on the street, shattered. The mark's second shot hit it, destroying the woman's phone. *I'm next; life's a bitch.* Sondra thought no other thought. Then, time began moving once again. The mark's footsteps thundered in her ears. No, he was running away from here. She swallowed. *I'm still alive, but. . .*

She mechanically knelt down beside the woman who looked identical to herself. Blood poured from the woman's chest. Sondra had no medical training and had no idea what she could do for the woman. *Was she shot instead of me? Why?*

The woman spoke in a whisper, "You . . . you? Who? Never mind. Give me your ID card. Take my purse. Mine is in there." Her voice was just as mellow as Sondra's, shocking Sondra even more. "Give me your ID card," the dying woman whispered again.

In shock, mechanically Sondra dug hers out of her purse and handed it to the woman, who clutched it in her right hand just as tightly as she could. "Take mine. Take my purse. Be me," she whispered. "Take it and go! Be me! Take it. . ." The woman's voice trailed away with her last breath of life, her hand still holding Sondra's ID card in a death grip.

Shocked, Sondra took the dead woman's purse in her hands. Later when asked why she did this, she had no answer at all. It just happened. Sondra stared at the woman's face— her own it seemed to her. No, the woman had traces of makeup still on her face, residue she'd not completely removed. Her lips had worn a bright red lipstick. Her eyes still had traces of mascara and a light blue eye shadow, though some attempt had been made to remove them, perhaps in a hurry. *But who was she? Why? Why had she been shot?*

Sondra tried to remove her own ID card from the woman's hand, but she held on to it in a death grip that Sondra couldn't break. Just then, she heard other noises and decided to flee the scene. One thing was certain; she didn't want to be caught standing beside this dead woman, a woman who looked identical to her! Quietly, she rose, making sure her hoodie was in place before speeding on down this side street, not looking back. Adrenaline finally pumped into her system. She broke into a mad dash to get away from that horrible scene, though the image of the dead woman—herself—permanently blazed in her mind!

Around twelve thirty, she arrived outside the closed pub. No one was in sight and Sondra hastily dug out her key, but her nervously shaking hands almost dropped them. Only with an effort did she finally manage to get the key into the hole and stepped inside, out of breath from her long run. For a minute, she just stood there in the dark behind the closed door.

"Well, you're back. Got out of helping me close down, I see," the friendly voice of Ben startled her, all the more so when he turned on a light. "What the hell? You have blood on you! Are you hurt? What the hell happened?" he exclaimed, startled at what he was seeing.

"No, I'm all right. Oh Ben! Something horrible just happened. He shot and killed her!" Sondra said in a rush of words.

"Shot who? Okay, come on; sit down. Have a stiff ale. Tell me what happened, sis!" Ben insisted, an arm pushing her towards a chair. As she slumped into the chair, he rushed off, filling two mugs with stout ale. "Here, drink!" he ordered. Mechanically, Sondra did as ordered. The familiar taste of the ale helped bring her around, settling her stomach, which now believed that it was some kind of Gordian Knot.

"She was me, Ben, me!" Sondra exclaimed.

"Who was? How can she be you? Better start at the beginning, sis," Ben said, growing more confused than ever. What had happened to his little sister?

Sondra took another long drink. "It all went as planned. I followed him for a block and cloned his phone. Then, I turned down a side street, and it happened. Ben, it went so fast! There I was. It was me. Coming towards me, but it wasn't me. Ben, she looked exactly like me! Long, wavy, light brown hair, sky blue eyes—me, I tell you, she was me, only she wore an expensive dress, possibly satin from the way it reflected the street lights. I think she was texting. She had her cell in her right hand and was typing I think."

"Then, I heard a gunshot. Muffled. More like a ping. She took a bullet in her chest. Blood flew everywhere. She dropped the phone and fell to the ground. Slow motion like. Ben, time just seemed to slow way down. I turned a bit and saw the man with a gun in his hand. It had one of those silencers on it. I saw smoke coming from it. It was my mark who killed her! Then he fired again. Crazy. I thought I was dead too, but it shattered her cell phone into bits. It was awful."

She took another long drink. "He turned and left. I could hear his leather shoes. Running away. I bent down. She was whispering something to me. Ben, she was still alive! But I froze. I didn't know what to do."

"What did she say?" Ben asked, his face now white as a sheet.

"Ben, it was really weird, really weird! 'Give me your ID card. Take my purse. Mine is in there. Be me.' She was insistent. Ben, she was dying right there in the street. She looked exactly like me, and she was dying. How could I refuse her? What does she mean by 'be me?' Why did she want my ID card? She didn't even look at it, just grabbed it in her hand. I tried to get it back after she died, but I couldn't pull it from her hand. Like it was glued to her somehow. I don't understand, Ben. None of this."

Ben wiped his face, took another long drink. "She looked like you? How can that be?"

"Yes, that was the weirdest, spookiest thing I've ever seen. It was like I was looking at myself in the mirror. It was me, but not me. She had traces of makeup on her face, as if she hastily removed most of it. Fancy clothes too. But, Ben, she looked like me. If she wore my clothes, you couldn't tell us apart. And her voice! Ben, she sounded like me. My voice. Only she could only whisper, barely. How is any of this possible?" Sondra wailed and finished the mug.

Ben hastily refilled it for her. None of this made any sense to him. None. "Okay. Let's go over all this again. You met the mark and cloned his phone?"

"Yes, that went precisely as I planned, but I've not

contacted the client about it yet," Sondra replied.

"You said this other woman came up the side street?"

"Yes, I turned and headed down it. I saw my face—er hers—at once. Ben, I've never been so shocked in my life! There was me staring back at me! Her face is frozen in my mind! She had her phone out and was probably texting with one hand as I sometimes do. Bang. It happened so fast, Ben, so fast!" Images swept through Sondra's mind like some uncontrolled tornado. She gulped down half of the mug, while Ben sat there trying to figure out what was going on.

"So he fired again? Did he say anything?" Ben asked.

"The hell you are. That's all he said. Ben, did he mean— did he think she was cloning his phone? Is she dead because of me? Is she dead because he could see her phone was in her hand? Am I responsible for her death? My god, Ben, what have I done? Who is she? Why? Who murders someone over a simple phone cloning anyway? Why not ditch that phone?" Sondra began crying. *I've caused her to die. It's all my fault. He thought she was cloning his phone! I should be dead not her.* "I killed her, just as though I fired that damned gun!"

"No, no, sis. You aren't to blame, not really. He shot her. He's the murderer, not you," Ben attempted to console her and shift the blame to where he thought it belonged. *What does she mean? This woman looked exactly like her? How can that be? Twins perhaps. She'd never spoken of her birth family, but then she was only two when their parents died in the plague.* He couldn't remember anything from when he was two, so why should Sondra? No, there was never any mention of her having a twin sister, not from their foster parents. That much he felt certain of, if very little else just about now.

He then said, "So her dying wish was to hold onto your ID card?"

Between sobs, Sondra replied, "Yes. Why? Lord, I don't know. What did she mean by be me? Why take her purse?"

"Sondra, I surely don't know. Come on; let's see what she has in her purse. Who was she? Did you have a twin sister? That is the only reasonable explanation, you know," Ben suggested.

*A twin? Now she's gone too!* Sondra began crying

harder. If she miraculously had a twin sister. . . *Life's a bitch.* Now she was gone even before she knew who she was. Mechanically, Sondra dumped out the contents of the woman's purse. She had a wallet with her ID card and various other cards. At least the ID card provided a name and where she lived. Sable Lorraine Hampton. 1542 Plum Street. Twenty-two. Keys, makeup, and a couple of handkerchiefs were all that was in the purse. Not much to go on.

"She was my age," Sondra whispered. "I've never heard of her name before. No similarities at all—Sondra Sofia Shelley—Sable Lorraine Hampton. But, Ben, she looked exactly like me, and I got her killed," she added, breaking down into another fit of crying.

Ben sat back and finished his second ale, before refilling both their mugs. "That ID card thing has me puzzled. Look, if she is found with your ID card, they're going to believe it was you who was killed. As far as the system is concerned, Sondra, you're now dead, unless you come forward and explain everything."

"But why? Why did she have to be killed? What's going on anyway?"

"Damned if I know. Your client started this thing. We have a bigger mystery on our hands, sis. Who was she? What bothers me even more is what did she mean by 'be me' anyway? Her dying words, 'be me.' That's the wildest thing I've ever heard." He took another long drink. "You know, she probably saw you as herself too—I mean in that split second when you first saw her. She had to be as shocked and startled as you were, Sondra. And yet, she had the presence of mind while in all that pain and dying to ask for your ID card and telling you to be her. Sis, I think that is somehow very important. Very important," he added for emphasis or was it the three beers speaking. Ben wasn't quite sure.

"But why would she want me to be her?" Sondra wailed, now also rather drunk. None of this made any sense to her, but the pain of her loss was very real. *Have I an unknown sister? Was my sister's dying wish for me to find out about my sister's life? Could that be what she wanted?* The more Sondra thought about it, the more she felt that must have been what

Sable had meant in those last seconds of her life—for her to learn about her now dead sister. That had to be it.

"I guess we'll just have to pay a visit to her home and see what we can find out about this Sable," Ben suggested.

"I'll do it in the morning. I'm too upset and drunk to do it now," Sondra admitted.

"Go take a bath, and we'll talk more in the morning—first thing," Ben advised.

She put the things back into Sable's purse and headed up to her tiny apartment, more drunk than she'd been in a long while. She took a quick bath and fell into bed. Morning came far too soon. Still reeling from the confusion and shock of the previous evening, Sondra mumbled, "Coming, coming." Ben had just yelled for her to come to his apartment. Something about the news. Her head felt like mush, but she slipped on a robe and walked into his living room, where the TV was blaring.

"I'll replay it for you, sis. You're officially dead now," Ben announced in a teasing manner. She glared at him.

"This just in. Late last night, a Snake Town resident, one Sondra Sofia Shelley was run over by a truck on Plum Street. While authorities indicate her body was pretty well mangled, identification was made by her ID card." The news reporter moved on to other stories.

"That's all the mention that I get?" an annoyed Sondra exclaimed. "Life's a bitch! Ten seconds. That's all my life is worth, a stupid ten seconds!" She sat down and rubbed her forehead.

"Well, you have a few minutes yet. The police will likely come here this morning, probably wanting me to show them your apartment and maybe identify the body. What do you want me to do?" Ben asked rather worried about her.

"Well, I need to check out her place—find out who she was. Are or were we related? Ben, I just have to know. I got her killed. I know I did. It's what she wanted, I think. Okay, I'll pack a few things and get out ASAP. I'll play dead, until I can find out about Sable. Thanks for covering for me," Sondra said with a sigh. *This is so hard. I owe it to her. Her dying wish was for me to be her, whatever that means.*

14

She ambled out of the living room and began stuffing a few things into her pack. She still had the two cloned phones, but decided against calling up her client just yet. She had too many unanswered questions, the biggest of which was why the mark chose to murder her. Now she added another one. *Run over by a truck? No, the woman was shot with a silenced gun. How could the police get that so utterly wrong? What the hell is going on?* Her head spinning with unanswered questions and dressed in the same dress she wore last night, Sondra slipped out of the pub and into the bright morning light. She took a deep breath and headed off to pay a visit to the home of her double.

She traced her previous night's path and an hour later arrived at the junction of Plum Street and West Side Boulevard, where she'd first made contact with the mysterious mark. She shivered involuntarily, before heading west down Plum Street. All around her, well-dressed men and women moved along, driven by their own pursuits. None seemed to pay any attention to the site where the murder took place, only Sondra did, reeling slightly as she passed by that corner.

She hesitated a moment, checking once more on the address of Sable, before heading on down the street some six blocks, more determined than ever. She entered a zone of smaller commercial establishments before drawing close to 1542 Plum Street. As she approached the building, Sondra spotted a sign in front of it: Madam Sable. *What the heck does this mean?* Before she could even frame an answer, a middle-aged woman with bright red hair and painted nails stepped out of the shop just before Madam Sable's.

"Oh here you are, Madam Sable. I've been texting you. Your special order of nail extensions has come in. I know you were very anxious to get them on before the big meeting. Do you have time now? I can squeeze you in. My, you look, well unusual. I can't recall seeing you without your makeup and fetish outfits. Please, come on in. I'll get your new nails done up right now," she insisted, ushering Sondra into her small nails shop. Sondra glanced about and saw two other women were already here, getting their hair and nails done. They glanced her way but quickly ignored her.

Lilly ushered Sondra to an empty seat near the back of the store. "You sit right down. We'll have you all fancied up in no time. Say, would you like me to do your hair too? It needs a good washing, don't you think?" Before Sondra could really reply, Lilly began working on her. "So how come you are looking, well so ordinary this morning?"

Sondra thought fast. "Had some private errands to run. Didn't want to be so easily recognized."

Nodding knowingly and as though this happened every day, Lilly replied. "Ah, right you are. Say, did you hear about that poor woman who was run over by a truck last night? They say it happened only six blocks from here. Honestly, that truck driver must have been asleep at the wheel or drunk. Bet he was drunk. That's what I think. It's not safe for anyone to be on the streets anymore, don't you think?"

Finally, Sondra had a chance to get in a word, though she was grateful that she didn't need to say much. Obviously, Lilly was used to chatting away while doing her work. "It was really terrible. Did they catch the driver who did it?" *That should give her something more to talk about.*

"Oh no. Don't expect they will. Something about the cameras were out. Fine time for them to go out. I always keep my surveillance cameras in good working order. I know; there's not much to steal in here, just small change. We don't keep any real cash here, but I suppose someone could rob us for all of our expensive shampoos and conditioners and such, but then perhaps not. What would someone do with ten bottles, partially used? A year's supply?" Lilly chuckled at her own joke, and then tested the softness of Sondra's immersed fingernails. "Ah, perfect. Mind you, I'll be very careful to sterilize your nails first. We don't want to remove the extensions later on and find an awful fungus has grown under them." On she chatted.

When she finally brought out the nail extensions, Sondra swallowed hard. They were three inches long! *Well, I can hardly stop her from putting them on, since Sable obviously special ordered them. Still, why? Why would she want such long nails?* Sondra had no answers and continued to relax and allow Lilly and her helper to do their work. Only once had she been able to have a professional do her hair. *Well, this is a luxury, so I might as well enjoy it,* she decided. *The more Lilly talks, the more I may find out about Sable and who she is or was, rather.*

# Chapter 2—The Mystery Deepens

Around eleven, Lilly finished up. Her new nails were bright red and very long. "Now remember, they need about a day to harden up. So you don't be doing much until tomorrow afternoon. Here, I'll get your ID card out and swipe it for you. I sure don't want you coming in tomorrow with a nail off. That'll never do, not for your big day." Lilly chatted and handled the payment. Finally, Sondra left her shop and walked next door to Sable's place, her heart beginning to race, anticipating finding some much-needed answers.

As she walked up the two steps to the front porch, she saw a buzzer and a small sign that read: Press for assistance. *Well, someone could well be inside. She could be married and have a husband and children! What will I do then?* Panic swept over Sondra. She swallowed hard and decided to press the button. With luck, Sable lived alone and no one would answer. Of course, she'd then have to be extra careful of the nails trying to dig out the keys from her purse. While Sondra was debating how to do that, a young woman about her own age opened the door.

She had curly blonde hair and an infectious smile. "Oh here you are at last! My God, Madam Sable, you've given me quite a worry. I came by this morning to help you get dressed and your breakfast made, and you weren't here! I almost called the police and reported you missing, but then I didn't. Oh, come on in. I see Lilly got to you. Those nails look fabulous. They will go very well with your new outfit. Do you want me to dress you in it so you can get used to it? You tell everyone else to do just that, so I suppose that you do. Come on in. I'll get you all dolled up and then warm your breakfast up. I guess you can use it as your lunch."

Sondra panicked. The house and this woman were strange to her. She had no idea what was inside, or where anything was! The woman was well dressed and wore black pumps with perhaps four-inch heels. Sondra stepped inside and allowed her to close the door. Thankfully, she said, "Now you just follow me, Madam Sable. At least, you don't have any appointments today. Your calendar is clear. I just don't know what I would have done if a client dropped by while you were gone. At least, tell me when you are going to be out, please."

"Yes, of course I will. In the future, that is. Sorry. Something urgent came up. I had to go out on very short notice," Sondra tried to make up something that sounded plausible.

The woman giggled. "Things are always coming up with you. Okay. Apology accepted." She led her into a very elegant bedroom. Sondra had never even seen such a fancy bed, let alone the ornate cabinetry and bed, whose head was polished oak with a pair of dolphins carved in it. A canopy of light gauze was rolled up, but ready to be lowered at bedtime. For an instant, Sondra thought she was in some princess palace.

"Now you have to let those nails harden. I know. Lilly told me about that yesterday, so you don't do a thing. Let me dress you as always, Madam Sable," she insisted, much to Sondra's relief. She opened a huge walk-in closet. Sondra stifled a gasp, turning it into a swallow! Before her eyes were countless elegant outfits and heels, a wardrobe fit for a princess! She'd never even seen such fine dresses close up. *Wait a second.* She caught herself. *What are they made of? Plastic? Oh, latex and satin. Just what was Madam Sable anyway? Fabulously wealthy?*

With remarkable efficiency, she stripped Sondra and began dressing her in what appeared to Sondra to be a brand new red dress, tight fitting, and likely satin. She brought out a corset and began cinching up Sondra, who had never worn such a garment. "Oh, it's so tight. I can barely breathe," she gushed at the intense pressure around her waist.

That only brought a laugh. "Silly. That will teach you not to follow your own advice to your clients, Madam Sable. 24/7. That's what you are always telling them. Miss a day and you pay dearly for it, so I guess now you get to pay for it yourself." The woman laughed again, but added, "Don't worry. I remember. Don't fully tighten it at first. Do it partially and give the body time to adjust before you chinch it tight. See? I pay attention, even though you probably didn't think I ever did," she chatted gaily.

Gasping slightly, Sondra replied, "Thank you. I'm sorry if I gave you that impression. It's just that I've had a lot on my mind." Then she added, "Lately that is."

"Oh, I'm sure you have, what with that invitation to the Galactic Dynamics' CEO Ball tomorrow night. Heavens, who would have ever thought that these off-worlders would even know about you, West Port's Fetish Queen, eh? None at all. Sometimes, I wonder how those stupid men ever found out about you and the service that you provide to young women. Oh well, good thing you recorded all those sessions. That way, they can't argue that you didn't warn them and all that sort of thing."

She chatted on, but Sondra began to think. *So she recorded her sessions, whatever they were. I wonder where she keeps the recordings. I best try to find them and watch. Maybe I will find a clue in them. Oh, this corset thing is awful!*

"Okay, half hour is up. Time to get it securely tightened," she explained. With an awful lot of pulling and effort, she finally got the corset fully closed, leaving Sondra gasping and near fainting from the intense pressure. "See, you should follow your own advice and wear it all the time, even while you sleep. If you want my opinion, you had darn well better leave it on until at least after this fancy ball tomorrow night. Now, let's get you finished up." Before long, she had the finest black, seamed nylons on Sondra, held up by eight garters. After putting a white slip on her, she then helped Sondra into her new red, form fitting satin gown, which now barely closed in the back. Without the corset, there wasn't any chance the zipper could be closed. Just when Sondra thought the woman was done, she produced yet another corset, the outer one, in a matching red satin. Once it was fully secured, Sondra could not bend much at all, except at her waist.

At last, she slipped a pair of matching red oxford heels on Sondra's feet. Even though she tried to keep from gasping, Sondra inhaled. Their spiked heels were at least six inches tall. She'd never worn heels of any height before. "Stop gasping. These are your usual heels, Sable. Now then, you look fabulous, but let me do your makeup. Remember what Lilly said about letting the nails harden." A few minutes later, the woman finished up.

"One last thing, Madam Sable," she asked, as she was getting ready to leave, "did you want me to put your matching ruby earrings on you as well? Completes the outfit." While Sondra adjusted her hair, she nodded. At least, this wouldn't be a torture. Shortly after birth, every girl born on Virge-C had her ear lobes fitted with a small grommet, a permanent tiny disk whose central hole allowed all manner of earrings to be easily worn at any time. Sondra wasn't an exception. However, she never had any earrings actually to wear. The woman fastened a pair of heavy earrings on her, each one holding five rubies in a gold setting. Sondra couldn't even guess their worth, but it had to be a fortune. *Just who was Sable anyway?*

"Okay time for me to be off. I'll be back around five to fix your supper. You've no appointments today. I checked the black book on the hall desk. Just remember to take it easy with those nails. Bye, bye for now," she added cheerily and headed out the door, leaving a gasping Sondra still sitting on her fancy bed.

*Well, alone at last. My god, what was Sable into anyway? I have five hours to find out! Come on, up and at it, Sondra. God, I can't even breathe in this. Shit, I can't even walk in these heels! What have I gotten myself into? Life's a damned bitch! Slow and easy does it.* She started with the room she was in, searching it carefully. The clothes closet held two dozen different outfits, all nearly as elegant as the one she wore. She checked on the heels and found little variation in heel heights, all extremely tall, though the platform heels were taller and more striking. *Thank God, she didn't put those on me.*

Having found nothing useful there, she moved over to the desk and began going through the drawers. Bingo! She found Sable's last bank statement and gasped, this time not from the intense pressure around her waist. *She has a fortune!* The balance was a little over ten thousand gold credits. Beyond that, she found a note reminding herself that she'd ordered the nail extensions and an engraved invitation to the CEO's ball. She noted it began at seven tomorrow night. Beneath all this, she found a small ledger that indicated weekly payments of a hundred credits to a Beth Ferguson. *Perhaps that's her name. I'll remember it and see if it is. I wonder how I am supposed to pay her and on what day?* She went back over the last bank statement and breathed a sigh of relief. The woman's pay was being handled automatically each Friday.

Feeling a bit relieved at what she'd discovered so far, Sondra began exploring the other nearby rooms. Soon, she found if she took small steps she could manage in these impossible heels. The bathroom with its fancy fixtures spoke of true elegance, something she'd never known before. *Oh, cool it, Sondra. You know you have nothing to compare this to. Ben's place is the dumps.* The kitchen had newer appliances, and the smallish dining room had a nice table and chairs, service for four. Beth had left a small breakfast on a china plate for her. The aroma of coffee filled the room. Just now, Sondra knew that she couldn't eat or drink anything. She moved on into the outer hallway.

She spotted the mahogany reception desk and its ledger. *Damn these nails,* she cursed silently, trying to open the black book. Weeknights of the previous week held names of women and times, usually seven at night. Hastily, she flipped back a few pages and saw more names. Apparently, these women came by for something around ten times. Just what, Sondra had no idea. The living room had a hardwood floor, rather like a ballroom. A music console was up against the far wall, but there were some expensive furniture around one side, sofas, and lounges as well. She moved on and found the back study. Here, her heart skipped a beat. A laptop computer sat prominently on the small desk. Bookshelves contained numerous books and fashion magazines, many showing gorgeous women dolled up similar to her. She glanced at some of the titles. Most contained the word *fetish* in some manner. *Fetish Queen. So Sable was a fetish queen. What the hell is that?* Sondra couldn't answer that question. She had no idea at all.

However, the computer was something else again. For

the first time since she entered this house, Sondra felt at home. Computers and electronics—those were her specialties, if she cared to tell anyone, which she didn't. Only Ben knew what an expert she actually was with them. Shortly, she fired it up, but needed a password. On a hunch and again cursing the long nails, she typed in Fetish Queen. Bingo, the computer finished booting up. "So much for a secure password, Sable," she explained to the air around her. "Let's see what you have here."

The first thing she uncovered was the voluminous recorded private sessions Sable held with her clients. She opened one and watched the video. Quickly, she saw that Sable made her living by teaching young women how to be elegant, fashionable women, wearing fetish apparel, or these extreme heels. Sable was saying, "No Marge. Yes, you are taking small steps. That part is right. However, you want to swing each foot over past the other foot as you step forward. That motion will really swivel your hips. Here, watch my hips." Sable then moved gracefully across the hardwood floor of her living room. Sondra watched, enchanted both by the vitally necessary tips she realized she needed just to get by while wearing this outfit, and more importantly how close she felt she was getting to Sable, who could well be her identical twin sister!

Tears welled up in her eyes, but even though she'd never worn much makeup, she had seen what watering eyes did to other women who did. Hence, she continually suppressed her swelling grief. Time flew by, as she watched this woman educating these younger women, all the while looking just like she now did, even more so now, since Sondra couldn't tell the difference between the dead woman and herself. *That isn't entirely true;* she corrected her thought. *I'm more like a fish out of water, clumsy and nervous, while Sable moves about with the grace of a natural born dancer! I have a whole lot to learn and learn quickly.*

Just then, the disposable cell phone of Sable's sounded back in the bedroom. A text message arrived. It took Sondra several minutes to return to the bedroom to fetch the phone. "I sure can't move fast in this outfit," she declared, gasping as she retrieved the phone and opened it up to see the message.

It read: Did u get it last night?

*Get what? Hell, what was Sable doing out there?* She sighed, knowing she had no clue. *What do I do now? The text is coming from Sandy, whoever that is. I can do some sleuthing and find out I suppose. Should I answer it? If so, what the hell do I say? Sable is dead. I saw her shot.*

After a minute and once more cursing the long nails, Sondra typed a reply. No. Got interrupted by the truck running over that woman. After hitting Send, she waited. What would this Sandy person say next? *God, I hope she gives me something to go on.* While she was waiting for Sandy's reply, she quickly checked what else was still in the phone's memory. All she found was an address. Apparently, Sable had erased everything else, assuming she'd used the phone before. The phone buzzed again, startling Sondra from her musing.

The text read: Sit tight 4 now. Will txt u l8r. *So much for that exchange,* Sondra thought, and headed back to the computer, this time bringing the purse and phone with her. She was still watching some of the recorded sessions when Beth arrived, letting herself in.

"Hi ya. Busy day at the Academy. Now I have an impossible Web assignment to do by this weekend. Worse, I've no idea how to do it. I know. I should pay more attention in class. But why do art and music majors have to take a Web course? I'm not going to make web pages," Beth complained, heading for the kitchen and not really expecting Madam Sable to reply.

Slowly, Sondra followed her. "Beth?" she asked tentatively testing her theory of the woman's name. Beth turned around, holding a head of lettuce in one hand. "I'm sorry I've not paid much attention to you lately. I've been rather preoccupied with my own things. So you are going to the Academy, right?"

"Duh? Yeh. Of course. That's why I'm working part time for you, silly. Damned expensive."

"Oh," Sondra said rather surprised. An idea just popped into her head. "Beth, I've a confession to make. It's about last night," she began hesitantly. Suddenly, Beth was all ears. She put down the head of lettuce and the large knife she'd just

24

picked up. Stiffly, Sondra sat down and swallowed again.

"You see, something happened to me last night. I remember being near where that poor woman was run over by the truck. Someone came up behind me and hit me on the back of my head, knocking me out. I woke up around dawn. I was just lying there in the street. I still had my purse. I checked. I wasn't robbed or raped or well anything that I could tell. But," she paused for dramatic effect, "but I couldn't remember anything, not my name or anything. I found my ID card in my purse and my address was on it. So I headed home."

"Oh my God, Madam Sofia! Did you report it to the police?" Beth exclaimed, her voice full of concern, at least Sondra thought Beth was expressing honest concern.

"No, what could I say? Nothing was taken. I wasn't hurt, not really. So I walked home. Thank goodness, Lilly spotted me when I drew close and ushered me into her salon, fixing my nails and washing my hair. Bit by bit, memories are returning. This morning, I couldn't remember your name, but this evening at least that much more has come back. Beth, this is scaring me—not remembering much—who I am—what I am supposed to be doing. I can't remember what I was doing out there last night or why I even went out."

"I'm so sorry, Madam Sofia. This is just terrible. You should go to the doctor or the hospital," Beth replied. "Concussion maybe."

"No. I thought so early this morning, but my head doesn't hurt any more. If I had a concussion, I would think my head would still hurt, and it doesn't, but I'll go if I start having headaches or dizziness. No, what is truly frightening, Beth, is I can't remember things, things I should know. Like you. Am I paying you enough? Am I over working you?"

Beth laughed. "No silly. You're overpaying me, if anything. I'm here weekday mornings and early evenings. I make your breakfasts and suppers, but on the weekends, you fend for yourself. Honestly, though, I have no idea how you manage. About the only thing I've seen you cook, successfully that is, is a cup of tea from a tea bag." Both women chuckled.

"I'm that bad eh?" Sondra added. Beth nodded.

After a pause and while watching Beth cut up the lettuce, she asked, "Beth, do I have any relatives that I should notify? About my memory loss, I mean. I can't remember if I'm even married. God, I hope not."

Beth laughed. "No, your aren't married. No boyfriends I've ever seen. You are an very private person, and you've never mentioned any relatives, to me anyway. I don't think you should see any clients for a couple of weeks, until your memory comes back."

"Good idea. I did find some of the sessions that I recorded. They seemed somewhat familiar, but not entirely. This is awful, Beth, not being able to remember the simple, normal things."

"I can't imagine how you must feel. Oh, I do all of your booking of clients, so I won't book any until you get your memory back. How's that?" Beth suggested.

"Oh that would be very helpful." Sondra laughed and added, "The clients might end up teaching me." Both women chuckled.

While Beth made them their dinner, Sondra pumped her for other details of Sofia's life, but learned nothing of importance. So she asked about this formal CEO ball she was supposed to go to tomorrow night.

"Oh that. Yes, you were extremely surprised at the invitation. All that you are aware of—well, all that you told me anyway—was that you were supposed to go all dolled up in your fetish outfit. Something about showing other women your fancy, seductive style. That's about it. Not much to go on, is it?" Beth answered.

"No, it isn't. Say, do I usually take a taxi when I go out or do I have my own car?"

"A taxi. The number is in your cell phone and on the first page of the black book."

"Thanks." She could think of nothing else to question Beth about, and the two chatted while Beth fixed supper and ate. After that, Beth helped her change into a nightgown, though she still wore the tight inner corset. Her oxfords were exchanged for slip-on mules. That done, Beth departed, reminding her that she'd be back around seven in the morning.

Alone again, Sondra called up Ben to report in. "So what have you found out?" Ben asked, holding the phone against his shoulder while tending bar. "The police came by and took a look at your apartment, but they didn't say much."

Quickly, Sondra relayed what she'd learned about Sofia, along with the fact that she had ten thousand in her bank account and that she was to attend a fancy CEO Ball tomorrow night, dressed as a fetish queen, though she had to explain what that was to him. Until now, neither had ever even heard of such. "Well, you be extra careful. That man is dangerous, sis. If he murdered Sofia over something as simple as cloning a cell phone, he'll be even more ruthless if—well, you know what I mean," Ben cautioned. "Gotta go. Busy night."

Sondra hung up and headed back to the computer to see what else she could find on it. Clues. She desperately needed something to go on if she had any chance of unraveling what had happened to Sofia. *Maybe it really is my fault she was murdered,* she sighed. *It's damned hard to get that notion out of my mind. After all, I did clone that man's phone, not Sofia—she just appeared on the side street, probably texting someone. If only he hadn't destroyed her phone, maybe I could get a clue from it.*

She got out all her accumulated phones. She had one disposable cell of Sable's, another normal cell of Sable's, her own cell, and the two disposable ones which were now clones of the "mark" who murdered Sable in cold blood. "I wonder what is on the cloned phones?" she muttered. She had been too harried since the shooting even to look at what she'd gotten on the cloned cell phones. Just as she was about to examine them, Sable's disposable cell vibrated. A new text message appeared. She inhaled sharply as she read it: Get out of your house now! Gunmen are coming to kill you. Txt more l8tr. Get out!

"Shit!" Sondra exclaimed. She stuffed all the phones into her purse. With only her nightgown on and this damned corset, Sondra knew she couldn't flee quickly. *Life's a bitch,* she thought, but then an idea popped into her head. Hastily, she jotted a note to Beth on a blank computer paper, sticking in on top of the black book on the entryway reception table. It read: Beth. Had to go out. Left lights on for you. Later, Sable.

As fast as she could move in the tall mules, she and her purse headed to the fancy bedroom. There, she stepped into the walk-in closet and moved back into the far corner, hiding behind racks of fetish gowns. Now she waited. *I know the front door is locked, but that's not likely to stop them. Who wants to kill me, or Sable rather? How did this Sandy person know about the gunmen? What is going on anyway?* Sondra had no answers and had to content herself with merely asking the questions while she waited silently in the closet.

Time more or less froze for her. She didn't have a watch, and the room was dark. Straining her ears, she eventually thought she heard someone at the front door. She imagine them using lock picks to undo the lock. It was a simple one, and she'd picked locks like it twice before. Voices. Men's voices. Muttering something. Yes, she picked out two men, probably reading the fake note to Beth; at least, she prayed that was what they were discussing. Sondra kept still and crossed her fingers. Footsteps. Yes, they were moving around the home. *Can't muffle hard soles on that hardwood floor.* Then, she heard someone stepping into the bedroom. The lights turned on, and she imagined the gunman looking about for her, verifying that she wasn't in the house. Holding her breath as though even the sound of breathing might give her location away, Sondra stood as still as a statue, frozen inside the clothes closet.

Off went the light. Out went Sondra's breath. *It worked! My God, it worked,* she thought as the rush of adrenaline swept through her body. She heard the front door close and finally relaxed, though she waited quite some time before stepping out of her hiding place. Quietly, she darted about the home, verifying the men were in fact gone. Finding no signs of them, Sondra finally relaxed.

Too wound up to sleep just yet, she texted the mysterious Sandy, thanking her for the warning and that she had eluded them. Then, she decided to see what was on the cell phone of the man who killed Sable. A bit of reverse engineering with the phone's Simm card and she had a name:

Rodrigo Vegas. The name sounds off-world to me, like I've heard those kind of names before, the newcomers, she thought. The phone was registered to Galactic Dynamics, the huge off-world corporation that had relatively recently come to Virge-C and was slowly buying up all available property.

She sat back wondering why someone from Galactic Dynamics wanted Sable dead or if she had been the target because she'd cloned his phone. Sondra still had no rational answer. The day of the killing, this Rodrigo received six phone calls from another unlisted number, probably another burner phone. Looking over the call list, she spotted Rodrigo calling that number back around eleven that night, probably right after he murdered Sable! That, she found interesting, though it gave her no real clues. He'd not made any further calls after that nor had he received any. No texts either. Possibly, he'd dumped that phone, she concluded, though she continued to check for new calls and texts for the next week. *Well,* Sondra concluded, *this phone wasn't used to arrange the gunmen to come here tonight.*

"Wake up sleepyhead," the youthful voice of Beth roused Sondra. After her tinkering with the cloned phones, the adrenaline rush was gone, and she'd finally gotten to sleep; only now it must be morning. Oh how she wanted to sleep in. Sondra moaned and got up, wishing she'd gotten more sleep. "The big CEO Ball is tonight. You certainly want to look your best," Beth rattled on, efficiently going about getting Sondra dressed up in the new red satin dress once more. After Beth departed for her classes, she again practiced her walking, particularly crossing each foot in front of the other as she walked, swiveling her hips rather seductively. The day passed quickly.

After a light supper, Beth's final touches on her appearance, and with a nervous stomach, Sondra climbed into the waiting taxi. "Galactic Dynamics headquarters, please," she notified the driver, settled back, and tried to calm her nerves. She had no idea what to expect, why she was invited, or what might be expected of her. Still Sondra's curiosity would not let her decline the invitation. Sable was supposed to go to this ball, so there was some chance she might learn more about the woman.

# Chapter 3—The CEO Ball

"Madam Sable Hampton," a tuxedo-clad older man announced, presenting her to the well-packed room. She'd been directed to the second floor's ballroom and had handed her invitation to the doorman. As she peered into the elegant and spacious ballroom complete with hardwood floors that reflected the ten giant chandeliers hanging from the twelve-foot tall ceiling, Sondra saw perhaps a hundred very well dressed men and women. A few she recognized from newscasts, local heads of Virge-C companies, such as Mr. Marshal Tucker of Aerostar Engines and Mr. Sam Decker of Rosewood Homecare, but many were definitely off-worlders, including the host of the party, Mr. Diego de la Vasco, the head of Galactic Dynamics.

Uniformly, the men all wore expensive, black tuxedos, rather boring she thought. The women wore various party gowns, adding a rainbow of color to the gala affair. Many wore elaborate earrings and jewelry, denoting their wealth and the importance of their husbands, for the most part. Few women actually ran Virge-C companies, the larger ones, that is.

Quite unexpectedly, Diego quickly strode over to her, taking her arm in his. "Ah, Madam Sable, so very good of you to come. I heard a rumor you might not. I am so glad you could make this formal ball. Besides getting to dance with all the most eligible bachelors on Virge-C, you will complete our display of the most ultimate in feminine beauty. Come. Let me introduce you to your four other competitors." He urged her towards the back of the room, while the throng gave way and stared at her in her fancy fetish outfit. Many whispered among themselves, but Sondra focused her attention on walking as gracefully as possible in the impossible heels.

"I didn't know this was a competition," she whispered.

He chuckled, "None did, except for my wife, Luisa. Allow me to explain, Madam Sable. You see, we are trying to establish precisely what constitutes the absolute ultimate in feminine beauty. Back on my world of 9-Gamma-C, we have

31

long ago agreed upon just what that ultimate is. My wife, Luisa, is highly honored to be one such woman. Note I *am* trying to be quite fair in this competition. I have judges from your world and from mine here tonight; each one will be appraising each of you five candidates. It is our wish that we can come to some agreement as to that ultimate." He then added, "Please, I would like very much to discuss another matter with you later this evening before you leave."

"Of course, Mr. De la Vasco. Did I say that right? We're not too up on your off-worlder's names," Sondra asked. She couldn't help but signal to him that she too wasn't happy with the surprise competition, as well as the ever-growing presence of so many foreigners on her world.

"Yes, just Diego, please, Madam Sable," he replied. She detected a twinge of covertness in his voice. "Ah, here she is, most elegant ladies, the fifth candidate for the contest." She stood gaping before four other beautiful women, only one did she recognize, but that wasn't the reason she stared. No, it was the two obviously off-world women that caused her to react visibly. Neither had arms.

Either Diego couldn't see her shocked face or he didn't care. "Madam Sable Hampton, this is my charming wife, a true UFB woman, Luisa de la Vasco." Before her was a tall stunning woman, who had thick, lush, shiny black hair that fell to her knees. Her face was round and angelic, with thick lips, and long black eyelashes. Her breasts were perhaps the largest Sondra had ever seen, at least as large as her head. Her tight corseted waist stood in stark contrast to her bosom and hips. Her gown was a shiny blue sea of perhaps satin, shimmering in the ballroom lights. Her feet, Sondra noticed, were somehow misshaped. She was standing on the flat of her toes, but her heel was arched high above them, as though someone had cracked the arch of her foot in half. A tiny spiked heel rested on the floor perhaps a half-inch behind the back of her toes, but her black nylons were nearly identical to those that Sondra wore.

"So very pleased to meet you at long last, Madam Sable. We've heard so very much about you and your fetish style. I must say I am in love with your dress, most delightful. Later, you simply must tell me where I can find such fabulous dresses. Diego dear, you make sure that you find out for me, won't you?" she batted her long lashes at him, and he smiled approvingly.

"And this is Mrs. Juanita los Santos, the wife of my second in command." She looked very much like Luisa, same knee-length, thick black hair, same enormous bosom, though hers was definitely larger than Luisa's, and the same malformed feet. Sondra wondered how these helpless women could even stand up, let alone walk, but obviously they must be able to do so. What set Juanita apart was her fabulous jewelry, if that's what they were called. First, she wore an emerald green, satin gown, form fitting, though revealing her knees. Her earrings were huge. Tiers of gold fittings holding large emeralds draped downwards, touching her shoulders, threatening, Sondra thought, to pull off her ears. Even more shocking were the woman's lips. Both were slit and a pair of golden disks, perhaps five inches in diameter, drooped downwards touching her chest while holding the lip loops nicely taught. Her speech, however, was almost unintelligible.

"So very pleased to meet you, Fetish Queen of Virge-C," she said, repeating it three times. "Everyone finds it so hard to understand me, but aren't these lip loops just fantastic?"

Searching for some polite response, Sondra declared, "They are most stunning! I've never seen anything quite like them."

"Moving on," Diego interrupted her attempts to say anything further, "you will recognize your very own Miss Universe, Miss Victoria Silvers." Here, Sondra was on familiar ground, since she recognized the beauty queen, having seen her images on the news many times. She was a gorgeous blonde, whose ringlets were nicely arranged over her shoulders, touching her ample breasts; she wore a light red gown that billowed out a few feet starting at her waist, revealing her black nylons and reasonable pumps, perhaps five inches tall.

"So pleased to meet you, Madam Sable. I've heard of what you do for some of the young women of our city. Thank you so much and best of luck with this competition," she said politely, her smile never wavering. She was an old hand at beauty pageants and acted as though this ball was just another one of them.

"Finally, this is Miss Rene Harvester. I believe your title is Miss West Port," he added and she nodded. Rene had waist length, wavy, black hair, and charming eyes. Her gown was a loose-fitting, gauze done in pink and barely reaching her knees. What struck Sondra was the woman's shoes or boots rather. The woman was standing on the tips of her toes with the tallest spiked heel she'd ever seen, like a ballerina! She had no idea how the woman could possibly stand or walk in them.

"Wow, and I thought my heels were fetish," Sondra exclaimed.

Rene giggled. "I know. Most striking. Normally, these are bedroom boots, but I've taken ballet and am able to wear them as you wear yours, though I must admit that I had better sit down soon."

"Don't they cramp your toes and feet some?" Sondra could not help asking.

"Yes, of course, but with lots of practice, they can be worn like normal heels. Sexy eh?" Rene teased her. Sondra nodded. "I do so like your evocative look, Madam Sable. Fabulous." She sounded sincere and not fake, as Victoria had. Sondra smiled.

"Now then, allow me to pin these corsages on you five most elegant and beautiful women so the judges can identify you at a glance." As Diego set about pinning them onto their gowns, he added, "Don't worry. You will not know who the judges are. Please enjoy the dance. I know that many men and women wish to dance with each of you tonight. Above all, have fun. All eyes will be upon you—the five most perfect women in West Port."

As far as Sondra was concerned, Diego was pouring it on way too thick for her liking. She'd never considered herself a beauty queen, far, far from it. This was completely weird, and she felt very much out of place and also very worried about the two helpless women. What awful accident had happened to them to have destroyed their arms and so mutilated their feet? Didn't these supposedly advanced off-worlders have better medical equipment? Sondra's head was spinning with more unanswered questions than ever.

Music. Dozens of unfamiliar men took turns dancing with the five women, while the hundreds of others watched for a time and then bored, danced among themselves. At least they played familiar music, stately and regal, making the needed dance steps that formed a parallelogram easy enough to do, even for Rene who was standing on the tips of her toes. Sondra couldn't imagine how Rene could manage. By now, her toes and feet ought to be a mass of painful, debilitating cramps, and yet she continued to stump. As time passed, Sondra noticed Rene's face began reflecting the pain she was suppressing. While she wished she could find a way to help Rene, just now, she couldn't. Then, Diego broke in on her current dance partner, and she seized this opportunity. "Diego. Our feet are hurting from so much dancing. Couldn't we women have a bit of a break? Some refreshments, perhaps?"

"Quite right. Yes, in all this excitement, I've overlooked your well-being," he replied diplomatically. He signaled for a halt and announced refreshments would be served. Off he went to assist his wife, along with the other husband. Certainly, Luisa and Juanita needed help—of that Sondra was certain. She moved over to sit down beside Rene, whose face was taught and tense.

"How are your feet doing?" she asked politely.

"Bad. I don't normally stand on them for this long a time. I took some painkillers before I came. I'd best take another batch. How are you holding up?" Rene explained, slipping her hand into her purse. While Sondra accepted the two offered glasses of juice from a waiter, Rene popped several pills and hastily took a long drink. "Thanks. I should be okay by the time they resume. I think those who danced with us were the judges," she suggested.

Victoria whispered, "I think so too. Thanks for getting us this break, Madam Sable. I needed it. I hope this doesn't go on too long. Still, maybe we'll actually get a chance to meet some of these very important men. I hope so." She chatted for several minutes until the music began once more.

Diego announced, "This time, the floor is open for

everyone to dance with whom they please." Sondra took that as further evidence that Rene and Victoria were correct about the judges. This time, things got more interesting for her; the men and women who chose to dance with her introduced themselves. For Sondra, it was a whirlwind of unfamiliar and familiar names, and she tried hard to commit faces to names for the future.

Within the next half hour, Sondra met Mr. Marshal Tucker, head of Aerostar Engines, Mr. Sam Decker, head of Rosewood Homecare, Mr. Jason Miller, the Governor of West Point, and President John Johnson, who ruled Virge-C and who had close ties to the off-worlders. There were many lesser executives as well, along with a number of women, most of whom wanted to chat about the five contestants and their exoticness. After that, the five saw a drastic reduction in dance requests, which again gave them a much-needed break, except for Sondra.

A young man, rather dashing she thought, with short, black hair, and a handsome face, her own age, came up to her, quite a change from all the middle-aged men who had been her dancing partners. "Hello. I'm Detective Matt Homes. I must admit, you look stunning. If your feet can take more dancing, I'd love to offer you my hand," he said politely.

"Sure. Wow, a real detective," Sondra said, slightly hesitantly. Trouble with the authorities was the last thing she wanted just now. Still, it would be impolite to reject his offer, and she gave him her hand. At least the dances were slow, she thought.

"Yes, a real detective, though right now, my detective skills are not doing so good. I don't know how you women can even dance in these getups, but you do look fabulous."

"You dance well, detective."

"Matt, please just Matt. My sister taught me."

"Okay then Matt. Call me Sable. So what do you mean by your skills are not doing so well just now?"

"Funny that you ask. Well, this new case was dumped into my lap. You see, I'm the lowest ranking detective on the West Port's force. Hence, I get all the cold cases and those that no one else wants—you know—the kind that probably can't

Slow Comes the Dark Volume 2 Serendipity

ever be solved."

"Wow. Are there that many cold ones?" Sondra asked, becoming curious.

"Yes, I'm afraid there has been quite a rise in unsolved cases, particularly during the last five years. Murders mostly. Nasty business. If that wasn't enough, I got a fresh one dumped on me the other day. You probably heard about it—a woman got run over by a truck late at night near the Plum Street Bridge."

"Oh yes, yes, I heard about it on the news." Sondra did her best to keep from flushing and reacting visibly. She hoped he couldn't sense her rise in blood pressure!

"Nasty one. Say, could I possibly take you out for a cup of coffee tomorrow, like late morning? I've never met anyone quite like you, Sable. I rather thought these contestants would be, well you know, typical women interested in just looking pretty, but you're bright, alert, and intriguing. I'd love to get to know you better."

"Sure, why not? I've never met a detective before." *Is he hitting on me? What do I do now? I can't easily get out of this one. Maybe he thinks I look like the dead woman. In that case, I best play along and see what he really wants. Besides, he's darn handsome.*

To her amazement, Matt was the only person to dance more than one dance with her, dancing with her until the ball ended and impressing her even more. When the dance ended, Diego used the microphone to announce the results. "May I have your attention before you leave? Thank you. The results of the contest to define Virge-C's Ultimate in Feminine Beauty are in. The results are slightly mixed. For certain, Luisa's magnificent hair, lack of arms, gorgeous breasts, and small waist have gotten neatly unanimous choices. However, it is a tie between Luisa and Juanita's toe shoes and Rene's beautiful ballet boots. Likewise, it's a tie whether she should have Juanita's gorgeous lip disks. Finally, the judges agree; Madam Sable's gown wins. Thank you all for coming and participating in helping to define Virge-C's Ultimate in Feminine Beauty. Good night everyone."

As the crowd began to breakup, heading for the doors,

Matt was still holding onto Sondra. He commented, "Congratulations on having the best gown. Still, I can't see why they want women to have no arms, those obscene monster breasts, or even those crazy lip disks of Juanita's."

Sondra smiled and replied, "Neither do I, but I felt bad for Luisa and Juanita. They have to be so helpless. Rene's feet are probably throbbing madly about now, in spite of all her painkillers."

Overhearing Sondra, Rene chuckled, "I'm a little high on them right now. Tomorrow, I probably won't even be able to walk. Still, I did what I intended to do tonight—popularize these bedtime boots. Oh, I didn't tell you. My parents run the Shoe Box, a small company that makes all kinds of ballet boots and shoes, mostly for exotic times in the bedroom. My goal is to get more people to buy them. I think that will happen, and my parents will get lots more sales."

"Wow. I didn't know that. Good for you," Sondra replied.

"Well, they certainly would add spice to bedtimes," Matt commented with a wry smile.

Rene continued. "Yes, but did you know that Luisa and Juanita were once just like us, normal women? I heard they underwent some kind of genetic modifications to end up looking like they do now. Rumors suggest their arms dried up and fell off in the process, but that sounds impossible, doesn't it? Still, they chose to be as they are, but I can't imagine why. They are very nearly helpless," Rene explained.

Coming up to Sable Rene, and Matt, Diego broke in on their conversation, "Genetic mutation. On most worlds of the Galactic Federation, we have defined what we consider to be the Ultimate in Feminine Beauty, the UFB woman, for short. Our geneticists have perfected a genetic mutation agent that can convert any women, no matter how ugly she might be, into a magnificent super-model. My wife, Luisa, and Juanita underwent that procedure many years ago and have been stunning models of womanly perfection ever since. In addition, our daughters inherit Luisa's modified genes. I'm the proud father of two stunning young women, UFB women in their own right, though they are only thirteen and twelve right now. Of course, our son is normal, taking after me. However, the UFB women do require servants around them to assist them. Only those of us who can afford such magnificent women are able to have them."

He went on, "Most top executives of the major corporations on Federation worlds have UFB women for wives. Naturally, with Virge-C's acceptance into the Galactic Federation, your top men desire and deserve to have such women for their wives as well, hence, the competition tonight to help define what that should be on this world. Now then, Madam Sable, might I have a brief private word with you. I'll have her back with you two in just a minute," he explained to Matt and Rene, while pushing her slightly away from them.

Once out of earshot, he stated, "You have a secret admirer. He's a top corporate executive, a very wealthy young man, I believe only a bit older than you. He would like to marry you and have you become his UFB wife. Would you be interested? You would become even more beautiful than you are now, and you would become quite wealthy and very influential with other local women."

Sondra flushed. Of all the things she imagined Diego would say to her, this was not remotely one of them. "Definitely no, sir. I don't want to be helpless like Luisa is. I can't imagine how she can even survive."

"Oh, I assure you she has servants to assist her. She wants for nothing, best clothing, best shoes, best food—best everything. Did you know each of her modified strands of hair have neurons in them? She can feel with each strand of her hair, much as though they were tiny arms. She claims sex is now utterly incredible, but then Juanita claims her lip loops take sex to a completely new level. Luisa wants to get the fancy lip ornaments too, but we'll see about that."

"Still, the answer is no, sir. I'm not interested in becoming a helpless sex doll. I'm not interested in being wealthy either. Tell him thanks for the offer, but I'm not really interested."

"Okay. I will do so. I'm sure that he'll be disappointed, but then there are other women out there. I'm sure he will find a perfect match," Diego replied diplomatically while ushering her back to Matt and Rene. After he left them, Rene just had to know what he said. Sondra told them both.

"Well, I'm glad that you said no," Matt gushed.

"Me too. I can't imagine anyone wanting to be like Luisa and Juanita. They are almost completely helpless," Rene added.

Matt cautioned her, "Say, I would be extra careful. You don't know who this suitor is. Some of them never take no for an answer. He could have you kidnaped and this genetic modification done on you without your consent." Sondra's stomach knotted. She too had the same idea. "Be damned careful. Say, here's my card. Call me if you suspect anything going on."

"Can I have one too?" Rene asked. "Here's my card, er well, my parent's card. My number is on the bottom." She handed one to Sondra and Matt.

"Thanks. Both of you. I'll be extra careful. This is scary," Sondra admitted.

"Indeed. It has me worried too," Matt admitted. "Look, they could easily kidnap you, knock you out, and do this genetic modification thing to your body. When you woke up, it would be all over, and there wouldn't be any way to undo it. Damned scary if you ask me."

"Now I am worried!" Sondra countered. "Could I ask you to take me home tonight?"

"My incredible Sable, of course. I'd feel much better if I did just that. How about you, Rene? I have my car here. I can see you both safely home," Matt offered.

"Thank you!" Rene gushed. From her shake tone, Sondra suspected Rene was just as scared as she was. Certainly, no one would try anything while a police detective was taking them home.

"Oh! My feet!" Rene exclaimed, as she tried to rise from her chair. "I've really overdone it. My feet are throbbing fiercely."

"Can't you take your boots off?" Matt asked.

"Kind of risque, but I don't have much choice. Well, most everyone's gone, so I guess it won't be that embarrassing," Rene added. Carefully, she undid the laces and slipped her feet out. Matt and Sondra each took a nylon-clad foot and massaged the painful cramps out of them. Still, it was another half hour before she could put any weight on her bare feet. "What we women endure to look fabulous," she teased the pair, who laughed.

"Indeed, you both look just incredible to me," Matt complimented them. "Come on, lean on us, Rene; we'll get you safely home."

An hour later, Matt stopped before Sable's home. He helped her out and up to her door, even waiting until she was safely inside before leaving. "I'll be by around ten for coffee," he added.

"I'll be waiting," Sondra replied with a smile. *I do like him, even if he is the police. He's a real gentleman, well so far anyway. We'll just have to see what tomorrow brings.* She headed to bed, struggling to get herself undressed. *This is the pits. I can hardly do this by myself without Beth's help. Why did Sable want this lifestyle anyway? I can't see it. Mostly misery, but then Luisa and Juanita's life is vastly worse. Still, I don't want to keep this up much longer.* Sleep came quickly. Her body was exhausted.

# Chapter 4—Coffee and a Detective

"I am going out for coffee with a handsome police detective," Sondra explained to Beth the following morning. Although it was Saturday and Beth wasn't scheduled to work for her during the weekends, Beth just had to hear all about the CEO Ball. Sondra found an eager audience in Beth and enjoyed telling the young Academy student all about it, particularly the two most unusual UFB women, who were the wives of Galactic Dynamics top executives.

Besides, she wanted to hear Beth's reaction to the winning combination for Virge-C's Ultimate in Feminine Beauty. Her declaration was similar to her own. Beth declared, "They must be nuts! Women don't want to be helpless sex dolls. Whatever are those men thinking about?"

"They can't keep it in their pants," Sondra joked. Beth roared.

"So how about a tight-fitting pants suit?" Beth suggested. "It would look less formal and not quite so fetish."

"Good idea. Let's see what we have in the closet." An hour later, Sondra wore a white silk blouse, very form fitting over her slip-covered corset, and tight, black leather pants. A wide black velvet belt dramatically outlined her reduced waistline. She complimented the appearance with knee-high, black patent boots, whose heels were tiny metallic spikes, six inches tall of course. Sable didn't have any other foot apparel whose heels were lower than six inches. Sondra mused that Sable had probably died wearing the lowest heels she owned.

Promptly at ten, Detective Matt Homes arrived and rang the doorbell. As always, Beth answered it for the slow moving Sable. "Oh excuse me. I have an appointment," a flustered Matt began, obviously not expecting to see Beth answering the door.

"I'm coming. Matt, this is my part-time helper, Beth Ferguson. Beth, this is Detective Matt Homes," Sondra introduced the two, cleverly giving her time to cross the room to the doorway. *Life's a bitch in these heels,* she thought, thankful she'd found a way to stall until she reached the door.

"You look stunning this morning, Miss Hampton. I've brought my car. I know just the place to take coffee. Have you ever been to Mel's Diner?" Matt asked, slipping an arm around her when she reached him.

*I'm glad he took my suggestion and stopped calling me Madam Sable.* "No I haven't. Is it far? I do hope I'm not taking you away from your official business," she replied. "Oh, Beth, lock up when you leave."

"Not at all. I'm off-duty on the weekends," Matt answered. "It's about two blocks from the Plum Street Bridge—this side of it."

Inwardly, Sondra groaned. *That stupid bridge! Does everything revolve around that place?* She hoped she didn't flush at the mention of it.

A short while later, the two took a private booth in the quaint diner. Mel, if that was truly the owner's name, took pride in all things old. Antiques lined the walls. Even the soft leather booths were antiques, but the coffee was extremely good. Matt bought them both a large cup, served in antique coffee mugs, each one of which probably cost Mel ten gold dollars—at least that was Sondra's estimate.

They chatted pleasantly for a time. Then, Matt cleverly said, "Sondra, I've been thinking."

"What?" she replied automatically. Suddenly, her face turned beet red. *Shit! Now the game is up! He knows I am not Sable. Shit. What do I do now? Is he going to be arresting me? Life's a bitch.*

"I thought so. I apologize for taking you by surprise just now. I rather figured you were not Sable Lorraine Hampton, but Sondra Sofia Shelley," Matt explained.

"How did you know that?" Sondra struggled to control her wild emotions and say something intelligent.

"Well, it began when I finally found a photo of you, of Sondra, the woman who was presumably run over by a truck in the middle of the night. Then, when I saw you at the ball last night, well, I began to wonder what was going on. So I did some checking; everyone there who knew you swore you were Sable Lorraine Hampton. I concluded you two must be identical twins. And yet, neither Sable nor Sondra seemed to be related. As I danced with you, I had a hunch and played it. From all that I could find out about the presumed dead woman, Sondra Shelley, she was bright, intelligent, highly independent, and something of a private investigator down in the Snake Town. As we danced, you seemed to fit that profile well. Apparently, Sable was something of a fetish queen and a flirt, very extroverted. I had to find out. This case has far more to it than meets the eye, and I took a gamble."

"Well, yes, I'm Sondra Sofia Shelley. I was orphaned when I was two, I think. Ben Blackwater took me under his wing when we lived with our foster parents who mistreated us."

"Yes, I got that much out of Ben. Moreover, when I looked over your small apartment, I realized Sondra was bright and intelligent. A bit of digging revealed that in Snake Town, you have quite a reputation for helping others—an unofficial private detective."

"Yes, that's me." *I best see what else he knows about me. This is darn spooky. What does he want from me? Is he going to arrest me? Should I tell him everything and beg for mercy?*

"Good. Now then about the dead woman, I presume she is the real Sable Lorraine Hampton."

"As far as I know, she was," Sondra agreed.

"What's so strange is the autopsy showed she was not killed by being run over by a truck. No, she was shot. The MD found a 9mm slug in her chest. The heavy truck tires that crushed her head beyond recognition occurred post-mortem—an estimated two hours after her death, making any attempt at facial recognition darn near impossible. May I ask why she had your ID card in her hand?"

*He's not taking me into the police station. Maybe I should just tell him everything.* Sondra began, "You may, but it's a longer story. I accepted a job for a client, a rather unusual one. I'm something of an electronics and computer person. I was hired to clone a mark's cell phone. I know, it's illegal, but I needed the cash. Anyway, the client gave me a very precise route that the mark would be following, complete with times. I spotted him walking across Plum Street Bridge around eleven. I moved out and followed him for a block, while using my two phone systems to clone his. I stayed ten feet behind him all the way, and he didn't see me."

"As I approached the first side street, the phones in my purse vibrated, telling me they'd finished cloning his phone, so I veered to the left, heading down that street. I hadn't gone but a few feet when I suddenly came face to face with Sable. Mind you, I was shocked. It was like looking at yourself in a mirror! I had a hoodie pulled up, but still she saw my face, which was her face. We each had similar hair and voices. Really weird. Just then, the mark called out and fired his gun. It had a silencer on it. He shot her in the chest, and she fell to the ground, dropping her cell phone. Oh, I forgot to tell you that as she came walking up the street towards Plum Street, she was holding a phone in her right hand and texting, I think."

Anyway, she dropped the phone, and the mark fired a second time, hitting the phone and destroying it. He then fled, and I went to help my double. She was just as shocked to see me, as I was to see her. She begged me to give her my ID card so I eventually gave it to her. She told me to take her purse and for me to be her. She said, 'Be me!' Look, it was her dying words, and besides, she looked just like me. Did I have an identical twin sister? I can't begin to tell you the wild thoughts I had, but she begged me to take her purse and to be her, so I did. Once she had my ID card in her hand, she died. I tried to retrieve it, but she had a death grip on it. So I did as she asked."

"Anyway, the next morning when I got up, it was on the news that Sondra Shelley was run over by a truck, that I was dead. So I found her ID card with her address on it and headed over to her place in hopes of finding out about her. Was she my unknown identical sister? Were we separated when our parents died? Who was she? Worse, I felt guilty. After all, if I hadn't cloned the mark's phone, he wouldn't have shot her by mistake, only now maybe that wasn't the reason he shot Sable, but I'm getting ahead of myself again. Let's just say I had a thousand questions that needed answering, and I thought just by going through her things I might find out about her and who our parents were."

"As I was walking up to the home, Lilly, who runs a nail and hair salon next door, spotted me and came out, telling me that my special order of nail extensions had come in. Well, she insisted I come inside and get them done right then, so I did. Honestly, I was shocked she believed that I was Sable. Once I got these awful claws on, I finally got to Sable's door. However, Beth was there waiting for me, and she too believed I was Sable."

"I had to think fast, so I explained I'd gotten hit on my head and spent the night behind a garbage bin, that I wasn't robbed or raped, just mugged and had lost most of my memories. That Beth could handle, and she began filling me in on many things, such as Sable often took in clients, young women, and taught them how to walk elegantly in these heels. Mind you, I do need her help getting into these impossible fetish outfits! She works part-time and comes in the morning to fix breakfast and get Sable dressed. She returns around suppertime to fix dinner and to help get her undressed. Anyway, with her help, I began to fill in some of the pieces of Sable's life."

"However, Sable was invited to attend this CEO ball last night. That's why she special ordered the long nail extensions. Before I go on, I should also tell you that I didn't call my client to tell him that I cloned the mark's cell phone. I figured if I did that, then he'd know I wasn't the woman who was run over by the truck. I didn't want him or her knowing that it might be Sable who died. Besides, the mark did the killing. And I still haven't let the client know I have two clones of the mark's phones. I did check, and the mark's phone and my client's phone are both untraceable disposable phones."

"Now I wasn't going to go to this CEO Ball, but I needed more days to go through Sable's things to learn more about her. I also had Sable's second phone with me in her purse. This one is registered to her. While I was trying to adapt to the situation and deal with learning what I could from Beth, I got a text message on Sable's phone. The caller ID said simply Sally. It read: Did u get it last night?"

"Get what? Hell, what was Sable doing out there? I

suddenly had a zillion questions, like what was Sable doing there at night alone on the street. So I quickly replied back: No. Got interrupted by the truck running over that woman. After a minute, this Sally person sent back: Sit tight 4 now. Will txt u l8r. Weird, but it gets weirder. Anyway, after Beth left for the night, I was in my nightgown and this impossibly tight corset and with no shoes in the house whose heels are lower than what I'm wearing, when I got another text message from Sally. It said: Get out of your house now! Gunmen are coming to kill you. Txt more l8tr."

Matt suddenly straightened up, paying very close attention to every word that Sondra said. "So I freaked out for a minute. I couldn't leave the house. Even if I could get these boots on, I can only just barely walk in them. I'd not get five feet before the gunmen would shoot me down as the mark did Sable. I used my head. Most of the lights were still on in the house. I wrote a note to Beth saying I had gone out and left the lights on for her. I put it on that reception desk just inside the front door, the one that you saw when you came to pick me up a bit ago. Then, I headed to the bedroom. Sable has a huge walk-in closet filled with all her fancy fetish outfits, and I hid in a back corner behind them and waited."

"Sure enough, a few minutes later, two men must have picked the front lock, because later the door wasn't locked and wasn't broken. They searched the house. One came into the bedroom, but didn't see me hiding in the closet. I waited there for quite a while until I was sure that they had gone. You know, the funny thing is at the ball, that Mr. Diego de la Vasco told me that he was surprised to see me at the ball, because he had heard a rumor that I wasn't going to come. Weird."

"So after that, I began to wonder if Sable died because I cloned the mark's phone or whether the mark was actually after her? I need answers, Matt, so I went to the ball last night hoping to find out more. All I got for my trouble was sore feet, but I sure wouldn't want to be Rene this morning. I bet her feet are black and blue."

"Anyway, I guess you can arrest me now. I have so darn many questions without answers that it isn't funny."

"Arrest you for what?" Matt teased her. "Well, I suppose

for failing to report a murder. Did you see the mark's face? Can you identify him?"

"Nope, it was dark, and I was behind him. Couldn't see his face."

"Well, this case has definitely gotten stranger, Sondra. I certainly am not going to arrest you. We need to get to the bottom of all this. I agree with you. There are just too many vitally important questions. Was Sable into some shady dealings? Drug dealer? Prostitution ring? Escort service? A client gone bad? Why would two gunmen break into her home to kill her? From what I have learned, she was a Fetish Queen."

"I agree. I can't figure out why someone wants her dead. No on the drugs. She recorded all her sessions with her clients. She was just teaching them how to walk properly. If she was into something illegal, I've not yet found any trace of it, but then I haven't had enough time to search her place thoroughly for clues."

"Excellent. Sondra, how would you like to work for me officially as my confidential, undercover informant and investigator? We need to uncover what really is going on here and why Sable was murdered and by whom. You take all the time you need to investigate everything in Sable's home. Meanwhile, if you will give me access to those phones, I'll see what I can discover." Sondra gave him one of the two clones and the number of Sable's phone.

"While I am at it, let me double check on you two women. Sondra Sofia Shelley and Sable Lorraine Hampton, correct? Orphaned when you were two?" Matt asked.

"Yes. That's right, at least what I was told by the foster parents. I have a birth certificate backing that up," she added.

"Okay. One more thing, if you don't mind, I'll take a sample of your DNA as well. I can compare it to Sable's and tell for sure if you were sisters. How old are you now?"

"Twenty-three."

Matt smiled. "Same as me." He swabbed her mouth for the sample. "Okay, I'll take you back now. Keep in touch. I'll call you later with what I can find out. For now, please continue to be Sable, all right?"

"Thanks for not arresting me, Matt. I have far too many questions that I simply must get answered. Was she my identical sister? Why did they split us up? Why didn't they tell us that we had a sister? Life's a bitch, isn't it?" Sondra replied.

Matt chuckled. "Well, this is indeed a strange case."

After dropping her off at Sable's, he headed downtown. He knew much more than before he awoke this morning. Perhaps, this case was solvable and soon.

Back at Sable's home, Beth had gone. *That's good. Now to search this home thoroughly. I wonder if Sable kept her valuables in some kind of safe? Damned these boots and nails anyway,* she cursed her slowness and clumsiness as well, but began her search in the living room, discovering the hidden camera.

Sondra always had hunches. Sometimes they panned out, which in part accounted for her remarkable success helping others with difficult situations. She acted on her hunch and replaced the camera so that it would capture whoever entered the front door. She activated the recorder and continued her search, this time going through the entire registry black book before moving on to the rest of the reception area, unfortunately uncovering nothing new.

She stopped for a light lunch. Just as she was eating, Sable's phone vibrated once more. Hampered by the long nails, she nearly dropped it before getting it out of the purse. She cursed again and read the text: Get out. Gunmen are on their way to kill you! The text was from the mysterious Sally. Her stomach knotted and her legs felt like mush. However, she reacted, taking her purse and heading for the backdoor. She had no idea where it led, but her hunch was that she'd be safer going out this way than going out the front, since the gunmen had entered the front door last night.

She found herself in the alley that ran behind the buildings. Lilly's Nails was painted in red letters on the door next to hers. Acting on impulse, she opened it and entered the rear of the salon, taking some of the women by surprise. They were huddled around a small table eating takeout lunches of fish and chips. "Well, this is a surprise," Lilly spoke up, swallowing her last bite.

"Er, sorry to intrude, Lilly, but is it possible to get these extensions removed? I've decided I really don't like my nails this long. They keep interfering with everything, and I haven't got time to get used to them."

"Sure, but while we do it, you simply *must* tell us about how the fancy ball went last night," Lilly declared emphatically, definitely insisting on a complete report. All her other employees were just as interested, and they all worked on the nails while Sondra told them about the dance, including why she'd been invited and the results of the competition.

"What? You mean these top men want armless sex dolls with monster boobs?" Lilly exclaimed. "Well, I never."

"Idiots, that's what they are," another put in.

"Bunch of sadists, I say. Let them carry around another twenty pounds on their chests." Several women giggled at that notion.

"Well, we'll definitely have to increase our rates for these women with knee-length hair," another suggested.

Lilly agreed, but added, "Honestly, what are those men thinking? We women hardly want to be helpless sex dolls for them. Who do they think they are? God's gift to women or something?"

"More like ultimate power corrupts," Sondra suggested. "Life's a bitch, but these lunatics want to make it even worse." She got no argument from the others. An hour later, her nails were done, back to their usual length, but with a clear coat over them. Before she left, she sent a quick text to Detective Matt. Got warned that two gunmen were coming to my house to kill me. I ducked out to Lilly's next door. Mind dropping by now?

"Damn! On my way. Stay out of your house til I get there," Matt texted back, and Sondra was more than willing to do as he asked. This was getting out of hand. Why kill Sable now? That dance was over or was there far more to all this than she knew about? That had to be it, she concluded, and waited patiently for Matt to arrive. Spotting his car pulling up out front, she stepped out of Lilly's. "Whew. You all right?" he asked, worried.

"Yes, no sign of the men. Thanks for coming. This is getting to be a bit scary, Matt."

"You're right. Come on; let me make sure they aren't hiding inside your place," he suggested, drawing his own gun. Sondra stayed back while he went inside. A bit later, he called out, "All clear. Come on in."

"Thanks for coming by so quickly, Matt. Now let's see if we can see who these gunmen are," Sondra said, moving into the study as quickly as she could, which wasn't fast in these boots. She noticed Matt had continually to adjust his steps not to move ahead of her, further embarrassing her. "I can't see what Sable ever saw in heels this high. We can hardly walk in them. Ah, here's the computer. Let's see."

"What do you mean by seeing who the gunmen are?" Matt asked. "I like the boots, Sondra. They look quite good on you."

She ignored the compliment. "Sable always recorded her sessions with her clients. I found her spy camera in the living room and moved it into the hallway, facing the doors. It was on all this time, so maybe we have these men recorded." She ended the recording, and hit Play and Fast Forward. Suddenly she stopped and backed it up a bit. For a second, all they could see was the front door. Then, it opened, and two men wearing ski masks entered cautiously. Both carried a gun with a silencer on it, raised and pointing ahead of them. One gave a hand signal to the other, and they moved off in two directions out of the camera range. Matt cursed. Several minutes later, the backs of the men appeared in the video, and they left, closing the door behind them.

"Well, you weren't lying about the hit men, Sondra. I think that you should have a gun yourself," Matt suggested.

"I was thinking that too, but I don't know how to shoot one or what kind to get. Guns aren't my thing," Sondra replied.

"Well, I can handle both. It's not safe for you here. Someone wants Sable dead, and I want to know who and why," Matt explained.

Sensing that he was sincere and honestly wanting to help her, Sondra agreed, "Okay Mr. Detective. Let's get me a gun and show me how to shoot. I agree. I certainly don't feel safe in this house. I would be dead twice now, if this mysterious Sandy woman had not alerted me to their coming.

I wonder who she is and how she knows when the gunmen are coming."

"Come on. To my car. Lock the door first. Oh, and reset the video recorder. I have to hand it to you, Sondra; you're quite brilliant. I don't know of any other woman who would have had the presence of mind to do what you've done—elude them and capture them on video. Shame they wore gloves and masks. Identification is next to impossible."

After helping her into the car, even though she really didn't need such assistance, he added, "As far as this Sandy woman goes, my theory is that she must somehow be working for or close to those who are ordering the hit on Sable. We're going to have to discover just who she is. Okay, first stop, Able's Guns and Ammunition. Then, we're going to the police range and get you trained up a bit."

An hour later, Able wrapped up Sondra's new purchases: a 9mm automatic with five clips holding a dozen shots each, a legal silencer signed off by Matt personally, and ten boxes of ammunition. While Matt tried to pay for them, Sondra insisted on paying. "Look, this is my gun, and I should be paying for it."

"Independent aren't we?" he teased.

"You bet your bottom I'm that—and more," she teased and flirted with him a bit. *I do like him. A whole lot. I wonder if he has a girlfriend or fiancé. Best not ask outright, though.*

They spent two hours at the firing range, just outside the city. While she had never held a gun, let alone fired one before, Matt claimed that she was a natural at it. By the time they left the range, she was able to place an entire clip in the middle of the chest of the man's image on the target. She felt good about that much. *If they come again, I'll make them pay for killing me. Life's a bitch, but this bitch is getting bitchy.*

It was well past lunchtime. Heading back, Matt suggested they stop for a burger. "My treat, Madam," he teased her.

"Okay. But I should be treating you, Matt. You keep coming to my rescue."

"Hey, I like coming to the rescue of a hot lady," he teased her.

Sondra grinned. "Bet you say that to all the women you meet."

Matt laughed heartily. "Fat chance of that. With few exceptions, all the women I meet are corpses. It's nice to deal with a live chick, especially a hot one."

Sondra flushed at the compliment. "Say, I've no right to ask this of you, but could you possibly stay the night at my place? I'd feel far more secure with you around, especially if the gunmen come back again."

"Thought you would never ask," he teased. "Of course. Consider it police protection of a valuable witness. I'll handle some things and be by around seven. How's that? Text me right away if you get another warning or see anyone suspicious hanging around, okay?"

"Absolutely. Seven is fine. Thanks, Matt. I owe you." He smiled and dropped her off at the house.

Sondra spent the long afternoon continuing her thorough search of Sable's home. She finally found a concealed box, hidden in the back of her walk-in closet. In it were Sable's important papers, one being her birth certificate. *She has the same birthday as I do. How strange is that? Can she be my sister somehow? Were we separated when our parents died? Why? Now I have even more unanswered questions. I'm going bonkers by the minute here. What else has she got in her box?*

Old bank statements, a degree from a fashion model school, and a yellowed photo of her parents. Sondra stared hard at the photo. She had one somewhat like it and dug it out of her purse, one of the few things she brought with her when she abandoned her apartment with Ben. While hers was not the same photograph as Sable's, the similarities in the rather faded images were striking. They could be the same two people, she concluded, sticking both back into her purse.

With her thorough search done, the only thing left was Sable's computer. Munching on a light, cold supper, she began to explore what else was on Sable's computer besides the mountain of recorded client sessions. Finally, she found a text document, but it was encrypted. She spent a half hour trying to crack the password, before she hit upon it, a lucky guess:

Parents.

Anxiously, she read the document. There were date notations and short partial sentences.

Contacted by mysterious woman. Sandy.

Possible twin sister, must investigate further.

Shocking. She looked just like me!

Waiting on the DNA tests.

Confirmed. We're going to meet, but someone has been watching this place. Can't tell who it is. Sandy urges caution.

Secret meeting arranged tonight. Must make sure I'm not followed. Sandy texted me a map to follow.

That was all. However, the date of the last entry was the very night that Sondra ran into Sable and Sable was killed. *So she was going to meet this Sandy person and her sister. Wait! Meet her sister? Is there another one of us out there? Triplets? Oh my God, I might have another sister! Wait. Why was Sable killed trying to meet up with our sister? Damn, life sure is a bitch. Now I have even more questions than before! I need a hot tea.*

While she was sipping her tea and pondering the significance of what she'd discovered, Sable's phone vibrated again. She picked it up, smiling because she no longer had those giant claws to interfere. It was from Sandy. Her heart skipped a beat. She read the text: Must meet. Tomorrow noon. The Steak Grill on Plum Street, four blocks west of the bridge. Make damned sure you aren't followed. I'll contact you there.

After reading it twice, she replied with a simple "K." While she wanted to ask this Sandy a zillion questions, text messages could be intercepted. *Hell, I've done that once or twice.* She knew that Sandy was taking a huge risk by sending all that information in a text message. The unknown enemies could well be monitoring her phone. Had someone cloned it, as she'd done with her mark? *Shit! I keep on getting more unanswered questions. This has to stop! I need answers, not more questions.*

Promptly at seven, Matt arrived, bringing a duffle bag inside with him. "Change of clothes and some more guns. Take no chances, eh, hot one?" he teased her. "Find out anything while I was gone?"

"Well, as a matter of fact, yes I have, but damn it, Matt, it only raises more questions. Tomorrow, I'm supposed to meet this Sandy person. Noon. At the Steak Grill on Plum Street, four blocks west of the bridge. She wants me to make damned sure I'm not followed. She'll probably keep an eye out to make sure I'm not followed and then make contact with me, but I've found out some more things too. Look." She showed him Sable's birth certificate, the old photograph, and then her own well-worn photo.

"She has the same birthday as me. Compare these two keepsake photos. They look like the same parents, but they are so fuzzy I can't quite be sure of that. Still, she could well be my sister. Matt, there's more. Come look at this. I found an encrypted file on her computer." She showed him the document, which she had left open just to show him. "So triplets maybe? What do you think?"

"Triplets? Wow. Yes, that could well be the answer. The DNA results won't be back until Monday morning. They're done at the labs at Rosewood Homecare. Then, we will know a lot more. Say, I also brought you a deadbolt for your front door. I'll install it now. I want you to keep the deadbolt locked when you're here. Beth can just knock to get entry. This is a strong one, so they won't be able to break in very easily next time."

"Thank you, Matt. You are saving my life." She watched as he installed the new, heavy-duty deadbolt and then showed her how to use it, but that part was obvious. That done, they headed to the kitchen to brew a pot of coffee and chat.

Sipping the fresh brew, she asked, "So what's your wife saying about your spending the night here?"

Matt chuckled. "Sorry, not married. No fiancé either. No girlfriends. Just me."

Sondra flushed. *I shouldn't have been so direct, but he's single. God, I do like that.* "Me either," she replied, flushing. *Now why did I say that?*

Breaking the awkward silence, Matt suggested, "We have lots of questions. I was thinking about them on my way here. Why don't we start making a list of the events and the questions that we both have?" They did just that, filling two pages with their observations and resultant questions. He ended with, "So Sondra, it's my hunch that Sable wasn't killed by your mark because he thought she cloned his phone. I think she was purposely targeted by him, but we lack the reason why."

"It does make me feel a bit better. Matt, I don't know how I could live with myself if I was the cause of her death, even indirectly," Sondra admitted.

"I know. You've a good heart, Sondra. Now, let's see what we can find out from the two birth certificates, shall we? Maybe there are some clues in them," Matt replied.

For several minutes, the pair studied the two documents, side by side. Different parents, different addresses, different hospitals, and different names. Matt sat back. "Well, you are right. This doesn't help. Only more questions. What say I take these with me and have the lab boys go over them."

"Fine with me. We need answers, lots of them, Matt. I have a feeling we're into something terribly sinister," Sondra admitted.

" I rather think you might be right. After all, running a dead woman's head over with a truck to disguise her face is very unusual. Do you often have hunches on the cases that you work?" he asked curiously.

"Well yes, I do. I go with them. I'm right more than I'm wrong," she admitted. Recalling one, she chuckled. "One client, Fred, hired me to find his lost car. It seems he went out drinking and lost track of his car. He had stubs from six bars and was in a tizzy because he couldn't find his car when he sobered up. I had a hunch it was probably somewhere near the first pub he visited. Based on the time stamps on the bar stubs, I went directly to the first one. Found his car two minutes later, two blocks from it."

Matt chuckled. "At least he wasn't drinking and driving." Both laughed.

The next morning, Matt put Sondra into a taxi. Once she was on her way to the secret meeting with the mysterious Sandy, he took another route, parking across the street from the restaurant. He got his camera with telephoto lens ready. If nothing else, he intended to get a photo of this woman. Besides, he wanted to make sure that Sondra was truly safe.

# Chapter 5—Coffee and a Donut

Sondra's taxi let her out in front of the steak house. After paying the driver, she headed inside. She had her waist length, light brown hair tied back in a ponytail, but wore the same outfit that she had yesterday. Besides, she felt more at ease wearing pants, even if they were leather, than Sable's highly restrictive gowns with their outer corsets that so limited her mobility. Wearing the damned overly tight inner one was bad enough, though now she was starting to get used to its constant pressure. Her metal heels clicked on the granite floor as she made her way inside. Following Matt's advice, she took a booth by the front window, knowing that eventually Matt would be across the street, watching out for her.

She ordered coffee and a donut, along with a child's steak sandwich. No one appeared, but soon the waiter brought her the order. *Where is this Sandy person? Can't she see that I wasn't followed? I don't see anyone out there, and I didn't see any cars following the taxi. What do I ask her first?*

Just then, a blonde woman wearing what looked to be a professional woman's outfit slipped into the leather bench opposite her. Her curly tresses barely touched her shoulders, and her lips were red; eyes, blue. Her blouse was white, probably silk, expensive with some kind of interlocked chains embossed upon the fine cloth. Her grey skirt fell to her knees, revealing black nylons and low patent pumps. Sensible. She carried a matching purse, which she placed on her lap. Her face, though stern, was quite attractive. One thing was certain. If this was Sandy, she didn't look remotely like Sondra or Sable.

The woman sat down and faced Sable. Seconds later, she spoke softly, but very forcibly, "Okay. I'm Sandy. Now who are you? You're not Sable. Mind you, I have a gun pointed at you beneath the table! One wrong move, and I will not hesitate to shoot! Who are you?"

"What do you mean I'm not Sable?" Sondra replied, sizing up the woman sitting across from her. *Surely, she wouldn't dare shoot inside this restaurant. That would attract far too much attention. Besides, they probably have security cameras in place.* Sondra didn't feel particularly threatened, more like curious.

Sandy continued, "Look, I was at the CEO Ball and watched you all night. I know Sable, and you're an imposter. I admit you look amazingly like her, but you totally lack the poise and grace of Sable. So answer me. Who are you and what have you done with Sable?"

"Are you Sandy?" Sondra asked. *I sure am not saying anything until I know if this is really Sandy. But wait. How will I know if she's the right Sandy? Shit. Life's a bitch as always.*

"Yes, I'm Sandy. Now talk woman, talk! I warn you. I will shoot."

"Okay then. Long story. I'm Sondra Sofia Shelley."

"You can't be. She was run over by a truck. Saw it on the news."

"Well, I am. That was Sable who was run over by the truck, but they did that to her after she was shot dead. Now will you please let me explain?" Sondra retorted. Seeing how shocked Sandy suddenly looked, she knew Sandy was no longer on the offensive and would listen.

"I am Sondra. I took a job for a client. I live down in Snake Town where I sometimes do private investigations for people. He wanted me to clone a mark's cell phone. He gave me the time and route the mark would be taking, and I waited for him by Plum Street Bridge." Bit by bit, Sondra explained what had happened, including Sable's weird request to hold her ID card and then Sable's dying plea that Sondra become her, Sable.

"Look," she continued, "I was utterly shocked to see myself lying there in the street. I always thought I was an orphan with no sisters or family. She looked just like me. That was the freakiest thing ever—to be looking at yourself, hair and all. So I did as she asked and gave her my ID card, which she clenched in her fist. After she died, I couldn't get it out of her hand. Her grip was that tight on it. So I headed home, more shocked than anything else." She went on to say that in the morning, the news carried her "death" and that she subsequently headed over to Sable's home to find out who she was and if she was perhaps her sister. She related the experience with Lilly and the nail extensions, and then what transpired with Beth. "So you see, I pretended I'd been hit over the head and lost part of my memories. Beth accepted that and went along with me. I needed time to go through Sable's things to try to find out if we were related and all that, but she had this CEO Ball to go to, and I had no choice but to go to it so I could buy more time to learn about Sable."

She described how she'd been able to avoid the gunmen twice now, thanks to Sandy's timely warnings, and how she'd captured their images on video this last time. However, she kept Matt out of her story. No sense revealing everything to this unknown woman, despite her timely warnings.

Sandy's face paled more and more before the color returned. The waiter brought her a coffee and a donut, which allowed her to relax some. When Sondra finished up, Sandy was quiet for a minute. "Well, you have to admit, this is all a pretty wild story you're telling, Sondra, if that's truly your name."

"Well, it is, though I don't have my ID card any longer." She decided against saying anything about her birth certificate, since Matt now had possession of it.

"If you continue to impersonate Sable, then your life is in grave danger."

"So what's new? I saw her shot right before my eyes, and I've seen gunmen break into her house twice now."

"And they will continue." Sandy bit her lip, hard in thought. At last, she decided something. "This is a whole lot to take in. You'll have to admit that. So while my," she paused, thinking of the right word to use, "*client* and I decide what to do about you, give me a DNA sample. We'll have it tested and then get back to you. If you pass, someone else would like to meet you, but in total secrecy. Don't worry. I'll use Jane Doe for your name. No one will know your identity."

"Fine with me, but can I ask you some questions? I have zillions about now, like why you are helping Sable? Is she my sister?"

"This is a very dangerous business. We don't know why yet. All I dare say is that Sable was with us. We'll discuss what you've told me, check on your DNA, and then I'll contact you again. Meanwhile, watch your back. I might not always know when the gunmen are being sent after you." With that, she rose and left the restaurant, leaving Sondra with most all her questions still unanswered. Since Sandy hadn't touched her donut, she wrapped it up to give to Matt, whom she spotted in his car just across the street. After paying the tab, she headed over to him.

"Here, have a donut. Well, that was interesting," Sondra said, handing him the untouched pastry, which he gobbled.

"So tell me what she said. I'm as curious as you are. I did get some photos of her," Matt replied. "Thanks. Good donut."

She smiled and related what little Sandy had said. "No, I didn't actually see her gun, but she went through the motions I would have expected if she were taking it out of her purse. It's interesting that she too wanted a DNA sample and even brought the stick thing with her to do it. She said she was at the CEO Ball and that I totally lacked the poise and graceful movements of Sable. Honestly, I was just trying not to fall down and make a complete fool of myself. But how did she know that much about Sable? Was I really a klutz on the dance floor?"

Matt chuckled. "Oh brother. Do I dare answer that one?" He laughed. "If I answer one way, you'll bean me. If I answer the other way, you won't believe me. So I lose no matter what I answer." Both laughed heartily.

"Okay, Matt. I'm a big girl. I can take it. Was I that bad at the dance?"

"Okay, okay. Truthfully, Sondra, you looked very ill at ease, uncomfortable, like a fish out of water. At first, I thought that must just be nerves over the competition, but later I saw that wasn't the case. Still, you were a knock out, Sondra. A real hot shot. Probably the only real woman there at the dance."

"Okay, you're redeemed. I was all that and more. So if Sandy was familiar with Sable, then she could also see I wasn't Sable. Okay, I'll buy that much, but who is she working for?

Was Sable part of her group? What were they up to or into?"

Matt chuckled. "More unanswered questions, my dear. We simply have to continue our detective work. Eventually, the truth will come out. It always does, you know, though on some cold cases that might not happen for years."

"Well, I don't have years to wait. I'm too impatient for that. Besides, someone is gunning for me or Sable rather," Sondra admitted.

"I know. Patience isn't part of your vocabulary. That's what I like about you," Matt replied. "Come on. I'll drop you off at Sable's place. Then, I'm going to run Sandy's photo by facial recognition software. Maybe we will get a lucky break."

"I make my own luck. Thank you very much," Sondra replied, half-teasing, but half-serious as well.

"Say, why don't we take a walk along the river? We can chat and get to know each other better," Matt suggested, looking her in her eyes.

"Sure, that sounds like fun. The river walkway is always beautiful," Sondra replied. *Does he really want to get to know me because I'm me? He's quite handsome. Walk? Hell, in these boots? Best not say anything about them though.*

He parked in the walkway lot where another dozen cars were also parked. It was Sunday, and strolling the river walkway was a nice getaway for those who appreciated what bit of Nature was still available within this city of ten million. Once, it had been a railroad line, but with the expansion of West Port, a new and dual set of lines had been built. Now, the ties were gone, replaced with an asphalt path filled with people walking, jogging, and exercising their pets, even some riding bicycles. It paralleled the wide Boca River, and here and there patches of grass-covered areas held picnic facilities. Swimming in the river was outlawed because of its high level of pollution. Industrial wastes and agricultural fertilizer runoff had long ago fouled its waters, though reclamation procedures were now in effect. River trout had returned as had fishing, though the waters had yet to be proven safe for humans.

Arm in arm, the two headed down the trail. "So tell me about yourself, Sondra. About all that I know is you were orphaned when you were two years old. How does the man who runs the pub where your apartment is at figure into it?"

"Not much to tell. He and I ended up with a pair of nasty foster parents," Sondra began, outlining her messed up childhood and how Ben always looked out for her, since no one else ever had. She finished some time later, "So you see, I do have a sort of a knack for helping others, especially if it involves electronics and the Internet."

"Interesting. Do you do any hacking?" he asked.

"I know. That's illegal, but yes, a bit, only when there are no other avenues available to help the client," she admitted. "So tell me about yourself. How come you became a detective?"

Matt chuckled. "Well, I guess I am lucky. I've a brother and a sister. My folks are retired now, living on the southeastern edge of the city. Dad was a building inspector for many years, and I used to tag along with him. I didn't go to the Academy though. Book learning and I didn't get along, and I just barely made it through high school. In my senior year, one friend of mine was beaten and robbed, but the police couldn't find the culprits. So I got interested and eventually tracked them down. I can't tell you how great the feeling of satisfaction I had was when they were arrested and thrown into jail for their crimes. After that, I knew I had to become a cop, a detective actually. So Sondra, I know exactly how you feel when you help someone. Makes life worth living, I think."

"Yes, life's a bitch, but helping others kind of makes up for it. At least, it does more or less for me," Sondra admitted. "I hate to cut our walk short, but my feet are starting to protest. God, why did Sable always have to wear such high heels anyway?"

"Cause they look really sexy?" Matt suggested teasingly. "You best keep on wearing them. We need you being Sable for a while longer, until we catch these criminals." He purposely stopped at one small concession stand by one of the grassy picnic areas and bought them each a soda. Together, they sat down on the grass and watched the giant river barges moving up and down the Boca, transporting grains into the city, while taking manufactured goods up north on their return trips.

Neither said much for a time, merely sipping their

sodas and watching the sunny day pass by. Suddenly, Matt whispered, "Don't look up. There are two men shadowing us. Slowly, let's get up and head back. I've my gun ready. Is yours in your purse?"

"Yes, right where I can get at it. Where are the men? Can you help me up? This damned corset is a royal pain too, you know."

Matt laughed. "Yes, you women do have to look fabulous, don't you."

"Sable did, not me," Sondra retorted, and they both laughed. Meanwhile, she noticed the two men, but didn't recognize them. "Are you sure they're watching us?"

"Yes. It took a while for me to confirm it. At first, I thought they were just looking at you—you know, because you look fabulous, but my gut tells me differently. I doubt they're going to try anything out here in public," Matt whispered.

"Well, perhaps they recognize you. My being with a police detective might give them pause to think about shooting me," Sondra whispered hopefully.

"I'm not that well known around the city, but you could have a point. Keep alert," he replied. An hour later, they entered Sable's home again. The men had followed them down the trail, but apparently, they lost them once they took off in Matt's car.

Matt suggested, "Mind if I spend tonight here? I don't want anything to happen to you."

"I'd love to have you with me, Matt. I'll see what I can fix up for supper, but I might have to order something. Sable wasn't big on cooking; at least that's what I think."

Nothing further happened that night, though the two kept watch while pretending to watch a movie on Sable's big screen. Beth merely giggled when she arrived Monday morning and found Matt was still here. After he left and she and Sondra had breakfast, she said, "Now that's a fine catch, Sable. He's really handsome, isn't he?"

Sondra blushed. "Well, yes he is. He's been guarding me. I had another scare with the gunmen over the weekend." Beth insisted on hearing all about it while she dressed Sondra in a new outfit.

That handled, Beth again complained about her impossible homework again. "Say," Sondra suggested, "bring it with you when you come by this evening. I bet I can help you out with the web page design assignment."

"Really? I didn't think you knew anything about that," Beth replied, but gladly accepted her help. "I'll bring all of it."

During the day, Sondra decided to do a bit of hacking. The men who were trying to kill her had to be identified somehow. The only clue she had was the cloned phone and the text messages from her supposed "client." Already, she'd discovered they were burner phones, discardable and untraceable. However, someone had to have purchased them. She sat down at Sable's computer to do a bit of hacking and sleuthing. An hour later, she sat back looking at what she'd uncovered.

Aerostar Engines Corporation had purchased the phone used by her "client" along with a dozen others, while the Galactic Dynamics Corporation had purchased her mark's phone. *So Aerostar is spying on the off-worlders, GD, who are slowly buying up all of West Port properties. Interesting. Corporate espionage, I'll wager, but what has this to do with Sable? Was she involved in spying for maybe Aerostar? I can't imagine her spying for GD. Hell, no one really likes them, except for our political leaders. Well, I'll text this info to Matt.* She did just that.

That done, she called up Ben to let him know she was okay, but still hadn't figured out what was going on. They chatted for twenty minutes before Ben was finally convinced she was all right. At this point, Sondra couldn't think of any other avenue she could pursue and decided to sit back and see what Matt could turn up.

# Chapter 6—Weird DNA

Sable only had the one pants outfit. Hence, Sondra wore another one of her red satin fetish outfits, chosen by Beth. This one fit her tightly down to her knees, but allowed her more freedom of motion, except the matching red outer corset made her nearly immobile except for waist bends. Still, she knew she did look good and couldn't wait for Matt to see her in this outfit.

Beth came by around 4:30 and fixed their supper. After that, as promised, Sondra lent her a hand with her first web page design. "Look Beth. I know you are an artist in training. When you finally get your art done and ready for sale, you are going to need a web page to promote it. That's why you need to know the basics. So let's get going." For the next hour, Sondra went over the basics, pointing out why the user guidelines were necessary to follow.

"Look, when someone finds your pages, they will expect your pages to operate the same way as everyone else's do. If you have it set up differently, that's going to upset them considerably."

"I think I see. So how's this?" Beth replied. An hour later, Beth had her first major web assignment completely finished and a week ahead of its due date. "I never knew you knew so much about the web stuff, Sable. This is incredible. Thank you, thank you."

Just then, Matt rang the doorbell, and Beth, giving Sondra a wink, said, "I'll be running along and leave you two alone. Go for it," she giggled.

When they were alone, Matt said, "Thanks for the text. So we now know that Aerostar Engines and Galactic Dynamics are involved. Corporate espionage perhaps. Everyone knows GD isn't well liked by our local corporations. Come. Sit down. I have a bit of startling news to share with you too." They sat down in her living room. She noticed he couldn't take his eyes off her legs and dress.

"I look good, eh?" she decided to tease him.

Matt swallowed. "Damn good, Sondra. A knockout. How am I going to keep my attention on the business at hand?" Both chuckled.

Then he began quite seriously. "Okay, the DNA results came back from Rosewood. I brought along copies for you." He laid the two nicely labeled pages on the couch between them.

"Sorry, I don't know anything about DNA stuff."

"Neither do I, so I had them explain it to me. It goes like this. Your DNA and Sable's are very nearly identical. So yes, this proves that Sable Lorraine Hampton is or was your biological sister."

"I knew it had to be. I wish she wasn't dead though."

"So do I, but there's more. Your two samples should not be very nearly identical, Sondra. There is always some variation even among identical twins. Yet, you two are so darn close that there's only .001% difference, literally unheard of."

"What does that mean, Matt? We looked identical as far as I could tell in that brief encounter."

"Clones. It is possible you are clones of each other or someone else."

"But cloning and genetic experimenting on humans is highly illegal. Even I know that much," Sondra gushed, trying to grasp what this all meant.

"Quite true, highly illegal, and totally unethical. As far as I can tell, no one has ever actually cloned another human being, so while that's what the DNA tests are suggesting, we know that can't be the right interpretation. Rather, we think you and Sable are very identical twins, very identical twins," he repeated for emphasis.

"Is that possible?"

"No one at Rosewood could say for sure, only that must be the explanation for these results. I'm inclined to believe that explanation, since the results came back on your two birth certificates. Guess what? Both certificates are forgeries!"

"What? I'm not me?" Sondra gushed. "But I'm twenty-two. I can't be much older than that. I went to school with other kids my own age."

"No, you are likely twenty-two, dear. What it means is

that someone has purposely fabricated fake birth certificates, hiding your actual birth parents and making it impossible to track your birth. Obviously, they couldn't lie about your age. I suspect the date of birth might be accurate or nearly so, give or take a few months. That much can't be faked," Matt explained.

"So what does this mean? Sable was my sister and someone covered up our records? What happened to our parents? Maybe they were murdered too? Why send twins to different foster homes and with very different names? Matt, this is making even less sense to me."

Matt sighed, "To you and me both. Someone went to an enormous amount of trouble and clearly way outside the law to disguise your birth information. So yes, you can say it again, Sondra, life's a bitch. What a curve we've been thrown. Still, we will keep doggedly at it. Someone out there knows what actually happened. We just have to find that person. And we will. I promise you that we will, Sondra."

She leaned over and hugged him tightly. Acting on impulse, she gave him a passionate kiss. He responded in kind, sliding his hands over her satin gown and exciting her even more. Feelings and emotions long dormant in Sondra suddenly arose and came to the fore. Before long, by mutual consent, they ended up sharing the master bed that evening.

In the morning, Matt whispered in her ear as they lay beside each other and rather tangled in her long hair, "I've never met anyone like you, Sondra. I'm falling in love with you."

"Same here. I falling in love with you too, Matt." She gave him another passionate kiss, but both had to get up since Beth wisely announced her arrival by making noise in the kitchen. She'd seen his car out front and his makeshift bed untouched. When the two came down for breakfast, arm in arm, she giggled.

Later after Matt had showered and left for work, she said, "Now you *have* to tell me all about it!"

Sondra flushed. "I think we're in love, Beth. I've never been in love before. I feel so different!" The two chatted until Beth left for her classes.

Around noon, she received a text from Sandy. It read:

Come to the symphony concert Friday night at seven. A box seat will be provided in the name of Sable Hampton.

She reread it twice. *The symphony?* She'd never been to one, but had some idea of where the concert hall was located over in the east side of the city. Obviously, she was to go alone; the singular was used. At last, she replied: K. That done, she headed for the computer to look up all she could find on the symphony. She'd never been exposed to classical music, not living in Snake Town. From the photos on the web page, she was able to see that people dressed up to go to this concert thing.

That done, she texted Matt with this news. He replied he'd go along and keep an eye on her. She smiled while reading his reply. *I feel so light,* she thought. *I want him around me all the time. How silly of me. Get your head back on,* Sondra. *Get back to sleuthing.*

After another digression to make a cup of hot tea, Sondra decided she had two avenues she could explore. One, she could research babies being born in West Port around the time of her birth and see if somehow she could find her real parents. Two, there was this conflict between Galactic Dynamics and Aerostar Engines to study. She opted to look for her parents.

Records were kept at a dozen hospitals around the sprawling city. She decided to bracket the date by two months on either side of the theoretical birth date. In a city of ten million, many babies were born on the same day. However, she was looking for records of multiple births, hoping that would narrow down her search. The two birth certificates came from different hospitals and different delivery doctors, so that didn't help either, besides, a quick check revealed neither doctor actually existed.

Soon, she realized she was going to have to hack into each hospital's database, which was illegal, and she decided against that just now. There was Matt to consider now. Instead, the newspaper, the West Port Times, carried birth records daily. A few minutes later, she found all their papers for the last fifty years were available online. However, she'd have to go through each one visually, painstakingly slow and tedious. Sighing, she began at two months before the recorded birth date. By evening, she estimated she would need at least a week to go through each one, but Sondra was determined to do it, and Matt encouraged her as well. It was something positive that she could do.

Friday arrived without event. No gunmen had returned. Sondra now had a new theory why that was. The enemy now knew that she was being watched over by the police, but Matt didn't buy that explanation. On their detective front, neither had uncovered any more significant clues, much to their annoyance. Still, Matt urged patience.

"So what do you want to wear to the concert tonight?" Beth asked. They'd finished supper. It was time to get Sondra ready for the affair. In addition, as soon as she was done here, Beth had her own date waiting to take her to the movies.

"You decide. What looks the best on me? From the images I saw, everyone dresses up fancy."

"You got it boss. This one is my favorite, and you look fabulous in it." Beth soon had her zipped up into a sky blue satin gown that had only one thin strap over her left shoulder. It fit her curves tightly down to her knees, where a flair began, expanding to nearly two feet across near the floor. Her pumps were matching, as was her outer corset. "Now drape your hair over your right shoulder. There. Take a look. I think you look stunning in this one."

"Wow. I do look good, don't I?" For the first time, Sondra realized that she actually did look quite stunning in these uncomfortable fetish gowns.

While she continued to admire her new look, Beth said, "See, told you. Now, I'm off. Bill's taking me to the movies tonight. Hot date. Hope yours turns out hot too." She giggled, turned, and left. Sondra continued to admire new looks in the mirror for a time. *What will Matt say when he sees me in this one? Now why am I worried about what he thinks? What matters is what I think, Sondra, and I think I look good in this one. Come on; get it together. You still have to change purses.*

Soon, she had her matching purse ready to go, and she headed down to the front door to wait for Matt to show up. As always, he was punctual. As he entered, his eyes met hers.

"Wow!" they exclaimed in unison.

"You look great," Sondra quickly said, before he could get another word out. He wore a rented black suit that was obviously very carefully matched to his measurements. His polished black shoes reflected the overhead lights.

"You've out done yourself this time, Sondra. You look fantastic, but we best hurry up. I checked on the box seats. They are on the second floor, so I may be able to spot you from down there. Have you ever heard a symphony concert?"

"Er, no. We Snake Town folks don't get over on the east side of town much. Besides, I expect that we couldn't afford tickets. How about you?" she asked as they waited for her taxi to arrive.

"Same here. Nope. Never been to one before. I hope it isn't too boring. You can make a paper airplane and toss it down on me if I fall asleep," Matt jested. She smiled. "Ah, taxi's here. Remember, if you run into trouble, just scream."

*Like that's going to happen. I can take care of myself, well mostly.* "Okay. I do hope we learn something tonight. This is incredibly frustrating for me and for you too." Matt nodded and got her into the waiting cab. Once it was off, he followed her in his car, thankful that no one was watching her place. He'd been very alert for just that, but so far, the gunmen continued to stay away from her place.

An attendant opened the taxi door for her and gave her a hand getting out, for which Sondra was quite grateful, since she was quite confined in her outfit. As she walked into the entrance, she spotted a ticket area and headed there. "I believe you have a box seat for me, Miss Sable Hampton."

"Of course, madam. One moment," the well-dressed man said, scrolling down the reservations. Shortly, he produced a ticket for her, Box Seat 10. "To your right, madam. Show this to usher, and he will escort you to your seat." She thanked him and soon found the usher, who was dressed in a fine suit and carried a flashlight in one hand. The whole entry area was done in plush red carpeting, with golden chandeliers providing the warm illumination. Climbing the stairs was just barely manageable. The tight-fitting gown only barely permitted her to take each step, and then only slowly.

At last, she arrived at an oak door with the number 10 on it. The usher opened it for her, and she stepped inside. As she stepped into her box, she forgot to breathe! The box hung in space far above the giant fan shaped arena. Down below her lay rows and rows of soft seats. There were only a few seats to a row up front, but fanning out to far too many to count at the rear. Up front behind a red curtain lay the stage. She counted twenty box seats on each side of the concert hall. Somewhere down there would be Matt.

The box was small, just two very plush chairs done in red velvet. She sat down on one. Incredibly soft. *I bet this chair cost a fortune! Wow. I wish Matt could see them. I wonder if I can spot him down there?* Just then, a dozen more golden chandeliers illuminated the main floor, and she watched as the well-dressed men and women in their elegant gowns filed in and took their seats. *Why here?* Sondra wondered. None of this made the slightest sense to her. *Why does Sandy want me here of all places?* She sat stiffly waiting for the music to begin. The dual corsets forced her to sit with very good posture. Then, the lights flashed once, and she wondered what that meant. Less than a minute later, the lights slowly dimmed, and the giant curtain moved aside, revealing the hundred twenty member orchestra on the large stage.

Uniformly, the musicians wore black, as though this was a funeral, she thought. Plus, each had a black stand in front of them. A few instruments she recognized, the drums and horns, similar to those she'd played with in grade school. A man dressed in a black tuxedo walked out on stage, accompanied by a loud round of applause. Mechanically, Sondra clapped along with them, though she didn't know why they were clapping. He'd done nothing but walk on stage. He carried a small stick, which he waved about a bit. Then, suddenly the music began, loud and thunderous, but also very upbeat and joyful—at least that's how she described it. Only then did she realize that the usher had handed her a program. There was a dim light illuminating the box, just enough for her to read: Leonardo: Violin Concerto Number 3 in D Minor. Soloist: Alice Middleton.

She looked up only to see that Sandy had somehow

slipped into her box seat, silent as a cat! Sandy whispered, "Look at the soloist. There," she pointed to a young woman with light brown hair, quite short. She held a violin and watched the man with the stick. Suddenly, Sondra wanted to shriek! To cry out! But she dare not. The young woman looked exactly like herself! Sandy whispered, "That's Alice, your sister, we think. You'll meet her after the concert. She's a fantastic violinist! Best in West Port and maybe all Virge-C."

Sondra simply stared at Alice, committing her image to her memory for all time. Part of her believed that soon Alice would be dead, just as Sable was, before she could even talk to her. Wild emotions flooded through her, but the music itself soon took control of her emotions, forcing them to flow along the lines the composer had intended. The second movement was slow and mournful, though somehow capturing the grief Sondra felt standing over the dying Sable. The sounds coming from Alice's violin commanded her in a way that she'd never felt before. Soaring, graceful, and yet commanding—all at the same time. Her eyes watered continuously. For once, Sondra was glad she had stopped wearing the makeup that Sable always wore. Beth had complained, but went along with her request to abandon it.

The final movement was more like a rousing dance, celebrating life, and yet with a dark overtone that in spite of everything, life was still a bitch. Sondra smiled as she thought this. Beautiful and sad at the same time. *God, Alice sure is good.*

When the piece finished, the audience responded with a thunderous applause. Alice took numerous bows before returning to her position as first violinist in the West Port Symphonic Orchestra. A short march-like piece came next and then intermission. The house lights went up.

"Well, what do you think of my mate? Alice. She and I are married," Sandy said softly.

"I cried all through it. She looked just like me and like Sable. Is she really my sister? When can I meet her?" Sondra gushed rapidly.

"After the concert is done, we'll meet her in her dressing room. That's the only safe, secure place we can meet. No one is allowed backstage. Someone is trying to kill her, so we are being extra careful about everything. We'll explain later. You weren't followed here, were you?" Sandy asked, suddenly remembering to ask that key question.

"I took a taxi, but I didn't see anyone. No one has tried to kill me this week, not since your last warning. Maybe they won't try any more. I have a thousand questions."

Sandy smiled. "I bet you do. Sable did too. I told her to take a taxi but no, she had to walk. She was on her way to meet up with us when she was killed." At that, Sandy's eyes watered, and both women remained lost in their own thoughts for a minute. Finally, she was able to repeat, "We'll talk more when the concert's done." Sondra took that as ending this chance to ask questions. Instead, she asked about the concert, the hall, and the music, explaining she'd never heard this kind of music. That gave Sandy something comfortable to chat about, which she did willingly.

The lights dimmed again. All through the second half, Sondra kept wishing they'd hurry up and get done. Time seemed to move along slower than a snail; she was so anxious to meet Alice, praying that no one would suddenly stand up and shoot her before her eyes. Only now did Sondra realize just how that incident had affected her mental well-being! Finally, the concert was over. The curtain closed, and Sondra hoped with all her might that Alice was still alive!

"We wait a bit to allow the crowd to disperse some. Then, we'll head backstage to her dressing room. Only a few performers have their own private dressing room. I must say, I do like your outfit. I think it suits you better than it did Sable, who favored red gowns, but you probably have figured that out already."

Sondra chuckled. "Honestly, I've not paid that much attention to Sable's wardrobe, except that it sure isn't what I'm used to wearing."

Shortly, Sandy rose. "Follow me. I'll go slowly for you." She led her out and down a back way. To Sondra, it seemed they were in some kind of maze with no way out. That was an exaggeration. She saw clearly marked Exit signs periodically, but they pointed in opposite directions to their travel. Sandy wore a rather plain blue dress, elegant in its own right, loose fitting and flowing, but she wore practical low heels. Still, she was considerate of Sondra's slow pace.

Finally, they reached a door, and Sandy knocked. "It's us, Alice." She heard someone unlocking the door and it opened, revealing the black-gowned Alice. The two women stared at each other's faces, identical to each other. Sandy pushed Sondra on inside, shut the door, and slid the lock shut. She was taking no chances.

Sondra threw her arms around Alice, who did likewise. For a time, the two stood there hugging each other for all time. Just then, all three were startled by a knock on the door. "Miss Alice, a policeman is here for you."

"That's Henry. Open it. Police? What's up?" Sandy whispered, but opened the door, revealing Matt standing beside the usher named Henry.

"Hello. Detective Matt Homes. I'm with her. May I come in?"

"You bet! Matt, this is my sister, Alice," Sondra gushed, pulling him in, ignoring the astonished looks on the other two women's faces. Mechanically, Sandy locked the door.

"Oh, I should explain. Matt and I are working together to find out who killed Sable. He's my boyfriend now too. So anything you wanted to say to me you can say to him. He knows everything that I know. We have so many questions for you two. Are we really sisters? That would make us triplets, wouldn't it?"

Sandy and Alice looked relieved and accepted her explanation for Matt's presence. "Come sit. We've probably got as many questions as you do," Alice said, motioning to some chairs, while Sandy hastily got out folding chairs for her and Matt to use.

"We got the DNA results back Tuesday. It's a match," Alice began. "In fact, Sable's DNA and ours are nearly identical, so we're sisters; triplets is our best guess. Oh, I'm Alice Middleton. She's Sandy Wade-Middleton, my mate. So you're really Sondra Sofia Shelley. Sandy said you didn't act right at the dance and was going to challenge you. Glad she did, but what happened to Sable? Was she really shot right in front of you? At least that's what Sandy told me."

"I'll go first, since my story is short," Sondra suggested. Quickly, she again relived that terrible night, telling Alice all about it. Meanwhile, Matt quietly compared their DNA test results with the pair he had in his pocket. When she finally finished her tale, Matt spoke up.

"I've been comparing Alice's DNA report with those I have from Sondra and Sable. Honestly, ladies, they are all three identical, and they shouldn't be this darn close. As I told Sondra, this could well be more indicative of clones than it is for identical triplets. I suspect that when we examine your birth certificate, Alice, we will find that it too is a fake."

"What? A fake? That can't be. Well, maybe it could be. I'm about ready to believe anything about now," Alice exclaimed. Sandy quickly put a supporting arm around her mate. "I suppose I should tell you everything that we know."

"Please, that would save us having to ask many questions," Matt said softly and considerately.

"Well, I'm an orphan, just as Sable was. The Middleton's, who were musicians, raised me. I took to the violin when I was five and am now the first violinist for the West Port Symphony Orchestra. Five years ago, I met Sandy here in school, and we, well, we fell in love and got married two years ago. I guess it was about six months ago now, Sandy here ran into Sable and did a double take. Sable looked just like me, except that she had hair as long as yours, Sondra. I keep mine short so it doesn't get in the way of my playing."

After Sandy told me about Sable, I just had to see for myself, and we paid a call on her. I can't begin to tell you how spooky that was—looking into her face, which was my face! Anyway, Sable insisted we must be identical sisters. Her theory was we were separated when our parents died. We compared birth certificates, but that suggested we weren't even related. Well, eventually, we decided to have our DNA tested."

"That way, they would know for sure," Sandy interrupted. "It was my idea they do it. I wish now I'd never suggested it. All the trouble happened after that."

Alice continued. "We got it done, and the results told us

what we just knew. We were identical twins sisters. Shortly after that, Sable began seeing a man following her around. As the days went by, accidents began to happen around her. I think she narrowly missed being killed four times. By then, we were paranoid that someone was trying to kill us. I lucked out. When I submitted my DNA sample, I used a fake name. If only I'd done that with Sable's sample, then maybe she'd still be alive. I just know that's what got her killed and not me."

"Hey, honey, it's not your fault. Besides, I've been taking every precaution I can think of to keep you safe," Sandy declared emphatically.

"Alice, I know how you must feel. When Sable was shot right in front of me, I thought it was my fault, because she had her phone in her hand and I'd just cloned my mark's phone. It's taken me days to get over my feelings of guilt, but even if that was the reason she was murdered, I didn't pull the trigger. Maybe I was just a bystander, and she was his real target. Why? Life's a bitch. I don't know, but I'll spend the rest of my life trying to find out why and who."

"Tell me about these accidents," Matt probed a little.

"It was really spooky," Alice said, wiping a trace of water from her eyes. "One day, she was returning from shopping with her arms full of packages—down on Main Street where all the fashion shops are at. She accidentally dropped one and stopped to pick it up. As she did so, workers accidentally dropped a heavy crate from the roof. It landed two feet from where she stopped. If she hadn't dropped the package, she would have been crushed to death."

Sandy broke in, "So you see, they failed to kill her by staging an 'accident,' so they had to shoot her. Someone wanted her dead, but for the life of us, we can't figure out why. I mean she was just being a Fetish Queen. Why kill her for wearing exotic outfits? Lots of men and women think she looked fabulous and very sexy. Makes no sense."

"I know. It doesn't," Sondra agreed with her, but changed the topic. "Sandy, how come you knew some gunmen were coming to Sable's house to shoot her? You sent me two very timely warnings. If you hadn't, why, I would be dead too."

Sandy flushed. "I work as a secretary-receptionist for

Galactic Dynamics' group of top executives, including Mr. Diego de la Vasco. Twice, I overheard them calling someone on a cell phone, ordering them to break in and shoot Sable Hampton. When it wouldn't rouse their suspicions, I went to the restroom and sent you a quick text. I don't know if they are on to me or not, but they haven't done that this week. Why would the head of GD want to kill Sable? He invited her to his fancy CEO Ball."

"Incredible! Well done, Sandy," Matt praised her. "But you be careful. If they find out that you are tipping Sable off, they'll kill you too."

"This is getting weirder by the minute," Sondra broke in. "Look, I was able to get a partial trace on the burner phones of my supposed client and the mark, who murdered Sable. The phones themselves are untraceable, but I found they were sold in batches. The phone used by the guy who shot Sable was part of a lot purchased by Galactic Dynamics. The phone used by my client was part of a lot purchased by Aerostar Engines. Was Sable involved in corporate spying or something?"

"Hardly, Sondra. She was nothing more than she seemed," Sandy defended Sable. "If she was, she never told us."

"Well, I went through all her things and didn't find anything suspicious either. I think we can rule out that she was spying for someone. So why are the two big corporations involved in this?" Sondra asked rhetorically, knowing that none here had an answer. The topic changed to one of sharing much about themselves, and Matt quietly stepped out of the room to allow the two sisters time to get acquainted and with Alice's mate.

*What's going on here? Some kind of conspiracy among the corporations, I'll bet anything,* Matt thought. *We have the two biggest corporations fighting against each other. Everyone knows that's been going on for years, but why involved these women? No sense. We must be missing something key, but what? Damn, I have to find out or Sondra is doomed. Best not tell her that though; she has enough worries of her own. So just what do I do next? There's nothing in the detective's manual that covers this kind of mess.*

An hour later, Sondra finally joined Matt. "Oh, you're still here. Watching my back big boy?" she asked teasingly.

"It's such a pretty back," he teased her and gave her a loving kiss.

"Best get me home quickly, that is if you still want me all hot," she joked, but dared not say that she truly meant it!

***

During the following week, nothing unusual occurred. The three women had exchanged phone numbers and sent texts to each other regularly. Matt continued to look into unexplained "accidents" and found well over a dozen such incidents that were at least reported to the police, though nothing was actually done about them. Now he had a stack of these files on his desk along with a mountain of cold cases. He began to wonder if many of these cold cases and accident cases were related to the ongoing conflict between the off-worlders and the locals.

For her part, Sondra continued going through the ancient newspapers, checking birth records, but now focusing on triplets being born. Such was quite rare, and she hoped this would narrow down the search. When she finally finished her survey of births two months on either side of her birthday, she had uncovered four sets of triplets being born. Unfortunately, each of these four sets was well documented and was still alive, though most were married and had families of their own. She'd struck out.

Sighing, she turned her research efforts down another path. This feud between Galactic Dynamics and Aerostar Engines lay somehow behind the killing—at least the shooter worked for GD. Just what had been going on? History wasn't one of those things that interested her in school. Staying alive was. So with little else to do, Sondra began researching this area.

# Chapter 7—Corporate Wars

Sondra's research began to pay off in that a larger picture of corporate greed and brutality emerged. Space travel finally became commonplace on Virge-C some seventy years ago. True, years before that, they had been able to send men to the two moons of Virge-C, but until seventy years ago, they'd not had the technology to travel much beyond there. It was at this point that Aerostar Engines developed their revolutionary EM engine, which allowed spaceships to travel drastically farther out into their planetary system, exploring the four gas giants and countless moons, bringing back extremely valuable ores, which fueled further research and development.

Then, fifty years ago, representatives of the Galactic Federation landed on Virge-C. The stir that their arrival caused was remarkable. The newspaper's headlines occupied half of the page! A photo of the aliens covered the rest of the front page. Everything changed after that encounter.

After a diplomatic rush pushed primarily by Governor Thomas Miller, the current governor's father, Virge-C was admitted into the Galactic Federation, joining hundreds of other space-faring worlds. Sondra focused on what concessions Governor Miller had to make for Virge-C to be allowed into the federation, as this seemed to her to be the most fruitful approach to take, since these people were aliens.

She was sidetracked by descriptions of other worlds of the federation. Virge-C was run by President John Johnson, a Legislature, and Courts of Law. In sharp contrast, these federation worlds were wholly run by the giant corporations. All land, all buildings, and all companies were owned by the corporations, with Galactic Dynamics, Galactic Electronics, and General Robotics being the three largest, followed by General Goods and several others. These corporations made the world's laws, enforced them, and handled violators.

The normal citizen worked for one of these corporations and paid rent to the appropriate corporation for their home or small business, paid for their food, clothing, and other essentials of life. Even the banking system was controlled by the corporations, who had their hands in every facet of life on these federation worlds.

The corporations justified their methods by claiming exorbitant costs of finding and colonizing new worlds. *Well, that surely is a costly enterprise,* Sondra thought, *but still. . . Who keeps the corporations in line?* She could not discover an answer. The top executives of these corporations actually ran their worlds. They could and did whatever they desired, as long as their actions didn't severely affect overall corporate profits. The only thing that truly mattered to these CEOs was maintaining a goodly profit, but expansion to new worlds was secondary, as it was a sure way to enlarge corporate profits.

So what had Governor Miller had to give up in order for Virge-C to be admitted into the Galactic Federation? She soon discovered the answer, though indirectly at first. Initially, the corporations were allowed to purchased land and buildings to begin their presence on Virge-C. After that, they were permitted to buy up all the land and buildings they desired. No local company could compete with the seemingly unlimited finances these off-world corporations had.

Some forty years ago, Aerostar Engines wanted to buy up one of its smaller competitors, Eagle Engines Limited. They offered the owners a fair price for the company. However, just as the deal was about to be accepted by the owners, Galactic Dynamics stepped in and doubled Aerostar's offer, which the owners eagerly accepted. Who wouldn't accept twice what the company was worth? Sondra believed this incident might have been the starting point of the conflict between these two corporations.

She looked into what became of Eagle Engines Limited after the purchase and found the company had been disbanded, though key personnel were hired by Galactic Dynamics. Embolden by this discovery, she began to search West Port's landowner and tax records. Her idea was to get some kind of idea just how much of her city was now owned by GD.

Two days later, she sat back shocked at what she'd found. One of these off-world corporations owned nearly half of all skyscrapers in West Port. Nearly all the manufacturing plants, save a very few, were likewise owned by them. These corporations owned fully half of the smaller land parcels with their apartments, homes, and small businesses. Galactic Dynamics held even Ben's mortgage! That shocked her considerably.

In just fifty years, these off-world corporations owned outright nearly half of West Port! What about the rest of Virge-C, she wondered. She spent another week researching this aspect, focusing first on the major mines and industries scattered about her world. What she found amazed her. Nearly half of the companies whose gross income exceeded five million gold dollars were now owned by one of these off-world corporations!

That night when Matt dropped by, she gushed, "Matt, do you realize that in another fifty years, these off-world corporations will own everything on Virge-C that is worth anything? It's astounding what they now own. Here, look at what I've uncovered. Our leaders and company owners are systematically selling off our world to these beastly corporations!"

Matt looked over her accumulated results and slumped into a sofa. "My God, Sondra, this is beyond belief! These corporations control almost half of West Port. No wonder I'm not getting a raise or a promotion. I have been rather vocal against allowing the corporate executives to dictate new laws for the force to carry out. Damn, this is bad, really bad. They are taking over our world and the average person knows nothing about this."

"Probably won't until it is too late," Sondra added, thankful that Matt saw this the way she did, the destruction of their world.

"Creeping control, that's what it is. Little by little. Mark my words, Sondra, one of these days, these executives will simply issue new laws and no one will own enough of anything themselves to do anything about it," Matt declared, running his hands through his hair.

"So I bet Aerostar Engines people are trying to do something about it," Sondra expressed her newest theory.

"You know," Matt said after a moment's reflection, "this is beginning to explain my pile of cold cases."

"Huh? What do you mean?"

"Well, on those cases where the victim was an off-worlder, our force has been pushed really hard to solve the crime, and yet where the victim was a local, our force has only paid it lip service, as far as I am concerned. Take Sable's case. It was marked a cold case two days after it happened. I barely got to search your apartment at Ben's place before I was told it was now a low priority cold case. I protested, but the bosses said to treat it as any other cold case on my desk."

"I see what you mean. The corporation executives now have undue influence over our own police force. Matt, this isn't good at all!" Sondra declared.

"No, I am afraid things are going to get a whole lot worse."

The two chatted for some time over these findings, before they were interrupted by an incoming text message. "Oh, it's from Rene. You remember her from the CEO Ball? She wore those incredible ballet boots. Her parents own that small company that makes them. Shit! Matt! Look," she turned her phone so he could read the message: Help!

That was all it said. Sondra sent back several more replies, but got nothing more back from Rene. "Come on; get your gun. We're heading over to her place now," Matt ordered. As quickly as she could, Sondra complied and shortly with blazing siren, the pair flew through the streets of West Port, arriving some ten minutes later at the small combination home and factory called the Shoe Box. Lights were on, but the front doors were splintered. Guns drawn, the pair entered, Sondra staying well back, constrained to taking small steps in her spike heeled boots.

"Shit! Homicide. Best stay back, dear. It's grim in here," Matt called out, holstering his gun. She ignored him and entered anyway. There on the living room couch lay two older people, presumably the parents of Rene.

"Where's Rene?" she asked, fearing the worst. While Matt called in for backup and the crime response team, Sondra moved from room to room as quickly as she could, calling out for Rene. Suddenly, her voice stopped, worrying Matt, who headed towards where he'd last heard her voice coming from. He found her holding Rene's phone.

"Her phone. She's been kidnaped, Matt. I just know it. We have to find her."

"We will, as soon as help gets here. Look around. See if her parents have any kind of surveillance systems in place. I'd expect they would. This place is also their small shoe factory," Matt advised.

"On it," she acknowledged. This she could do and quickly she spotted the nearly hidden cameras. By the time many others arrived including the medical examiner, she found their control panel in a back room. She queued up the video and was ready to replay it when Matt entered, slipping a steadying arm around her.

"Good going, hot shot. Let's see if the video can tell us anything," he whispered.

Before long, another officer joined them, watching as well. Two men appeared before the front door. They had a battering ram in their hands and smashed the door open. Another camera showed the two men entering the living room and murdering the older couple at point blank range, execution style. "Hey, I recognize that man," the officer exclaimed. "He works for Galactic Dynamics. I've seen him around, a real trouble maker."

"Excellent. Take charge, find him, and arrest him for cold blooded murder," Matt ordered. "We'll watch the rest and see what happened to their daughter. I'll have someone take this video in for evidence. Once you catch him, from this recording, he'll be tried, convicted, and executed."

"You got it, detective!" The officer rushed out on fire. Meanwhile, the pair continued to watch the grizzly scene. Soon, the two men carried an unconscious Rene out of her back bedroom, past her dead parents in the living room, and on out the front door, where they stuffed her into what looked to be an emergency rescue vehicle.

"Can you zoom in on that vehicle?" Matt asked.

"Already working the controls," she replied sternly. Soon, they could see the company logo and the license plate.

Matt copied them down and then carefully collected the video disks, marked them as evidence, and handed them to another one of the officers, who promised to get it into the evidence locker, along with all the other forensics evidence the crime crew was gathering. Matt and Sondra then departed the scene, heading for headquarters.

"We're going to check the city-wide traffic cameras and see if we can follow where they went with that emergency rescue vehicle. Only police are allowed inside, so I'll drop you off at home, okay?"

Sondra grumbled, but couldn't argue the point. Once she was safely home, Matt left in a big hurry. She texted Sandy and Alice the awful news and then called for a taxi. On a hunch, she had the driver take her to the Galactic Dynamics skyscraper. "Now drive around the block please." He did so, watching the fare slowly increasing by the minute. "Wait. Stop here a minute." Hastily, she sent Matt a text message: Vehicle is parked outside GD skyscraper, west side. "Okay, take me home please." The driver smiled; the fare just doubled, making him a happy man.

He sent back: Thought u were home. Got 2 make a chain of evidence. Will c if she's there. Hours later, Matt returned to Sable's home, exhausted. He no more than got inside when Sondra fired questions at him.

Holding his hands up in protest, he said, "Yes, I found video surveillance evidence that they did carry her body out of that vehicle and into that skyscraper. It has been put in the evidence locker as well. I double-checked everything. It's all there down in lockup. Now we just have to wait until morning and see if this man can be found and arrested. We will have Rene back in the morning. I'm exhausted. Come on. let's get some sleep."

Sondra was up at dawn and even had coffee waiting for Matt, surprising Beth when she arrived. "Oh, taking over for me now are you?" Beth teased, nodding towards her bedroom where Matt was still sleeping.

With a somber face, Sondra relayed what had happened last night, scaring Beth more than a little. "They just broke in, killed her parents, and kidnaped her? Unbelievable. Is no one safe around here anymore?" After fixing them breakfast, watching the handsome Matt eat, and then leave for work, she announced, "Sondra, I've changed my major."

"What?"

"Yes, what with everything going down the drain and the future being up there in the stars, I'm taking up being a shuttle pilot, er that's not quite right; they call it a transport pilot. Yes, I'm going to be a transport pilot. There's a future in that, not in drawing pretty pictures," Beth declared.

"Hey, go for it," Sondra exclaimed. "I think you're right about that. There should be many more well-paying jobs doing that. Plus, you won't have to make web pages." Both laughed at that.

"I get my first simulator run today. I'm so excited. Wish me luck," Beth gushed excitedly. Sondra did so and watched her scamper out of the home. *She really is excited about her career change. That's a good sign—being enthusiastic about your work. I wish Matt would hurry up and text me about Rene.*

Sondra paced the living room, around and around, but still no word came from Matt. She knew better than to text him needlessly. He was probably very busy with this very nasty crime. Still, she was very worried about Rene's welfare. What did they want with her anyway? Why kidnap her? Why kill her parents? This brutal crime made no sense at all.

When Matt arrived at headquarters, he found a new file sitting on his desk. Cold Case was stamped across its front. The tab read: the Harvester Murders. He opened it. There were the grizzly photos of last night's crime scene! "What the hell is going on?" he cried and with folder in hand, rushed into his boss' office.

"Ah, I see you found the newest cold case file. Nasty business. Hope you can solve it," he declared.

"Wait a minute. We know who shot the older couple and kidnaped their daughter, Rene. We know she was taken to the main GD skyscraper. We have video evidence down in lockup," Matt protested.

"Hardly. Sit down, Detective Homes. That's what you get by rushing things. Now the man who was supposedly identified in the surveillance footage has an airtight alibi. GD has ten men who swear he was on guard duty at their building all night long. And this video evidence you and Officer Henry claim to have seen simply doesn't exist. I checked the evidence locker myself this morning. No such video is there. True, someone made a paper trail error, logging them in as evidence, but they simply are not there."

Matt fumed, "You mean someone broke into our evidence locker and stole the incriminating evidence, don't you?"

"Now see here Detective Homes, that's an outrageous charge! Don't go fabricating evidence when there isn't any! It is officially a cold case now, so you better get busy and stop bothering those GD folks. It's obviously a local crime, burglary gone wrong or something. Dismissed."

Matt knew well enough not to press him any further. Obviously, someone had already gotten to the evidence and made it disappear! That could only mean someone who worked at police headquarters! Maybe even his boss was behind it! Matt was more than a little scared and headed back to his desk to think this through. It was obvious that someone from Galactic Dynamics ordered the hit on the parents and the kidnaping of Rene and that she was taken into their building late at night. But why? That led him nowhere, so he tried another angle. Someone at GD wanted this crime buried and called someone here at headquarters to do just that.

So who had the authority to go into the evidence locker and remove the video files? Who had the authority effectively to kill the case, marking it officially a Cold Case. Only his boss could do all that, and this scared Matt more than anything else did. The head of the police department of West Port was on the GD payroll! Suddenly, all the cold case files that he'd been given these past many weeks made sense. The boss was systematically burying those that GD wanted removed from active investigation! The man must be on GD's payroll!

He knew that Sondra was waiting anxiously for word on Rene and that he'd put off texting her for several hours. Reluctantly, Matt decided to speak to her personally. Stepping out of the building where he could not be overheard, he phoned her and told her what had just happened, knowing how she'd react. Sondra surprised him. Instead of an angry tirade, she said calmly, "This is to be expected, Matt. The CEOs now control our own police force. We're going to have to find Rene a different way. I'll see what I can do. Bye."

At first, while Matt was explaining what had happened at police headquarters, her anger seethed, but Sondra quickly realized this was a direct result of what her research suggested. Hence, she'd replied as she had. No, now it was back to her old ways of helping others, outside the police, outside the law.

*All right, we know she was taken into the GD skyscraper. Why? We don't know. Why were her parents killed? Again, don't know, unless they were simply in the way, but then that also doesn't make a whole lot of sense. Why not just knock them out and carry on with the kidnaping? Unless if not dead, they could raise a stink, preventing this one from being turned into a cold case. Pretty poor reason to take a gamble on murder and being caught. This time, the GD executives must have gotten very worried about how sloppy their thugs were—not only getting caught on video committing the murders but also bringing Rene into their building. No, I bet those men are seething with anger at the loused up job and having to call in heavy duty favors from Matt's boss to get it to go away.*

*First thing has to be finding a way to get into that building and search for Rene. That means I need the building's plans.* Satisfied of her first move, Sondra fired up Sable's computer and did a bit of hacking into public records. Galactic Dynamics bought the building from Best Hardware Corporate Headquarters. Hence, the building plans were on file, and she retrieved them.

Next, she needed a sample security pass for GD and that meant making a quick trip back into Snake Town, where she often conducted rather shady deals when needed. She changed into her old dress, the very one that she'd worn when she fled her apartment after Sable's death. She left Matt a note and headed off on foot, not wanting even a taxi to have a record of her movements. Once inside the boundaries of Snake Town, she make triply sure she wasn't being followed, before heading to the Goose, who had served her well in the past.

She returned well past suppertime, carrying quite a few packages. Both Matt and Beth were already there and were quite worried about her. "Where have you been? Don't you know it isn't safe out there?" Matt cried out.

"Madam, what's going on?" Beth wanted to know. "Supper is getting cold. And where on Virge-C did you get those awful rags you are wearing?"

"Sit down. Let's eat. Beth, I have to tell you something important, and I want you to swear to tell no one about this," Sondra replied, having already decided to let Beth in on just who she was and what was going on.

Over supper, she outlined everything to Beth, whose face grew whiter and whiter. "So you didn't have amnesia. Now things make so much more sense. You haven't behaved like the Sable I knew for two years. I promise I won't say anything, but do you still want me to work for you here like I have been?"

"Of course, I want you here, Beth. I, we need you, now more than ever. We must not let anyone know Sable is dead— not just yet. Besides somehow, I have to rescue Rene."

"Now how are you going to do that?" Matt barked, annoyed that she'd been off on her own and in Snake Town of all the nastiest places in West Port!

"Matt, I'm not sure of all the details yet. Trust me. I've done similar things for others who needed help. Rene certainly needs help, and the police aren't going to do anything at all. You know that. So give me time to work out the details," Sondra declared just as emphatically. Matt had no choice but to trust her. "Besides," she added, "I grew up in Snake Town. It's been my home for twenty years."

She knew the Goose would need a couple of days to get her what she needed. In the meantime, she needed clues about why Galactic Dynamics targeted these people. When Matt headed off to work the next day, she again went online, this time looking at newly filed legal briefs. Sure enough, she found what she desired. Galactic Dynamics filed a take-over bid to purchase the Shoe Box from Rene's parents, in gratuity as it were in this case, since the owners were now dead.

Checking the brief further, she found GD was paying one million gold dollars for the Shoe Box Company, to be paid to Rene or other nearest relatives should Rene be deceased. That seemed to be a huge sum, based on what Rene had told her at the CEO Ball, so Sondra then pulled up the Shoe Box's tax records for last year. They reported an income of a little under a hundred thousand. *Well, that's more like it,* she thought. *Take out operating expenses and they probably made fifty grand at most, enough to live comfortably. No wonder Rene was so keen on promoting their fancy, exotic boots. So GD paid ten times what the company was actually worth and to Rene no less. Does she know? Where is she? She's worth a million now.*

Sondra sat back pondering this new information. Then like a lightning bolt, it hit her. *Why kidnap Rene? To force her to marry a GD executive who would then have access to her million gold dollars!* "Follow the money trail," she cried out to the house. "With these greedy bastards, follow the money trail!"

Thus, Sondra reasoned, Rene must still be alive, at least long enough for some executive to marry her and abscond with her new fortune. Sondra was convinced that time was critical! Yet, she dared not hurry. She never, ever acted in haste. *No, slow and careful,* she reminded herself and then added, "Life's a bitch, especially if you're a bitch!" It seemed the walls of Sable's home fully agreed with her.

Next, she put her attention on working out just where inside that skyscraper Rene was being held. *First, I need to see if they have brought her out of there.* Sondra set to work, it being a simple matter for her to hack into the citywide surveillance system, an action she'd done even when in high school, only then it was for fun. She spent hours fast forwarding through several strategically placed street cams, watching men and women walking at enormous speeds into and out of the building and from several doorways.

After two days of eyestrain, she concluded Rene was still being held within that skyscraper, but where. She took a taxi downtown, but departed it several blocks from the Galactic Dynamics skyscraper. Slowly, she walked all around the block-wide, square building, covertly taking pictures of it as she went. An hour later and back home once more, she uploaded them all to Sable's computer and brought them all up, tiled nicely side by side. Sondra sat back and studied them.

Nearly a hundred stories tall with thousands of glass windows, this GD building was formidable with thousands of places inside where they could hide Rene. Still, she reasoned they would need to keep her away from the normal people who worked in the building, thousands of them. They would have to feed her as well. That meant she could not be just anywhere inside, but in some relatively isolated, but secure location, one which few had access to, but where?

After some study, one floor on one side got her attention. This particular set of windows was blacked out, opaque. All the other thousands of glass panes allowed light and visibility inside. She could barely make out some desks and possible people behind some. Had she a better camera than her phone's, she probably could have actually seen the people, maybe even well enough for Matt's photo id program.

"Why black out these windows?" she asked the computer, not expecting it to answer her. Sondra often asked questions aloud, hoping that would jar some detail she'd overlooked into view. "I wonder if they were always blacked out," An hour later, she'd found some old photos of the building before GD bought it. Presto, the windows were not blacked out. She counted the floors and discovered they were on the southwest corner of the thirteenth floor. Superstitious? Sondra wondered if these aliens actually kept a floor numbered thirteen. Looking at the original building plans, there wasn't a thirteenth floor. Was there now? She decided to ask Sandy about that the next time they chatted.

On the fourth day after Rene's abduction, Sondra again visited Snake Town. The Goose came through. She now had a *valid* security card that would allow her access to secured sections of the building, as well as open other doors, but the Goose only guaranteed it would work for one day. However, she'd already figured she'd enter via an entirely different route, perhaps one they wouldn't anticipate. First, she needed to construct her electronic *bomb*. This, she'd done several times before.

When Matt came home that night, he found Sondra dressed in men's clothes, all in black. She had a small backpack ready to go as well. "What's up?" he asked, looking her over.

"Time for action. Rene must be rescued tonight. You with me or not? It will be very risky, but I have the bases covered, I hope, dear."

He chuckled. "Dear, you aren't going anywhere without me. I take it I need to look like a thug as well?"

"Yes, unless you want to be recognized," she teased him. "Here, put these on. I hope they are the right size. I sort of guessed." A few minutes later, another black-clad man joined her. She explained further, "I have a rented car waiting a few blocks from here. Rented it under a fictitious name and paid cash. Can't be traced as long as we don't leave DNA in it, so we wear gloves and masks and take care of that detail."

"Okay. You think of everything. So what's the plan anyway? How are we going to get in there? How do we even know where she's being held? I have a whole lot of questions for you, if you hadn't guessed."

She showed him the blacked out thirteenth floor, there on the southwest side. "I suspect she's being held in there. As to getting in, I have a security pass that will work, but it might not by tomorrow. We're going in via the sewer system. Once inside, I will release my special electronic bomb, which will wreak havoc with their security camera system. We'll take the elevator to the thirteenth floor and see if we can find her. If she's not where I think she is, then we'll have to improvise from there. Once we have her, we'll take her out via the sewer to the waiting car. Sound good, dear?"

"Incredibly illegal, but these are aliens and have committed murder, kidnaping, and a police cover up, so in my book, this isn't illegal, but payback. Let's do it. I take it we take our guns with silencers on them?"

"Absolutely. Lord knows what we're going to find in there. We move out around ten, when it's good and dark. Now let's eat."

Sondra parked the rented car two blocks south of the

skyscraper and close to a sewer manhole cover. From her pack, she produced a lift tool, but let the stronger Matt lift the cover up. Donning a hat with a light on it, the pair descended the steps, though Matt put the cover back in place before he finally joined her at the bottom. "Gosh, it stinks!" he whispered. She grinned and led the way. Before long, she paused at a side tunnel, one that led into the basement of the GD skyscraper. Using the ID card, she opened the grate.

"So far so good. The card is working. Now let me install my special bomb."

Matt sounded worried. "Explosions?"

"No, it is going to basically freeze all the video streams going into the central console. Most all the buildings have identical systems. This program of mine will simply freeze the signals, so anyone watching will see the same image for the next three hours. It's not too likely they'll catch on, and if they do, there's not much they can do except reboot the entire system, which will also chew up the time we need."

Matt watched as she plugged a small thumb drive into the card reader. A light flashed twice, and she removed it, stowing it in her pocket. "Okay. Cameras are frozen. Don your mask. Leave the hats here." She got out her phone and brought up the map she'd installed on it. "This way to the elevators, unless they've completely redone the interior, which isn't likely." Matt dutifully followed her, his gun drawn.

They got into the elevator and examined the buttons. As she expected there wasn't a thirteenth floor, so she guessed they called it fourteen and pressed that one. Cleverly, they were already in the southwestern section of the skyscraper, just where she wanted to be. Up they went in silence. *God, I hope I'm right and Rene's being kept here. I don't know what I'll tell Matt if she isn't!*

Ding. A small bell announced they'd arrived. Both pressed up against either side of the doors, just as they opened. This way, if there were guards outside, they'd see an empty elevator. Sondra had a small video camera attached to a flexible rod that sent its signal to a tiny hand held monitor. She could see a desk and console just beyond the doors, but no one was around. Silently, both stepped out. From her pack, she took out a metal jam, forcing it into the rails at the bottom of the elevator doors, preventing them from opening. While she could have pressed the elevator's stop button, she didn't want to risk that action sounding an alarm, which often was installed with the stop switch. Together, guns drawn, the pair stepped out.

They were in an isolated section of the building. This was the only elevator that serviced this section. Sondra pointed to a side door labeled Exit, a stairwell that could be used in case of a fire or other emergency. Behind the desk were a set of locked doors, but a sign over them read: Genetic Research Department.

Sondra's heart skipped a beat, and she stifled a gasp. What had they done to Rene? It couldn't be good. She used her ID card, swiping it in the slot, but this time, it failed to open the doors. Expecting this, she dug a small electronic device from her pack, hooked it up to the side of the card reader, and activated it. Matt saw several diode lights blink, and then magically the doors opened. She unhooked it, stuffing it back in her pack. Together, the pair stepped into the genetics lab. Everything around them was wholly unfamiliar, and they stood there a minute trying to make some sense of all this equipment. Then, she spotted a light coming from a crack beneath a door and moved silently over to it.

Both put their ears against the door, trying to hear any voices inside. Sondra thought that she heard sobbing. Was that Rene? Only one way to find out. Again, she got out her camera system and carefully slid it beneath the door and floor. It barely fit. While she fiddled with it, moving it this way and that, she kept her eyes on the tiny monitor. Matt, looking over her shoulders, whispered, "That's her. Rene." Taking a deep breath, she retracted her camera and stowed it. Then they tested the doors. They were unlocked. *Funny, Rene could have opened the door and walked out of here on her own,* Sondra thought. Together, they entered and saw a sobbing Rene sitting on the edge of a hospital bed. She was fully dressed. Both involuntarily gasped at the sight of her!

# Chapter 8—Rene's Ordeal

Rene was in her bedroom, getting ready for bed. She'd had a long day helping her parents with their shoe making operation. Ever since the CEO Ball, weekly orders had doubled. Rene was very pleased that her promotional scheme had actually worked, though for the next three days after the ball, she wasn't able to walk. Her feet had taken quite a beating. The black and blue patches took nearly ten days to fully clear up. Still, they were rolling in orders, and she was quite tired from the day's work. She heard her parents in the living room watching the late news, just as they always did just before bed. Quite why they wanted to hear all of that bad news before bed eluded her.

The thunderous sound of their front door being smashed in startled her. She heard her parents cry out, followed by several gunshots. She screamed involuntarily and began texting Sondra. Two masked men came dashing into her bedroom, guns in their hands. Then, one started laughing and put his gun away. The next thing she knew, he was forcing a smelly rag over her face, and she blacked out, but only after hitting Send.

When she awoke, her head felt like mush. Her mouth was terribly dry; her face itched; her upper and lower lips throbbed with a dull pain; she could scarcely breathe as her chest felt as though it was under some kind of terrific compression. She tried to sit up, but her arms failed to lift her. Again, she tried and failed. She was lying down in a small bed—that much she sensed. Turning her head to the right, she saw only her shoulders. Dumbly, she said, "Where's my arm?" but the words were almost unintelligible. She turned her head the other way and saw her other empty shoulder. Recognition finally came. Rene screamed! She screamed louder than she ever thought possible, but passed out almost at once.

She smelled something terrible, a hideous stench. She turned her nose away from it, regaining consciousness. Glancing right and left, panic swelled, and she screamed wildly and passed out once more. *This is some hideous nightmare. I have to wake up. I just have to.* The smell returned, and she again tried to move her nose away from that awful smell, regaining consciousness once more. She saw a nurse—at least she wore a nurse's white uniform—standing over her, while holding a tiny vial in her hand.

The nurse said, "Stop screaming Rene. You are alive and well, so stop screaming. Take shallow breaths or you will faint again. Stop screaming."

Rene managed to stop screaming, but began panting like a dog, gasping for breath. "There now. This is much better, Rene. It is done. You're now a very special young woman. You are officially a UFB woman, that is, one of the Ultimate in Feminine Beauty women! An incredibly high honor. Mr. Greeley will be your new husband in a few days, once you get adapted to your new life. You are also quite wealthy, I'm told. It seems Mr. Diego himself purchased your parent's Shoe Box Company for a million gold dollars, which is now in your bank account."

Rene gasped, "My parents—what happened to them? Are they all right? Where am I? What's happened to me?" She suddenly stopped talking. She didn't understand a word of what she'd just uttered! Her lips didn't work!

"There, there, Rene, don't try to talk just yet. I can't understand what you're saying. Later on, Mrs. Juanita los Santos will pay you a visit. She will be able to understand you, or so I'm told. Now, let's get you up, dressed, and ready for Mr. Greeley to see. He's made all the decisions for you, making you his perfect UFB woman. I'm sure that you two will be very happy with each other."

Absolutely nothing made any sense to Rene. *Married? I don't even know anyone named Greeley. What does she mean he made all the decisions for me? What decisions? What's happening to me? I need to wake up from this nightmare!*

The nurse got her up into a sitting position on her bed. She now faced a huge mirror on the wall just in front of her. Rene saw a female figure, but knew it couldn't possibly be her! The woman's lips were slit, and large lip loops dangled down, her white teeth showing prominently. The woman's hair was incredibly long, touching the floor as she sat on the bed, but it was much thicker than her own hair, and she felt strange tactile sensations coming from the individual hairs. That strange woman's breasts were gigantic, the same size as the poor woman's head! They weighed a ton. The woman's waist was shockingly small. No, she wore a very heavily boned corset, Rene observed. The woman had no arms and her feet were pointed downwards like an arrow, plus they didn't bend like a real foot did. No, this image in the mirror wasn't herself, probably a reflection of someone else in the room. She turned her head to see this stranger, but only saw the stranger's head partially turning.

As she turned back to the mirror, Rene's mental fog finally lifted. She remembered Juanita's appearance from the CEO Ball. No, she wasn't seeing Juanita looking at her! It was her self! "Oh my God! No!" Rene shrieked, nearly fainting again, but the nurse was swift and caught her before she fell over.

"Yes, your new female form is absolutely stunning, if I do say so myself—the epitome of feminine beauty. I'm told you need to wear that tight corset to help your back support the weight of your incredible bosom. Your feet have been altered so that you can always wear those fancy ballet boots that your company sells. I did see you wearing them at the CEO Ball, and you looked absolutely stunning in them—the talk of many women who were there."

She went on, "Mr. Greeley also wanted your lips to show great beauty, and had them prepared like Juanita's. Let's get you properly dressed, and then let's get you to the bathroom. I expect you need to go badly, after all, you've been in a coma for four days. That's typical of the genetic bio agent. Nothing to worry about. We fed you intravenously until just a while ago, so your body isn't lacking any nourishment or vitamins." Slowly, the nurse began to dress her, beginning with black nylon socks. She then laced up a pair of ankle-high ballet boots, done in red patent leather.

"Now then, you can walk. Let's get you to the bathroom. It's this way. With your fused feet, you'll always have to wear your shoes or boots to be able to walk." Gently, the nurse forced her to rise. Rene tried to use her arms to get her balance as she always had, but panic set in at once. They weren't there. She wiggled and wobbled wildly, but the nurse kept her steady.

Once sitting on the toilet, Rene discovered she really did have to go and go badly. That handled, the nurse helped her back to the bed and into a sitting position again. Along the way, Rene noticed her hair was no longer waist length, but now touched her knees. It had grown considerably if four days had passed. In addition, it was much thicker and shinier, though just as wavy as before. However, now she couldn't push it away from her face as she always had.

The nurse got her into a white, silk slip, and then with some effort, got a red satin gown on her and zipped up. It was quite form fitting, holding her upper legs tightly together, but it was hemmed at her knees, revealing her shiny black nylons and red ankle boots. Foggily, Rene though, *At least, they had the fashion done right*. That done, the nurse stretched out her lower lip loop, inserting a large, golden metal disk in it. Then, she did the same to her upper lip loop. Rene saw herself in the mirror. She looked much as Juanita had at the ball. Worse, it finally struck home; she was now completely helpless in all ways, and probably not even able to walk on her own!

The nurse had a soothing voice, and she began brushing out Rene's hair, eventually draping it over her left shoulder. "There, how's that look? Why, you look ravishing, don't you think so?" Rene wanted to scream no, but knew she'd not be understood. She remembered trying to understand what Juanita said at the ball when she was close to her. It was darn near impossible to grasp anything the poor woman had said. She made a gurgling noise, trying desperately to let the nurse know how thirsty she was, how dry her mouth was. Finally, the woman understood or perhaps this was the next item on her checklist of things to be done. Rene noticed she was checking things off on a clipboard beside the bed.

While she sat erect on the edge of the bed, the nurse brought her a glass of water and a spoon. She lifted the top plate up and carefully inserted a spoonful of water into her mouth. Much of it dribbled out, since Rene no longer had any lips to hold in inside her mouth. "Oh do be a bit more careful,

Rene; you're drooling on your dress." Eventually, she got most of the water into her mouth, and Rene was grateful for that kindness.

"Now then, there's one final touch. Mr. Greeley purchased some fabulous new earrings for you. Gold with red rubies. I'll get them on you now." She retrieved a velvet-lined box and opened it, showing the expensive earrings to Rene. Each one was huge and heavy. Once attached to her ear lobe's permanent grommet, the bottoms of them rested lightly upon her shoulders, though Rene felt they were so heavy that at any moment they were going to rip her ears off.

"Okay, we're all done, Rene. I'll fetch Mr. Greeley so he can see just how incredibly beautiful you really are. I must say, Rene, you're simply stunning. I'm sure Juanita and Luisa are both going to be highly jealous of you! You sit right there." She darted out of the room with a swish of her uniform's dress.

A minute later, she entered bringing a man with her. Rene thought he had to be in his late forties. "Rene, this is going to be your new husband, Mr. Greeley. Sir, isn't she just fantastic? I'm sure she's going to make Juanita very jealous. Rene is the best looking UFB woman we've ever produced, don't you think so?"

"Ah Rene. Incredible, far more beautiful than I anticipated! Indeed, she is the epitome of beauty! I'm very much impressed, very much! Rene, don't worry. I'll give you several days to get accustomed to your new life before we take our wedding vows. I'll have servants to attend you at all times. You'll lack and want for absolutely nothing. Besides, you're now a very wealthy young woman. Did she tell you about the million gold dollars in your account? Mr. Diego de la Vasco bought the Shoe Box for that amount, many times more than it was worth. So you will always have everything your heart desires. No, don't try to speak just yet. I'm told Juanita will come by later and help you learn to speak some. Just know I believe you to be the finest, prettiest young woman in the galaxy! I just know we'll be eternally happy with each other." He leaned over and placed a loving kiss on her forehead.

Rene was grateful for the debilitating lip disks. He couldn't kiss her lips, so she didn't have to flinch in revulsion from that. A forehead kiss was tolerable, but little else was. After he left, the nurse insisted, "Let's get you up and walking about. You have to be able to walk on your own, of course. They told me they've removed the one problem you had with these boots at the CEO Ball. They said your feet cramped and throbbed in pain. That will no longer be a problem. Your foot bones have been fused, and many nerves in them severed, so you'll feel no pain at all; at least that's what the podiatrist claims. Let's get you up and walking on your own. Then, we'll have our lunch."

Shortly, Rene saw she really didn't have much feeling in her en pointe feet. She could still bend her ankles, but nothing below her ankles responded in any way to her attempts to bend or flex her feet and toes. In fact, she couldn't feel her toes any longer, which rather scared her. However, walking around the large room without any arms to help keep her balance terrified her! She pleaded with the nurse to keep an arm around her, but the nurse couldn't understand her. This terrible nightmare only continued unabated. *If only I can somehow wake up. Then, things will finally be all right again, but I can't even pinch myself awake.*

Later, someone entered with a lunch tray. The nurse had quite a difficult time attempting to feed Rene. One hand had to hold the upper plate up, while the other hand got the food bite into Rene's mouth. Lacking lips to help keep food and liquids inside her mouth, Rene slobbered madly, much like a young infant struggling to take its first solid food, rather embarrassing both herself and the nurse, who couldn't wait for this assignment to be over. After cleaning Rene up, the nurse insisted she walk some more on her own and get used to tossing her hair to either the front or back when she intended to sit down or stand up. Meanwhile, the nurse handled the mess that they'd made with the lunch.

All afternoon, Rene's nightmare continued unabated by anything or anyone. *If only the nurse would leave me alone, then I might stand a chance of waking up from this awful dream!* Rene didn't wake up. Finally, nearly exhausted from the constant fear and nervous strain of having to stand and walk by herself, Rene was allowed to sit down on the bed, but only after she tossed her head about, trying to get her hair out from behind her. Already, she'd endured intense pain while sitting on several strands. Then, the nurse fed her supper, generating a sloppy mess before Rene was full. *At least with this terribly tight corset I can't eat as much. If only I can wake myself up.*

Once cleaned up again from many drools, the nurse explained, "It's time for rest. I'm exhausted, so I'm going to leave you fully dressed and the lights on so you can see. When you get tired, simply lie down, and sleep. If you really do need something during the night, which I sincerely hope you don't, then press that red button there by the door. Eventually, someone will come to help you. Really, this has been entirely too much work for a nurse. Good night, Rene." She turned and left the room.

Rene looked at the red button and sighed. *How am I supposed to press it if I haven't any hands? Bet you didn't think about that! At last, I'm alone. Now I can focus all my will power on waking up from this terrible nightmare. This can't be real. I must be drugged or something, hallucinating perhaps. Yes, that's probably what has been happening. I'm hallucinating. So all I have to do is wake myself up. Come on, Rene, you can do it. Wake up. Wake up!*

After trying hard for some time, finally the awful truth registered in her conscious mind. She wasn't hallucinating. No, her body had been genetically modified and turned into this helpless thing that these insane aliens called the ultimate in feminine beauty! When she fully realized this, intense grief flooded her. Beginning as a tiny trickle, grief swept over her entire body like a tidal wave suddenly released by a shattered dam, the dam being her resistance to this entire situation. Rene cried. She simply sat erect on the edge of the bed, sobbing and wailing, while wishing with all her might that she was dead, for all possibility of life had been taken from her by these sadistic, vicious aliens.

The door opened, and two masked people entered, dressed entirely in black. *Maybe they've come to kill me. I'm ready to die now, but I can't even speak well enough to tell them to go ahead and shoot me. Please, put me out of my* misery. *I can't live like this. I have to try.* "Please, shoot me. Put me out of my misery," Rene said, but couldn't even understand her own voice; she continued to sob bitterly.

"Rene, it's Sable and a police detective. We're here to rescue you," Sondra whispered, trying hard to stifle her overwhelming surge of conflicting emotions! She felt total outrage at what these beasts had done to Rene, intense sympathy for Rene and her awful condition, bitter anger at these corporate executives who sponsored such mutilations of women, and an overwhelming urge to lash out at these aliens. Had one been in this room, she would have emptied her gun in him!

Fortunately, Matt responded more appropriately. "Sondra, I'll carry her. You take the lead." Sondra whirled around, ready and willing to empty her gun into anyone who appeared, while Matt went to Rene and carefully picked her up in his arms, but her long hair dragged the floor. "Sondra, little help here." She turned, saw the ends of Rene's long hair on the floor, and quickly gathered it up, placing it in Rene's lap. He had her cradled much like a small child. He nodded, and she began moving out of the room, heading for the elevator.

*I'll kill them! I'll kill them! Show yourselves. I swear I'll kill you all!* Sondra saw nothing but the empty hall and open elevator doors. She moved over to them, removing her steel bar, allowing the doors to close as soon as Matt entered. She pressed B for basement. Matt moved to one side of the doors. "If the doors open," he began, but Sondra planted her feet squarely in front of the door, her gun aimed at them, ready and willing to empty her gun into anyone who appeared when the doors opened. Matt groaned. This wasn't the best move on her part, but right now, he couldn't think of anything to say to her. Rene continued to sob, though at least she was doing it quieter.

Matt thought, *This could end in one of two ways. If the guards are alerted, they'll be on this elevator when the doors open. We'll probably all be killed. On the other hand, if they still don't know we're in here, we might get out of this alive. But what about Rene? Damn, she's a total basket case now. There's nothing we can truly do for her. She's completely helpless, dependent upon us for everything. I doubt she can even talk any more. These aliens have to be stopped before it's too late. Maybe it is too late, and we just haven't realized that yet. Crap. If it is too late, what then? Go down with all guns blazing? Damn.*

The elevator doors opened in basement. Sondra wished the elevator had stopped at other floors just so she could empty her gun into these beasts—let them know they couldn't get away with this brutality. Seeing no one around, she whispered a silent curse, and led the way back to the sewer exit, once more opening it with her ID card. Five minutes later, they reached the ladder that led up to the manhole cover close to where she'd left the rental car.

Reaching the ladder, Matt carefully sat Rene down on her toes. "We hadn't thought of this, Sondra. Now what? How are we going to get her up there?"

She looked at the ladder and sighed. *So close and yet so far.* Then, she remembered a game she and Ben had played when they were kids. A smile appeared beneath her ski mask, visible to Matt even in the dim light. She'd put their miner's hats back on them when they entered the sewer, and it was enough for him to see that telltale smile of her, one he truly loved to see. It meant she had an idea. That much he already knew about this powerhouse of a woman. "Out with it," he teased her, attempting to soften this harsh situation. Rene continued to whimper softly to herself.

"When Ben and I were ten, we used to play this game of climb the ladder at school, after hours mind you when we weren't supposed to be there. One of us would climb the ladder using only our feet, while the other put their body around ours and using their hands and feet kept the other up against the ladder so they didn't need their arms. I know, it was a silly game, but we had fun doing it. Rene, you have to climb, but Matt will keep his body over yours, pressing you against the ladder. I'll be below you and guide your feet up to the next rung. Got it?" She didn't expect Rene to be able to answer, nor did she really expect Rene even to comprehend what she'd said, but hoped that Matt did.

"Got it." He pushed Rene's body into the ladder and put

his hands around her body, latching onto the ladder rungs. Sondra squatted down and lifted up one of Rene's boots, placing it over the first rung. She and Matt pushed Rene upwards. Bit by bit, up the trio went some twelve feet. Near the top, with their bodies sticking halfway out of the manhole, Sondra squeezed herself around them and climbed out. She found a support point on Rene, just below her giant breasts, and was able to help pull her on up and out, supporting her while Matt climbed out and put the manhole cover back in place. He then lifted Rene into the backseat, while Sondra fired up the engine. Ten minutes later, she pulled in the back alley behind Sable's home, and shortly after that, she had Rene safe inside her home. Matt volunteered to drop the rental car off and left to do so. No way did he want to have to deal with the pitiful Rene just now. He needed to clear his own head some.

Sondra helped Rene into the kitchen and got her safely seated, her knee-length hair in front of her. "There now, Rene, you are finally safe from those beasts! We'll look after you. Are you hungry? Thirsty? In pain? Need to use the bathroom? Can you even talk?" She fired off what she guessed might be uppermost in Rene's mind.

"Shoot me now, please. I beg you," Rene said, but her outburst only brought on renewed sobbing. She couldn't understand her own words.

"Say that again, Rene. I almost got it, I think. Was it shoot? You need something shot? Like a doctor's shot?" Sondra fumbled around trying to work it out. The split lips and disks removed all traces of any vocal sound that in any way involved her lips and the front of her mouth. Those sounds simply were not present any longer. "Tell me again."

Rene repeated it two more times, and Sondra finally thought she understood. She felt an overwhelming surge of sympathy for Rene. "You want me to shoot you? Put you out of your misery? Is that it?"

Rene nodded vigorously, her heavy earrings threatening to rip her ear lobes, but just now she didn't care. She'd finally made herself understood to another human being.

"I understand Rene. What they have done to you is, is,

well I don't even have words to describe it. But you are alive and healthy; that's something positive. Don't worry; we'll find a way to make a go of it. If you don't mind, I'd rather shoot those Galactic Dynamics executives who probably ordered this done to you. I'll kill them all!" She let her pent up anger surface, and Rene again nodded vigorously. "Right, Rene. We'll get those aliens good! It's hard, but I did understand what you were saying. So let's try this some more. I'll ask, and you nod your answer." She asked again, "Are you hungry? Thirsty? In pain? Need to use the bathroom?" However, she asked them one at a time, allowing Rene to nod yes or no for each one. She wasn't hungry but was thirsty. No pain, but she did need to use the bathroom.

Together, the pair handled her bathroom need, though Sondra mostly fumbled her way through it. She'd never had to be another's hands before. That done, back in the kitchen, Sondra finally worked out how to get some water into Rene. Obviously, she had to lift up the upper lip plate. She saw at once that Rene couldn't sip from the glass, so she got a spoon and tried that. With a half a glass of water in her, Rene settled down some, and Sondra then wiped the young woman's wet face, gently dabbing it here and there.

"Okay Rene. Let's see if we can make you more comfortable. Those earrings are spectacular, but they look far too heavy. Do you want me to take them off?" Rene nodded yes, and Sondra finally figured out how to undo them. "Well, they are locked on. Clever. Guess they didn't want you accidentally losing them. Okay better?" She cut them off with a wire cutter. Rene nodded.

"How about those boots? I know you like to wear this kind, but aren't your feet hurting now? Like they did at the CEO Ball?"

Rene nodded no. She tried to say, "Corset," but the word wasn't clear, even though she repeated it several times.

"Oh, I get it. You want that tight corset off. Okay, let's get you undressed a bit," Sondra suggested. To undo the corset, she had to strip Rene. By the time she was down to just the corset still on Rene, Sondra could really see what all had been done to her body. Her breasts were enormous, as far as

Sondra was concerned, easily the same size as Rene's head, but they were perky and not droopy, dangling weights. However, Rene's feet got her complete attention. She still held them vertical, the tips of her toes touching the floor. Gently, Sondra explored them.

Shocked. That was how she later explained it to Matt when he returned. Her feet now seemed to be one solid, inflexible mass. The only movement was at her ankles, which bent as much as Sondra's ankles. Yet, nothing below that point could move, not even a hair. Matt theorized they'd fused the bones in her feet, which was later proven to be the case.

After Sondra got the extremely tight corset off her, Rene nodded yes vigorously. She breathed in deeply, while Sondra noticed Rene's waist seemed far smaller than she recalled from their meeting at the ball. Then, something Luisa had said back then came to mind. Sondra asked, "Rene, do you need to wear this tight corset to help support the heavy weight of your breasts? I think I recall Luisa saying something to that effect."

Rene shrugged her shoulders. "Don't know?" Sondra asked. Rene nodded yes. "Okay. I know how hard it is to live while wearing these things. So let's leave it off and see how you do. If your back aches too badly, we'll have to leave it on. Okay?" Again, she nodded yes. "I suppose we should put your boots back on you. You're not going to be able to walk at all without them."

That done, she said, "Rene, it's way past bed time. Let's get you into my bed. You'll sleep with me tonight. Matt will have to use the couch." Matt chuckled, more than willing not to have to deal with Rene. Rene nodded yes. However, as Sondra got Rene into position to lower her onto her bed, she saw the lip plates. "Probably those disks should come out too. I can't imagine sleeping in them." Gently, Sondra experimented with the upper plate and figured out how to remove it. Then, she took out the lower one. Sondra stared at how Rene now looked, while Rene stared into the mirror beside the bed. Two large loops draped down from either side of her mouth, the remnants of her lips. They looked so incongruous that both women began laughing at them. In that slightly lightened mood, Sondra helped Rene lay down, and she snuggled up to the virtually helpless young woman, pulling up the light covers.

Shock and surprise. That was Beth's reaction the following morning when she found they had a new houseguest, though she was quite shocked at what had been done to Rene. She had seen her when she won the Miss West Port beauty pageant but now—well, she kept her opinion to herself and tried not to stare at the woman, who was mostly naked. Sondra had to put the lip plates back in, since it became obvious to both women that the dangling loops of flesh would interfere with eating. However, without the tight corset on, the gown that she had on last night wouldn't remotely fit her, and Sondra had nothing that would fit her enormous bosom. So she draped a bathrobe around her when she brought her to the kitchen for breakfast.

Matt explained what they'd done last night, and Beth was most impressed with them. She asked, "Now what? She doesn't even have any clothes that will fit."

Matt suggested, "We should make a list of actions that need to be done and their priority. She obviously needs clothing and shoes, but I'm worried about her huge bank account. I expect those unethical aliens will attempt to drain her bank account soon. Tell you what. I'll handle the bank for you. Can you see about getting her clothing?" Sondra agreed, and they added a few more things to the to do list. Rene needed a constant helper, unless Sondra stayed with her. To help, Beth volunteered to watch after Rene while Sondra headed off to see about clothing and shoes. The other items on the list were of much lesser importance.

That morning, Matt used a little-used police action. Under specific circumstances, a duly appointed police officer could withdraw a person's funds from their bank account. He filled out dozens of forms, indicating the Rene was no longer physically able to handle her own account. He cited lack of arms as the primary reason, which was promptly accepted by the bank. He withdrew slightly over a million gold dollars in large denomination bills, which the bank manager put into a bag for him. However, as Matt saw the large volume this much cash involved, he decided to go another route.

From the bank, he went directly to Ace Jewelers. There, he converted the cash into a number of large diamonds. His reasoning was that in every culture, diamonds were considered quite valuable and could be used as a means of exchange. He did place some funds in Sondra's account so she could help pay for their living costs. He returned around noon with a small bag of the stones and a heavy new safe in which to store them.

Meanwhile, Sondra donned her Snake Town dress and headed off shortly after breakfast. Having taken Rene's new measurements, Sondra knew just the dress maker to visit. The wealthy women of West Port always purchased very expensive and well-made clothing from one of ten high-class boutiques. However, these boutiques didn't actually manufacture these elegant gowns. No, that would have been prohibitively expensive. While they could charge ten times more for such gowns, competition forced far lower prices, though to one like Sondra, even these lower prices were exorbitant. Hence, these boutiques farmed out the actual construction of these incredible gowns to seamstresses who lived in Snake Town. Thus, they were able to keep their cost of these fabulous outfits down and their profits way up.

As a lifelong resident of Snake Town, Sondra knew all about this arrangement, having sometimes window gazed at elegant gowns being made by these poor women of Snake Town. Within an hour, she arrived at the one she was most familiar with and where she had often window-gazed at the gowns under construction. After explaining what she desired, the seamstress didn't believe her.

"Look, the material for these gowns is extremely expensive. These measurements, why, they look almost like one of those alien UFB women we sometimes see in the background on TV."

"She is almost like them, but her waist isn't that small. I'll pay you up front. Cash. No questions asked. How's that?" Sondra said the magic words, which from long experience, she knew was needed. Cash. The seamstress wouldn't have to report the sale, or pay any taxes on the funds. No one would know about it. Thus, she had every reason not to say a word about these dresses. Sondra ordered sixteen complete outfits in varying colors, styles, and fabrics. She didn't know Rene's favorite colors, but judged what they might be from her wavy black hair. She paid two thousand gold dollars up front, pleasing the seamstress enormously.

"For you, I will work on these right away. The boutiques can wait a while for their next batch," she replied, covertly counting the bills Sondra handed her.

That handled, she paid a visit to the fetish shop Sable often used, but first she had to make a quick trip back home to change into an appropriate Sable-like outfit. Once more intensely uncomfortable, Sondra visited the fetish shop and bought seven pairs of ballet boots and shoes, noting that all had been made by Rene's parents, the Shoe Box. Thus, she knew these were quality footwear. Another thousand spent, she returned home to await their deliveryman.

Once Sondra returned and changed into more comfortable clothing, Beth headed off to her classes. "Today, I actually get to fly a transport, though the instructor will be right there beside me. Wish me luck."

"Best of luck, Beth! Go for it," Sondra encourage her and watched her bounce out of the front door, very much excited by the day's prospects. She returned to Rene, who was still sitting at the kitchen table, morose as ever, though she wasn't sobbing like last night. *What a difference in emotions,* Sondra thought, sitting down beside Rene. *If only there was something I could do for Rene. She was so full of life at the ball, and now she's mostly a vegetable.*

"Well, Rene, it's just us now. Why don't you tell me what happened to you. We saw some of it on your parent's surveillance footage, but not what happened to you. Talk slowly, and I'll try to understand you."

Rene nodded and began relating what had happened to her, at least what she remembered. "I was in my bed when I heard this loud explosion sound, then gunfire. Two armed men with masks on their faces came into my room. They put a rag over my face and everything went dark." Rene began her tale. At first, Sondra only caught a word here and there. She had her repeat each sentence several times, and each time she understood more and more of what Rene was saying.

Then, it happened. Rene seemed to drift into unconsciousness, just as she had when they put the smelly rag over her nose. *What do I do now? It's as if she is reliving it right now!* Sondra had no idea what she should do and so wisely did nothing but wait. Later one, Rene woke up and continued her explanation, beginning with her screams and the nurse's response. "Then I woke up in that room where you found me," Rene finished. Sondra had her repeat it all again, and this time, she noticed Rene was able to remember more details about it.

At this point, what Rene began to tell her rather startled her. The woman was supposedly unconscious from the ether. "They are carrying me out of the house, past the living room. I see a dark car—no, it's more like one of those emergency vehicles. Yes, that's it. They put me in the back and covered me up with a blanket. One said, 'No one can see her now.' I wondered why anyone would want to see me."

Sondra knew that Rene must be unconscious, but somehow she was still aware of what was going on around her! *How is this possible?* Rene continued to surprise her. "Now they are carrying me inside a skyscraper. I'm lying on a bed now. Someone says, 'Good. She's still unconscious. Put that mask over her face. Careful.' So weird. They are wearing spacemen's suits. That's what they sort of look like to me. They have plastic walls around me. Weird. Now I smell something. Sort of a sick smell. Everything gets blacker. 'There. That's the proper dose.' A man says that. He's in a spacesuit kind of thing. 'She'll be in a coma for four days. Hook up the tubes now, nurse.'" Rene then described that part in detail and went silent for a time once again before waking up and saying that was all.

At this point, it was noon and Matt returned carrying the new safe. While Sondra fixed their lunch, he explained to both women what he'd done. "This way, Rene, no one can steal your money." After lunch, he headed off to work.

During the long afternoon, Sondra continued having Rene tell her all about the abduction and genetic operation. With each passage through the four days, Rene continued to add more and more information that an unconscious person shouldn't even recall. Further, Sondra noticed subtle changes in Rene's emotions. At first, Rene spoke in an apathetic manner. That changed to grief. Later on, grief was replaced by fear, then anger and hate, which gave way to extreme antagonism. A period of boredom followed that and then Rene was somewhat cheerful about this part of the terrible incident. However, once she reached the point when she awoke with the nurse helping get her out of bed, she continued to hit an overwhelming wall of utter grief.

Hence, the next day, Sondra had Rene go over and over that part of her ordeal. As before, each time she went through that fourth day, Rene was able to *see* more and more detail, and slowly, the incredible wall of grief and sadness began to change into intense, terrifying fear. Rene's whole body shook with the fear she was experiencing. Then, that gave way to vitriolic anger against these aliens, which slowly morphed into open hostility towards them, and then boredom. "He was forty or more, an old man. Marry me? The hell he's going to do that. He could be my grandfather," Rene exaggerated some.

When Beth and Matt arrived around suppertime, they were shocked to see Rene actually laughing. Her lips prevented any form of smile from being observable, but her laughter was unmistakable, even though those two couldn't understand what she was saying. Sondra, however, did.

"I don't know what you've done for me, Sable, but I feel light as a feather. I feel happy. I don't know why I should though. I'm completely helpless now. I can't do a damned thing for myself. Still, I'm happy. Whatever did you do?"

Sondra translated what Rene was saying for Beth and Matt. He said, "You can understand her?"

"Yes, it was very hard at first, but if she talks slowly and repeats everything, you can catch on to what she's saying. I'm getting good at getting what she says the first time she says it now. If you listen to her lots, you'll catch on too. It's hard, but you can get what she's saying," Sondra answered.

Sondra decided to tell Rene she wasn't Sable, but her twin sister, Sondra. Over supper, she outlined what had happened, what all they'd done, and discovered so far. Rene looked very pleased to be trusted with this delicate and critical information, promising never to tell anyone about it. She laughed, "They couldn't understand me anyway!"

"What's she saying?" Matt asked.

"They couldn't understand me anyway," Sondra repeated. Matt roared with laughter, and Beth grinned.

"Say, how come you are so, I don't know, cheerful today? When we found you, you were crying your heart out and rightly so!" Matt asked.

"Sondra did something to me," Rene explained, and Sondra translated for them.

"I just had her tell me about what she went through. We had to go over it many times so I could get what she was saying. Somehow, she had mind images of everything that happened to her, even when she was unconscious and in that coma. It's incredible, but true," Sondra explained.

Rene added, "It is almost as if she erased all that from me, and I feel happy now." Again, Sondra translated for the others.

"Incredible, simply incredible. Who would have thought that was even possible?" Matt declared. "You should look into it more, dear."

"Well, I need to pick up the first of Rene's new outfits tomorrow morning. Beth has an early morning flight, so can you watch over Rene here for an hour or so, Matt?"

"Sure. Things are rather quiet. Interestingly enough, I've not heard anything about our rescue of Rene here at headquarters. GD certainly hasn't reported it," Matt replied.

Sondra added, "Also, I've located a Snake Town doctor. I want him to examine Rene and see if there is anything we can do for her to undo what those beasts have done to her body, Matt. I'll bring him back with me and the dresses. He is totally against these aliens, and we can count on his discretion," Sondra explained.

"Dear, you never cease to amaze me with what you know. Go for it. If there is anything that can be done for Rene, we have to try it," Matt replied.

***

Around ten the following morning, Sondra arrived back

home, bringing the first of the new outfits for Rene, along with a doctor who wished to remain anonymous. "Just call me Doc Smith," he explained to Rene and Matt, when she introduced him. He'd brought along a lot of medical gear, which Matt brought in from the car.

He took one look at Rene and exclaimed, "Oh my! She's been exposed to the alien's genetic biological mutation agent! You know, they're now training some of the unscrupulous doctors at the ritzy East Side Hospital in how to deliver this mutation agent. So much for their pledge to do no harm to their patients. If this isn't harmful, then I don't know what is!"

"She has, but can anything be done to reverse or undo these awful changes?" Sondra asked what she desperately wanted to know. *Can he do anything for her?*

Doc Smith gave Rene a complete medical examination, including taking x-rays of her feet. "It's like we suspected. Here, look at the x-rays of her feet. You can see they've fused all the bones in her feet. We sometimes do that to vertebrae when the disks rupture and can't be repaired. I'm afraid there is nothing medically that can be done for her. Her lips have already healed as well. I'm afraid these evil aliens have left us no way to undo any of these awful changes. Perhaps, out there in the Galactic Federation, someone might know more about how to undo these modifications. From what little I know of this mess, the changes are genetic in nature, meaning that her children will inherit these changes from her."

Doc Smith continued, "I've heard from a fellow doctor who heard this rumor from another doctor close to the aliens that girl children of these genetically modified women look precisely like their mothers, while boy children look like their fathers. If this is truly accurate, then one could speculate that Rene's new, modified genes are dominant over the father's X chromosome, but the father's Y chromosome is dominant over the Rene's X chromosome. Mind you, this is mere speculation on my part. I do wish there was something that I could do for you, Rene, but there simply isn't. We have these damned aliens to thank for that. May they rot in hell." They chatted a bit longer before Sondra took him back to his Snake Town residence.

On her way back, she reflected on what he'd said. *Perhaps, out there in the Galactic Federation, someone might know more about how to undo these modifications. That's it! I need to search the federation's Internet. That means I'll have to go to the library. Hardly anyone has a direct hookup to the federation's internet, except the libraries.* Once back, she began spending several hours each day at the library looking for clues for any kind of cure for Rene.

# Chapter 9—Alice's Trip in Drug Land

Several weeks had passed since her last concert after which Alice had met Sondra for the first time and learned the startling fact that they had once been triplets, not merely identical twins as she'd previously thought. Sable was dead, and Alice felt a sadness she'd never known before. Still, concerts must go on. In two more weeks, the orchestra had its next one in the summer series, and Alice had to practice if she intended to maintain her first-chair position. One day, she fully anticipated being promoted to concertmaster.

In the quiet of her home, Alice began her morning practice, running rapidly through warm up scales as she always did. Sandy had left for work an hour ago. Now it was time for her to work on her technique, even if she didn't feel much like playing. She was just running through the D Major scale, when two men burst through her front door, shocking her. Two men, their faces hidden by masks, rushed into the living room, pointing guns with silencers at her. Alice froze, unsure what to do. *Are they here to murder me too, like Sable? How did they find me? Is Sandy in danger too?* A myriad of thoughts flooded the musician's mind.

"What—what do you want?" she managed to get the words out of her dry mouth.

"We don't want to harm you, but we will if you don't obey us. Here, drink this or we'll smash your precious violin to pieces," the taller man ordered gruffly.

In the back of her mind, she wondered how did these thugs know how precious her violin was to her? Carefully, she laid the instrument down. "Please, it's a rare violin."

The man thrust a small vial into her hands. "Drink it, and we won't smash it." Mechanically, she swallowed the sweet liquid. It wasn't much, only a small amount. *Probably won't kill me,* she thought crazily, as wild thoughts streamed through her mind.

The light blue wall in front of her morphed into a giant spiral pattern, swirling around and around and around. Dizzy.

Out of its center a giant caterpillar appeared, smiling lovingly at her. *This can't be real*, she thought. In fact, it was simply a photograph of Sandy. "Come with me," said the caterpillar. Alice rose, or at least believed that she rose.

Somehow, the caterpillar seemed to be flying now, moving effortlessly through space. *Wings. I have winds*, Alice thought, and stretched them out. She jumped up and began flying after the caterpillar. "Oh don't fly so fast! I can't keep up," she called out to the disappearing creature. The blue swirls gave way to grey wonderland of giant cactuses, each one stretching their appendages upwards, trying valiantly to reach the blue swirling oceans overhead. *Where has the caterpillar gone?* She looked about and forgot to flap her wings. Crunch, she landed on the brown ground, studded with enormous green spikes, soft spikes though.

Stunned briefly, her eyes focused on a shiny, greenish bug of enormous proportions. "And who are you?" asked the bug.

"I don't know anymore. When I awoke this morning, I was Alice, but now I don't know. I have wings. Perhaps I'm an angel, do you suppose?" she replied.

"I don't often suppose, though I suppose you should play in G Major," the bug replied.

"But I can't see the F Sharp anywhere," Alice protested, growing confused with all the green spikes around her. None looked particularly sharp to her eyes.

"Then you must look sharp," the bug declared, growing rather annoyed with Alice.

"Please, don't be so sharp with me," Alice replied. "I can't see it, that's all. But it must be here somewhere, if we're in G Major."

"Well, I'm a major and you are seeing me, so why not follow me," the bug said, promptly scurrying down from its perch on the side of the green spike. Rapidly, the bug began moving through the walls of green spikes.

"Wait for me," Alice called out, her wings becoming entangled in all the spikes. "Wait for me, I'm getting stuck."

The bug stopped and looked back at Alice who was prone on the ground. "No, you are B Flat now. Oh, stop playing around. Do keep up. I haven't got all day," he complained, bitterly annoyed with Alice.

Confused, Alice complained, "But I thought that we were in G Major not F Major. Please make up your mind." The major bug vanished from sight, and Alice struggled to her feet, quite dizzy. "I wish the world would stop spinning. I need a rest."

A voice above her head called out, "Very well. You may have a half rest now, but no more. The show must go on. Everyone is waiting for you." She looked upwards and saw what she believed to be a giant toucan, resplendent in its multicolored plumage. "Time's up. Let's get moving again. This isn't a dirge, you know. Quick time. Make up for lost time, Alice. Flap those wings." In a flash of brilliant colors, the toucan flew off into the distance. Alice tried her best to flap her wings and follow the toucan, who rapidly left her far behind.

"Wait. I'm going to slowly."

From seemingly far ahead of her, she heard the toucan reply, "Then make it triple time."

"But I can't fly that fast, can I?" Still, Alice felt she was moving. The sea of green spikes became a blur in her eyes. "Oh now I'm really moving," she explained to no one in particular. Still the toucan seemed to vanish in the distance ahead of her, which now turned into a sea of grey. *Water perhaps? I can't swim,* thought Alice as panic began swelling in her stomach. As her attention drifted towards her nervous stomach, the grey gave way to a light pink, but the pink was solid, and Alice collided with it, unable to stop her speedy flight. "Ouch. That hurt," she exclaimed.

"Oh you are all right so far," a voice said. She was lying on the ground again. *I must have fallen to the ground when I hit the pink.* She looked up and saw a butterfly, perhaps a zebra butterfly, all black and white, such pretty wings, so soft and delicate.

"No I'm not. I can't breathe. I don't know how to swim. I'll drown. I just know it. I can't breathe water," Alice protested and struggled to get to her feet, but found that perhaps she was inside some room, one that she didn't recognize. "Where am I?"

"Will she be able to breathe in that?" someone unseen asked the butterfly.

"Of course, but she will need practice," the butterfly answered politely, as though breathing water was something that anyone could get used to doing.

Alice continued to be nervous and fearful. *I can't breathe water. I remember falling into a pool once and choking. No, definitely not. I can't breathe it,* she decided, *but how to tell them that?*

The unseen voice then commented, "My, these are quite heavy, yet very costly. Can she actually safely wear them?"

"She's strong enough to wear them. They are beautiful. Alice will look beautiful in them, I'll give you that," the butterfly replied.

"Of course, I'm strong. Just look at my arms and fingers," Alice tried to say, noticing that her arms now appeared as well-muscled as a wrestler's. Her fingers seemed to swell up, each becoming a foot long. "See, they are big and strong for me to play, but I am beautiful. Sandy says so."

"She won't be able to play though," the butterfly explained.

"But I want to play. See?" Alice got up and found herself in a field of yellow buttercups. She pranced and danced gaily among the heady fragrances, though being careful not to harm any of the delicate flowers. She did notice her arms had shrunk some, as had her fingers. "See, I'm playing the field."

As though answering her, the butterfly added, "Yes, she should play the field. There'll be plenty of suitors seeking her. She shouldn't go with the first one she sees."

Just then, Alice thought she saw a red mantis standing close to her. "Oh, I should not go with the first one I see. I do hope that is all right with you," she explained to the mantis, who seemed to be ignoring her. Then, she spotted what must have been a brown cricket of enormous proportions. "Oh hello. You're not the first one I see, but perhaps I should not go with you either. I should play in the field some more, only I can't seem to find the field of buttercups any longer. Where did it go anyway? And where has that caterpillar gotten to? I just remembered I was to follow him."

From overhead now, the zebra butterfly spoke up, "Well, there's plenty of time to make the proper choices. No one knows she is here. We will take our time and do it right. She should probably sleep now."

"Well, yes, there is plenty of time, at least two dozen measures, maybe more, but I must be ready to play when it is time for me to come in," Alice answered the butterfly. "I play first, so when I come in, everyone will know I'm here, you see, but yes, it is always best to take your time and get it right. Who wants to hear it wrongly? Sleep? Say, am I tired? I expect so. All that flying about has made me terribly tired. Would it be all right for me to take a nap now? But please wake me when it is time for me to enter and play my part."

The butterfly answered, "Yes, it would be perfect for you to take a nap now. I'll wake you when it is time for you to make your entrance. Sleep now, Alice. Sleep."

Alice's eyes closed. The butterfly vanished, as did the pink room. A deathly silence fell, but Alice couldn't fall asleep, but neither could she move her body. At last, she gave up trying and did fall asleep.

***

Roxane Stevens, a twenty-two year old nurse at Rosewood Homecare corporate headquarters in south West Port, was frightened by what she saw and what she now knew. She was a direct assistant to Dr. Sam Decker, who headed up this rather large company, which specialized in a number of medical arenas, not the least of which was care for the elderly and infirm. The company had ten other smaller facilities scattered around the sprawling capital city. Under Dr. Decker's guidance, Rosewood also provided DNA analysis services for West Port and many surrounding smaller cities, which could not afford the expensive and sophisticated equipment needed to perform these studies. They also had a contract with the police, handling any needed DNA studies.

Roxane handled much of the mundane paperwork for Dr. Decker, who couldn't be bothered with such trivia. While he was a hard man to work for, until recently, Roxane felt that he was fair. Today, everything was in doubt, serious doubt. Moreover, she felt fear, real, unadulterated fear.

Some time ago, she'd sent off the DNA comparisons of one Sable Lorraine Hampton and a Jane Smith. What was utterly remarkable about the results was the degree of identicalness in their DNA. While Roxane wasn't a geneticist, she'd been around Dr. Decker long enough to have picked up quite a bit of knowledge. While on the surface, it did appear these were identical twins, the degree of identity in their DNA suggested something far deeper, something quite sinister and highly illegal, human cloning. Hence, when Dr. Decker gave her the results to handle, she paid close attention to his comments about the striking results. He'd told her to ignore it, "Probably a fluke. Twins."

She accepted it at the time. Months later, she had to handle the paperwork on another DNA comparison. Once more, the two women had virtually identical DNA. That raised a red flag, and she dug out the older results. Staring at the two comparisons, it was obvious to her that all three women had identical DNA. Triplets, possibly, but clones might be a more reasonable explanation. She examined the physical characteristics of the three women. All had different names, but all were the same age, remarkably her own age. All had the same hair color. Did they look alike, she wondered.

Roxane did a bit of digging and found photographs of two of the three women. The Jane Smith woman didn't exist and was probably an alias, she presumed correctly. However, staring at the images of Sable and Sondra, Roxane gasped! The two women looked exactly like her! Sondra had apparently been run over by a truck. Rosewood had performed a DNA test for the police, verifying Sondra's identity. Now, however, Roxane knew better. That test wasn't conclusive. The dead woman could also be Sable or this unknown Jane Smith!

Secretly, she ran her own DNA through the machine and compared it to the three women. Looking at the results for the first time, Roxane nearly fainted! Her DNA was an exact match for all three women. Quadruplets? Possibly. She was an orphan. Her parents died in a car crash when she was two years old, or so her foster parents claimed. However, if they were in fact clones, then something beyond awful had gone on somewhere in West Port.

Since most genetic research was carried out in the well-equipped labs of Rosewood, such illegal work would have likely been carried out here. Worse, Dr. Decker had been the head of the corporation for twenty-five years now! He had to have known about it. That alone gave her cause to be very concerned, but not frightened. Not yet. Since Dr. Decker paid no attention to those two DNA reports, she wasn't too concerned at that time.

Then, on Monday, Dr. Decker held a special meeting of all the top doctors and personnel here at the headquarters. Nurse Roxane attended, since she was his special assistant. Dr. Decker explained, "This is Dr. Vega from Galactic Dynamics. He is here to train us in an entirely new genetic procedure. It is with very great pride that I'm able to announce to all of you that, as of today, GD is licensing Rosewood to be able to perform their genetic bio agent mutations used to create the UFB women. Yes, Rosewood will now be able to create these ultimate in feminine beauty women right here in our own facilities. In time, we can expect many of West Port's top leaders to be bringing their wives and daughters here for this special procedure that will make these women into absolutely stunning super-models." Many began wildly clapping. Roxane cringed. She'd seen pictures of some of these alien leader's wives. True they were incredibly beautiful. One could find not the slightest blemish or imperfection in their bodies, but they were helpless women with grossly exaggerated physical forms.

True, many women passed through Rosewood, getting breast enhancements, but nothing as gigantic as these UFB women had. Face lifts, yes, but not the rest of it. She began to worry. Where was Rosewood headed with this new procedure? Just how many women were they planning to do this to? The alien doctor did give a short speech in which he explained that out there in the Galactic Federation, any executive of any standing had a UFB woman as his wife. It was quite commonplace and very much the thing to do. Were they planning to turn many of West Port's women into these helpless sex dolls? That was the only thing they could now do, or so Roxane believed—be a sex doll.

During the week, training sessions were held. One thing

became very clear to everyone: this genetic bio agent was virulent. Great care had to be taken. The slightest exposure to the gas resulted in that person becoming infected and falling into the required coma. What shocked her even more was the fact this bio agent could also affect men. So yes, she observed the men involved with this new procedure exercised the highest degree of caution and care that she'd ever witnessed at Rosewood! She wondered what such affected men would look like, but dared not ask.

Around ten on Friday morning, Roxane was ordered to report to one of these newly build labs where this new procedure would be carried out. When she arrived, Dr. Decker was already there and merely nodded to her. A man from GD was also present, though she'd never met him. His badge identified him as being from GD—that much she could tell. Shortly after that, two men wheeled a drugged woman into the room and left her. "Check her vitals," Dr. Decker whispered to her, "and draw some blood for a test sample. We will be performing this new procedure on her."

Dutifully, she began drawing the requisite blood. The drugged woman cried out, "Ouch. That hurt."

"Oh you're all right so far," Roxane said softly and politely. She was wearing her white nurse uniform, which had several black bars, indicating she was Dr. Decker's nurse. She continued with her routine exam of the woman.

As though answering her unspoken question, Dr. Decker whispered, "She was given a psychedelic drug. Note that on her chart. She did so. The chart was now resting on Alice's chest.

"No I'm not. I can't breathe. I don't know how to swim. I will drown. I just know it. I can't breathe water. Where am I?" the protesting Alice said and asked.

Just then, the man from GD held up a heavily boned, tiny corset, whispering to Dr. Decker, "She'll need to wear this when she first awakens."

"Will she be able to breathe in that?" Dr. Decker asked. It seemed terribly small, considering the waist of the woman on the table. It couldn't possibly fit her now.

The GD man explained her waistline would be reducing

as part of the mutation process and that it would eventually fit.

"Of course, but she will need practice," Roxane added, recalling how she once had tried one on when she was in nursing school.

The GD man then brought out a box and displayed the earrings they were to put on the woman when she came out of her coma. Dr. Decker looked at them, as did Roxane. She'd never seen such huge earrings. Gold and rubies galore. She figured that these must have cost this man an incredible fortune!

Dr. Decker was also impressed and he lifted one up, commenting, "My, these are really heavy, yet very costly. Can she actually safely wear them?"

"She's strong enough to wear them. They are beautiful. Alice will look beautiful in them, I'll give you that," Roxane replied.

"Of course I'm strong. Just look at my arms and fingers," Alice muttered softly. Only Roxane could hear her though. "See, they are big and strong for me to play, but I am beautiful. Sandy says so." At the mention of Sandy, something clicked in the back of Roxane's mind. That was the name of the woman to whom she'd sent the two sets of DNA results. Could this woman on the table be one of them?

The GD man whispered to Dr. Decker, "I believe she was a violinist in the orchestra."

Standing close to Alice, Dr. Decker replied, "Well, after this, she won't be able to play though." He backed away from Alice and asked, "Are you sure you want this procedure done on this woman?" The GD man merely nodded affirmatively.

"But I want to play. See?" Alice said quietly, though Roxane heard her. "See, I'm playing the field."

Out of the hearing of Alice, Dr. Decker said, "Well, she will certainly soon be the ultimate in feminine beauty."

The GD man replied, "Absolutely! Of course, there are a dozen top executives that would love to marry her, but she should play the field a bit and see with of them is best suited to her, don't you think? With her incredible new beauty, she deserves only the best man."

Dr. Decker nodded and Roxane said, "Yes, she should

play the field. There will be plenty of suitors seeking her out. She shouldn't just go with the first one she sees." In her mind, she was sticking up for Alice, about the only way that she could right now.

Alice whispered dreamily, "Oh, I shouldn't go with the first one I see. I do hope that is all right with you." At this point, the man from GD moved closer to Alice and bent over her, taking one last look at her. "Oh hello. You're not the first one I see, but perhaps I shouldn't go with you either. I should play in the field some more, only I can't seem to find the field of buttercups any longer. Where did it go anyway? And where has that caterpillar gotten to? I just remembered I was to follow him." The GD man looked a bit startled until Dr. Decker whispered that it was the psychedelic drug speaking. He moved away from Alice.

Roxane added, "Well, there's plenty of time to make the proper choices. No one knows that she is here?" She asked. Both men shook their heads no. Looking at Dr. Decker, she added, "We'll take our time and do it right. She should probably sleep now."

Dr. Decker agreed with her, "Well, yes, there's plenty of time." Turning away from Alice, he added, "We want to let that drug work its way out of her system before we perform the procedure. She should sleep a while before we begin, nurse. Sir, if you will come with me, I've a few questions to ask before we commence." He and the GD man left the room.

As Roxane finished up, Alice whispered, "I play first, so when I come in, everyone will know I'm here, you see, but yes it's always best to take your time and get it right. Who wants to hear it wrongly? Sleep? Say, am I tired? I expect so. All that flying about has made me terribly tired. Would it be all right for me to take a nap now? But please wake me when it is time for me to enter and play my part."

Roxane answered, "Yes, it would be perfect for you to take a nap now. I will wake you when it is time. Sleep now, Alice. Sleep."

Her duties here done, a very frightened Roxane headed to her own private office. This woman just had to be that mysterious Jane Smith! Sandy. That was the name of the contact person and to whom she'd sent the DNA results. Worse, Alice was her own sister, and now she realized just who Alice was—the principle violinist of the West Port Symphonic Orchestra! These evil men were about to genetically modify her, and she'd never be able to play the violin again. They were about to rob the world of one of its greatest musicians!

Roxane knew she had to act, had to do something to save Alice from these men, but what? The only thing she could think of was to text Sandy and tell her what was about to happen and where. Maybe Sandy could mount some kind of rescue. She knew she couldn't call the police. This whole procedure was legal. Besides, Alice was in no condition to know what was about to happen to her, that her life was about to be destroyed. She sent the text.

Her hands shook wildly. Although she tried to calm herself down, nothing kept her fears from growing. *What if Dr. Decker already knows about Alice? That she is one of the four clones? Does he know about me too? He obviously must know. When is he going to come after me? If he's willing to wipe out the stellar career of Alice, why not me? We look identical except my hair is much longer than hers. Oh God. If Sandy mounts a rescue, he'll know I tipped them off! He'll get to me for sure. God, if Alice is rescued, then he'll likely substitute me for her, since we are identical in all ways! Oh dear God, what's happening to me? I have to flee somehow. Where will I go?*

*Pull it together, Roxane! Look, you are a nurse. You are honor bound to save lives. You can't flee until Alice is rescued. If she isn't, she'll be desperate for your aid when she wakes from her coma as a helpless sex doll. I can't abandon my post yet. No, I'll flee once this is over, one way or another. Pull it together and stop shaking like a leaf!*

\*\*\*

Across town, Sandy was at work on the top floor of the GD headquarters skyscraper when Roxane's text message came in on her private phone, set on vibrate mode. Only a few people had this number, and she immediately began to worry. No one was around. She pulled out the phone and read the message. Sandy panicked and very nearly fainted. They had taken Alice! The only thing she could think of doing was to forward the entire message to Sondra, which she did as fast as she could hit the buttons. That done, she sat back. *What can I do to save her?* She wanted to rush right over to Rosewood and demand to see her mate. *This is illegal. We are married, after all. This couldn't and shouldn't be happening. What is happening to the world?*

Then, a thought came into her mind from some distant part of her. They know about you. Her stomach knotted, threatening to upchuck her breakfast! Her arms and fingers began shaking, wildly out of control. *They know. They know. They know Alice is my mate and that Alice is an identical twin to Sable. They want her dead too or worse. What will they do to me? I have to get out of here!*

Sandy had halfway gotten her things together to flee when she sat back down. *No, if I flee now, they will know that I know about Alice. That will give us both away. If only Sondra will be able to do something.* Her cell vibrated, and she hastily read the incoming message from Sondra.

It read: Wait a half hour and then get yourself over to my place. Use the backdoor. It's unlocked. We're going after Alice now. Give us a half hour to get to her.

Finally, Sandy began to relax just a bit. She let go of her purse and pretended to shuffle some papers, looking busy. From the corners of her eyes, she kept looking to see if security guards were coming after her, but saw nothing out of the ordinary. Slowly, the panic began to lessen. The horrible knot in her stomach finally eased off, and she took a long drink of water. *I need a plan to get out of here without attracting notice.*

***

"Matt! They've taken Alice!" Sondra yelled loudly. She'd just received the forwarded text from Sandy. Matt dropped everything and ran into the kitchen where Rene and Sondra were chatting. Beth had already headed off to the Academy for more flying lessons. He read the text on Sondra's phone, which she'd placed flat on the table where Rene could also see it.

"Save her," Rene begged. "Don't let her become like me." While Sondra understood her, Matt wasn't used to

126

hearing her talk yet and didn't.

"Okay, we raid the place," Matt made a hasty decision. "Look, we can't use a sneak approach this time. They haven't yet administered the genetic agent thing to Alice, but they will within hours. So we move now, Sondra. Rene will just have to get by on her own while we're gone."

"Okay, what do I tell Sandy? God, they must know about her now. She isn't safe any longer. The GD bastards will come after her too," Sondra declared emphatically.

"Let's think this through. If she flees now, then they will be alerted to trouble and that might make it impossible for us to get to Alice. How far is Rosewood from here? Cross town. Probably fifteen minutes. It's not rush hour. Okay, give us say fifteen minutes to get in and get her. Tell Sandy to get the hell out of GD headquarters in a half hour from now," Matt ordered. Sondra typed the reply and hit Send.

"Let me get my purse and gun," Sondra requested. Matt was already checking his gun, chambering the first round, ready for action.

When she joined him, she had calmed down and so had Matt. He volunteered, "Look, we can't go charging in there. We don't know the layout or where their security guard posts are."

"Let's see if whoever sent Sandy this message is willing to help some more. My guess is that she will. I'll text her while you drive," Sondra suggested. Two minutes later, Matt took off, driving as fast as he dared, without turning on his siren, which would alert far too many people.

Sondra reported a couple minutes later, "Okay, this Roxane nurse says to go around back to the service and supply entrance. She'll meet us there and take us up the back way. Might not be too many guards, she says."

Matt was quite good on his time estimate. They arrived at the back entrance off 43rd street in a little over sixteen minutes. They got out of the car and walked up to the entrance. No one was around. Just then, the door opened, and the two stepped inside and got their first look at their benefactor, Roxane. "Oh my God!" Sondra gushed, unable to contain her reaction. Once more, she was staring at herself! Roxane looked exactly like her, Alice, and Sable, only her hair was shoulder length and she wore a nurse's uniform, white with black stripes.

"You? Sondra is it? They have Alice. She's drugged. On a psychedelic trip right now. That's why they are delaying the procedure. It's up on the fourteenth floor. We can take this service elevator up. After that, lord knows how many guards we will find. I have to come with you. Dr. Decker is going to know I'm behind this, since only he and I were present with the GD man when they brought her in. I'll be next if I don't flee. Come on."

Finally having decided upon a course of action, Roxane's nerves steeled. The terror and fear left her, and she now had her usual calm presence of mind, befitting a trauma nurse. She'd seen it all in her years as a nurse, from vomit messes, to gargantuan feces piles, to gunshot victims, to major surgeries. They rode up the elevator in silence. As they approached the floor, Roxane whispered, "There might be security guards around the room now."

She watched as both pulled out their guns with silencers attached. *Well,* she thought, *we have to save Alice somehow. These men don't deserve to live, not with what they are doing to defenseless women.* When the door opened, Roxane stepped out first, but she was right. Two burly GD security guards sat on a pair of chairs just outside the entrance to this new genetic biological agent facility.

Pop! Pop! Matt and Sondra fired at nearly the same time, each one aiming for the guard on their side of Roxane. Neither guard knew what hit them, slumping over, and then falling onto the floor. Roxane's instincts as a nurse kicked in; she just had to check on them. Matt's man was dead; Sondra's man was only wounded. "He'll live. Come on; she's inside." She swiped her ID card, opening the doors.

Alice lay on the narrow hospital bed, sleeping off the heavy psychedelic drug she had been forced to drink. Matt simply picked her up and tossed her over his shoulder. The two headed back outside, where Roxane was standing holding the elevator's doors open. They stepped inside, but somewhere within Rosewood, the alarms had sounded. Evidently, someone was monitoring this area and had seen the two guards being shot. At least, the elevator responded, and they headed downward.

Shortly, they reached the ground level, and the doors opened. However, a dozen security guards came rushing towards the elevators, guns drawn. Matt fired and hit one, while Sondra hit the Basement button. The doors closed with a cacophony from a rain of bullets from the guards.

"I'm hit!" Matt exclaimed, dropping Alice onto the elevator's floor. Blood was oozing from a leg wound. "We're going to have to blast our way out of here! Why go down?"

"I saw a sloping loading dock just to the right of the doors we entered," Sondra replied. "Must have another entrance—basement likely. Okay, Roxane, get Alice up. Put her between us, an arm on each of us. We'll see if we can walk her out of here. Matt, try to walk if you can."

When the doors opened, no one was present. Sondra glanced around and saw her theory was correct. Heavy equipment entrance doors lead out onto the sloping ramp. Struggling to keep the un-cooperating Alice walking between them, they headed to the big doors. They didn't open when Roxane swiped her ID card, so Sondra simply shot it with her gun. The doors opened.

However, they heard thundering footsteps coming down a nearby stairwell. "Matt, give me your gun and clips. I'll hold them off. You get the others to our car. Yell when you have the motor running," Sondra ordered.

Matt wasn't in any position to argue. He could only just barely walk and was losing blood rapidly. The slug had hit an artery, but right now, he couldn't take time to wrap his belt around his leg to slow its flow. Neither could Roxane, who could barely keep Alice on her feet. The poor woman was ranting about some caterpillar. Between Matt and Roxane, they began the long trek up the ramp, while Sondra took cover behind a metal trash bin, just inside the doors. An idea formed. She pulled the bin over to the doors and used it to keep them open, and then ducked behind it, laying six ammo clips out on the concrete floor.

Guards came bursting out of the stairwell doors. Sondra fired both guns emptying her clips in short order. The hail of fire kept the guards back behind the doors, while she hastily reloaded both. A bit later, the guards made another rush, trying to break out of the stairwell. Again, Sondra gaily emptied both clips. She wasn't really aiming, merely convincing the guards not to come out. Buy them time was her sole goal. She reloaded another pair of clips.

Three more times she hit them with a hail of 9mm slugs, before she ran out. After loosening her last set of clips, she dashed out of the door, shoving the trash bin inside. As she expected, the doors shut long before the guards realized that she'd fled. The closed doors with the shattered opening mechanism slowed them down even further.

When she reached the car, Roxane had the motor running. Alice was slumped in the back seat moaning about butterflies, but Matt was unconscious. "Drive. I'll try to save him," Roxane ordered, squeezing over in the front seat and applying pressure to his wound. Sondra pealed out of the lot and into the streets of south West Port. Then, she slowed down. No sense in being stopped for speeding or running a red light.

"He needs a doctor soon," Roxane said mechanically. "Losing blood."

"Okay. On it," Sondra replied, her throat dry. She couldn't lose Matt, not now, not after all he had done for her and her sisters, not when she finally found someone to love. She crossed South Bridge and headed into Snake Town. She had only one thought right now, Doc Smith. Ten minutes later, she pulled around back of his small medical practice, a slummy looking building and entered the back way.

While Roxane fretted over Matt and wondering what they were doing in the slums, Sondra came running back out with Doc Smith in tow. "Oh dear me. He really has been shot. Oh, are you a nurse?" he asked. "Doc Smith here." Roxane nodded. "Then, you can assist me. Come on; we need to get him on my operating table fast." Between the three of them, they carried Matt inside and got him on the table.

"Well, this is more like it," Roxane commented upon seeing a clean, sterile operating room. She'd been expecting the worst.

"I do what I can," Doc Smith replied. He and Roxane set to work, while Sondra headed back out to watch over Alice and text Rene and Sandy. She'd left a phone on the top of the kitchen table in hopes that Rene could manage to press the View message button. She sent word they'd rescued Alice, that she would be all right, but that Matt had been shot.

Finally, she had time to think about their next move. Should they gamble and all stay at Sable's place? Perhaps not, since that would be the first place they might search for her, assuming they were able to identify her as one of the attackers. On the other hand, Matt was in big trouble. He couldn't return to the police force. How could he explain his wound? If he too were recognized as one of the attackers, he'd be arrested, and shot too.

In desperation, she phoned Ben. "Hi big brother. Say, I'm in a whole lot of trouble. We all are. I've found and rescued my sisters, but Matt's been shot, and they might be on to us. We need a place to stay for a little while until we can figure things out."

"What? Tell me all about it. I'm not busy now and can talk," Ben responded. He sounded very worried, and Sondra told him everything. Finally, she sensed he'd calmed down.

"Okay sis. I know an unused warehouse nearby my place. I have extra blankets as you well know. You can stay there. I can bring you all food and water from time to time. How's that?"

"Perfect, big brother!" With a place to stay, she texted Sandy, asking her to pick up Rene and bring her to Ben's pub in Snake Town. She also texted Beth, telling her roughly what happened and for her not to show up for work until she contacted her again. Two hours later, Doc Smith and Roxane brought a limping, weak Matt back out to the car.

"Thank you, thank you, thank you," Sondra gushed, running up to them and grabbing a hold of Matt. "I'll get you some funds soon," she added. He smiled and headed back inside.

A few minutes later, they parked outside Ben's pub. "This was my home after Ben and I moved out of our foster parent's place," Sondra explained, while they were waiting for

Sandy and Rene to arrive. Ten anxious minutes passed before Sandy arrived, with Rene sitting in the passenger seat, taking everything in.

Sandy just had to see Alice, but found her mate still heavily under the influence of the drug. Meanwhile, Sondra headed on inside to get directions from Ben. Another ten minutes passed before both cars entered the large, rusting doors of the abandoned warehouse. Once the doors were shut, Sondra finally felt safe. "Crude, but no one will find us here. Now we can plan some. Let's see what we can get setup," she ordered.

"We need to get our things and Alice's violin," Sandy pointed out.

"I should get mine too," Roxane added.

"Well, so do we all," Sondra admitted. "Okay. Here's what we'll do. I'll drive Sandy and Roxane to your places. If it looks safe, you can rush in and grab what you can carry out to the car. If I honk, you drop everything and come running. That will mean immediate trouble is coming. Agreed?"

First, she drove Sandy to her place. While Sandy dashed inside, Sondra, her guns reloaded and in her lap, kept watch from the driver's seat, the motor running. Fifteen minutes later, Sandy came out lugging many bags. Sondra had to laugh. *A few things, ha!* Once she stowed them in the back seat, she said, "Stop by one of the ATM machines. I want to see if I can withdraw our funds."

An hour later, with Sandy and her pile of possessions back at the safe house, Sondra drove Roxane to her small apartment. Again, she waited while Roxane grabbed quite a few of her possessions. Then, they visited some ATM machines, and she withdrew her own funds.

After dropping off her bags, Roxane volunteered to go with Sondra so she could retrieve what she could from Sable's home. She didn't want to leave Rene's diamonds there, for one thing. In addition, she needed more ammunition, to say nothing of clothes for the three of them. Matt would have to wear dirty clothes until he was able to get around on his own and make a trip to his place.

# Chapter 10—The Move

Diego de la Vasco listened to the call from Dr. Sam Decker, who described the brazen attack on Rosewood, resulting in the death of two security guards, the wounding of four others, and the kidnaping of Alice Middleton, who was supposed to be made into another UFB woman tomorrow. When the doctor finished, Diego made a critical decision. "Okay. It is time to implement Phase II. Doctor, please report here tomorrow morning at nine for a special briefing." He hung up and placed a number of other calls, pulling in numerous key individuals, including Governor Jason Miller.

Fifty men assembled in the GD auditorium just before nine the next morning. Diego walked up to the podium. "Gentlemen. It is time we commence Phase II of the Virge-C long-range plan. Attendants are handing out specific plans to you while I talk. At this time, we are disbanding the local police. Our corporation security guards are far better equipped to deal with the situation, as it develops. Governor Miller will be declaring martial law within West Port, as our security men begin to take over control of the city. The corporations now own more than half of the largest industries on Virge-C, controlling some sixty percent of them."

"This is expected to be a clean transfer of power to the Galactic Federation corporations, and in return, Virge-C will be receiving a large number of new space vehicles to enable Virge-C to open extensive trading deals with many other federation planets. I don't have to tell you the enormous benefits this new trade will bring to Virge-C. Within months, you may expect to have all manner of new and fancy devices to market to the population, including widespread access to the Federation Internet, which has been limited only to the public library to this point. In short, gentlemen, Virge-C is now entering a whole new era of its history, one that promises to bring tremendous new inventions and procedures to this world."

"Along those lines, I'm proud to announce that

Rosewood Homecare is now officially authorized to create UFB women. No longer is this being done only in the GD facilities here. Now, this incredible beautification program is being made available to all those who wish to have their wives and daughters turned into the agreed upon ultimate in feminine beauty. Soon, gentlemen, you will be seeing many absolutely stunning women walking the streets of West Port. Each of you here today is encouraged to get your wives and daughters signed up to receive this incredible medical procedure. There will shortly be a waiting list. So the sooner you get your women signed up, the sooner you can have these, the ultimate women, in your lives. Take it from me, you will never regret it."

"On another note, Rosewood will now become the official site for genetic experimentation. Gone are the superstitious prohibitions on genetic testing and development. In time, new genetic research will yield many new medical cures, just as it has on many other Federation worlds."

He talked on for another half hour before opening it up for questions. Marshal Tucker of Aerostar Engines asked the pointed question, "Excuse me, but will President John Johnson go along with this? After all he controls the armed forces of Virge-C."

"What President Johnson does is of no consequence. The Federation corporations now totally control the skies over all Virge-C. We are prepared for any use of the local armed forces. No, this should be a clean takeover. So why don't you drop by my office and discuss how we can merge your company into Galactic Dynamics?" Diego responded. He had still been unable to get Tucker to either sell his company or merge it, but even that didn't matter, not any longer. In time, he could force the issue. Best let the old man come to terms with the inevitability of it all.

Around noon, Dr. Decker met with his top staff, relaying the incredibly good news. Then, he took his chief of security aside. "Okay. We no longer need to locate and kill the clones. That project is terminated. We are now the sole authorized center for human genetic experimentation, so there's no need for the cover up, no need to get rid of the evidence of our past experiments."

"Okay boss. That's just as well. Roxane has gone into hiding, as have the other two. We don't have to waste our resources trying to track them down. Good move, boss." Dr. Decker smiled. Not all of that experiment had failed. He had the use of the nurse for a number of years. Besides, he had proved that clones growing up in different home situations developed along very different lines. He officially closed that old case. Now, he could legally begin entirely new lines of genetic research and manipulation. Making a superman was his lifelong goal, only now he was finally in a position to do so. Dr. Decker was a very happy man this day.

***

That same day, Sondra decided to see if Matt responded the way that Rene had. After all, there wasn't much else they could do. Sandy was looking after Alice who felt horrible. The drug had worn off, leaving her groggy, confused, and with a splitting headache. Roxane busied herself helping Rene and everyone set up housekeeping in the warehouse, no matter how crude. "Okay, Matt. I want you to close your eyes and go back to when we went to rescue Alice. Tell me everything you're seeing and feeling."

"This is silly. My leg is throbbing, dear, but okay if it'll appease you," Matt reluctantly agreed and began reliving the experience. On the fifth pass over the day's events, suddenly Matt felt a sharp throbbing pain when the slug hit his leg. After that, he began to see more and more details. Then, he even surprised himself, relating everything that had happened after he lost consciousness and was operated upon by Doc Smith. Roxane suddenly got interested when he began describing Doc Smith's operation on his leg.

Around noon, Matt was laughing about the whole thing, but Roxane was flabbergasted. "You were unconscious. Yet, you described exactly what Doc Smith and I did on your leg. Matt, that's incredible." She and Matt began discussing how this was even possible.

Sondra had no idea how it was possible, only that it was and that the person felt a whole lot better when they finally began laughing about it. Hence, she took on Alice next. She spent the afternoon working with Alice, who began talking about caterpillars, butterflies, and bugs, obviously hallucinations. However, Roxane recognized some of the phrases as those that Dr. Decker and she had said around Alice while she was totally out of it on the hospital bed. Once more, she paid close attention to the pair.

After a half dozen passes over the drugged day, the caterpillar turned into one of the men who had abducted her. Later, the butterfly turned into the nurse, embarrassing Roxane somewhat. Near suppertime, Alice was laughing about her wild trip, having seen what really had happened to her. Even more significant, when Roxane changed the bandages on Matt's leg, the wound had miraculously healed far more than it should have.

"Look at it, Matt! This is what I should see around the sixth day of healing. How can this be?" Roxane exclaimed, very much surprised. "I've never seen anything like this."

"Damned if I know, but it has stopped throbbing. That's what matters to me. I'm still a bit weak," Matt replied.

"Well, whatever you did, Sondra, I think you've stumbled upon something very significant," Roxane insisted. "So you aren't Sable. Have you got time to fill me in?"

Just then, Ben showed up carrying a large tray of food. Sondra gave him a big hug and the others thanked him repeatedly. "Say, you need to get a TV in here. Something big is going on. No one is really sure just what it all means."

"Okay, I'll get us one tonight," Roxane promised.

After they finished supper, Beth showed up, guided here by Ben. "Wow! Three of you," Beth exclaimed, looking from Sondra to Alice to Roxane. "Incredible. Oh hi boss," she added to Sondra. I came by because I just thought of something. My parents have recently moved out of their old farmhouse just a couple miles west of the spaceport. It's empty now, and they've not yet been able to sell it. You could all move in there. I checked with them today, and they like the idea of having someone living there watching over the place. What do you think? Besides, I'm now officially stationed at the spaceport until I graduate, so you'd be closer to me and I wouldn't have to drive around so much." She chatted away, but Sondra thought this was an ideal solution for the present.

She interrupted Beth. "You can stop convincing us. I love the idea. We'll do it. Need directions though."

"I'll come by first thing in the morning and drive out there with you. You can't miss it. I know you're going to love the place, rural, and all that," she continued to chat.

***

True to her promise, Beth returned around seven the next morning and helped everyone pack their few bags. Then, she proudly led the caravan of three cars west through the rest of Snake Town before veering north on Spaceport Road. Just at the edge of the spaceport itself, she veered left or west onto Highway 41. Two miles further along, she turned right up a farmer's lane. Ahead lay rolling pastureland and an old farmhouse, two stories tall, white clapboard, rustic, but safe. *Surely, no one could track us here,* Sondra concluded.

Inside, old sheets covered the well-worn furniture of her grandparents. There were far more bedrooms than they needed, and all opted to stay on the first floor. A very pleased Beth showed them where everything was located before she headed back to the spaceport.

Sandy declared, "Well, this is perfect, if only we could move more of our stuff out here." Even Rene wanted to retrieve some of her possessions, particularly photographs of her slain parents. Sondra had very little choice but to allow everyone an opportunity to return to their home or apartment and fetch what they could. The only exception was Matt. His leg, though healing well, still didn't permit him to do much walking, but his strength was returning rapidly. She guessed in a few days, he'd be able to make the trip to his apartment for his things.

However, Sondra insisted they follow the same routine they'd used before. One person drove and stayed in the car with the motor running while the other went inside to pack up. A honk meant extreme danger and to get out immediately. She got everyone's agreement on this point. Just as they were trying to decide who would go first, Matt's phone rang. He took the call, but as he listened, his face turned white. "Well?" Sondra pressured him the instant he hung up.

"It's bad. The aliens are taking over, officially. The entire police department has been disbanded. We're to go get our things out of there today. The corporations are providing their own security men to take our place. Governor Miller has declared martial law, with the aliens providing security. I can't believe President Johnson will stand for this."

"Well, Matt, we rather figured this day would be coming from all our research," Sondra argued. "Sooner than expected."

"What's it all mean?" asked Roxane.

"Don't know. Maybe war with the aliens?" Matt theorized. "We best get everyone's stuff out here today. No telling how bad things might get a week from now. We have two cars, so let's make two parallel runs."

His idea was accepted. Sondra drove Roxane to her apartment, while Sandy took Alice back to their small home. Matt looked after Rene while they were gone on this first run. Together, the two sat down to watch the newscasts, which now replaced all the regular daytime shows. The alien takeover was big news, and Matt wanted to know as much about it as possible, even wild rumors. He had a bad feeling about it.

Sondra and Roxane cased her apartment building for several minutes. Satisfied that no one was lurking about to get Roxane, Sondra finally allowed her to leave the car and head inside. This time, she was armed with many bags, picked up at a shop in Snake Town for very little money. Hastily, she began tossing all her clothes and shoes into the bags. Meanwhile, Sondra sat in the car, motor running, watching the street.

A lone man came walking up the street. At first, she didn't pay much attention to him. There were quite a number of people going about their business. As he approached her, she recognized the man. She'd seen him before. Where? Ah, the CEO Ball. Who was he? Ah, now that she couldn't answer, but he recognized her and came on up to the car.

"Madam Sable Hampton, if I'm not mistaken? Marshal Tucker, CEO of Aerostar Engines. We met at the CEO Ball."

"Oh yes, I remember your face. Sorry about not remembering your name. I met so darn many men that night that I couldn't keep them all straight," Sondra replied truthfully.

"Of course, nasty business—that alien contest thing. Have you heard? They're now proposing that all local business leaders turn their wives and daughters into those freakish UFB women."

"No, I hadn't heard. That's awful. Inhumane. Downright criminal," Sondra replied sounding the man out. He seemed very much against this genetic mutation and his reply convinced her of that.

"Unethical, evil, wicked. I could go on, but not in front of a fine young woman. You've heard the aliens are taking over, disbanding our own police force?"

"Yes, we just heard about it. Why?"

"Before I answer that, might I inquire, is Miss Roxane Stevens inside? I would like a word with her, if I may."

Sondra had to make a snap decision to trust him or not. Her intuition hinted at trust. "Only if you will allow me to be present. I do have a gun with me, so don't try anything."

"A very wise precaution, Madam Sable, very wise. Thank you. This won't take long, and it might interest you. Lead the way," he said politely.

Roxane was startled to see the older man walking into her apartment, but Sondra was behind him, and she knew she had her gun in her purse. "Packing? Yes, a very good idea, Miss Stevens. I would like to have a word with you, if I may."

"Well, make it fast. We don't know if they are watching for me or not. Oh do sit down wherever you can," Roxane insisted.

"I will be brief. Several years before you both were born, Dr. Decker of Rosewood Homecare was secretly involved in highly illegal human genetic experimentations, actions carried out at the very building in which you worked. His work resulted in untold deaths and mutilations of our people. I learned of his nightmare experiments on humans from your mother, my first wife. Yes, she was persuaded to donate a number of her eggs to his diabolical program. We had no idea of his real intentions or the awful things his experiments did to human volunteers, who often simply vanished without a trace. Rumors of men with two heads, men with four arms, men with no heads, men without any lungs or stomach. Hideous, malformed creatures—those were the results of his inhuman experiments."

"Yet, he had charisma and talked my wife into donating eggs for science. Later, when the awful rumors of his mad experiments began surfacing, she asked him what he had done with her eggs. All she ever got out of him was that she would be proud of what her eggs had become. Believe me; we tried to find out what happened. I've spent a fortune trying to get the necessary evidence to convict this monster of his myriad crimes. Then, I finally discovered what he'd done. One of her eggs had been used to produce four identical clones, you girls. While we had no proof of this, we demanded to be allowed to raise and to see our daughters. He refused and denied any such thing had occurred."

"Only recently, I've finally found out what he did. You were raised there in the Rosewood labs until you were around two years old. At that point, he sent each girl off to different foster parents, widely scattered around West Port. Why? Lord knows. Finally, I discovered the identity of one of you, Sable. Unfortunately, Dr. Decker found out that I'd found out, and he sent out orders to terminate all four of you. The man who told me that lost his life in a mysterious accident several months ago. And then just when I was trying to arrange a meeting with Sable, his henchmen attacked her, but somehow killed one of the other sisters, Sondra, according to the news."

"That set me back considerably. Only last week, I finally discovered you, Roxane. I've been researching your position and know that you know where Decker keeps his records. Now timing has become critical. The aliens are giving Decker carte blanche to continue his evil experiments under the guise of genetic research. I have to stop this maniac. All I need from you is the location of where he stores those records and his security precautions. In return, I'm prepared to give you a hundred thousand gold dollars, but I must know today. Time is critical. War will soon be upon us. I promised my wife I'd take this evil man down before I die, and I aim to keep that promise. Will you help me bring this fiend to justice?"

Sondra couldn't believe what she was hearing. It was

beyond incredible. "So, so you mean that we, we the four sisters, we're your daughters?"

The old man sighed, "That goes beyond rational knowledge. I suppose you are, in a way, since you somehow all came from her egg. Genetically, that would make you her daughters, but I have no idea if that relationship holds with whatever he did to make the four of you."

"Well, I've seen enough of his fiendish ways, Mr. Tucker. I don't know if the records you want are in his vault or if he has them secreted away in some other location, but I'll tell you what I do know," Roxane declared. "I can hardly believe all this either, but the man is a fiend. He was ready to destroy Alice's life, one of West Port's finest musicians."

She dug out a paper pad and began sketching a map. "His records vaults is here, in the basement, northwest sector. It's in a fireproof, waterproof, bombproof bunker." She outlined the points of entry and the complex security measures surrounding the vault. Handing the papers over to him, she added, "I wrote my number on there too. If you should find any records of us among them, I'd appreciate getting my hands on them."

"Thank you, Roxane, thank you. Here," he pulled an envelope from his jacket pocket. It contained a large stack of thousand gold dollar bills. Hastily, he turned and left them. Sondra finished helping her pack, worrying that they'd spent too long in her apartment.

As they headed home, Sondra commented, "Well, finally, I know it wasn't me that got Sable killed. For a long time, I thought I was somehow responsible. This sure is weird about us, I mean. We are sisters, aren't we?"

"Damned if I know for sure, but I feel better saying that we are. Clone sounds inhuman, like we're aliens or something. I guess the money will come in handy if things go bad," Roxane replied.

"Sorry, I was raised in Snake Town and barely got through high school. I'm not like you and Alice who know many things and all that. What does it mean to be a clone anyway? It sounds bad, but I haven't a clue what it really means; only everyone seems to think it is something really bad, evil perhaps."

"Look sis—it sure feels wonderful to say that, Sondra. I've gone my whole life alone, no parents, no brothers, no sisters, no relatives, just me. Now, I feel so lucky that I have two sisters," Roxane gushed. "But realistically, we only have what that man said happened. He could be lying just as much as Decker. I'm not going to take his word for all this. Right now, what we know for sure is that we are identical triplets, and that is more than enough for me," Roxane declared emphatically.

After a pause, she said, "But I didn't answer your question, did I? Well human cloning is illegal and doesn't actually exist, not in our medical arena. With animals, as I understand it, sometimes, they take cells from one animal and use them to make a duplicate animal. I think the best way to think of it is like a copy machine. You put your original document in, press the Copy button, and out comes an exact copy of the original."

Sondra thought about this a moment before replying, "Okay, we four look exactly alike, except for our hair styles, but wait, Sable was into exotic fashions, a Fetish Queen, wearing lots of latex or satin apparel. Alice is an incredible musician; you are a nurse and know much about medicine, and me? Well, I don't know much of anything. We're all so very different, not copies at all, not remotely."

"I see what you mean, but don't sell yourself short. You have survival skills the rest of us don't have. If it wasn't for you, Alice and I would be dead by now as well or worse," her voice trailed off, as she thought of Rene and what almost became of Alice.

When they got back to the farm, Matt insisted on having Sondra drive him into town next. "Look dear, I have to get to police headquarters. Things are going downhill rapidly. The alien corporations only own half of West Port and certainly not the rest of our world. Protests are springing up around the city. Eventually, someone is going to start shooting."

"Well, I kind of figured that, Matt. We're almost out of ammo," Sondra replied, turning south from the spaceport before heading into the city.

"That's why we need to get to the station. We have an armory there, if it hasn't already been looted. We have to lay in a supply of guns and ammo; we just have to," he insisted. They rode along in silence for a time. Since Matt seemed preoccupied with keeping watch on what was going on out on the streets, she decided not to interrupt him. Every few blocks, they spotted an unusually large number of people. Some groups were obviously locals, but several groups wore the grey and black uniforms of GD security guards, and they held what Sondra thought were big guns. She'd never been exposed to any firearm larger than a 9mm pistol. They were, in fact, automatic-firing riot guns and rifles. That fact wasn't missed on Matt, however.

When they approached the twenty-five story police headquarters building, she saw that barricades had been set up out front and were manned by some of the *disbanded* police. Matt recognized several and had Sondra pull up closer. He stuck his head out of the window and called out, "Hey Bill, what's going on? Are we officially disbanded? How can those aliens do this? What's up?"

"Yes, where 'ya been? Orders came down yesterday. We're disbanded, but some of us aren't going to give in to these alien thugs. Go around back. They'll let you in. We can use all the firepower we can get. They haven't tried to storm us yet," the man yelled back. Matt didn't have to tell her. Sondra turned the car and headed around to the backside of this building, which, like so many of the taller skyscrapers here in the heart of east West Port, occupied an entire city block. As she pulled in between several marked police cars, two more men stepped out, guns at the ready.

Matt stepped out and waved. "Ah, good. It's you, Matt. Where have you been? All hell's broken loose. We can use more of you. Hey, what happened to your leg? Who's that with you?"

"I got shot. She's with me, an undercover cop. We're out of ammo," Matt replied. He was limping on his right leg badly, a dead giveaway he'd been shot. Sondra came around to his right side and insisted her put an arm over her shoulder.

"Sure. Come on in. You know where the armory is. Head down there and load up. Some of us are holding out until—well, hell, we're just holding out," the man said. From that, Sondra guessed these men didn't really have a plan, other than to put on a show of resistance to the disbanding order.

"Damn, this place is nearly empty," Matt whispered, as the two made their way through the main floor to the elevators. "Usually, there are hundreds of us around, but we've only spotted a few. There's my boss's office." Sondra glanced and saw a man inside, sorting through piles of folders.

"What's he doing?" she whispered as they moved on down the hallway.

"Looks like he's collecting certain key files. Probably doesn't want them to fall into the wrong hands or something. We'll take the elevators up to the tenth floor. That's where the armory and firing range is located," he replied.

Minutes later, the two walked into what once had been a huge armory, countless shelves packed with all manner of police equipment. The locked gates were propped open and one man was already in there stuffing things into a bag. "Oh hi Matt. Good to see you with us. What a nasty mess, eh? Shit man, you're hurt!"

"Yes, I was shot the other day, but we decided we best get in here and armed while we still can. We've seen many GD security men out on the streets on our way in. Anyone have a plan?" Matt asked.

"Help yourself to whatever. Plan? Not really. Boss is here, planning to keep certain records safe. Some of us are manning a barricade out front. The idea is to hold them off from taking over our headquarters for as long as we can. Some say President Johnson will send in the army soon, so we hold until they get here. Gotta go. Cya." He slung the heavy bag over his shoulder and headed out of the armory.

Once the two were alone, Matt commented, "Wow, half the stuff is already gone. Okay, look around and see if you can find boxes of 9mm ammunition. I'll see what else might be useful for us."

Matt added six more semiautomatic 9mm guns with silencers to their arsenal, along with one high-powered rifle with a spotting scope. He found a box of stun grenades and added them to his bag, before meeting up with Sondra, who finally found the racks of ammunition and was stuffing her second bag with boxes of 9mm ammunition and clips. "Say, I saw a long rack with really big guns back there. Do we need any of those or shot guns? I saw a bunch of them too," Sondra asked.

"No, those are way too big for our needs. We're not an army. Let them bring on the heavy-duty firepower. We're just trying to defend ourselves, if we have to, not fight a war." Ten minutes later, they had all they could carry and headed out to her car.

"We have to get this stuff home. I'll try to get back as soon as I can, Henry," Matt explained to one of the men just outside. "Have someone text me if there's something going on. I have to let my leg heal some. No good limping around like this."

"Right, Matt. I'll spread the word. My money is on a good fight, once the army gets here. We'll be ready for the aliens. Never should have let them land on Virge-C, that's what I say."

"No argument from us!" Sondra agreed with him. She fired up the car and headed back to their new retreat on the farm. Once there, Matt insisted Roxane, Sandy, and Alice each have a 9mm gun with silencer for their protection. Thus, part of the afternoon, Matt spent teaching the three women to shoot. The abandoned farm was a perfect place to do just that.

Around five o'clock, Beth drove up, but had a young man with her. "Hi everyone. This is my big brother, Tom. He's just come home from the army." Tom was a tall, thin young man of twenty-two. His hair was just growing out from the typical buzz cut of the soldiers. His enlistment term was over, and he'd returned home to a city in turmoil. Tom had a distinct accent though.

"Hi ya, laddies, lassies. Looks like I gotta out of the army just in time. War's coming, I canna feel it," he announced his arrival.

One by one, Beth introduced Tom to the group. When she got to Rene, Tom exclaimed, "Wow! Will you look at you!

I'd recognize you anywhere! Miss West Port. Well, you do look a bit different and all that, but wow anyway. Very pleased ta meet ya. Canna see why ya wanta go an look like the aliens though. You was just perfect before. Still, ya look like the finest Miss West Port ever. Thomas Ferguson, at your service, lassie. Ya canna count on old Tom ta protect ya, now that's fa sure!"

"Well, I didn't want to look like this," Rene replied.

"What's that? Dinna quite get it. Oh, da lip things. Can ya say it a'gin?" he asked.

"I didn't want to look like this," she repeated. The grin on Tom's face was quite broad. His smile was infectious, and she didn't mind having to repeat things.

"Ya dona want ta look like this?" he guessed. She nodded. "Well, I dona blame ya none fer that. Still, ya gotta love your curves. Mighty impressive, Miss West Port. If'en I do say so myself, you look better than the photos I got of ya when ya won the pageant last fall."

"Oh stop flirting with Rene," Beth broke in. "Ignore him, Rene. Look, Tom, she was kidnaped by the aliens, who murdered her parents in cold blood and stole their Shoe Box Company. They turned her into what they call a UFB woman against her will, but Sondra here and Matt—well, they rescued her. Now we're looking after her. So stop messing with Rene. She's been through utter hell."

"Sissy, I'm not messin' with her. She was already an ultimate beauty before they laid their miserable hands on her. We guys know. Lot's of soldiers have her pic up on their lockers. Rene is our inspiration, donna ya see? Probably, ya don't, sis, cause you's a girl. This is a guy thing. Donna pay her any mind, Rene. We all think ya is one fantastic woman, but we dina know ya got kidnaped and all this done ta ya. Rene, I promise ya that I'll kill those who done this to ya. Ya got Tom's word ona that."

"Tom, she doesn't need revenge. She needs her arms back and more. Revenge isn't going to help her any," Beth retorted.

"Well, okay, sissy. Point taken," Tom backed off, his face slightly red. "Well then, Tom will just have ta be ya arms and hands for now, Miss West Port."

Beth giggled. "You don't have any *idea* what you're getting yourself into, big brother. You'll soon regret it. Come on; we need to get supper going. Any news from today?"

"Well, actually quite a lot," Roxane said, as they headed into the kitchen. She began to relate what she'd learned from the CEO of Aerostar Engines.

At the supper table, Beth finally announced, "Gang, I've an announcement to make. You are looking at the newest deep space transport pilot! I just passed my solo flight today. I have my official license to pilot any transport!"

"Incredible. Well done," Sondra praised her, while everyone clapped and cheered.

"Well now that's really somethin', sissy, because I was a navigator in the service," Tom added. "Don't that beat all?"

"So now I can fly a transport anywhere in the galaxy," Beth said proudly.

"Except'n ya donna have a transport," Tom added, busting her bubble. She pouted a little.

After the noise settled down, she added, "So now I can stay here with you and help all the time, except for once in a while when I have a job interview. I don't think I want to work for the aliens though, but I did hear they're going to bring or make the Federation Internet available everywhere, not just the library, but I expect that won't happen for a while. Once it does, we can really see what worlds are out there. I can hardly wait to go exploring. Do you suppose it's possible to visit all them? Will they speak our language?" Beth chatted on gaily through the rest of dinner and then some.

The next morning, Roxane received a text message from Marshal Tucker, the CEO of Aerostar Engines. Puzzled by what it meant, she showed it at once to Sondra and Matt. It read: Meet me at Lou's Chicken & Grits in Snake Town at eleven. I've a proposition for you and your sisters.

"Well, you aren't going alone," Sondra declared. "Matt and I will come with you. This could be a trap. I don't trust any of these CEOs."

Roxane grinned. "Thanks. I don't either. Funny, when I was younger, I looked up to Dr. Decker as a medical genius. How little did I know then? Why Snake Town?"

Sondra laughed. "Because it's the slums of West Port. All the seedier things live there. The respectable folks avoid that section of the city as though the people there had the plague or something. Probably, the aliens are giving Snake Town a very wide birth. If I know Snake Town, no alien would be safe walking those streets."

***

"Don't recommend eating anything here, just the coffee," Tucker said. It was just after eleven, and Roxane, Sondra, and Matt found Lou's diner. Mr. Tucker was already there. Six of his armed guards stood guard outside. He'd already paid the manager a sizeable sum to compensate him for vacating the diner, so only the four of them were sitting at one table in the vacant eatery. The place smelled of rancid grease. Even the tables had a film of something slimy on their surface. One just didn't look closely at the floor.

Hastily, the manager, who was pleased to have just made a week's salary, poured them three cups, and rapidly vanished from sight. "Okay. Thanks for coming. War is brewing. I've heard President Johnson has ordered full mobilization of Virge-C's armed forces. Meanwhile, Roxane, I need to get to those records of Dr. Decker's. My spies tell me he now has a dozen, well-armed Galactic Dynamics security guards bolstering his own forces. My original plan of snatch and grab has gone by the boards. We're going to have to assault the place."

He continued, "Lord knows what's going to be happening in the near future. I've no sons now. Peter died in an accident last year. All that I have left are you daughters. I know, I'm probably not your father, but Helen—she was your mother. That much I know, but I can't prove it until I get my hands on Decker's records. However, I'm really more interested in his other records, those of his evil, wicked genetic experiments. Anyway, I wanted you to have this disposable phone, Roxane. It can't be traced, like your current phone. If you will take my advice, get rid of all phones that aren't disposable. I'll be sending you messages on this new phone." He handed her the phone.

"Now then, I figured to get to those records of his, I'll

148

need a distraction. Some of my men will openly attack Rosewood Homecare headquarters, tying up lots of their men. While they are busy fighting, I'll lead a second force into Rosewood and get those records. I was hoping you might be interested in coming along. Your knowledge of the building would be invaluable. Besides, the records you and your sisters need to see have to be in there as well. You can search for them at the same time as I look for those that I need to get my hands on. What say you?"

"But I'm a nurse, Mr. Tucker, not a fighter. True, I know where things are at, but I can't fight or anything," Roxane protested. Going back into Rosewood was the very last thing she wanted to do. If she never visited that place again, she'd be happy.

Sondra felt torn. On the one hand, she desperately wanted to know more about their history or creation—that sounding so utterly alien to her—and on the other, she didn't want to go near these sadistic people. Weighing what they could possibly learn about themselves against the obvious danger they'd be facing, Sondra made her decision. "Look, it's too dangerous for Roxane to go in there. She's a nurse. I'll go in her place. I can fight. I think we all want to see those records about us."

"But you can't," protested Roxane. "You'll be killed. I don't want to lose another sister. It's too dangerous. He's utterly ruthless, I tell you, utterly."

"I know, Roxane, but somehow we have to know about ourselves," Sondra insisted. "This might be our only chance ever to find out the truth about us."

Obviously quite afraid, Roxane sighed. "Okay. I'll go with you. You don't know the layout or where things are at. Besides, you wouldn't know one record from another. I'll have to look over the records."

"Hey, I'm not letting either of you go in there alone. I'll come with you as well," Matt insisted. Sondra already knew that if she went, Matt would insist upon coming as well. She counted on that, and he didn't disappoint her.

"Good. I promise you I will one day make this right with you. I'll send word to you on this new phone. The attack must come soon, before the army gets here and all hell breaks loose," Mr. Tucker explained. "We best get out of here now. Lord knows how many spies GD has got around our city." With that, he rose and left. Matt waited a minute and ushered them out as well.

"Where are we going now?" Matt asked. Sondra wasn't heading directly back to the farm.

"He's right. We all should get new disposable phones. I know just the place to get them," she replied, pulling up beside a rundown building. "I'll be back in a bit. You all stay in the car. It's much safer for you inside than out there on the street. This is Snake Town, after all. They know me here." Matt couldn't argue with that point. This place looked very creepy to him. He drew his gun, just in case.

She returned some twenty minutes later, a bag over her shoulder. "Mission accomplished. Home James," she teased everyone with an old move reference that the other two didn't get.

Once back at the farm, she spent an hour setting up the pile of phones. Each one had everyone else on speed dial, which she explained as she carefully handed specific phones to everyone. Tom, Beth, Matt, Sally, Alice, Roxane, and even Rene received new phones. "Look, I think Rene might be able to use her nose to push a button if she has to," Sondra explained, noticing Rene's eyes reflected the smile that she had, though her lips never would again. "All eight of us are on speed dial so we can reach each other as fast as possible if we need to. Don't give out these numbers to anyone you don't trust with your life. Got it?"

"Aye, lassie, got it," Tom replied, adding to Rene, "See lassie, even ya canna speed dial. I'll help ya practice it. I know ya canna do it."

Again, Sondra saw the helpless young woman's smile in her eyes. *As strange as Tom is*, she thought, *he's good for her.*

Sondra then said, "Okay this assault on Rosewood is likely to be nasty. We might become split up. If that happens, we need a safe house as a rendezvous point. We'll use Sable's place. I will place another one of these phones in her walk-in clothes closet. If we are separated, make for Sable's. Use the back door, which I'll leave unlocked. Hell, there's not much there that's worth stealing except her latex and leather apparel. Remember, if we are separated, eventually make your way to Sable's. Got it?"

"Yes, but I'm not too familiar with where her place is," Roxane spoke up.

"No problem. We'll go there this afternoon, and I'll drive you around some," Sondra suggested. "Remember, the phone will be in the walk-in closet in Sable's bedroom. You can't miss it."

Sondra spent an hour driving Roxane around the area of Sable's home and the streets from there to Rosewood, making sure Roxane could find her way there on foot if needed. However, both women were very surprised to see the number of GD security men out patrolling the streets of their city. It was unnerving to say the least. However, they didn't see any signs of an armed rebellion, which both took as a very good sign.

On Monday, Roxane received a text message on the phone Mr. Tucker had given her. The raid was planned for noon. Tucker and his secondary group, which included Roxane, were to meet at eleven at Lou's diner for further instructions. Matt checked both his 9mm guns and triple checked his bag of clips. Taking a hint from him, Sondra did the same. Both wore dark shirts and pants and soft-soled shoes.

Roxane gingerly kept her gun in her purse, hoping and praying she wouldn't need it. "I hope we're doing the right thing," she whispered to Sondra and Matt, as they left their car and entered the diner, where Mr. Tucker and six other men waited.

"Good. You're here. Now then, here's the plan." He spread out a crude map of Rosewood headquarters on the greasy table, compiled from what Roxane told him and from his other spies. "The main attack force will be striking here at the front entrance. We give them fifteen minutes to get all their guards committed to the battle. Then, we go in the back way, here. This elevator supposedly will take us directly to the records vault. I have charges that will blow the doors open if we have to. Once inside, we'll split up. Roxane, you look for your records, and I'll look for the ones I want. Call out when you have found the ones you want. With luck, we will be in and out before they know what hit them. Questions?"

"Matt and I will play rear guard while you search. I haven't the faintest idea what to look for. We'll be more useful guarding your rear," Sondra volunteered. "After Roxane finds our records, are we to depart or should we stay until you find yours? What about the other way around? Will you be staying until she finds our?"

"Good point. The honorable thing to do is stay together until we both have what we want. We're stronger united," Mr. Tucker stated. All agreed with him.

***

Parked a block away from the Rosewood headquarters skyscraper, Mr. Tucker stared at his watch. "Now," he whispered. Shortly, the sound of gunfire erupted. He smiled and gave an unneeded signal to Matt in the second car.

"It sounds like a war's going on!" Sondra exclaimed. The noise was quite loud even a block away. On the streets, over fifty people raced into any available building. This was not the time to be out on any street anywhere near Rosewood!

Roxane whispered, "That's a good sign. We don't want innocent people getting hurt."

"Right. No collateral damage," Matt stated.

"Is that what you call it, when innocent people get in the way?" she asked testily.

"Yes. Five more minutes," he replied.

Matt started the car and followed Tucker's vehicle. Both pulled into the back loading dock area. One other truck was already there, but no one was around. Roxane swiped her ID card to open the doors, but it failed to work. "So much for my ID card," she whispered.

"Not a problem," Tucker said, firing two shots into the glass surrounding the latch. They made their noisy entrance. One of his men shot the lone security guard still at his back post, while everyone ran to the elevator.

*So far, so good,* Sondra thought. Still, this wasn't her style raid. If she could have had her own raid, no one would

152

even know they were here. She banished such thoughts and focused on keeping alert. After all Roxane was totally out of her comfort zone on this raid.

As they approached the records vault, his men shot the two guards watching the vault and then set off the explosive charges, blowing the doors inward. Now there was no chance they could be trapped inside. Matt and Sondra took up positions on either side of the doors, along with two of Tucker's men. The rest entered the impressive vault, designed to resist fire, bombs, and floods.

"Think they will find anything useful?" Matt whispered.

"I have to hope so, dear. You can't imagine what it's like not to know your own history, your own life, your own parents, if we even had parents, Matt. The unknown is eating us alive. We have to know," she whispered back. "I do wish they'd hurry up. I have a very bad feeling about this."

***

In the top floor CEO office of Galactic Dynamics, Diego summoned his two seconds in command, Juan los Santos and Fernando Gabinio. Diego and Juan were middle aged and married to two beautiful UFB women, Luisa and Juanita. In stark contrast, twenty-three old Fernando was single. He had risen in the corporate ranks by displaying a superior intelligence, a remarkable knack for political subterfuge, and outstanding business acumen. He counted his lucky stars to have been chosen to become a part of GD's corporation on Virge-C under Diego. However, he needed only one thing to complete his image of Diego's second in command—a fine UFB wife.

Importing one from his home world wasn't practical. At the recent CEO Ball, he kept his eyes on the many local, high class women, knowing that marrying one of them, who was a UFB woman, would gain him even more status, particularly when GD made its takeover move. He'd spotted the Fetish Queen, Sable Hampton, danced once with her, and decided she was the one for him. He relayed his choice to Diego.

However, all attempts to apprehend her and convert her into his UFB woman had met with failure, one way or another. Next, he decided on Rene, Miss West Port. Her

153

conversion went perfectly. He'd see how she looked after she'd awakened from her coma, stunning! But someone snatched her out of GD headquarters and no one knew what happened. Then with a stroke of uncommon luck, Dr. Decker informed Diego, and thus Fernando, that Sable was a clone and that there were other copies of her in West Port, one of which was first violinist in the orchestra. Yet, even the attempt to kidnap her met with failure. Someone had snatched her out from underneath Decker's hands, only hours from the UFB conversion process.

With Diego's current preoccupation with the takeover move, Fernando decided to take matters into his own hands. If he were to have the UFB woman of his choice, then he'd have to go get her personally. He still had the two hundred thousand gold dollar earrings he was going to adorn Alice with, and he swore that would not be wasted. He began his own search, quietly using a few men whose loyalty to him could be counted upon.

An extra thousand in these men's accounts kept them from complaining about becoming bug-eyed from looking at so many hours of street cam video! Indeed, the woman of his dreams was spotted here and there around the city on various days and times—Sable or Sondra—he wasn't quite sure just what her name actually was. However, he was certain this was the same woman he'd met at the ball. All he needed now was to predict when and where she might next appear or to get advance warning of where she was. He kept his six men working on this project on the side.

Fernando was a handsome man, with black hair and a striking moustache. His black eyes gave him a fierce appearance, formidable some said. He entered Diego's office, joining Juan and wondering what was up. "Ah. Okay, this just in. Decker reports that his Rosewood headquarters is now under serious assault by parties unknown. I've checked some video streams and agree with him. This is some kind of all-out assault. We can't allow this to happen. We need his genetics lab facilities. So take some men and get down there and put an end to this uprising." Both Juan and Fernando nodded and left together to comply.

First, Fernando dropped by his private office where his special men were working. "Hey, focus in on the Rosewood headquarters. There's a battle raging there." Shortly, they could see at least fifty men assaulting the main entrance. Shattered glass covered the ground, but the attackers had the protection of many cars and trucks. On a hunch, Fernando said, "Zoom in on the rear of that building. Keep an eye on things there. I can't imagine why anyone would be assaulting Rosewood. The police station or GD headquarters—that would make sense, but not this place. There must be something else going on."

Just then, one of his men spoke up, "Boss, isn't this the woman we've been looking for?" He zoomed in the video as much as possible. While fuzzy, it certainly did look like her.

"Finally! Got you at last, 'Sable or Sondra or whatever your name is! Okay, gear up. We're going to get her alive and unharmed," Fernando ordered. "Join Assault Squad Two, but once we hit the ground, you and I will head around back with the truck. Make sure you bring the tranq gun!" He turned and left to get his own PDS on, that is, his personal defense shield. No sense taking a chance that one of these primitive weapons might harm him. His men didn't bother with a PDS, figuring this was a snatch job.

Juan ordered his Assault Squad to come at the main attackers from their left flank, since there wasn't any way to get at them from the rear or right side. Meanwhile, Fernando ordered his squad to join Juan's, while he and his six men drove the truck around to the rear. There, he spotted the getaway vehicles and one man guarding them, who was quickly eliminated. Carefully, Fernando and his six men entered the building following the trail left by the raiders.

Once inside, he had no idea where they went. Frustrated, he ordered his men to tap into the building's comm center. "Find out where trouble is being reported inside the building. Ignore all else. We must find where they are at inside," he ordered.

Minutes passed before Fernando learned the Records Vault was being attacked. Even more time passed before he could figure out where that was and how to get there, but their path had to have started here at the loading dock entrance, that much was certain.

"We have company," Matt called out the obvious. The elevator doors opened and gunfire erupted. Four Rosewood men fell out of the elevator even before they could get off any shots. Carefully, one of the Tucker's men dragged the men out of the way and propped the doors open so no more could come down this way.

There were two stairwells, one on each end of the long entrance hallway to this secluded Records Vault. Now, they only had to guard these two entrances, the elevator being temporarily inoperable. "Hurry up in there," Matt yelled into the room, suspecting Tucker wouldn't pay any attention to his warning. *That man is driven,* he thought. *I do wonder what he is after. Must be incredibly damming.*

Tucker received word over his phone that his outside forces were now taking fire from two assault teams on their flank and that they couldn't hold out too much longer. At last, he yelled, "Found them!" He joined Roxane and looked over her shoulder. "Yes, those are what you are looking for. Let's get out of here." Roxane held a manila folder with numerous documents inside along with a small thumb drive. She stuffed it into her purse and followed Mr. Tucker.

As they reached the destroyed doors, suddenly chaos broke out. From both side stairway doors, security men came rushing and firing wildly. More importantly, Fernando's men tossed several smoke grenades, which exploded, flooding the confined hallway with a dense smoke. Sondra emptied two clips, firing towards the door on her left, while Matt grabbed Roxane's arm and Tucker's as well. "We're making a break for the right doors," he yelled to Sondra. Three of Tucker's men led the way, firing constantly, as they made their blind way towards these doors, luckily downing three of Fernando's men who were at that entrance. However, they managed to wound severely those three men of Tucker's. "Come on, Sondra," Matt yelled, completely unable to see anything in the dense smoke.

The other two of Tucker's men were with Sondra on the left side. While she clumsily tried to reload in the smoke, unable to see her guns, Fernando and two others moved out into the room, making contact with the two remaining men, dropping them. Just as she got her guns ready, she spotted Fernando moving towards her. She began backing up towards where Matt's voice had come from, while emptying both guns at Fernando. Twenty-eight bullets fired in rapid succession. To her shock, even though she couldn't possibly miss a target this close to her, the bullets seemed to ricochet off him somehow. He fired a strange looking gun at her. Anticipating the heavy hit of a slug, she flinched, but felt only a tiny pinprick. Sondra continued to backup, but tripped over the body of one of the fallen men. She landed hard and lost her grip on both guns, which went sailing out of sight across the floor.

She felt weak and stunned, but struggled to continue moving backwards over the dead man, using her arms and legs. Slowly, they weakened, and darkness swept over her. Sondra slipped into unconsciousness. "Mine at last. You are one impressive woman, Sondra or Sable or whatever you call yourself. I must make you as impressive as I can, for you will be looked upon as the ultimate woman on all of Virge-C, the ultimate woman. Okay, pick her up, and let's get out of here."

"Where's Sondra?" Matt yelled. He'd gotten them up the stairs and out to their cars. Roxane looked all around, but saw only the three of them.

"Son, you have to get out of here now. Look there, that's a GD vehicle. Those men will be coming back out of the building in no time. If you value your life and Roxane's, get her out of here now! If Sondra were able, she'd be here already. She's probably shot or captured," Tucker yelled, making a dash for his car and yelling over his phone for his men to break off their frontal attack. He wisely didn't tell Matt that she was probably dead. Hell, he'd lost six of his own men. He was lucky to have gotten out of there alive.

"What do we do?" wailed Roxane.

"Go get in the car. Here are the keys. Get the motor going. I'll wait here until the last possible moment for her. Otherwise, I have to hope she can find a way to get to Sable's," Matt ordered. He couldn't bring himself to think she might be dead inside this building! He just couldn't. Only now did he realize the depth of his love for this most remarkable woman.

One of the GD security men appeared, running out of the stairway. Matt fired and ran over to the car. Once inside, he peeled out of the lot as fast as he could go, avoiding a number of other emergency vehicles and trucks on their way here. A precarious half hour later, he pulled into their remote farm. "Okay, Roxane, I'm leaving you here. I'll be back at Sable's waiting for Sondra to make her way there." Rather than explain to the anxious others, he loaded up a bag with a change of clothes, more ammunition, some water bottles, and a bit of food, before dashing back out to the car. He parked the car in the back alley, out of the way, but where Sondra could easily see it, when she made her way up the alley to the back door. Satisfied, he went inside to wait for her, vowing to wait for weeks if need be.

He made a pot of coffee and sat down to think. He knew he had no idea of what happened to her. The smoke was too thick to see anything. He turned on the news, hoping to get some clues. Naturally, coverage of the attack was all that was on. What he most wanted to hear was the casualties report. All day, Matt listened. No one had any idea who these attackers were, though in time, he knew they would be identified. No one had any workable theory why they had attacked Rosewood Homecare. It seemed inexplicable to these newscasters.

Late in the evening, they began reporting on the casualties. Ten attacking men were dead, and another dozen men were wounded and in various hospitals, and would be charged with various crimes. Twenty-six defenders were dead, and another twenty were taken to local hospitals. There was no mention of any woman killed or wounded on either side! Hearing that, Matt relaxed slightly for the first time since the battle began. He was certain if a woman were found dead or wounded, the press would be making a big deal over it. Had she somehow gotten out of that chaos? If so, where was she? If she was on foot, by now she should have made it here. Perhaps, she was wounded, had crawled off, and that was why she was late getting back to Sable's. Try as he might, he couldn't get rid of images of her lying in some dark alley bleeding to death.

Leg cramps woke Matt. It was morning. The TV was

still on. He'd fallen asleep on the couch while watching. He stretched and massaged the cramps out of his legs, particularly his right leg where his wound was nearly healed. He made a fresh pot of coffee and watched the news again. More accurate figures were given along with the theory that some of the attackers used to work for Aerostar Engines. Still, not one woman was reported as being either dead or wounded. They had taken no prisoners either, but during the night, the hospitals had been raided and the wounded attackers had vanished. Matt grinned upon hearing that tidbit. Old Tucker didn't let his men down, he thought. But what happened to Sondra?

After eating a poor lunch, he decided he had other ways to find out. If the police force was still operational, he could have gone in and asked Bill, their video hot shot, to cue up surveillance video around the rear of that building. However, the police force was no more. Still, Bill might be able to help. He headed out to his car, stopping at a fast burger joint for something more substantial.

He found Bill at his home, nicely barricaded against any threats to his family. "Oh, hi Matt. What brings you around here? Wasn't that something yesterday?" After some pleasant chat, Matt turned to conversation to what he needed.

"Say Bill. Is there any way you can cue up surveillance video that shows the rear of that Rosewood building?"

Bill laughed. "Of course. You don't think this video whiz is stopped by GD now do you? Come on into my workshop." He led Matt into a converted back bedroom, filled with electronic gear. An hour later, he had hacked into a promising feed from the bank across the street. "Mind you, I'm not going to sit here and watch video all day. Besides, if I don't know what you are looking for, then I can't be made to squeal on you. Just turn it off when you are done. I'll be out with the misses."

"Thanks, Bill. You're a lifesaver! I owe you a big one," Matt replied, extremely grateful for Bill's openness and assistance without asking any questions. Probably, Bill was wise in not knowing, not with all that was going on and probably would be happening soon when the army arrived.

For hours, Matt sifted through the video and finally began watching in earnest. He spotted them going into the building. One thing was certain; no one could really identify them from this video. It was too fuzzy. He watched, biting his nails with worry and anticipation. Finally, he saw the three of them rushing out. Now he sat up and paid very close attention. He spotted himself racing to the car and smiled, watching the car peeling out of the loading bay parking lot.

He saw the GD man come out, look around, and then drive their truck up closer to the dock. Then, he looked closer at the screen. Sure enough, he saw two other GD men coming out. Wait! They were carrying someone! He stopped the video and replayed it in slow motion, freezing it at one point. While he could have called Bill in to have him work his magic and get a close up shot of the person, he decided to experiment a bit with the controls. After some trial and error, he found out how to zoom in. Bingo. There was Sondra!

Swallowing hard, he looked for signs of bleeding. He didn't find anything obvious. "So she wasn't shot. They certainly wouldn't be carrying a dead woman out of there. Unconscious. Now who are these men?" He zoomed in on one and saw the man had a distinctive set of patches on his uniform upper sleeves. Someone in authority, he presumed. He watched as the truck departed, while many other vehicles drove up. So they were leaving. That also didn't fit. Why not stay and handle mop up actions? No, they must have taken her prisoner somehow. Where are they taking her?

"Hey Bill. Got another question for you?" Matt broke down and called for his former co-worker again. "See this truck leaving? Can you access traffic cams and see where it goes?"

"If we weren't disbanded, you bet. Simple matter. Might take some time, but easily done. Not anymore. They've changed all the access codes. I can't get into the traffic cam system any longer. They think I might get in there and screw with all the stop lights timing, creating a mammoth traffic snarl." Bill roared with laughter. "No can do that. About all you could do would be to make a guess of their route and try to hack into some nearby systems. Hit or miss. Sorry."

"Okay. Then I'm done here. Thanks." He jotted down the date and time that the truck left the back lot and headed back to Sable's, stopping along the way to pick up a few groceries. Sondra wasn't there, but after what he'd seen, he didn't expect to see her here yet. *Give her time to escape,* he told himself.

Around suppertime, Beth called him. "Any word on Sondra?" she asked timidly, but very worried about her boss.

Matt explained what he had uncovered. "So I'm close but no pie. I can see her being loaded into a GD truck and driving away, but we can't access the traffic cams any longer to follow that truck's travel."

Beth jotted down the exact time and place. "Well, maybe I can find out something." She hung up. Matt didn't know how Beth could possible find out something and promptly put that out of his mind. He toyed with going door to door along the possible route, asking around if anyone had seen that truck passing by, but realized that was unlikely to produce any results except worn out shoes.

The next day, he drove over to the GD skyscraper with the idea of looking around for that truck, but found the place surrounded by GD guards and no access to their underground parking deck. Somberly, he drove back to Sable's. Next, he decided to focus on identifying the man who was in charge of that small group. He fired up Sable's old laptop and began surfing, focusing on GD personnel. An hour later, his efforts were rewarded.

Fernando Gabino read the caption below the man. Apparently, he was one of the top executives of Galactic Dynamics. Only Diego was above him. *Damn.* He read the brief bio, much of which involved off-world stuff, which was meaningless to Matt, but one fact struck him. The man was single. Suddenly, Matt's heart skipped a beat! *Is this Fernando's objective to marry Sondra?* "My God, Sondra, I should have asked you to marry me long ago! I'm sorry. I will marry you at once, if only I can get you back," he called out to the unfeeling walls of Sable's workroom.

As he sat back still staring at his enemy, he realized if Fernando were planning to marry Sondra, first he would turn her into a UFB woman. All these top Federation corporation executives had a UFB woman as their wives. Matt felt crushed. He cried himself to sleep that night.

The morning of the fourth day after the attack, Beth called him up. "Hi Matt. I got some news for you. I followed that truck you told me about. It went into the underground parking deck at the GD headquarters about fifteen minutes after you saw it. Does this help? Is Sondra there? What can we do?"

"How on Virge did you ever find that out?" he exclaimed, his worst fears now confirmed beyond all doubts.

"Oh, I'm an official transport pilot. I have access to the spaceport. So I used their system, a geo-tracking and imaging system. Pretty easy actually, what with the precise location and time to begin looking for the truck," Beth replied.

"Okay, then the man who took her is Fernando Gabino, a young top GD executive. He alone of those top men is not married. I have a bad feeling that he's turning Sondra into another one of those UFB women, but just where Sondra is now, I have no idea." The two chatted a bit longer, but neither could come up with any way to get into the GD building. It was now impressively heavily guarded, a veritable fortress. Matt spent the rest of the day and far into the night trying to figure out how he could get in there and rescue Sondra, who by now was probably as helpless as Rene was. Still, Matt simply wouldn't give up. "I love you, dear. Somehow, someway, I will get you back," he swore to the walls of Sable's place. His last thought before falling asleep was, "Well, at least, I can sort of understand Rene now."

# Chapter 11—Down, Not Out

Sondra felt a pinprick. She recalled that much and then stumbling backwards over one of the dead men. She remembered how weak her arms and legs were and then that awful darkness came. Now, she believed she saw light. *Am I waking up?* Her mind struggled with conflicting thoughts and emotions. *Have the others gotten away?* The last thing she remembered was Matt leading them towards the right stairwell and calling out for her. *I tried to come to you,* she thought. Then, she saw that GD man coming towards her. She saw herself emptying both clips into him, the bullets merely bouncing off him as though by some unknown magical effect. Then, she blacked out. *I think I see light now. It must be later on because that's back then, I think.* Her fuzzy mind struggled to assert itself.

Slowly, her mind began to sense her body once more. Even though her eyes were closed, she sensed light on the other side of her lids. *I must be waking. Oh, I hurt. My lips are throbbing. I can't breathe. No, that's not true. It's hard to breathe. Must be that tight corset again. Have I gone back in time? Can anyone go back in time? Is there time travel? Oh get real Sondra. Wake up. How? My mouth—so dry, so hungry. Why do I ache so? No, lips ache. Weird. I'm feeling some airflow over me, but that's not possible. Have to get my eyes open. Yes, that's what I must do. Come on. Open. Ah there. It is light.*

"She's finally coming around," a nearby voice said—rather quietly, Sondra thought.

*Coming around? Yes, I was unconscious. I'm waking up. Light.* In a rush of sensations, at last Sondra's body responded or was it that her mind finally connected with her body? Either way, sensations, good and bad, flooded into her mind in one giant rush, nearly overwhelming her for a moment. Her lips throbbed and felt stretched somehow. Her mouth felt as though she'd swallowed sand. Breathing was extremely difficult, even worse than it had been when she was wearing Sable's fancy fetish outfits, but she had just enough presence of mind to take shallow breaths and not fight the incredible compression forces around her waist. Her chest felt as though someone placed a heavy weight on it. Her feet felt funny, but right now, her mind couldn't work out what they were trying to tell her. Above all this, she felt the constant, gentle, yet cool flow of air over her body, well most of it down to her knees anyway. Her mind finally registered that she was lying on her back and that the light was coming from overhead. Slowly, Sondra reoriented herself to the universe.

She blinked from the bright lights and tried to sit up. Somehow, her arms failed to push her up. She tried again, nothing. "She's coming around. Let's get her sitting up," the voice said.

*Yes, I've heard that voice before, just a bit ago, yes. I'm trying to sit up, but my arms must be still paralyzed or something.* She felt arms sliding beneath her back, lifting her up into a sitting position. Finally, the world came into focus, though she found herself staring at a total stranger.

The voice attached itself to a body—a nurse from the uniform she was wearing. She was standing beside her. "Welcome. You're finally awake. As you can see, we have you positioned before a mirror so you can see your incredibly, fabulous, new appearance, one of our fantastic UFB women!"

Sondra thought. *The nurse seems terribly excited about this, but why? UFB women are completely helpless, but pretty though.* Suddenly, recognition came into her mind. She wasn't looking at a stranger; she was looking at herself. They had put her through their genetic bio agent modification procedure. She was as helpless as Rene was. A wave of panic swept over her entire body. For a moment, she felt like vomiting, but it passed. *Get a hold of yourself, Sondra. It's not the end of the world. You got Rene doing well enough.* "Can't breathe," she mumbled, not recognizing her own voice for a second. "Thirsty," she added, wondering if the nurse could even understand her. *I can't wait for weeks until they learn what I'm saying. Can I?*

"Yes, we'll bring you some water shortly. Take shallow breaths. Very good on not passing out. So many new UFB women do that—pass out a few times when they first awake. It's the tight corset, which you must always wear now. Besides giving you a fabulously small waistline, the envy of all women, it gives you proper back support for your impressive bosom. No need for plastic surgery or those awful breast implants. Your breasts are all natural and just perfect, don't you think? The envy of all women," the nurse chatted away as though all this was simply the popular rage. Sondra didn't have the energy to protest, not just yet.

Looking at her image and forcing herself to take short, shallow breaths, she finally saw her face. Several blemishes were gone, and the slightly off-center nose of hers was now perfectly symmetrical, but her lips commanded her total attention. Now she saw why they were throbbing and feeling stretched. Her lips had been sliced from one side of her mouth to the other. Two large, golden lip disks stretched the loops of flesh out very taught. The loops had been her lips. The plates drooped downward, almost touching her chest, and did so if she lowered her head even slightly. Her mind registered a small detail; her disks were larger than Rene's were.

Then, she spotted why her ears were complaining. Two enormous earrings dangled down from her tiny ear lobe grommets, filled with gold settings and red rubies, in tier after tier, the bottom group resting heavily upon her shoulders. For a moment, Sondra admired her earrings, something that she always wanted, but could never, ever afford such luxury. Food was more important than pretty earrings of any kind, though like all girls born on Virge-C, she had the grommets punched into her ear lobes shortly after birth. *Well, they will either pull my ears off or they won't,* her mind more or less concluded as her eyes drifted downward, halting at the children's soccer balls.

*No, those aren't soccer balls. Those are my breasts! Good God, they're even bigger than Rene's are!* She swallowed involuntarily. As her eyes again moved slightly downward, she saw that she was right; she was wearing a corset, only this one had an overly large number of heavy steel bones, twice as many as Sable's fetish ones. In fact, there seemed to be more bones than cloth, but her waist couldn't be real. Her mind simply couldn't grasp that her waist was only twelve inches across!

The incredible contrast between her bosom and waist was shocking to Sondra, but then she saw her hips were wider than they used to be, adding to the unreal shapely form that her body now had. She had the thought: *Men must really like curves.* However, it vanished almost as soon as it came, partly because the nurse was now trying to get her to raise one foot. She wanted to slip some fine, black nylons on her.

In a panic, Sondra's eyes now focused on her feet, hoping and praying they were not fused like Rene's had been. She relaxed at once. *No, I am wiggling my toes, but what happened to my feet?* She stared in total disbelief at what her eyes were sending her mind. Just after her heel, her foot arch turned nearly ninety degrees downward and yet her toes would still lie flat on the ground. Then, images of Luisa and Juanita's feet at the CEO Ball flashed in her mind. Sondra finally grasped what her feet were telling her. Only her toes would rest upon the ground. She tested this conclusion, annoying the nurse who was trying her best to get the nylons on her feet. *Yes,* she thought, *only my toes can touch the ground.*

As if sensing what Sondra was thinking, the nurse said, "You can only stand on your toes now. That is very difficult to do and keep from falling down. So you must always wear these special toe shoes. They have a heel, giving you much more support, though you will find walking a bit tricky to do at first. Luisa and Juanita will come by and give you pointers and such in a little while. So don't worry about that yet. Now stand up so I can get the garters attached. Lean on me. I won't let you fall."

Sondra did as asked and would have fallen over had the nurse not caught her and used her body to keep Sondra in a precarious balance. *This is a disaster. I can't even stand up. Oh, neither can Rene unless she's wearing her special boots. At least my feet are not fused. That's something. Not much, I admit. Oh, the nylons are tight.* The nurse finished attaching the eight garters, stretching the nylons, which were made from high tensile strength, very sheer polymers, quite tight over her legs. Thankfully, the nurse allowed her to sit back down.

At this point, a more benign sensation got her attention. It came from her hair, which she noticed was about a foot longer, reaching her knees, just like Rene's hair. Her hair was still its natural light brown, but it was different, much thicker and so shiny. *Oh! I can feel with it.* Her mind finally worked out what the tactile sensations the neurons and axons in her hair were sending. Touch. She had a delicate sense of touch from each strand. She focused on the sensations coming in and found there were so many slightly different sensations being reported that she couldn't sort them all out. Some were feeling the slight chill of the air. Others were feeling the slight air motion brushing against them. Others felt the warmth coming from the nurse's body as she leaned into Sondra. For a moment, Sondra lost complete track of the universe, so wrapped up in this utterly new set of sensations flooding into her mind.

"There. Now let's get you dressed. I've an expensive, white silk slip to put on next. Then, your new fiancé has picked out a really gorgeous red satin gown for you." She chatted away, as she struggled to get the slip over her head, her hair out of the way, and the slip pulled down to her knees. Both women had quite a struggle getting the gown on her, mostly because it fit her new body form very tightly. There was virtually no ease in it until a little below her knees. It had no walking slit and was hemmed just at her ankles. It was so tight at her ankles that she could only just put one foot in front of the other.

Fortunately, the nurse began chatting about the dress. "You see, Juanita and Luisa suggested this type of dress for you to wear for your first weeks. It forces you to take the very tiny steps you must learn to do. In your heels, you simply can't afford to take larger steps. You'll lose your balance, so you must trust in the wisdom of Luisa and Juanita. They certainly know all about getting adjusted to walking in your new heels, which are red patent to match your dress and the rubies in your earrings. Now you sit there while I get your new shoes."

She returned in a moment with the pair. "These are oxfords. I'll tie them on securely and even double knot them so they can't come untied or come off. Luisa says these are the best for new UFB women to begin wearing. Once you are fully adapt in them, you can then have and wear heels that are more daring. Just ask Luisa or Juanita about them." She secured the heels and tied them up. Meanwhile, Sondra stared at her new heels. Only her toes were on the ground. *At least, it has a spiked metal heel,* she thought, *but it's so close to the back end of the toes. I don't think it'll give me much support. These are worse than Sable's six-inch heels. Why did I ever complain about them? Oh focus, Sondra, focus.*

"There you go. Don't you just look fabulous, better than most super-models! Wow. Okay, now let's get you up and over to the table, and I'll get you that drink you wanted. Up you go. Of course, you're going to have to practice tossing your hair. You need to get it to your front side before you sit down and to the side when you stand up. According to Luisa, you'll get quite a pain from your hair if you sit or step on it. I have you. Let's go over there," she pointed to a chair and small hospital table on wheels. A bottle of water was sitting on it, very inviting.

As she stood up, Sondra realized just how bad this was going to be. She had very little of her feet actually on the ground. The area occupied by her toes was less than a quarter of what had been the soles of her feet. Her heels did help some, but because the heel was so close to the back of her toes, there wasn't all that much support. Walking in Sable's six-inch heels was a breeze compared to these. With almost no ease in the gown, she had to pivot her lower leg to the front of the other to take one step. For a moment, her mind laughed at some of the images of Sable teaching her clients how to walk this way, so that their hips swivelled seductively with each step. That bit of brevity lasted but a split second.

"This is impossible," Sondra gushed, wobbling about wildly and utterly dependent upon the nurse to keep from falling. The upper half of her legs almost couldn't move at all, and the minuscule ease in the lower part of the gown forced her very carefully  to swing one lower leg and foot out in front of the other foot, all the while trying to keep her balance on the other toes and its tiny heel.

"Luisa and Juanita manage walking just fine, but they

wanted me to remind you that you will need to practice walking quite a lot for at least a week. Just between you and me," she lowered her voice, as though she was about to admit some deep secret, and Sondra bought it, listening carefully, "I think you look and wiggle far more sexily than either of those two women, and your breasts are just to die for. I mean Luisa has always been terribly jealous of Juanita's larger breasts. Now the tables are turned on Juanita, because yours turned out larger than hers did. I overheard them both complaining about that. Once you are walking on your own, you'll make them both mad with lust and jealousy over your seductive walk, which I can tell already, is so much better than either of theirs is. I know it must be a bit scary right now, but we'll do lots of practicing. I can't wait to see the envy on their faces when they see you walking so much better than they can manage. Now just a bit further. Good. Now see if you can toss your hair to the front. You don't want to sit on it."

After the nurse's first mention of the look and wiggle bit, Sondra tuned her out. That was ludicrous, and she focused on taking one step without falling and then another. Only with a great effort and nearly falling did Sondra get her hair to slip over her left shoulder, and she more or less fell into the chair, somewhat out of breath as well. Worse, in tossing her head about, she swore her earrings were going to pull her ears off her head. Wisely, Sondra said nothing about that. *Either this nurse is the dumbest woman on the planet or she is under orders to play up the supposed benefits of this whole UFB woman thing. Either way, I'll ignore her, but I need that drink!*

Sondra sat perfectly erect on the chair. She couldn't do otherwise—too much steel. She watched as the nurse lifted the upper plate with one hand and then fumbled with a spoon trying to get water into her open mouth, much as she did with Rene every day. This much was quite familiar to her, but from the nurse's viewpoint. Quickly, she saw two problems. First, the nurse was having trouble because the spoon was too short compared to the size of the lip plates, Second, without lips, she was having a hard time keeping the liquid in her mouth and swallowing it. Still, Sondra's body craved the water, and she did her best to cooperate, although the nurse grew more and more frustrated with it. Sondra resisted the temptation to tell her these lip plates were absolutely the dumbest idea yet. The only positive aspect was this nurse seemed to understand what she was saying. Sondra concluded she probably had much experience dealing with Juanita.

Minutes passed before she'd drunk nearly half a bottle of water, one partial spoonful at a time, dribbling some down her lower lip plate, much to the nurse's annoyance. That done, the nurse ordered her up and made her begin walking around the room again. Even with the security of the nurse's arm around her waist, Sondra still felt waves of panic sweeping over her. She could do almost nothing to keep her balance, which she lost with nearly every step. Plus, after one circuit around the room, she was gasping for breath. At least, the nurse wisely let her pause to catch it. "Don't worry, you'll get accustomed to all this in no time," she said cheerily.

While standing, Sondra appraised her new surroundings. She was obviously in some kind of relatively small, hospital-like bedroom. Certainly, the bed was quite narrow. Everything spoke of a hospital room. *But where? What hospital? Just where am I?* Wisely, she didn't ask the nurse.

They had made two precarious circuits around the small room when the door opened, and a man in a white doctor's jacket walked in. "Ah, up and about. Have her sit, and I'll conduct my last medical check. Sable is it?" he asked. She nodded, focusing on trying not to fall while heading for the bed. Then, she had to swing her head several times to her hair out of the way. Sondra was more than pleased to sit down again and quietly put up with the man's tests. "Yes, you came through the UFB woman procedure with flying colors, Sable. I must say you're truly a stellar example of the perfection of womanhood. You should be very, very proud and pleased with your new appearance. Has she told you that you'll need a week of practice to get used to everything?"

Sondra nodded. "Good. Good. I'm releasing you now. Your fiancé, Fernando Gabino, will join you shortly and escort you to your new living quarters. Obviously, you can't do much practicing here in this medical room. Will you tell Mr. Gabino he may enter now? I'm finished here." The doctor, if that's what he actually was, rose and left, taking his clipboard with him. Shortly, the nurse returned with the very man she'd emptied two 9mm clips into during the battle at Rosewood!

Sondra gasped slightly when she recognized him. Twenty-eight bullets had bounced off him. *I need to find out why my bullets didn't harm him.* Fernando mistook her gasp. "Oh, I see you find me quite handsome. I'm so glad I take your breath away, Sable. You certainly do take mine away. My, the good doctor has outdone himself. You are fantastically beautiful! Those earrings I had made specially for you look absolutely perfect on you. Sable, you're the very model of perfection, though I'm told I must give you a week to get accustomed to walking and your new form, though I surely don't know why that is. Anyway, in a week, we can be married, and then you'll get the most fabulous sexual stimulation ever. You won't believe how fantastic sex is for you UFB women, but you'll soon get to experience that as well. Oh, I'm supposed to escort you to our new home. Well, I won't be staying there with you, not until we're married. Protocols must be followed or Luisa will have my head. 'Give her time to adapt, Fernando, or you will regret it.' I'm a patient man, Sable. Now up you go. Let's get you to your new home."

Sondra waited for him to help her up, but he didn't, just continued to wave his hand indicating she should rise. She tossed her head a bit, got her hair out of the way, and lunged to her feet. Unable to get her balance, she began to fall over. Only a frantic effort by Fernando kept her from hitting the floor hard. "Sorry. You're a bit wobbly," he said, placing the blame on her.

"I can't breathe or walk," Sondra finally said. *Hell, I'll never make five feet if he doesn't hold on to me. Is he blind or just stupid?*

"Sorry, I don't understand what you are saying, Sable. Come on; out the door." Again, he let go of her. Wobbling like mad, Sondra managed to take one step before losing her balance completely once more, forcing him to catch her at the last second. "My, you *are* having trouble, aren't you?"

"You try it," Sondra retorted. "You have to hold me." Sondra hated to have to say that, let alone *mean* it. Always, she was the independent one; she had to be. Now, she was not only helpless, but also unable to walk or stand up on her own. Humiliation swept over her.

Just then, Luisa and Juanita came shuffling up to the door. "Oh, I see you're taking her to your new quarters, Fernando. My, Sable, you look ravenous! Oh, Fernando, do put your arm around her waist. Can't you see she hasn't yet learned to walk on her own? Didn't we tell you she'll need at least a week of practice before she can get by on her own?" She definitely chastised him, and Sondra relished seeing his face turn red. At least now, he kept an arm around her.

Step, step, step. Sondra focused on taking one at a time. Excruciatingly slow, she thought. At last, she hazarded a glance at Luisa and Juanita's feet. They too were taking very tiny steps, barely one foot in front of the other. *So it really is done this way. Okay. I best learn to do this well. I have to get out of here before Fernando gets his way with me.*

The hallway seemed to go on forever, but she soon realized this was only an apparency due to the tiny steps she was taking. Pausing often to catch her breath didn't help speed either. Finally, they reached an elevator. *I'm in a skyscraper.* In a flash, she realized this detail. The elevator looked similar to the one she'd seen before. He pushed the 98 button. *So I'm going to be on nearly the top floor. Must be the GD headquarters building. Now we're getting somewhere. Crap. No chance Matt can rescue me. He probably doesn't even know where I am.* Waves of raw emotions swept over her causing her to lose her balance, forcing Fernando to catch her again. *Don't think about him. Don't think about him. Focus. Focus.*

As they rode the elevator up, Luisa chatted away. "The 98th floor is the living quarters for the top executives and us, their wives. Each of our three families has their own suite. You'll find yours is very luxurious indeed, as befitting your exalted status as one of us, a UFB woman. Throughout the Galactic Federation, we UFB women are always treated as the most elegant, well respected, and envied women, to say nothing of also being wealthy and always wearing the most expensive apparel. Fernando has given you those earrings, which are worth a quarter million of your dollars, a fabulous pair, I might add. I'm going to have to beg Diego to get me a similar pair. Ah, here we are. This hallway connects our three suites. Your suite is #3, to your right."

Luisa walked up to the doors as though they should open by magic. "What? Fernando, have you gone and locked these doors?"

"Well, yes," he replied, again slightly embarrassed.

"You silly man. Never lock the doors. Have you ever seen Juanita or me open a door that wasn't automatic? Now really your future wife isn't going to go around opening doors, now is she? If you haven't noticed, you are now her arms and hands. So don't be silly and go around locking doors and such," Luisa continued to chide him.

Hope. *If they don't lock the doors, then maybe there is a way out of here for me. I have to try. I just have to.* "Oh!" she exclaimed, stepping into the luxury suite. Nothing prepared her for the luxury she saw before her eyes. The contents of the suite probably cost several million gold dollars, perhaps far more. She'd never seen such wealth on display before. Plush, beyond all description.

"Yes of course, you're a local primitive. The corporate executives throughout the Federation are the wealthiest men in the galaxy. They make it a practice to surround themselves and us UFB women with only the very finest the galaxy has to offer. Mind you, Fernando, it is only right you men do this for us. After all, we're your UFB women and can't survive without your assistance in all things," Luisa chatted on, as though talking to a child, meaning both Sondra and Fernando.

"Now be a good boy, Fernando, and summon Sable's new servant for her and do help her get seated on the love couch, please," Luisa ordered. He helped Sondra sit down, though she mostly fell onto the couch. She watched Luisa and Juanita sit and was shocked to see that they did so quite gracefully. He pressed a button on an intercom and then excused himself, citing work calling.

"If I practice a lot, will I actually be able to walk and sit as gracefully as you both do?" Sondra hazard asking.

"Oh most definitely, Sable. Practice, practice, practice," Luisa said.

Juanita added, "It usually takes a good week to get reasonably comfortable with most actions, but certainly after a month you'll be an old hand at it. Your new servant is Adoria. She is eighteen now, and as soon as she gets you up to speed so you and Fernando can be married, then she will get her own heart's wish, becoming a UFB woman herself. She has a vested interest in helping you master everything as rapidly as possible. In addition, Juanita and I will come by to visit and give you other hints only us fellow UFB women know about. So you see, all will be just perfect in a short time."

"What about other clothes and shoes?" Sondra asked.

"Oh don't worry about that. Tomorrow, Adoria will walk you next door to Leonardo's. He runs a store that caters to all the special needs of us UFB women. If we need it, he has it, can acquire it, or make it. Of course, you'll need a whole wardrobe and soon. Yes, I know it'll be an exhausting walk and so soon after becoming a UFB woman, but it can't be helped. Adoria will take it slow and easy. You're to purchase a dozen outfits. Leonardo knows what you will need and will be ready to service you tomorrow. Ah, here comes Adoria now."

A very cute, black haired, young woman entered, curtsied to the three UFB women. "This is your charge, Sable. Sable, this is your servant for now, Adoria. We will leave you. Oh, Adoria, supper will come up around six tonight. Remember, Sable, practice, practice, practice." Sondra watched the two women carefully. Each tossed their hair to one side and rose gracefully, pausing a moment to secure their balance, before taking their tiny, shuffling steps across the room and out the door, which automatically opened as they approached it.

"Hi. I'm Adoria. Did they tell you as soon as you get married to handsome Fernando, I get my wish to become a UFB woman myself. My fiancé is most anxious for me to be transformed and to marry me. I'm so excited, but enough of silly me. Let's get you up and at it. You're probably very frightened and wobbly right now. That's to be expected. Every new UFB woman is. See, you did a good job tossing your hair to the left. Now up you go. Don't worry, I'll catch you if needed."

"Thank you, Adoria. Can you even understand me?" Sondra asked, hoping and praying that the teen could.

"Oh sure. I've been around Juanita since I was a little girl. Isn't she just incredibly beautiful? Well, so are you, perhaps even more so. I think you have made Juanita a tad jealous. Now let's take a complete tour of your fabulous suite. Everything in here is the most expensive item of its kind in the galaxy. You know executives. Only the very best for themselves and their UFB wives." Adoria was a chatterer, which Sondra appreciated right now, as it distracted her from her misery.

By the time supper arrived, Sondra was exhausted and starving. However, she had the layout of the suite memorized. As she sat down to eat at the superbly carved, teakwood dining table, she was pleased to discover she managed this tiny action on her own. Adoria missed that detail, engrossed in setting up their diner table. Soon, Sondra found Adoria was very competent, handling feeding her easily, presumably from helping Juanita for many years. Finally, eating wasn't so awful.

After eating, Adoria said, "You've had more than enough exercise for one day. Tomorrow will be a grueling day. We have to walk a long way and out in public as well, but it's only one block. We'll get lots of sleep tonight. How about chatting a while yet? I really can understand you. As I said, I've been assisting Juanita for years now. I bet you have many questions. I might know the answers, Sable. That's a pretty name, strange to my ears though, just as Adoria must seem to you."

Finally, Sondra found an opening to say something. "So we are on the 98th floor. Do all the doors open automatically for us?"

Adoria giggled, though Sondra didn't see the humor. "Yes, near the very top. I'll show you the spectacular view after the sun sets. All the doors in the part of this Galactic Dynamics headquarters skyscraper, which you UFB women are allowed to visit on your own, open automatically. Of course, you can operate the elevators by pressing the buttons with your noses.

Luisa often does that. You can wander all over this floor, though I would announce yourself before entering their private suites. Be polite. You can do down to medical anytime you want, in case you feel ill or something. That's where you were when you woke up, down on the 14<sup></sup>th floor. There is a canteen on the 20th floor, and someone there will always help you eat or drink. There is a formal garden on the 21st floor. Luisa spends a lot of time there. She rattled off several more floors.

"Now you don't have to try to remember them. Beside your main doors is a wall plaque, which has them all listed out. Oh, you probably can't read our writing. I've learned a bit of your writing. I'll paste some labels over them for you. You can read your own language, can't you?"

"Yes, of course. Thank you very much, Adoria."

"Oh, from time to time, you may be asked to visit some other floors without automatic doors. When that happens, a servant will always accompany you."

"Got it. Say, why do you want to become a UFB woman anyway? We are darn helpless."

She giggled. "You're a local so you don't know. Out there among the many worlds of the Federation, UFB women are the most respected, most beautiful women in the entire galaxy, wealthiest, and most everything. Plus," she leaned closer and lowered her voice, "it's said their sexual sensations are mind blowing. Some women have said sex is a hundred times better than before they became a UFB woman." She giggled again.

"I get it. So is there any such thing as a UFB man?"

Adoria giggled again. "Well yes there is. Very rare, very. Now I've never actually seen one in person, but I'm told they look exactly like you UFB women, exactly, except their maleness is still there and works just fine. Of course, men often don't want to look like you do now, so there are very few of them. There are other aspects, but I don't know what they are. With you UFB women, any daughters you have will be born as a UFB woman, just as you are, but if you have a boy, he will look like his father. All that has something to do with genetics, but I don't know anything about that. You should ask the nurse or doctor sometime. I'm sure they would know."

A while later, Sondra again tossed her hair to the left and lunged to her feet, wobbling wildly. This time Adoria allowed her to wobble, but was ready to catch her if she didn't finally get her balance. The long walk to the glass windows followed. "Isn't the view just spectacular?" Adoria chatted.

It was, but more importantly, Sondra was properly oriented in space. She was on the southeastern side of the building, and she knew precisely where the building was located. Finally, she felt more secure.

Later on, Adoria got her undressed, except for the corset. She carefully removed the lip disks and tucked Sondra in for the night. "Now I will leave you. If you need me during the night, just press that red button there. It's really big and easy to press. I live a floor down from here, close to where Fernando is staying. He's in #3 down on 97. I'll be up in a moment if you need me. I'll be here first thing in the morning to get you up and all that. Night, Sable."

"Thanks Adoria. Night."

She listened for Adoria, and heard the door open and close. She grinned, but realized it wasn't visible, just as it wasn't when Rene smiled. Carefully, she lunged a bit and got to a sitting position. Then, she carefully stood up. *Wow, it's much harder without the heels. Okay, let's see what I can do on my own.* Carefully and without the awful restriction of the gown, Sondra was able to keep her balance better, even though walking was far more difficult for her. She moved around her huge suite, going from room to room. "This is too easy," she whispered, barely recognizing her own voice.

The next day was just as terrible as Adoria had hinted. The normal one block walk took forever, and many people stopped to stare at her. At least, there wasn't any chance anyone would recognize her. Leonardo's was everything Luisa promised and more. Silently, Sondra made plans to rob this store to get her apparel once she escaped from these insane people.

Practice was precisely correct. Each day, Sondra found herself better able to cope with her heavy restrictions. However, when others were looking and monitoring her progress, she purposely fouled up some, a believable amount, anything to slow this process down. At night, she began a regime of falling down and then trying to regain her feet on her own. After all, if she were going to escape, she could well take a tumble or two before she got to Sable's house. She'd have no one to help her up.

Five days into her practice week, Sondra began to feel rather confident. She knew
she could likely escape on her own. However, she wanted revenge. Several times Fernando came by to visit and gloat over her. She learned why her bullets failed to harm him, his PDS. In addition, he became cockier, finally telling her how much he wanted her after first seeing her at the CEO Ball. *This man needs a lesson, and I'm going to give him one he'll never forget, I hope!*

During the daytime, she was now being encouraged to walk all over the *free* area of the building, that is, the areas with automatic doors for the UFB women. She took advantage of this, paying several visits to the medical room. She found the doctor more than willing to chat about their wonderful genetic bio agent and how it worked. In fact, samples were stored in the side room where she'd woken up! She discovered the door there wasn't even locked! Slowly, a plan formed, combining her escape and her revenge on Fernando.

It hinged on two valuable facts she had learned. First, when she had her feet free of the nylons and heels, she had full use of her toes. While not fingers, she was able to sit on the floor and manipulate the door latches with her feet. Further, with some effort, she was able to get her lip disks out by using her toes. Of course, she also saw the real need to wear them. It was extremely easy for her to get one of the lip loops caught on something. One rip would be terrible. Second, at night, there were very few security guards on duty, and those were mostly down at the building's main entrance. She had free run of the building at night. Even when a guard spotted her, he thought nothing of it, often merely smiling at her, lecherously though.

As the end of her training period approached, her plan solidified. The night before her planned escape, she waited until around one in the morning. Then, she got out of bed, made her slow, careful way down to the medical lab, and entered it, compliments of the automatic doors. Once inside, dim night-lights were on. She went over to the storeroom door, sat down, and manipulated the latch. After a little struggle, she was back on her toes again and stepped inside. Using her teeth, she carefully pulled out one vial of the genetic bio agent. Holding it between her teeth, she headed back.

Using her nose again, she pushed the elevator button and waited. When the doors opened, she entered carefully and then pressed 97. Leaning back against the wall for support and relief from her throbbing toes, she waited until the doors opened. No one was around, and she made her pathetically slow walk to #3. Here, she swung her head around sufficiently to get her hair out of the way and sat down. Now came the difficult part. Using her toes, she worked on Fernando's door latch. It opened. Carefully, she maneuvered her body around and very clumsily got to her feet once more.

She walked into his small quarters and found Fernando sleeping in his bed. The floor was ice cold concrete. All the better, she thought. Now came the moment of truth. She swung her head back and forth. At the last moment, she opened her mouth; her teeth let go of the delicate glass vial. It arced in the air. She turned and headed back to the door as fast as she dared move, not terribly fast, but fast enough she hoped. Behind her, she heard the vial shatter on the concrete. Then, she was out the door, pushing it shut with her body. Minutes later, she was back in her own room. With an invisible smile of satisfaction, Sondra maneuvered her body back into her bed.

Adonia arrived early, at dawn, just as she always did, ready to get Sondra up, dressed, and fed. With her usual efficiency, the many tasks were done in good time, and they sat down to breakfast, which as always was quite excellently prepared. During these past days, Sondra had never eaten such superlative cuisine. Yes, she had heard of people dining on roast pheasant, but such a meal would have cost her a week's wage when she was living in Snake Town. *I shall miss these meals, but nothing else,* she thought as Adonia spooned her morning coffee into her mouth. *At least, I'm getting better at not drooling while I eat. I suppose that's something.*

"Well, today, I should pass all their tests, don't you suppose?" she asked.

Adonia smiled. "Yes, I do believe you shall. You had a rocky start, but it was just as Luisa said, practice works wonders. If you pass, then tomorrow you can be married, and I will be free to get my heart's wish. I can't tell you how long I have looked forward to the day I can become one of you, the most important, most beautiful women in the entire galaxy."

"I do hope your heart's desire is all you want it to be. Do I look good? I want to make a good impression with Luisa when she comes by," Sondra pretended to play her role.

"I'll brush out your hair and see that it's properly draped just before Luisa comes. Best of luck."

An hour later, Luisa arrived, only slightly later than expected. Her face looked quite worried, perhaps whitish. "I'm afraid I bring you some very bad news, Sondra. It seems there has been some kind of terrible accident. It's Fernando."

"Oh no. He's not been killed, I hope," Sondra feigned extreme worry. With her facial features mostly nullified by the large lip plates, she couldn't be sure if Luisa was duplicating her expressions or not.

"Oh no, no. I'm afraid there's been some kind of genetic bio agent accident. He was found in his room this morning when someone went to check on him. He didn't show up for breakfast or Diego's morning briefing. A vial of our UFB agent was broken on the floor beside his bed. He's in a coma now, down in medical."

"Oh dear. He'll be all right, correct? He isn't going to die?" Sondra asked.

"No, no. He isn't going to die. However, I don't know how to tell you this. He'll become what is called a UFBMD, an Ultimate in Feminine Beauty Male Donor. He will look just like us UFB women, only his male organ will still be fully functional. UFBMDs are a very rare. I'm so sorry, Sondra," Luisa explained, her voice carrying a tone of sadness perhaps.

"Oh no, no. Now I understand. Luisa, didn't you know about Fernando's wishes? He told me all about it," Sondra replied.

"What? I don't understand you. What wishes?" she asked, her face distorted by confusion.

"Well, he told me his greatest wish, his heart's fondest desire was to be a proper UFBMD for me. He wanted to wear lip plates like mine and even magnificent earrings like mine. He said then we would be the greatest couple on Virge-C. Everyone would treat us with the highest honor and respect, that there wasn't anything more important he could do for me than to become—what did you call it—a UFBMD for me. I agreed we would postpone our wedding for a few days until you all said he was ready. Didn't he tell you his wishes? He told me he had told you, and that it was all arranged properly and for me not to worry. Should I be worried now? He isn't going to die or anything, is he?"

Luisa looked stunned and didn't reply for a moment. Even Adonia gasped. At last, Luisa found her voice, though it squeaked slightly, "No, he told us nothing about it. So it must have been he who broke the vial in his bedroom last night. I must relay this to Diego immediately. You say he wished to have lip plates like you have?"

"Why yes. Yes as large as mine, and earrings like mine or nearly so. He didn't say where he purchased mine. Won't red rubies look good on him?" Sondra answered, playing Luisa perfectly.

"Oh indeed. Red rubies would be ideal, a great contrast with his black hair. I'll speak with Diego at once. Thank you for being so forthright with me." She turned and left, wobbling more than Sondra had ever seen her wobble.

"She's really upset. She nearly took a tumble," Adonia whispered.

"Wait. We should follow her and make sure none of this prevents you from having your wish fulfilled, Adonia."

"Sondra. Thank you. That is very kind of you. Let's."

Later that morning, Diego and Luisa met with Sondra. He said, "Well, it is done then. I've ordered the lip plates. I believe I know where he got the earrings and will see he has them on him when he wakes from his coma. I do wish he'd come to me, requested it formally, and not taken it upon himself to do it to himself. He could have harmed others, you see. Still, it is done."

"Thank you. I would like to sit with him some, even though he is in a coma, if that's all right with the doctor."

"Of course, Sable. Perhaps, it is fitting that you do so, considering," Diego replied.

"And what about Adonia? She was so looking forward to having the procedure done on her today. I do hope Fernando's actions won't affect her chances to become one of us UFB women. Her heart is set upon having it done now," Sondra said. In a way, she felt honor bound to stick up for Adonia. She had been a true lifesaver these past days. Since she desperately wanted this, the least she could do was to plead her case. She knew almost nothing about the cultural aspects of these aliens, but if Adonia so wanted this, then she owed it to her to try.

Luisa spoke up, "Diego. You know we promised her she could have it done when Sable was trained. Obviously, Sable is now ready. Adonia should get her wish. After all, she's been a faithful servant to Juanita and me all these years. And we promised her."

"All right. Might as well get it started now. That will give the doctor two patients to look after and something to do. Adonia, report to the doctor after lunch. We will send in a temporary servant to assist you at supper, Sable," Diego replied. "Now if you ladies will excuse me, I have very important business to handle and am shorthanded now that Fernando has gone and done it." He turned and left.

"Oh thank you all," Adonia gushed. "Come on; let's get you back to your suite, Sable."

After lunch was done, a very excited Adonia left, and Sondra was finally alone for a time. She carefully rose and made her way to the full-length mirror to double-check her appearance. She was still wearing one of the training gowns that so severely restricted her walk, but at least now she could manage it, she hoped. Looking at her foreign face and body in the mirror, she thought, *Tonight's the night. Now to play my role.*

Carefully and slowly, Sondra made her way down to the medical lab. "Oh hello Sable. Come to see your fiancé?" the doctor asked.

"Yes, and to see Adonia. She has been such a help for me. Look, I made it down here by myself."

"Yes, yes, it just takes time to learn to adapt. I have them in the same room, in separate beds. I can put a chair between them, if you like. I'm afraid there isn't much to see. They're in a coma and can't hear you, of course. Still, I know both would appreciate your loving sentiments, particularly when they wake from the comas in about four days." He did as he said, and she made her careful way to the chair and sat down.

After a time, the doctor came by to make a visual check on his two patients. "Doctor, would it be all right for me to come down and sit with them some at night as well? I know Fernando is making such a huge sacrifice just to please me. I ought to be beside him if I may. I won't be a bother, not really."

"Of course, my dear. Come down anytime."

Midnight came. Thus far, all went according to Sondra's plan. She'd convinced the temporary servant who clumsily fed her supper to leave her fully dressed because she was going down to sit with Fernando and Adonia until late. She'd done just that. Around midnight, the doctor had long ago gone to bed himself, explaining that all was well and that the patients really didn't need monitoring during the night. She told him she'd sit a while longer before heading up to bed.

Instead, she headed to the elevator. Once inside, her nose pushed the button for the basement garage level. Down she went. *Nervous? Yes, I'm nervous. This has got to work or I'm doomed.* She knew the layout of the garage basement level, and hoped and prayed the doors pushed open from the inside. If they didn't, she could well be trapped inside. Yet, fire codes demanded doors open outwards. Unless the aliens modified the doors when they bought this building half a century ago, they should work as she hoped. The real question was security. Would there be guards here too?

When the doors opened, she heard nothing but utter silence. Her heels clicked on the concrete floor, but there wasn't anything she could do about that. If there were guards, that would certainly draw them to her. Her steps were barely four inches, a far cry from her usual three-foot stride, but at least now she was mostly used to taking such tiny steps, only the time it took to cross the twenty feet to the beckoning door seemed an eternity to Sondra. Sixty careful steps later, she reached the doors. One glance told her they pushed outward.

She leaned into the push bar and tried to open it. Her heels slipped on the concrete. Her feet had so little surface contact with the floor she simply couldn't generate enough force to open the door without slipping. Her mind trickled the word *friction* into her consciousness, but she ignored it. Finally, in desperation, she turned around and pushed into the doors backwards. Suddenly, the door opened, dumping her outside. She lost her balance and hit the ground on her butt.

Several minutes of frantic wiggling passed before she was finally get herself back on her feet. That exertion caused her very nearly to faint from lack of breath, and she stood motionless, gasping until she recovered. At last, she began her pathetically slow walk up the concrete ramp towards the dark street. There were no trucks parked here at the loading dock. She also knew, while she could go up the concrete ramp, she'd never be able to go down it, not in these heels. At last, Sondra breathed in the fresh air of freedom. *I may be down, but I sure am not out.*

# Chapter 12—I Do

Sondra glanced around, got her bearings, and began her long walk to freedom. She knew it was about three miles from GD headquarters to Sable's home on Plum Street, and she'd have to cross Plum Street Bridge. At first, she occupied her mind with calculating how many footsteps she needed to take. At four inches a step, that came to nearly fifty thousand! One misstep would result in a nasty tumble. Getting back up in this extraordinarily tight dress was extremely difficult to do, even if she had her arms and hands. Out on the street in the daytime—well, she didn't want to think about that.

Since there were still a few cars traveling the roads, her first action was to get to the first available alleyway. Her immediate plan was to make the journey via back alleyways, as much as possible, staying hidden from view. Often the alleyways were very rough with uneven surfaces and not well maintained, which made walking even more treacherous. Nevertheless that was better than being spotted by a car, reported, and then recaptured. In her favor, it was still summer, and the nighttime temperature was quite pleasant. She couldn't imagine making this excursion during the winter with snow on the ground.

By the time she traveled four blocks from GD headquarters, she knew her plan of escape had one fatal flaw—no two flaws, but the second was subject to the first. Her feet were throbbing. While she had spent days walking around the plush carpeted suite, walking on the hard, uneven, and sometimes crumbling asphalt of the street and alleys was an entirely different matter. After just four blocks, she knew she couldn't go much farther. If she were able to find a place to hide out during the day to rest up, then thirst and hunger would take their toll. She'd be days getting back to Sable's home.

Just as the stark reality of her failure sunk home and total depression replaced her elation, she saw a car's headlights ahead. The vehicle was moving very slowly, but directly towards her in this alleyway. She couldn't run. Fleeing was no longer a viable word in her vocabulary. Whoever it was, she knew she was totally at their mercy. If she was very lucky, the locals would probably only rape her and keep her as their sex doll. *Well, that's about all I'm good for now,* she though, resigning herself to the failure, which was plainly obvious. *At least I got away. That's something,* she thought, as the car stopped a few feet from her and a man got out.

"Sondra? Is it really you?"

*Matt's voice?* "Matt? Is it really you?" Sondra called out, before remembering that no one could now understand her. She repeated it a couple more times.

Matt rushed to her, putting his arms around her. "It *is* you!"

"It's you," she exclaimed. "I never expected to see you again! Take me home! Please."

Matt picked her up and carried her to the car, sitting her carefully in the passenger's seat. Seconds later, he pulled out onto the main streets and headed down Plum Street. "I've been out here every night for days," Matt explained in a rush. "I figured if you could find a way to escape, you'd probably stick to the alleys. Sondra, I can't tell you how much I've missed you. Please, marry me at once. I don't ever want to lose you again!"

"But Matt, look at me. I'm as helpless as Rene. Can you even understand me now?"

"Yes, it's hard, but I've been working with Rene. I'm catching most of what she says and you too. We can talk when we get to Sable's. The streets aren't safe. Things are getting a little crazy out here. That's why I'm taking this devious route back," he explained.

Emotions. Finally, she knew she was really back with Matt, safe in his car. For almost a week now, she had been suppressing everything, focused only on surviving and escaping their clutches. Now, a veritable avalanche of powerful, conflicting, and uncontrollable emotions swept over her. No, it was more like a tidal wave of feelings, and she was drowning. Sondra began sobbing, tears streaming down her cheeks. Elation of gaining her freedom, the satisfaction of revenge, intense grief over the loss of her arms and hands, feelings of near total helplessness, the patheticness of her mutilated body, the intense love she felt for Matt, and her unworthiness of Matt now that she was so dependent on others—all these and more flooded through her mind and body. The dam of suppressed emotions, feelings, and desires burst forth in a torrent of tears.

Wisely, Matt fell silent and focused on getting them safely home. A mile from Sable's place, Matt suddenly veered sharply to the left, ducking down a side street. Ahead on Plum Street, GD security forces had set up some kind of roadblock. While Matt had no idea what they were searching for, the thought that they might be after Sondra certainly was in the back of his mind. *Sable's place might be under surveillance,* he thought, and totally altered his plans. He wouldn't go back to Sable's where he'd been staying since Sondra had been kidnaped.

*If there is one roadblock, there's bound to be more.* He continued driving south and within a few blocks entered the northern streets of the slums known as Snake Town. Matt was certain the GD men would not be in Snake Town. That was far too dangerous. Reaching what he believed to be the central section of this district, Matt veered west once more, hoping to avoid all kinds of trouble. Tense minutes later filled with the continuous sobbing of Sondra, Matt reached the western edge of Snake Town and relaxed. He turned north and soon headed west. "A couple more minutes and we'll be safe at the farm," he whispered to her.

It was two in the morning when he finally pulled into the gravel lane leading up to the old farmhouse. Matt carried her into the home and into their bedroom, trying hard to be quiet and not wake all the others. He sat her on their bed and closed the door. "We're safe now, dearest."

By now, Sondra's face was drenched with salty tears; her wild emotions had run their course for now. "Get me out of all this, please," she whimpered. Her own voice sounded so strange; the words, almost unintelligible; she knew she'd be like this forever. She remembered she should say everything several times and began to repeat it.

Matt interrupted her, "Get you out of all this, right?"

An invisible smile flashed, as she nodded yes, followed by the realization her smile would never again be visible to anyone. Grief returned. Matt ignored that and asked, "Dress, shoes, lip things?" She nodded. If she wasn't so down, she might have laughed at his fumbling efforts to get her out of this incredibly tight dress. That much done, he asked, "Corset too?" She nodded yes. Finally, she could breathe freely again! That awful compression was gone. She felt as though some giant weight was suddenly lifted off her body.

She then said, "Earrings too. Earrings too."

Matt fiddled with them and gave up, explaining, "I can't see how they are undone. Not enough light. Can that wait until morning?" She nodded. "Okay, into bed with you. You have to be exhausted." He helped her into bed, adjusting her hair out of her way and then crawled in beside her, pulling her over onto his shoulder. "I love you, Sondra. I never gave up on you. Now you are safe. Sleep. Sleep."

Sondra exhaled deeply. The next thing she knew, sunlight was streaming into the room. Sandy had brought in some fresh flowers, and their odor filled the room with a unique freshness. "Morning sleepy head," Beth's voice broke the tranquility of the moment. Sondra turned her head and saw her friendly face, as she had so many times before. "Welcome back! Everyone's elated you escaped. Breakfast is waiting. Matt told me I'm to get you up only when you're ready. We have a zillion questions for you, but I admit most of us thought we'd never see you again. All except Matt. He's been out looking for you since the day you got kidnaped. So let's get you up. I bet you're starving. Oh, Rene thinks you might be able to wear one of her dresses for now."

A half hour later, a very embarrassed Sondra took her tiny steps into the dining room. Beth's steadying arm was around her waist, beneath her light brown hair. Sondra dreaded facing all her dear friends looking like this helpless freak, but she knew she just had to face them all, even if all she wanted to do was find some rock to hide under. Everyone was around the old table and began clapping or cheering as she made her slow entrance. Warmth. That's what she felt, but she also detected pity, just as Rene had, and that bothered her, though she couldn't say why just now.

"Sit down and tell us what happened to you," Rene spoke for all them. Sondra realized that her friends had asked Rene to speak first, since she had the awful lip plates too, believing this gesture would make Sondra feel more comfortable. "Oh," Rene added, "Beth will be stuffing you with pancakes and eggs at the same time."

Sondra replied briefly, too embarrassed about how terrible her speech now was. "Eat first, please." A half hour later, Beth began spooning Sondra her coffee, and Sondra knew that she couldn't put this off any longer. *If only I didn't have to repeat everything three or four times.* She sighed and began. To her amazement, only rarely did someone ask her to repeat something.

Well over an hour passed as she told them about it, beginning with her unloading two clips of 9mm slugs into Fernando as he came at her. She did jump ahead and explain why he was totally unharmed by them. Of course, no one knew anything about this alien protective device, and she could add little more, other than it was wholly effective. Alice was astounded to hear it was the same man who was trying to turn her into his UFB woman wife, and she pointed out the earrings that Sondra was wearing were the same ones that he had shown her while she was lying on the bed in her psychedelic haze.

Later on, when she described what she'd done to Fernando, she was forced to stop. Wild cheering, foot stomping, and clapping echoed around the room. "Well done Sondra!" yelled Alice loudly above the others.

"That's my girl!" Matt yelled, proudly.

When the noise died down, Rene asked, "So will he really look like us, like a woman, with our hair, monster boobs, and all?"

"That's what they told me would happen. Serves him right. Now he can experience what they've done to all the women and us, Rene," Sondra declared and then continued her tale.

When she finally finished, Alice commented, "Gosh,

Sondra, you're not as helpless as we all thought you would be. Incredible. I don't think I could've done any of that. I would have just given up and died. You're the strongest person I've ever met."

Roxane added her thoughts. "Sis, you're the strongest of all us sisters. We're here for you now. We've learned a whole lot about ourselves from the records we got from Rosewood. While our bodies are virtually identical, all four of us, being raised in different families and exposed to different educations and stuff, we've all developed into very different people. Me, I'm a very competent surgical nurse. Alice is one of the best musicians in West Port. Sable was a true fashion model. And you, you are the smartest, strongest of us all. I'm proud to have you as my sister."

Beth had to dab tears from Sondra's face. "Thanks, but I'm mostly helpless now, just like Rene. What did you learn from those records? I hope it was worth it."

Beth spoke up, "Roxane, you best tell her about it. None of us know much at all about this genetics stuff."

"Okay, but remember, I know almost nothing about it myself," Roxane protested slightly. "Apparently, long ago, Dr. Decker and Marshal Tucker were friends. Then, Marshal's wife was tragically killed in an automobile accident. Dr. Decker, with Marshal's permission, retrieved several of her eggs, promising to see if he couldn't use them to give Marshal some children from his deceased wife. Apparently, there were some initial failures, but then Dr. Decker was able to get one egg fertilized. At that point, he did the unspeakable! We aren't able to follow all the medical and genetic talk in the records, but it's clear that he cloned that fertilized egg, making five identical ones. Apparently, we were then grown in his lab, but the records aren't so clear how this was done. One didn't make it. However, once we four were around nine months along, he came up with this wild experiment to see how four clones would develop if brought up in entirely different circumstances. He gave us four to four different nursing mothers, and then when we were two, he placed us in the foster homes we know. However, as the years went by, he forgot all about us, until recently. So we are sisters ,and we know Marshal is actually our father!"

Alice spoke up, "And we told him about it. He broke down and cried though. He's spent his life looking for us. Dr. Decker told him that none of the eggs produced a live child. Wisely, he began to distrust Decker and began seeking answers. In fact, he'd just discovered we did exist and sent one of his men to hire Sondra to clone one of the GD men's phones in hopes that the man would lead him to us. It's no secret now that Decker is in bed with these aliens, but Marshal did tell us to keep an eye on the news."

"Well, of course we're sisters," Sondra said. "I never doubted it."

Matt then related what he had been doing. Apparently, he'd not kept in close contact with the others, Sondra surmised, since they were just as anxious to hear his brief tale as well. He explained how Beth had been able to confirm his theory about where Sondra had been taken. He described the incredible security now around GD headquarters. He laughed, "So they are dead set on not letting anyone in, but their security is so bad that anyone can get out!" Everyone roared at his jest, even Sondra.

"I just never gave up on my love. I know Sondra. If there was any way possible, I knew she would make a break for it and head to Sable's, just like we planned." He sighed. "I also suspected she'd be like she is now, like Rene. At first, I just hung around Sable's expecting her to show up any time. Then, I realized she too was probably exposed to their alien genetic bio agent thing and would be darn helpless. I cried myself to sleep at nights, but I just couldn't find any way to get inside the GD building. I had no idea where she was among the hundred floors there. So I waited. I just knew my Sondra would find a way to get out of there."

"Then, I realized she probably wouldn't be able to walk much, let alone open the back door to get into Sable's! I nearly lost it then and kept the back door open a crack at all times. Finally, it sunk in to my thick skull if she couldn't walk well, she'd never make it all that way. I got to thinking about what she'd do if she got out of the building and couldn't walk much or fast. She'd hit the dark alleyways. So I began patrolling them every night, all night long. I knew she'd not make a break for it in the daytime. Last night, I found her. Sondra, I'm going to marry you as soon as possible and never, ever let you out of my sight again! I can't live without you."

Sondra flushed. She wanted to respond, but this was a private thing between Matt and herself. She smiled, and then flushed again, realizing again that her smile wasn't visible. Breaking the awkward moment, Rene spoke up. "Cool. Tom here has asked me to marry him, Sondra."

"Aye, lassie, that I have. And I'll keep on a doin' it, until she says she will. Ya canna say no to me. I wona let ya, prettiest lassie ever," Tom declared. "Rene's the finest woman ever! No offence Sondra, but she's gotta ya beat."

"But Tom," Sondra decided to speak up for Rene, who must have similar feelings that she had, "we're almost helpless. You deserve much more."

Both Matt and Tom laughed heartily. Matt declared, "And you, my dear Sondra, are about the most un-helpless helpless person I've ever heard of! Not only did you escape GD, but you turned the tables on Fernando big time!"

"Besides," Tom added, "we're all gonna keep look'en for a cure for ya. Look, if these aliens invented this stuff to make ya into UFB women, then they gotta have a way to undo it. Stands to reason, only we just gotta find it for ya, lassies. We will, donna ya worry your pretty heads about that. Tom and Matt, we're gonna find ya a cure one day. Right Matt?"

"Right," Matt declared, though he had no idea how they could possible do it, only that he would move mountains to find a cure for her and Rene.

Beth spoke up, "Okay fellows. Let's get down to practical business. Sondra needs clothing and shoes. Rene's dress doesn't quite fit her. So let's be practical for a while, shall we?"

"I can get the same seamstress to make me some," Sondra volunteered. "Only you will have to measure me since I can't now, and one of you will have to go to the seamstress. There is a UFB woman's store a block from GD headquarters. They have all kinds of apparel for UFB women there. I doubt we could get any local shoemaker to fix me up. If only these didn't have to be tied, maybe I could slip them off and make more use of my toes. I sure wish Rene's feet weren't fused cause then she could do more."

Rene interjected, "At least, Sondra, we don't have to wear those awful corsets. True, I get back aches several times a day, but Tom's been giving me massages when it hurts too much. It's a whole lot better than wearing them."

"Thanks, good news to hear. I was so hoping I could be free of that terrible corset. I don't know how Sable ever got by, but she did," Sondra replied. "My back is aching some already so I suppose that's just another thing I have to live with."

"I'll give you a massage in a bit," Matt whispered. "Tom, you and I have some planning to do. We have to get them plenty of foot-ware. Beth, you and the others get Sondra all measured up, and we'll pay a visit to that seamstress."

"Aye, Sondra," Tom broke in, "Rene's new dresses make her look real dreamy, super good."

Rene teased him, "But I thought you said they make me look sexy."

Tom flushed, "Aye, lassie. I said that and meant it, but I was try'n to be polite in front of Miss Sondra here." Everyone roared again.

An hour later, Sandy and Beth headed off to find the seamstress. Sondra had given them specific directions and instructions to follow. Matt and Tom headed off to get all the remaining shoes and boots left in Rene's parents Shoe Box. They also intended to case out Leonardo's as well.

Alice and Roxane cleaned up the breakfast dishes, leaving Rene and Sondra sitting on the worn out living room couch. Rene took charge. "Okay Sondra. I remember what you did for me. Now it's my turn to do it for you. Let's see what happens. I want you to go back to the start of the gunfight and tell me everything that happened, just as you had me do. We have to go over it many times. Okay?"

"Well, most of it is just blackness, but okay, let's see what happens. It can't hurt," Sondra replied. She closed her eyes and began seeing again what had happened, relaying it to Rene. By evening, she was describing how it felt being unconscious, being carried out of the building, and tossed like a rag doll into the truck—something she hadn't seen before.

Rene continued the next day, and as she suspected from her own experiences, Sondra finally connected up to the huge suppressed mountain of grief. Once more, she cried and cried, as she told Rene what she was seeing. An hour later, Sondra felt more resentment than she knew it was possible to feel. Several passes later, she felt the pain of her arms shriveling up and falling off. Later, Sondra felt an intense hatred, a rage that had turned her on fire not only to escape but also to extract revenge on Fernando. After supper, she was so bored with the whole thing that Rene ran out of ideas to press her onward, but vowed to continue the next day. Finally, around noon the third day, Sondra began laughing wildly. All traces of the trauma vanished, and she felt wholly alive. Whatever this was that she discovered certainly worked wonders. She had subjective reality on it now.

The others were also successful. Rene now had dozens of her special boots to wear, a multitude of colors and styles to go with her dozen new dresses. A week later, Sondra too had a dozen new dresses that fit her modified body very well. Tom had insisted that half be made from satin and velvet. "Nothing is too good for you, my dear." However, the light cotton dresses were just fine with her.

During this time, with Sondra's guidance, Matt was able to access the construction plans for the low building that housed Leonardo's. As she expected, there was a way to get inside the store from the city sewer system. Tom and Matt then raided the place, late one night. They returned hours later with two dozen shoes and boots for Sondra. Some were knee high boots—to keep you warm in the winter, Matt explained. He'd picked out a wide variety of styles, including mules, and a number of colors, though most were black patent. One pair was white.

Once her dresses arrived, Matt said, "Okay. Now you have a fancy white dress and white heels to match. So there's no reason we can't get married now. Tom has white ones for Rene. We'll have a double wedding. You can't say no."

"Matt, I don't want to say no, but look what you are getting—half a woman, mostly helpless. Surely, you don't want to be saddle with this all your life."

"Don't be silly. I love you and that's that. Tom and I will bring a preacher here tomorrow."

Just then, Beth called out from the living room. "Hey everyone! Come quick. It's finally on the news! Dr. Decker is in big trouble!" Rene and Sondra silently cursed their incredibly slow speed, joining the others, who had already heard most of it. As usual with news reporters, they continually repeated everything. This was so hot that the station carried nothing but this breaking news all day long.

"The following contains graphic images, horrific images, not suitable for general viewing. Watch at your own risk. This just in. President John Johnson has ordered the arrest of Rosewood Homecare's Dr. Sam Decker. He is charged with fifty-nine crimes involving unethical and illegal genetic experimentation on human beings, resulting in many horrific deaths. These are some of the images of his victims." The screen showed what appeared to have once been a man, but now he had two heads. Another man had four arms. One had six legs. One had no lungs. A woman had no eyes or ears. A dozen terrible images were shown. "This is only a representative sample of the many victims. An arrest warrant has been issued. However, Dr. Decker's whereabouts at this time is unknown. Federal agents raided Rosewood headquarters in downtown West Port early this morning, but he wasn't there. Apparently, he has gone into hiding. Agents are combing the city as we speak. President Johnson has said that he will be caught and punished for his many crimes against humanity. This is the single worst case of its kind in Virge-C's history." The news reporter rattled on, but that was the essence of the news. Somehow, Decker managed to get word of the arrest warrant and fled.

Roxane spoke up. "I do hope they catch that evil man. I wonder where he went."

"Probably he's hold up in the GD building," Sondra theorized. She was right, only no one knew that just yet.

The next day, Sandy and Beth fussed over Sondra and Rene, dolling them up as fancy as possible for their big wedding day. Alice decorated the living room with flowers and played wedding music for them on her violin. As promised, Matt and Tom brought a preacher out from the city, from Snake Town, along with Sondra's "brother," Ben, who was shocked to see what had become of his little "sister." Ben had a very hard time accepting what had happened to her, though he saw that she was truly happy. He swore to her that he would help get revenge for her, ignoring her protests that she'd already done that. By the end of the wedding, Ben had finally calmed down.

Rene stood beside Tom, while next to them Sondra stood beside Matt. The men wore their best suits. Truly surprising everyone, Marshal Tucker showed up to attend the wedding. "I'm here to give away one of my daughters," he said proudly and with tears in his eyes.

The preacher had never seen UFB women before and was rather shocked by their appearance. Still, he performed the proper ceremony. Finally, Sondra said, "I do," in answer to his question. He looked baffled, not grasping what she'd said.

Sandy whispered to the preacher, "She said, 'I do.'"

"Oh, good. Now Rene," he continued and accepted her equally incomprehensible utterance as another "I do." Finally, the four heard the words they longed for. "I now pronounce you man and wife. You may kiss your brides."

The men placed a loving kiss on their foreheads. Sondra whispered, "I'll give you a proper kiss tonight when you take out my disks." Presumably, Rene said something similar to Tom, who flushed.

After that, the group partied some. Marshal chatted with his daughters and then had to leave. He said, "Big things are brewing. You all stay here out of trouble. It's going to be bad. I can feel it in my bones. My dears, you all look as lovely as your mother, Martha. I never thought I'd see this day. You've made an old man happier than he ever expected to be again. I'm going to send over some old photos of Martha." With that, he left them to continue their celebrations, but did take the preacher back to his place for them.

\*\*\*

In the medical room back at GD headquarters, Fernando finally came out of his coma. He had no idea he'd been exposed to the genetic bio agent or that he'd been in a coma for four days while his body mutated according to his modified genes. He awoke with a throbbing pain in his lips. He couldn't breathe. He couldn't get his arms to get himself up. His feet felt funny. The nurse got him sitting up, but he fainted and had to be revived not once, but six times before he stopped passing out. He stared at a gorgeous UFB woman in the mirror. Then, he shrieked wildly in a soprano voice and promptly fainted yet again. Slowly, recognition that he had somehow become a UFB woman hit him. No. He was a UFBMD. He finally saw his penis.

Like the other UFB women, his black hair reached down to his knees. His lips had been slit and he sported six-inch, golden disks, just like those on Sondra. His ears were being nearly pulled off by the weight of earrings that were similar to those that he'd given to Sondra. His tightly corseted waist was fourteen inches across, and his feet were as malformed as Sondra's were. He screamed and screamed, passing out repeatedly. Finally, the nurse gave up and called in the doctor for help. He was reacting badly.

Two hours later, finally dressed in a beautiful, form-fitting, red satin, training gown, similar to the one Sondra had worn, they had him walking a tad and got half a bottle of water in him. Now that he stopped screaming and fainting, Diego entered and began questioning him. "But Sondra claimed you wanted to become a UFBMD for her."

After several more minutes of complete confusion, Diego sent someone for Sondra. He knew something was wrong when she could not be found. He ordered a compete search of GD. An hour later, the truth finally began to appear. Sondra had fled, but no one knew how or where. Speculation suggested that she'd dropped the vial of the genetic bio agent onto Fernando's floor. However, Luisa and Juanita both claimed that was impossible. "Dear, we're truly helpless. We couldn't *possibly* have done that, assuming we even wanted to do it. Just how? We can't open doors, let alone pick up a vial. So don't be silly. Sondra couldn't possibly have done this. You should look for a traitor in our midst!"

Thus, Diego became convinced there was a traitor

working at GD headquarters. He spared no expense trying to find out just who the spy was, but he never did.

Fernando was in total misery. His life, his promising career ended. Worse, he looked like a UFB woman, completely helpless, dependent upon others for everything, but he was still a man. His embarrassment was monumental and crushing. For days, he cried until his body could no longer produce tears. Worse, his gorgeous fiancé had mysteriously vanished. Now, even Diego shunned him, locking him away in what was supposed to be his new bridal suite.

On the other hand, Adonia awoke very excited about finally achieving her heart's wish to become a UFB woman. Unlike Fernando, she didn't faint, not even once, though she too gasped for breath, complained, and ached. From her long service to these women, Adonia knew what to expect, though the stark reality took her by surprise, as did her complete helplessness. She finished learning to adapt in the usual week, just as Luisa told her. On the other hand, poor Fernando didn't get his final pass until well into his third week.

Like Fernando, things didn't work out as Adonia had expected. Major trouble was brewing. Some hinted war was about to break out. Diego delivered the crushing news to Adonia. "Look, we're in crisis mode right now. Your marriage will just have to be put on hold until I can get this situation under control. In the meantime, I have cordoned off half of suite #3. You may live there. Fernando will be in the other half, but he will not be allowed to interact with you, naturally. I will arrange your marriage later on."

"But Julio and I are fiancés," she protested, but to no avail. Instead of married bliss, Adonia found herself bored out of her mind, with nothing to do and nothing to look forward to at night. At least, they brought her few possessions into her new suite, including her old cell phone. The only highlight was her trip to Leonardo's, where she was able to purchase a dozen fancy gowns and heels. Days passed by her endlessly, compounding the intense boredom. This wasn't right. She should have been wedded to Julio as promised. She took her case to Luisa, but even Luisa couldn't do anything about it. Riots were breaking out, and all available men were needed to maintain order.

On the same day that Sondra was married, Adonia received the worst possible news, news that shattered her completely. Diego entered her new suite. From the stern look on his face, Adonia suspected he wasn't here to tell her that she could now get married. "Adonia, I've terrible news for you. It's about Julio. I know you were quite close. There was a gun battle today near Rosewood Homecare. Julio was shot and killed. I'm sorry. When all this mess clears up, I will arrange a suitable marriage for you." With that, he turned and left her alone. Right now, he didn't want to listen to women sobbing. He had far more important things to handle. Diego didn't tell her that Julio had died rescuing Dr. Decker from the Federal Agents sent to arrest him. It didn't concern her.

That night, Adonia sobbed herself to sleep. Her imagined life, her hopes, her dreams for the future—all was gone, gone forever. She imagined Diego marrying her off to some man who she didn't even know or care about. She knew this often happened with UFB women, but never, ever expected herself to be in this situation. On top of that, she was truly helpless now and had to depend upon them for everything.

A servant dressed her and fed her the next morning, but all Adonia could think of was how she could die. Later, the servant left her alone and wouldn't return until lunchtime, not unless she managed to push the big red button. She sat motionless on the plush, ultra-expensive couch. Her mind began to wander aimlessly.

Then suddenly, she recalled something Sondra had said to her the day before everything happened at once. "Put this number in your phone. If you ever need help, call it. Put it on speed dial." She remembered thinking that was a very strange thing to say, but she'd done as Sondra had asked, assigning it to Number 2. Julio's phone was Number 1. She had no other numbers on speed dial.

*Did Sondra know one day I'd be in this mess? I sure need help. I can't live like this, not really, not without Julio. I don't want to be married off to someone I don't love and care about. I don't want to be some man's sex doll. I do need help. I wonder what that number does. Don't be silly, Adonia, you can't even use a phone anymore. You can't do anything anymore. But I have to have help somehow. I can't stand this any longer. Oh, why did I ever want to become a UFB woman in the first place?*

She entered another sobbing fit. Eventually, she stopped crying. *I do need help. If she had me enter that number, she must have believed I would have some way to use the phone. But I'm helpless. How can I use it? Duh! Adonia, you are stupid. Use your nose as you do with the elevator buttons. Cool. I wonder where the phone is at now? They did bring all my stuff in here.*

She tossed her hair to one side and lunged upwards, catching her balance by wiggling some. Slowly, she headed off to find the pile of her old things. They had dumped the mess in one corner of her bedroom. She stood there looking at the bags and sacks, unable to figure out any way to open them, let alone get to the phone.

That night after her servant undressed her and had her ready for bed, Adonia realized she now had some use of her toes and her mouth. The lip plates prevented any such use during the day, but now she could perhaps. Emboldened, she wiggled and got herself out of bed, wobbling wildly on her toes for a moment. Then, she headed to the light switch and used her nose to turn it on. She carefully sat down beside the bags of her things, most of which were now useless to her, clothes that would never fit. Using her feet and toes, she got them open and the contents dumped out. Finally, she spotted her phone. It took some doing, but she finally got it between her teeth and held onto it.

She tried various moves to get herself back up. Adonia almost gave it up before she finally made it, once more wiggling about, steadying her precarious balance. Slowly, she walked over to her dining room table, laid the phone on it, and then got herself seated. Using her nose, she hit the right speed dial button and waited. *Who am I going to be talking to? Will there truly be any real help for me?* It rang many times before someone answered it.

"Hey, that's a phone ringing," Matt noticed. He and

Sondra were in bed.

"It's coming from one of the unused phones," Sondra said. Then, it dawned on her. It might be Adonia. "Pick it up and open it up for me, please."

"Sure, but it's probably a wrong number. No one has this number," Matt replied, opening it up, and sitting it beside Sondra, who had struggled to get into a sitting position.

"Hello," Sondra said as clearly as possible. *If it's a wrong number or a telemarketer, they won't understand anything I say. Ah well.*

"Hello. Who is this?" Adonia said timidly.

Sondra recognized the voice, though the slit lips now masked it. Adonia. "Hi. This is Sable. Is this Adonia?"

"Sable? Is this really you? Are you all right? So much bad has happened here."

"Yes, it's me. I'm very fine indeed. I just got married too. How are you doing? I can tell you've had the procedure you so wanted done. Is everything working out as you planned?"

"No, it's horrible!" Adonia sobbed. For nearly a half hour, Adonia talked away, finally having someone truly to speak to, someone who really listened to her. She finished up, "I can't live like this. I need help. I don't want to be forced to marry someone I don't love or even know, but I'm so helpless, just like you are."

"Okay Adonia. We can get you out of there. You can come and live with me. How's that?"

"That would be wonderful, Sable. But how? We're helpless."

"We have many people who help us and love us, our friends. Look. If you are serious about wanting out of there, we can do it. Just like I did."

"Okay. What do I do? I can't do much, but you know that."

They chatted a bit about where she was at and that she was undressed, ready for bed. The hour was getting on. Once more, Sondra went with her intuition. "We will arrange a rescue tonight. Here's what you have to do, if you want out of there. You can do it. I know because I did it." She explained what Adonia had to do for herself.

"I do so want to come and live with you. I do. Thank you," Adonia replied, her voice full of youthful sincerity, which Sondra didn't doubt. She knew this teen and her heart.

After they hung up, Sondra explained, "Matt, she has to do that much for herself. It will do wonders for her self-respect. I know. Been there, done that. Come on, you are going to have to get me dressed again."

Adonia sat at the table staring at the phone's time display, occasionally bumping it so its dial lights returned. It had taken her close to an hour to get her lip disks back into place, using her toes. Now, she had to wait. To her, two o'clock seemed to take forever to come! Finally, her phone showed 2:00, and she took as deep a breath as she could. Leaning over, she maneuvered her disks about until she could get her teeth onto the phone. Again, she bit down on the phone, holding it securely between her teeth. Her lip plates then plopped down over it. Carefully, she got to her toes. She knew that walking without her shoes was much more difficult, but she simply had to do it.

She reached the door, and it opened automatically. She stepped out and looked around. All was dark except for the faint night lights. Slowly, she moved to the elevators. Following Sable's advice, she used her nose, and soon the elevator arrived. Inside, she used her nose to press the basement button and down she went. For a moment, she imagined this was how Sable had made her escape. *Diego is entirely wrong,* she thought, *there isn't a traitor among them. Sable walked out on her own.* The doors opened, and she expected to be stopped by a guard, but this back entrance was deserted. No one could get in, but fire codes dictated those inside could escape in case of a fire.

She looked through the glass and saw a car parked close to the door. A door opened; a man got out and opened the other door. Adonia's heart skipped a beat. There was Sable! Following her instructions, she turned around and pressed her back onto the door. She pushed and pushed. Suddenly, the door opened, and she began falling over backwards, but Matt was there to catch her. "Got you. If you don't mind, I'll carry you. We don't want to get caught."

"Okay," she mumbled through clenched teeth.

Minutes later, she watched the streetlights stream past. Sable hadn't said much, but then they were not safe yet, she reasoned. Soon, Adonia had no idea where she was at, out in the county perhaps? They pulled up at a dark farmhouse.

"We're home, Adonia. Once we get inside, we can talk some, but I bet you are tired. It's quite late," Sondra said.

Adonia yawned sleepily. Matt carried her inside and into their bedroom for tonight. Almost as soon as he laid her down and removed her disks, the teen fell asleep. Sondra whispered, "I'll sleep beside her tonight. Thank you dear. We've rescued another one.

"Okay sleepy heads, time to rise and shine," Beth's cheery voice woke Sondra and Adonia.

"Oh. Oh, who are you?" Adonia asked, roused by the strange voice. She saw Sable lying beside her and relaxed.

"Beth. Longtime assistant for Sondra there."

"But she's Sable."

"Oops. Well, she can tell you all about it. Matt has told us you've come to live with us. Cool. Come on; we have to find something for you to wear. I'm sure you want out of that corset, right?"

Adonia looked confused, and Sondra suggested, "We get along tons better without it. While our backs do give us some trouble, the fellows give us massages when we need it. We'll get you new clothes made today. Thanks Beth."

Once their lip plates were in place, Beth proceeded to get them dressed, while Sondra explained briefly, "I'm really Sondra. Sable was one of my twin sisters, but GD had Sable murdered, and I took Sable's place so that we could find Sable's murderer. The world out there thinks Sondra is dead, but it was really my sister Sable. I pretended to be her, you see. In a bit, you can meet my other sisters, Alice and Roxane. I'll explain more over breakfast, Adonia. Wow, you do look great."

"Oh. Okay. Well, it did turn out as perfect as I had hoped, but then Julio was killed, and I did all this just for him, and now he's dead, and I have nothing left, and I'm really helpless. I didn't really think you were this helpless.

Everything seemed so wonderful, fancy clothes, and all that attention, but it's awful, isn't it, being so helpless like this. And how did you know I would need help? When you made me put your number on speed dial, that was brilliant." She would have gone on, but Beth made her stand up so she could finish dressing her.

"I had a hunch. I'll explain more over breakfast. Looks like one of my dresses will fit you well enough. We can do lots of things with our toes, as long as we aren't wearing those corsets." Sensing Adonia needed a boost of confidence, she complimented, "Your hair is really beautiful, Adonia." It wasn't erroneous, for her hair was coal black, thick, and very shiny, falling rich and full to her knees when she stood. Sondra also noticed the minor blemishes in Adonia's face were gone and the slight size difference between her ears wasn't there.

"Oh my, so many of you," Adoria gushed, following Sondra and Beth into the dining room. Introductions followed. While they ate, Sondra gave Adonia a brief version of their adventures, enough so she could understand why she had been pretending to be Sable and that she really was Sondra.

After hearing what she thought a grand adventure, she declared, "I'm so glad you're married, Sondra. That is what UFB women are supposed to do—marry a fine man, dress very well, look our best at all times, make our husbands proud, and have lots of children for him."

Rene laughed haughtily and poked, "That's all well and good for *him*, but what about *us* and the things that *we* want to do. Shouldn't he also make *us* happy, help *us* with our endeavors, or are we just supposed to be his sex doll?"

Adonia flushed. "But that's always been the role of the UFB women. We're perfect women, so we must look our best, dress very well, and make him happy, giving him lots of children." Then she paused a second. "But, I suppose we can be happy enough doing all that for him." Adonia suddenly had serious doubts about it. "What do you mean help us with the things we want to do? We can't actually *do* anything else, not now, I mean as we are as UFB women."

Rene saw that Adonia was actually taking her criticism seriously and decided to press it further. "Sondra told us you just became a UFB woman a couple weeks ago. Before that, weren't you doing all kinds of things? She told us how great you were helping her learn to adjust. Didn't you have some things you really enjoyed doing? Surely, you didn't always want to become a UFB woman."

"Well," Adonia answered slowly thinking this over, "I loved to help the other women. Oh, I see what you mean. The main chef at GD—he wasn't very good at all, so I often cooked up special meals for the women. Luisa said I was the best chef she'd ever had and that I should be the top chef for all of GD. I actually thought I might just do that, but that was before I met Julio and fell in love with him. He was going to be a top executive one day, so if I were to marry him, I would have to be a UFB woman, of course, so I changed my mind. And now," she broke down. Tears swelled.

"I know; he has passed away. I'm so sorry for you Adonia," Sondra stepped in, giving Rene a cold eye stare. *She shouldn't be reminding her of her great loss before we can have her go over all that trauma.*

Rene suggested, "Okay. Let's get organized. We'll need to get Adonia proper clothing and get her a nice room fixed up here. Let's get cracking, gang, and let Sondra work her magic on Adonia."

The group divided, working out the details for the day, while Sondra took Adonia aside into the living room. There, she explained what she was going to do and had Adonia start re-experiencing what she'd gone through. She had the huge emotional loss of her fiancé lying on top of the genetic bio agent trauma to her body, which Sondra now knew had a large amount of pain buried beneath the unconscious coma. Right away, Sondra saw she could not get near the coma portion. Adonia's bitter grief and loss was the only thing the teen could see and face. Buckets of tears flowed, as Rene relived that awful loss.

The second day, Adonia finally began to uncover the real pain that her body underwent during the long coma. She was quite surprised to discover she heard every silly word the doctor and nurse had said around her! By the end of the second day, Adonia had risen from grief, through fear and pain, to hatred and anger, reaching a violent antagonism that led to boredom, and finally around suppertime, to a cheerfulness about the whole thing.

"The loss doesn't seem important now and all that pain and unconsciousness—Sondra, it's just gone, vanished. I feel so good, better than ever. Oh, but I'm still helpless, but I guess that's the way it will always be now, though I wish I could still cook. I don't mean to criticize, but Beth's not the greatest cook. If she added a touch of spices, it would taste so much better."

"Why don't you lend her a hand in the kitchen?" Sondra suggested.

Adonia giggled, "But I don't have a hand to lend. Seriously, I could make some suggestions, if she doesn't mind."

# Chapter 13—Yours Is Now Mine

Diego met with his top executives and those of the other Federation corporations. "Okay, time to make our big push. We have about a week to get all of West Port consolidated under corporation rule. Marcos, you handle Ace Foods. We need to control Bectold's Transport, General Manufacturing, and Supermart."

"What about the Teacher's Union and the Union of Nursing?" Juan asked. These two female-controlled organizations had defied every attempt of GD's to join the corporation's parallel divisions, let alone take orders from the GD executives. Their usual intimidation methods and bribes had failed to sway these female executives, who completely rejected offers of substantial monetary *donations,* if they would merge with GD.

"Juan, I will handle these two personally. Fortune has just given us the means. Now, what other large companies do we need to complete our takeover?" Diego asked. For an hour, smaller companies were mentioned, and various other corporation leaders volunteered to "handle" them this week. Bit by bit, the final set of takeovers were established, though by mutual consent the awful mess that was Snake Town was left to the very end of the process.

Diego also promised to deal with the last major thorn in their side, the last large company on Virge-C, one that had continually defied them at every step of the process for almost fifty years now, the Aerostar Engines Company. *Old Marshal Tucker is a worthy adversary,* Diego thought, *but it is time to take the old man out of the equation.* Besides, rumors hinted he might be behind all the rebellious discontent. Certainly, he was behind the exposure of Dr. Decker, Virge-C's most brilliant doctor and geneticist. *That man has great potential, if only he wasn't totally constrained by this primitive world's twisted sense of ethics. Well, the doctor is now studying Federation genetics down on the twentieth floor.* In time, Diego intended to put Dr. Decker in charge of Virge-C's new genetic research program.

After the meeting broke up, Diego placed a call to Dr. Helen Albright, head of the Teacher's Union, and to Jane Longtree, head of the Union of Nursing. "Yes, I wish to meet with you both today. Yes, it can be at a place of your choosing. I have a very important offer to make to you both, an exclusive offer to your two unions only." He punched in the exclusiveness of the offer, but refused to give either woman any details. They agreed to hear his offer and set the meeting on neutral ground, Plantora's Diner, at one this afternoon.

Of course, Diego had a dozen security guards stationed around the popular diner, before he walked in to meet the two powerful women. Quite why the men of West Port would have ever allowed these women so much power and control over two vital industries—teaching and nursing—was beyond his reasoning. *They should be UFB women, focused solely on being proper sex dolls for their husbands. Well, things have to change,* he thought as he walked into the diner. The rich aroma of freshly baked bread greeted his olfactory senses, giving him a pleasant feeling. The two middle-aged women were already here and motioned him over to their table. The noontime rush crowd was gone, and they had the manager reserve all tables for the next hour, making this an exclusive meeting.

"Welcome ladies. I'm so glad you decided to at least listen to my offer." Diego sat down in a well-practiced elegant motion, designed to display the ultimate confidence. "Teachers and nurses are absolutely vital for any culture anywhere in the entire Federation," be began. "And here on Virge-C, your roles are even more important, as it will be your people who lead the common man into their bright future as a member of the Galactic Federation. As you have heard many times perhaps, soon the Federation will be bringing many new inventions and education to your world. I want you to be in the forefront of these incredible changes, particularly so in the medical arena."

"Look to the future. Now what would you say if some twenty years from now, each of you had many dozens of new people in your groups, each of which were super-geniuses? I'm talking IQs of well over 160. Yes, geniuses. It is in your power to have as many of these geniuses, these incredibly brilliant people, as you desire, or as few of them as you wish," he played them well. He saw their eyes register the significance and potential of having many true geniuses among them, and then he lowered their resistance by pointing out that somehow this would be under their control.

Helen responded as he anticipated. "Just what do you mean by this? Yes, geniuses are rare. Are you saying we could have as many geniuses as we desire?"

"Yes, as many as you both desire. This is a gift offer I'm making to your unions alone. No one else is going to get this incredible offer. Why your groups? As you and I both know, education and medical care are the two biggest factors in the well-being and growth of any society. In your hands lies the future, which could be stellar, led by an army of geniuses, that is, if you choose this path. Imagine the educational benefits of having nothing but geniuses teaching your young. Imagine the benefits of having all your nurses be geniuses. Perhaps, they would prefer becoming the doctors instead. Everyone benefits enormously from great teachers and great nurses. Surely, you cannot disagree with that statement."

Both nodded. Of course, they would agree with that statement. Diego knew that he finally had them on the hook. Now to reel them in. "So both of you have it within your power to bring this about: as many geniuses in your future as you desire. I'm not talking about one or two, but dozens, hundreds, thousands. It is all up to you and is your choice."

"Okay, Diego, I'll bite," Dr. Helen spoke up. "What are we to do to get these geniuses?"

"Before I answer that directly, let me tell you a bit about the Galactic Federation. You see, we too once faced this same problem: far too few true geniuses. We recognize all giant leaps forward have come in part through geniuses and their incredible minds. Hyperspace travel, the sub-light engines, which can refuel while traveling, the medical machines—the list is quite lengthy. Behind each of these was a genius."

"Long ago, the Federation realized this fact and set about finding a way to create geniuses, rather than leaving their creation to Nature's Chance. And yes, it has been found!

And yes, the major corporations of the Federation are right now making good use of this unbelievable breakthrough. Any normal human woman can bear children who are guaranteed to be true geniuses, IQs at least 150 or more."

"How is this possible?" asked Jane. "Birth rates for true geniuses are infinitesimal. We all know this."

"The answer, nurse, is genetics. The solution is both utterly simple and quite normal. All that must be done is for a normal human woman to copulate with a special genetically modified male. Her sons are guaranteed to be geniuses. That is pure fact now, not subject to speculation or whims of nature."

"I don't understand. You are saying that if Helen here got impregnated from one of these genetically modified males, then if she had a son by him, he would automatically be a genius or at least have a very high IQ?" Jane asked.

"You are completely correct. That is precisely the situation."

"But what about their girls? Wouldn't they be geniuses as well?" asked Helen.

"I'm sorry. No, they have not yet shown such high IQs, but they have other redeeming aspects," he replied. This was the tricky point, and he didn't know how they'd respond.

"Such as?" Helen continued to press the issue.

"As you know, a very, very few Federation women have become the Ultimate in Feminine Beauty, gorgeous super-models, physically perfect in all ways. The UFB woman. These rare beauties are prized by corporation executives. I'm so pleased to have one as my wife and mother of my children, the incredible Luisa. So, to answer your question, Helen, daughters of this union, while not geniuses, are true UFB women, highly prized for their rare beauty by all."

He rapidly continued, "So any normal woman who in impregnated by this special male will have either a genius son or an incredibly beautiful daughter. It is a win-win situation either way for the mother. Let me assure you that she would have many, many men knocking at her door to have the chance to win her UFB daughter's hand, figuratively of course."

"I would also like to point out that these special males

are incredibly rare, incredibly! Until very recently, I've never even seen one. Yet, recently, I have acquired one, Mr. Fernando. While I would dearly love to hang on to him and use his natural gifts—yes, I would love to have a dozen true geniuses in my employ, I've decided that Virge-C could make far better use of natural born geniuses than I could. So what I'm offering you is this. I will give you Mr. Fernando to use, as you desire. Have him impregnate as many volunteer women as you desire. Statistically, half of their children will be sons and thus your new cadre of true geniuses, while the other half will be extraordinary women who offer other tremendous benefits for you and your world. Plan for the future. Think what fifty geniuses could do for the teaching and nursing industries across your world. Or perhaps a hundred. How many or how few is your call, not mine."

He finished up with, "But if I were in your shoes, I'd try to have as many sons as I could possibly have. Twenty years down the road, tremendous things will result. I'm giving you this chance to have a total monopoly on this Federation gift."

"And what do we have to do to get this?" Helen asked.

"Just merge your unions with the corresponding corporation's sections. We all win this way. Plus history will show it was the Teacher's Union and the Union of Nurses that created the mountain of geniuses that will have brought so many tremendous benefits to Virge-C."

"So you want to dictate to us how we teach our children and how we handle nursing duties?" Helen asked pointedly.

"Of course not. We are the foreigners here. Our people need and want your invaluable input. We work together, for it is in our best interests, as it is yours, that Virge-C flourishes and prospers. Crudely then, more money results if you want to be crass about our motives."

"Let us talk this over. Please go over there and give us a private moment," Helen ordered. Diego did as asked, figuring he had a good likelihood of success, since they didn't outright reject the offer. Besides, here was a good way to get rid of Fernando. Right now, he didn't need or want a silly UFBMD around. Time enough for breeding later, once Virge-C was totally under corporation control.

"I don't like having helpless, dependent daughters," Helen whispered.

"True, but as we well know, these aliens greatly prize their UFB women. So the daughters would very likely end up being very well cared for, perhaps living lives of luxury. Think of the possibilities, Helen. Many geniuses. While it is debatable whether these aliens are good for our world, having hundreds of our own local geniuses can only be of enormous benefit," Jane responded.

"Point taken. Shall we accept his offer? If we do, how are we going to handle this?" Helen asked.

"We don't want to break up marriages, but I think we can sell having them having one or two children from this Fernando fellow. What woman wouldn't want another Al Jones in her family?" Jane replied. He was the man primarily responsible for bringing their world into the space age. "We should plan for at least a hundred pregnancies right away this year and perhaps that many for next year. With luck, in some twenty years, we'll have a cadre of a hundred geniuses working for us."

"Okay. We can't let this opportunity pass us by. If we do, I'm sure he'll make a similar offer to some other group. I'd prefer it if we were in control of this," Helen stated and motioned for Diego to return.

\*\*\*

"But I don't want to be their sex slave," Fernando cried out after Diego told him that he was being delivered to the Teacher's Union and the Union of Nurses an hour later.

"Oh suck it up man. You are going to have more sex than you ever dreamed possible. Enjoy yourself," Diego turned and left Fernando, who again broke down, sobbing, helpless to control any aspect of his life. He'd fallen far.

\*\*\*

Marcos took the elevator up to the eighty-first floor of the Ace Skyscraper, prepared for his meeting with Raymond Ace, the president and CEO of Ace Foods, one of the largest food distribution companies on Virge-C. "Ah, this way, sir," an executive in a brown suit met him and ushered him into the president's office. Ray sat behind the desk once used by his grandfather who had turned Ace Foods from a small company to a planet-wide corporation, servicing most large cities of the world.

After cordial but cold greetings were exchanged, Marcos got down to business. "Okay President Raymond, here's the deal. As you know, our negotiations these past months have gotten us nowhere at all. So I've come today to get your choice. Either you sell your corporation to us for ten million of your gold dollars today or you and your family will shortly meet a fatal accident. Look." He pulled out a small tablet computer and played a short video for the man.

Ray saw a number of men in black cars parked outside his home. His two sons were playing ball in the yard. He knew his wife was just inside. He swallowed. Marcos said coldly, "If I don't call them in an hour, a bomb will mysteriously go off, leveling your home. Although you will rush home to save them, I assure you your vehicle will not make it there. So accept my check for ten million or I'll leave and let you make your frantic rush to save them and yourself. What will it be?"

Reluctantly, Ray accepted the check. "Good choice. Now then, you may stay on as Vice-President for now. Sign here." Marcos slid the formal document over to him for his signature.

Ray signed his name slowly. He looked up and said, "If any harm comes to my family, there will not be any place in this galaxy where you can hide from me!"

Ignoring his angry threat, Marcos picked up the legal documents and left the office. *We should have done this months ago. Well, it's done. On to the next one.*

***

That afternoon, the newscast reported on a tragic accident. A gas line ruptured and the fiery explosion leveled the home of the head of Bectold's Transport. Tragically, Hans Bectold was killed in a traffic accident as he drove to the scene of the fire. The next day, ownership of Bectold's Transport was transferred to Galactic Transport.

During the week, one by one, the ownership of the remaining larger companies and corporations located in West Port were transferred to one of the alien corporations. As the week closed, Diego was quite pleased with the results. He had total control of West Port, except for the slums, Snake Town, but they hardly mattered. More direct action would handle them.

***

"Well ain't this a fine howdy-do, lassies!" Tom declared. He'd just returned from the Snake Town seamstress. "Only able to get seven dresses for ya, Miss Adonia. These nasty corporation blokes done moved her out of Snake Town, lock, stock, and barrel. Nothing left in her place, 'cepting some scraps. Sign says 'Moved to Leonardo's.' Ain't that somethun'!"

"Well, I guess we can always get more from Leonardo's if we have to," Sondra attempted to defuse everyone's anger.

"Bombings, strange accidents. What's the world com'in to?" Tom continued to gripe. True, nearly every day, some new catastrophe in West Port appeared on the news. It bothered Matt more than the others. He felt as though he could do nothing to stop this madness, but as a police officer, it had been his duty to at least try.

Sondra sensed he was once more thinking along these lines. "Look dear, we're all helpless in some ways. What's going on is bigger than we can possibly handle. If only they hadn't dissolved the police force, you might have had some chance, but not now."

"I know. I feel so helpless," Matt replied. Then, he flushed. "Sorry. I know you three are the helpless ones. I should be thankful for being whole."

"I know. We're all helpless in some ways. Ours is different from yours. What matters, Matt, is that we do what we can. I'm sure you're doing all you can to keep us all safe here. Without you, we would all probably be dead by now." Her words mollified him for now.

That night, Sondra's phone rang, and Matt retrieved it for her, setting it on the table before her. "Hello Ben, what's up?" she answered.

Something was terribly wrong. She could tell from his voice even before his words registered. "Help! Security men are here threatening to burn my pub down! Shit, gotta go and try to stop them!"

"Matt, we have to help him. He's like my big brother!"

214

Sondra cried, once more feeling her helplessness to come to his aid when he truly needed it.

"On our way. Tom, grab your guns!" Matt yelled. "Ben's in big trouble."

"Maybe I should come too in case someone gets hurt," Roxane volunteered.

"Okay. Good idea. You can help look after Sondra. We have to hurry. I think it wise to take both cars," Matt ordered. "Beth, Alice, Sandy, you look after things here."

Within a minute, Matt lifted Sondra up, carrying her rapidly to their car, while Tom and Roxane headed for the second one. He, like Matt, carried a bag full of guns and ammo clips. Tom yelled over to Sondra, "Donna ya worry, lassie, we'll be rescuing him. Gonna shoot me a bunch of them creeps!"

She didn't doubt he would, but felt miserable having to be carried to the car, but she knew Matt had to do it. She was just too darn slow on her own. She blanked out the question of just what she could possibly actually do to help Ben.

When they arrived some ten minutes later, five GD guards were just coming out of the pub, but already Sondra could see some flames in one corner where the tables were located. Matt stopped the car, got out, and began unloading two guns into the guards, who were taken by surprise. Two dropped to the ground. Tom, on the other hand, went ballistic. He floored the engine and drove into the group of guards, running over the two that Matt had shot, but more importantly, the car smashed into the backs of the three others, killing them instantly.

As Tom got out, drawing his guns, he yelled, "Take that, ya filthy beasts!"

"Matt, Ben must be inside! It's on fire!" Sondra cried, acutely feeling her helplessness now as never before.

Roxane put her arm around Sondra, steadying her as they followed pitifully slowly behind the men, rushing inside the pub. The smell of petrol and burning wood filled the air. Ben was frantically emptying the contents of his fire extinguishers on the blaze, which had been ignited around the front tables.

As soon as Sondra entered the smoky pub, she knew it

was hopeless. "Ben! Grab whatever you can save before the fire gets too big!"

The look of frustration on Ben's face was heartbreaking. He turned to Matt and Tom, who stowed their guns and looked back at him. "We killed the five who did this," Tom yelled.

"Ben, start getting what you want saved out of here," Matt called out. He knew they only had minutes before they would have to evacuate or die from smoke inhalation. The fire wasn't stopable. Just then, five other men came running in. She recognized them as frequent customers and had even served them on a dozen occasions.

That was enough impetus for Ben. "Okay, grab what you can from behind the bar. I'll get things from my apartment upstairs. Matt, with me. We'll toss things down the back stairs." Tom found the cashbox and took it out of the growing inferno, while the other men grabbed various boxes of food supplies and raided the freezer for more frozen items, lugging them out of the burning pub.

Sondra and Roxane headed around back to see if there was anything they could do there to help. If nothing else, they could watch over the stuff the men were tossing out. One of the old timers followed them.

When Ben appeared at the top of the back stairs, he yelled, "Amos, you and the others can have all the booze you can get out of the place."

"Thank yea, Ben. I swear those GD folks ain't heard the last o' this!" He scurried around to the front, while Tom joined Sondra and began carrying piles of clothes to the cars. Roxane decided she could best help by doing the same thing. Sondra could only stand out of the way and watch. She had never felt so useless in her young life, but knew that Ben appreciated her even being here.

Fifteen rapid minutes passed before Matt and Ben came down the stairs. Already the entire main floor was engulfed, and they knew the place wasn't salvageable, though the sirens of fire trucks on their way pierced the night air. Grimly, Matt and Ben finished carrying the last of Ben's things around to the cars. Tom and Roxane headed off back home, just as the fire trucks arrived.

Ben stuck around a minute to tell the firemen what had happened. "Sorry son, don't think we can save the building," one said.

"I know. Keep it from spreading to other buildings if you can. They've gotten a lot of the booze out already, so maybe it won't explode on you," Ben replied. Sadly, he squeezed his way into the nearly full backseat, and Matt headed for home as well.

For a few minutes, no one said anything. At last, Sondra said, "Ben, I'm so sorry for you."

"Thanks little sis. I knew it would come to this one day. There's been a lot of talk about the corporations blowing up family homes and murdering those who won't sell their companies to them. Now, they are making their move on Snake Town. I figured they would come after me, since many locals meet at the pub each evening. At least, I don't have to make any more loan payments. They can have what's left," he added grimly.

When they got to the farmhouse, Roxane insisted on checking Ben, rightly so, for he had a few burns that needed tending. Meanwhile, the others carried Ben's things into another spare room; this one was beside Adonia's. Alice joked, "Well, if we take in more people, we are going to have to open up the upstairs."

Sandy barked, "Okay. Baths all around. You're stinking up the place. You all smell like smoke."

Hours later and cleaned up, they gathered around the old dining room table for a late night snack. Adonia asked, "So what did you used to do at your pub thing?"

Ben laughed, "Well, I owned it. I cooked people three square meals a day and at a low cost to them, cause the folks in Snake Town are so poor. Usually, all the locals came by at night, and I served up good ale. It was a meeting place for the folks in several blocks around me. Now that's gone, thanks to GD's hit men."

"Wow, so you were a cook too. I used to cook for all the women, that is, before I became one of them, a UFB woman," Adonia chatted. "They said I would have made a great chef."

The others were tired, and one by one, left the two, who continued to chat. "So you're understanding me pretty well. Most people can't understand our speech. Well, I couldn't at first either, but after a while you sort of can. I know I do sound really bad. So many sounds simply aren't there, but you already know that. Still, I think your sister is just the greatest."

"She's not really my sister, Adonia. We were both orphans and placed with the same foster parents. They treated us really badly, so being the older one, I always looked after her. She calls me her big brother, and I call her my little sister. Hell, we didn't really have anyone else to look after us, so we took care of each other. When I turned twenty-one, I received a small inheritance from my dead parents and used it to buy that pub. I was able to move Sondra in there with me, out from our abusive foster parents. We've been looking after each other since."

"I think that is really great. I never had any brothers or sisters. My folks died when I was young too, but Luisa and Diego—they took me under their wing when I was twelve. At first, I helped her and Juanita, but then I also began cooking for them as well, since their old chef did a terrible job. Of course, now that's impossible for me to ever do again." She sighed, but was able to keep her eyes from watering too much.

"That's got to be awful for you, Adonia. Why did you ever get all this done to you? Did they make you do it, like they did Sondra and Rene?" he asked sympathetically.

"I was naive and rather foolish, looking back on it all. Sondra worked her magic on me, so I can now talk about it. I fell in love or thought I did with a young up and coming GD executive. He was handsome, but I knew all top executives only had UFB women for their wives. He promised to marry me as soon as I became one, but it wasn't allowed until I was eighteen. Not long after I did it, Julio was killed. Now here I am, completely helpless and for nothing at all. Stupid of me, I know."

"Well, you're still bright, young, and darn pretty," Ben validated what he saw in her.

"And completely helpless, well mostly anyway," she added. "If I could only somehow cook again, I would be worth something, only I can't. Obviously."

"Well, you can lend me your advice and such. I suspect I'll be appointed chief chef around here, probably tomorrow, if I know my sis."

"Can I? Oh I'd love that. I won't get in your way. You can't imagine what it is like to be as we are, so completely dependent upon everyone for everything. Maybe it's all right for the executive's wives, but not for anyone else. Rene has it even worse, what with her fused feet and all, but Tom's good for her, you know. He treats her as his beauty queen, which of course she was. I saw her once when she won Miss West Port. I can't believe GD men killed her parents and did that to her just to get control of her parent's Shoe Box Company, but of course I don't understand why GD does all the bad things that they do."

"Greed, Adonia, greed. Some men just can't get enough money, and have to rob and steal it from everyone else," Ben answered angrily. His tone softened. *No sense taking this out on her.* "So it looks like you and I will just have to hang out together."

"Wow. I'd like that. I know many tips on making meals taste like treats. So where's your wife?" Adonia asked.

Ben laughed. "Don't have one. No time for a girlfriend either. It took all my time running the pub—dawn to dusk work. Sondra often helped me though, when I got too busy. She was always good about that, but now she's like you. I could tell her heart was breaking while she was there at the fire and unable to help me. I hope she gets over it."

"I know. Honestly, Ben, we do feel so helpless, and factually, we are. No sense pretending otherwise, not really." She sighed and then brightened up. "But she is really happy with Matt. Her eyes are brighter than I've ever seen them, after they got married that is. It is probably the sex, you see."

Ben chuckled. "No, I don't see. But I agree; she really is very happy with Matt. Blessed, I would say."

"Oh silly, that's one of the benefits of becoming a UFB woman. Besides all this," she shrugged her shoulders for the lack of any other way to make an expression, "we're supposed to have incredible sex. They say that it is supposed to be ten times better as a UFB woman than before. I've heard that from quite a few UFB women, you know the before and after comparisons, though I have no idea why that would be so." She sighed again, "But now I'll never know. Julio is dead and who is going to want to marry me, like I am now?" Again, she shrugged her shoulders.

"Oh I don't know. Trust me, Adonia, eventually, you'll meet the right one for you. Sondra did. Rene did. Give it time, and you will too. You are young, gorgeous, and bright. You should have many fellows begging to go out with you." He leaned over and teased her, "You better be careful. I might come after you too." Both giggled. "You have a cool sense of humor. Sondra and I always like to tease each other."

Adonia smiled invisibly. "Well, I still can laugh, Ben. I do like to laugh and talk."

Ben laughed. "I like that about you. I think people should talk more to each other. There would be lots less fighting if they did that, don't you think?"

"Probably. Getting them to talk, now that's the problem. Of course, most people can't even understand us. I hate having to repeat everything slowly and several times just so they can understand me, but I understand why they can't and why I do, but still it is annoying, not like us. You understand me pretty good, but that's probably because you've been around Sondra and Rene so much, right?"

"Yes, you're right. At first, I couldn't make out what they were saying. I could see how that really bothered both of them, but what else could I do if I couldn't understand what they were saying? Still, after a while, you sort of catch on to all the missing sounds and can piece the words together," Ben explained.

"I know what you mean. I was like that at first around Lady Juanita. I like you, Ben. I can talk to you, as if we are close friends or something, and we've only just met. Isn't that strange?"

"Not really. I like you too. You remind me of Sondra when she was your age—bright, inquisitive, always getting into things and figuring out mysteries. She never let anything get her down. She's never backed down from a fight either."

"Well, we sort of have to be that way now, Ben. The only other choice is to sit back and do nothing at all, wait to die. I did want to die you know, when they told me Julio died, but I suppose it is a good thing I'm so helpless because I might have killed myself, but then maybe not. I think not, because if I wasn't helpless like this, I could carry on and find someone else to love. Do you suppose that's so?"

"Sure thing. And you still can, Adonia—find someone to love. You just have to keep your eyes open. He'll turn up. I'll keep my eyes open too." She giggled.

Just then a sleepy-eyed Beth walked back in. "Are you two done talking? I need to get Adonia ready for bed before I fall asleep." Both chucked.

As Ben expected, he soon found himself appointed the group's cook, though he at once insisted the Adonia lend him a hand. Later when Sondra was alone with Ben, she said, "Thanks for taking Adonia under your wing. She needs all the support she can get."

Ben laughed. "I'm a sucker for a woman in need." Both laughed at that. He added seriously, "I really do like her, you know. She reminds me a lot of you as well. She might be the one for me. Can I ask you something personal, little sis?"

"Sure. When have you not?" she teased him.

"Quite true. Is there such a thing as love at first sight? Does that really exist?"

Sondra laughed. "Damned if I know, big brother, but I sure fell for Matt in a big way. Why?"

Ben flushed and looked at the floor a moment, before raising his eyes. "Adonia."

Sondra laughed. "She is a hot one. You could do far worse. I know she loves to talk, just as you do. She is a fighter, Ben. She got herself out of GD on her own steam. That tells me a whole lot about a person."

"I know. You told me all about it. I can't get her out of my thoughts and mind, not since we talked late into the night after the fire."

Sondra grinned invisibly. "Well, talk with her more. Get to know her better. Just realize that she, like Rene and me, are, well you know, a heavy responsibility. We can't do much of anything. We're basically helpless people now."

"Little sis, you are only helpless on some things that everyone else takes for granted. Yet, you are a powerhouse on many other things. I don't know of anyone who investigates better than you do, but I know what you mean."

After that, Ben and Adonia were seldom found apart. When they were not in the kitchen preparing meals, often they could be found strolling around the grassy patch of the farm, constantly chatting with each other. Although chaos was spreading around West Port, these two seemed oblivious to it all.

No one was surprised when the two announced at supper one night that they wanted to get married. Adonia giggled, "Ben asked me and I accepted. I never ever thought I'd feel this way again, but I do, I really do!"

The next day, with some difficulty, Matt managed to bring the preacher back out to the farm where the couple each got to say their "I do" to his questions. This time, even though he didn't understand a word that Adonia said, he accepted whatever she said as what was expected. He returned home happy with the additional hundred dollars. Within the city, things were quite a mess, and the money was helpful.

# Chapter 14—Conscience

According to the newscasts, the eastern portion of West Port was safe for business and travel. The streets were now safe. This also included the northern portion of the western part as well. All the conflict and riots were taking place in Snake Town. In fact, the reporters were very eager to explain that the aliens were now using their own weapons against the rebels. A new type of handgun called a d-gun, which the reporters carefully and with authority said stood for disintegrator gun and which could drill a three inch hole through a person's body, were now being used, but of course the reporters had no clue what or how that weapon was used.

Similarly, they all talked about the Personal Defense Shields that the guards wore, or PDS for short. This made them invulnerable to all local weapons. All alien security men were now wearing them or so the reporters claimed. It seemed backed up by the daily casualty reports they reported. Many more Snake Town men and women were dead, but few of the guards.

"Why didn't they give those to my Julio?" Adonia complained to Ben, while they watched the news after breakfast. "That Diego surely killed my Julio, because he should have given him these things."

"Point taken, Adonia," Ben replied. "I bet he just needed to have a number of his men killed in order to justify his using these killer weapons on us, don't you think?"

"Well, yes, that does sound like the reasoning Diego used," she admitted.

Matt spoke up, "Well, at least part of the city is now safe for travel. We need to get more groceries soon. So does everyone else in West Port, I expect."

"Hey everybody, we've now got access to the Federation galaxy-wide Internet!" Sondra called out. She often spent her mornings surfing for clues on her new computer. Matt placed it on the floor for her, and she used her toes to operate it. While terribly slow and clumsy, Sondra was able to operate it, giving her back some of her old self-confidence.

"Hey, now we can search the galaxy for a cure for all of you!" Alice declared rather excited, but then her face soured. "Er sorry, I wouldn't have the faintest notion of what to look for or do. Computers aren't my thing." Everyone laughed. Instead, she provided them with music, for she continued to practice nearly every day. Hearing the news that the streets were safe again, she asked, "Would it be safe for us to go back to my old place for a bit? I would like to grab all the music scores I have."

"Well, I'm going to have to make a grocery run," Matt replied. "You and Sandy can tag along and help with the groceries, and then we'll make a quick stop. How's that?"

Just then, Roxane walked into the room, a very puzzled look on her face. "Gang, I just received the strangest email I've ever gotten. I don't know what to make of it. I've printed it out so you can all read it, especially you Adonia. What does all this mean? Is it true what they are claiming?" She laid it out so that all could see, but helped Sondra get up gracefully.

Nurse Roxane Stevens,

The Teacher's Union and the Union of Nurses have recently acquired a special breeding male from the aliens. Apparently, this unique and strange male, if it really is male, is incredibly rare and very valuable, but its value lies in its offspring.

Its male children are guaranteed to have an IQ of at least 150 or more. That is in the high genius range for those of you who are not up these numbers. Dr. Helen Albright, head of the Teacher's Union, and I, Jane Longtree, head of the Union of Nurses, were given this special breeding male thing for our cooperation with the alien corporations. Why did we accept this "bribe?" Simple.

Imagine what our world would be like if there were a hundred Dr. Al Jones working as educators and in the medical arena. We all know what just one super-genius man has done for our world. Think what a hundred or two hundred of them might be able to accomplish. It's mind-boggling.

Thus, we leaped at this remarkable offer. We have now established an official breeding program for all female teachers and nurses on Virge-C, who are still able to bear children. If you would like to be the mother of one of these super-genius sons, all you need to do is sign up for an impregnation session to take place during your fertile time each month. We are limiting Phase One to the first one hundred women volunteers.

Of course, you would be expected to raise your son as your own, so if you are married, we will require your husband's signature as well as yours. If you are single, your signature is all that's needed. Women, this is an excellent opportunity for you to make perhaps the most valuable contribution to our world! Next year, we will be implementing Phase Two, which proposes three hundred more pregnancies.

Of course, having a male child cannot be guaranteed. If yours turns out to be female, you have two choices. It can be aborted, and you can try again with our blessings, or you can carry her full term. There is a catch, but only with female offspring. Males will be entirely normal, except for their brilliant intellects. Females, we are told, will be what the aliens call the Ultimate in Feminine Beauty or UFB women as they commonly are called. As most of us already know, the alien corporate executives all insist upon having UFB women as their wives. So should you chose to carry a daughter to full term, she is likely to also have a bright future ahead of her as a wife of a wealthy man, as we anticipate many of our local top leaders to parallel the alien leaders.

I can't begin to tell you how vitally important this project is for all of Virge-C. With hundreds of super-geniuses, our own men mind you, not alien men, the giant steps ahead that they could make for us all is mind-boggling. Thus, I personally would like to invite you seriously to consider taking this extraordinary step to help our world.

If you would like to be part of this first group of one hundred volunteers, please respond to this email. Positions are limited this year. Need I say first come, first served? I look forward to hearing from you.

Sincerely,

Jane Longtree

"Is any of this true, Adonia? You know more about these UFB women than any of us," Roxane asked.

"Gosh. This is strange. Let me think a moment," Adonia replied. She would have bitten her lip as she used to do when pondering something of importance, but that was now denied her. "Well, I remember Luisa once telling me that very rarely they used this same genetic bio agent on men. Oh right. That's what happened to Fernando. He became a UFBMD. Now I get it. That's an Ultimate in Feminine Beauty Male Donor. Right. I remember Luisa once telling me that—how did she put it—oh yes, children of one of those and a normal woman—by that she means not one of us UFB women, are special. Right, the males are terribly smart, her words. I suppose she meant geniuses. Females are like us, UFB women. Does this help?"

"Yes. So it is true. Incredible," Roxane replied, deep in thought. "You know," she then said, "I can see an ulterior motive behind Jane's program. She and Helen were always against the alien corporations taking over everything. That's why I was surprised to hear they had joined them. Now I can see what they are doing. Look, it's obvious that our men can't fight these aliens and win, not with these new weapons of theirs. So if suddenly, say twenty years from now, we have hundreds of extremely intelligent men arriving at maturity, why, their brains may well figure a way to throw off the alien yoke of oppression. That must be what those two have in mind. Read between the lines, I always say."

"Aye, lassie," Tom spoke up. "That-da make a whole lotta sense. If one genius got us into space, think what a hundred of them might-a do. They are smart lassies indeed."

Sondra remained silent. Fernando. She'd unleashed their genetic bio agent on him. Revenge. Make him suffer as she was suffering. She'd done just that. What had happened to him? Had Diego given him to these women to be used as a breeder? She swallowed hard. That wasn't what she had in mind at all. She listened to Roxane, who was speaking again.

"I'm inclined to give this a try. If I could have a son who is a genius, then that could really make a difference. I have nothing to lose and everything to gain," she theorized.

"But what if you have a girl child? She'd be like they are, helpless," Sandy pointed out. "That's as likely as having a son. Fifty-fifty."

Roxane didn't say why she was considering doing this. It was a private matter between herself and Sondra and Alice. They were clones. Were they even capable of bearing children? Alice had no worries, since she was married to Sandy and likely would never even try, but Sondra and Matt—well they were a different story entirely. *I have to do this for my sisters. I have to find out if our bodies are even capable of bearing a child. We ovulate like all women, but are we even fertile? I have to find out.*

Roxane replied, "I'll cross that bridge when I come to it. Besides, I can get more intelligence about this strange male and what's going on."

She replied to the email, volunteering herself. She was in luck. Subsequent emails indicated she was fifty-five in the queue and to notify them when her next fertile period was. A week later, Matt dropped Roxane off at the Union of Nurses headquarters in downtown West Port, a steel and glass skyscraper of some fifty floors, where she was to stay for a couple of days, until she tested positive for impregnation.

"You will be staying here," Jane personally showed her a small, private room. She showed her where to get her meals. Then, she took her into her office where Roxane signed the forms.

"Okay, here's how it works. We schedule four breeding sessions each day. One in the morning, one early afternoon, one before supper, and one at night. You are scheduled for the early afternoon session every day until fertilization is confirmed or your time expires. If we don't succeed this time, we'll try again next month. Having a hundred geniuses is vital for our long-term survival. Later on, if it is female, it is up to you whether to continue the pregnancy."

She continued, "Now I do need to give you some guidelines about this male thing."

"Why do you call him a male thing? Your email wasn't too clear on that point."

Jane laughed. "One look and you'll know. At first when I saw him, I didn't believe what I was seeing either. Honestly, have you seen any of these alien UFB women?"

"Yes, of course," Roxane replied, not saying she was

living with three of them.

"Well, he looks exactly like one of them—incredible hair, gigantic boobs, split lips, malformed feet. Even his voice sounds female, a soprano. They even have him wearing what must be expensive and heavy earrings. However, his maleness is intact and really does work, rather dramatically. He's been trying to protest some; at least we think that's what he's saying. None of us can understand a word he says—the lip disks you see. So we have worked out a way around any possible trouble he might give you. We leave his lip disks out all the time and never put those heels on his feet. Thus, he can't possibly walk much at all."

"Now here's the secret. You lick or suck on his lip loops, fondle his breasts and nipples, and boom! He's ready to mount. Honestly, we find his reactions to be rather startling and are studying them, medically that is. So when you get your turn, ignore his babbling, work on his lip loops and breasts for a bit, and you'll know what to do after that. It's darn amazing. You'll see what I mean soon enough. Roxane, we are planning for the future. One day, these sons will be smart enough to help our world throw off the yoke of suppression these aliens have us under. You are about to become a female freedom fighter in our own unique way."

Roxane laughed. "Hardly. I'm a nurse, but I guessed that this was actually what lay behind this project. If it works, I'm all for it. These aliens are truly evil beasts." Well, perhaps not all them, she thought, thinking of Adonia.

Her turn came that afternoon. However, she was able to understand what poor Fernando was saying, and it bothered her. Later, she told Sondra about it. "He was begging me to kill him. He couldn't live as he was. Honestly, Sondra, no human being should be treated as he is now. My God, forced to have sex with a different woman four times a day! Unreal. I know you wanted revenge on him for what he did to you, but isn't this going much too far?"

She'd returned pregnant with a male child, as verified by their staff doctor. After chatting with the others, she took Sondra aside for this private chat. Sondra's face reddened. "Roxane, that's not what I wanted or intended. I figured he'd be married to an alien woman and that would be that. I had no idea they would do this to him. You're right. This is utterly inhumane. Even if he was an unethical alien before, he doesn't deserve this. What have I done, Roxane? What have I done?"

Roxane chuckled, "Revenge isn't so sweet after all, is it?"

"I was angry. My life was ruined, but this—well this is going beyond too far," Sondra admitted. After a long pause, she added, "Well, I got him into this, so it's up to me to get him out. I suppose I'll have to bring him here with us. Give me some time to work it out, Roxane. Please tell the others for me, will you? I have some serious thinking to do. There must be a way to rescue him, though I never dreamed I'd be rescuing the man who did this to me." Roxane smiled and relaxed. The wrong might yet be righted somewhat.

Sondra spent an hour, finally hacking into the Union of Nurses computer system. Another hour passed as she scanned through their mountain of documents, cursing her slow speed. *This should have taken a couple of minutes.* At last, she found what looked promising. She opened the document and read it. She smiled invisibly, as a very simple plan jelled in her mind. No one would even get hurt.

Later, she outlined her plan to Matt, Tom, and Ben who would have to carry it out, since she simply couldn't, not anymore, thanks to the very man she was going to rescue. "After they impregnate their one hundredth woman, they are then going to move him from where he is to a more permanent home in the Teacher's Union Hall. Presumably, next year, they will move him back for the next round. Here's the route they will be taking. It's the most direct one. At that corner there— damn, I can't even point!" she growled.

After describing it and Matt pointing to it, she continued. "Yes, there. As their car comes down the street, one of you toss the tire deflator strip out across the road. The car runs over it and all four tires go flat. The car stops. Wearing grubby Snake Town clothing and masks, you step out with your guns and pull him from the car, put him in your car, and take off. A very simple snatch and grab. No one will be harmed. Very little risk. Done in less than a minute."

"Dear, you are a genius at this," Matt replied. "A master criminal." All four laughed. "Of course, in these times, it pays to be one."

***

From a street corner, Tom watched two women escorting what appeared to be another one of these UFB women out of the Union of Nurses' building, of that there could be no question. Tom relayed via his phone, "Got them. Putting her or him, looks like a woman really, into the car now." He described the car and followed them, just in case they decided to take a longer route to the Teacher's Union building. Luckily, they headed directly there. Thanks to Tom's constant relaying of their position, Matt and Ben had plenty of warning. Ben rolled out the strip just before the car rolled over them, puncturing all four tires. The car screeched to a halt, as the disguised pair stepped out, guns drawn. Silently, they opened the back door, and Ben lifted the confused UFB woman out, carrying her to their car in the alleyway, tossing her into the back seat. Seconds later, they were gone, leaving the two nurses completely shocked and confused.

"Sable? You?" the agitated and frightened Fernando asked, growing even more confused by the minute. First, he'd been kidnaped, and figured he'd be raped and killed, once they found he wasn't a woman. Now, he was staring at the women who he had been planning to marry before he blacked out in the coma and this horrid nightmare began.

"Sondra actually. Your GD people murdered Sable right in front of me. I took her place so I could find her murderer, your GD people. So how do you like being what you made me into, eh Fernando? Just incredibly wonderful isn't it?"

"But, but I was going to marry you," he protested.

"And make me your sex doll for life? Sorry, I'm nobody's sex toy. Besides, I married for love, not status or wealth or anything else," Sondra replied.

"But I don't understand any of this. Someone did this to me," he cried, as though somehow that would make her see reason. *Maybe it isn't too late. But she's married?*

"Look, just so you know, I stole a vial of that genetic agent stuff and dropped in on the floor of your room, breaking

230

it while you were asleep, and then I fled the GD building. Yes, I wanted and got revenge on you for what you did to me, and I escaped your clutches."

"You? You did this to me? But why? I was going to marry you and give you everything," he protested. It did sound funny hearing his high-pitched voice.

"Look, you ruined my life. I wanted you to experience firsthand what you made me into, a helpless freak of a woman. What's the matter, Fernando, don't you like being a UFB woman? Well I guess you're still a man down there."

Finally, Fernando understood. "I can't do anything, not really. I think I understand. You can't either, even though you would have had servants to help you. I—I never really thought about how UFB women felt about it. They live lives of luxury and never want for anything, except I now know they're completely helpless. I'm sorry, Sondra, truly sorry. I understand now, but it is too late for both of us. Please, have pity on me, and kill me now. You are more than justified. I really have ruined your life."

"Not likely, Fernando. I went to all this trouble to rescue you. I have to apologize to you for what you've had to endure these past weeks with all those women. I had no idea Diego would sell you into sexual slavery, certainly not of that magnitude. What those women were doing to you is inhumane. No human should be forced to go through what you have. I couldn't live with myself until I got you out of that mess. So I guess at this point, we're both sorry for what we've done to each other."

She went on, "Fernando, I've moved on. I've married the love of my life and am truly happy with that. I'm just not happy being forever  so utterly helpless and dependent on everyone. We're giving you the chance to move on as well."

"What do you mean?" he asked. "I can't convince you to have one of the men shoot me?"

"No, Fernando, that would also be wrong, and besides that would just be taking the easy way out. We both have to live with what we've done, make the best of it as we can, and carry on."

"But I can't do anything for myself. How can I move

on?"

Sondra nodded, and Matt signaled for Roxane to enter the room. "You recognize her? She's my sister, Roxane. She's now carrying your son. Both she and I agreed that you had to be rescued from those women. She'd like her son at least to know his father. So she's agreed to look after you, as long as you behave and act like a responsible father when the time comes."

"I don't have any choice," Fernando answered. "I can't survive on my own. I can't go back to GD even if I wanted to. Diego would just farm me out again. So I will do as you ask. I remember you, Roxane. Of all those women, you were the kindest to me."

"Good. Then that's settled. You best get her settled in, Roxane. Sorry Fernando, it's hard seeing you as a man," Sondra said, slightly embarrassed that she'd slipped.

"Please, can you think of me as a she?" Fernando whispered. "I get too embarrassed when others see me. I look like you UFB women."

"We will try," said Roxane. "Now then, you were a GD executive?"

"Yes, second tier, though I had hopes to one day make Diego's second in command."

"Good. Now then, I have one question for you. Is there any way to undo what your people have done to my sister, Sondra, and the others, Rene and Adonia?"

Fernando shook his head no, his heavy earrings tugging hard on his ears. "No, there is no cure I know about." He saw Roxane's crestfallen face and added quickly, "but I really don't know much at all about this whole genetics thing. I was a businessman, really, a facilitator. I know where to get things—supplies, equipment, that sort of thing. Science stuff—well, that's beyond me."

"Damn," Roxane cursed softly.

"What's going to happen to me now?" Fernando asked.

"Well, behave yourself, and you can stay here with us. When your son gets born, you can try to be a proper father to him, I suppose," Roxane replied.

"But that's not going to happen," he countered.

"What do you mean?" she asked pointedly.

"GD and the other corporations—they're going to take over this entire world. They are already in Phase Two of the standard takeover protocol. By the time you have your son, they will be in total control of this world, certainly this city. They will find us and dispose of us. They'll send me back into that breeding program. They'll remarry your UFB women to their executives and probably assign the rest of you to the jobs that they need filled," he explained. "So you might as well just kill me now. I don't ever what to go back to that—that nightmare."

"Laddie, that's notta gonna happen. Ya donna know our people," Tom declared. "Donna you worry, Rene. Tom wona let them getta ya."

Several very loud, but distant explosions interrupted their discussion. The chairs rattled on the floor. Coffee mugs jostled on the table, and one near the edge fell, shattering on the floor. Thankfully, it was mostly empty.

"What was that?" Sondra yelled above the other's startled cries. Several more explosions followed, but this time, they were not taken by surprise.

"It is not close," Matt theorized. "Probably near the edge of the city. The question is should we go investigate or stay put?"

"Stay here, Matt. Check the news. I need you," Sondra answered him, her masked voice quite worried. "Bombs?"

"Probably," Matt answered, "big ones. But whose? Okay, to the living room. Let's see if it makes the news."

"This just in to Channel 10 news. Serious fighting has broken out in Snake Town. Reports of several explosions were heard, even here in our studio. Our drone cameras are on their way to the scene. We have retired Field Commander Hank Williams on the line now. Commander, what do you make of these explosions?"

A tired voice was heard, "Likely the equivalent of a five hundred pound bomb. Of course, there are no aircraft in the skies, so it's likely these were set explosives."

"Aliens or rebels? Do either have this kind of destructive capabilities?" the reporter asked him.

"We've not seen such weapons from the aliens. It is my understanding they prefer to use their new disintegrator guns and their amazing defense shields. If I may make a wild guess, I would suggest perhaps the rebels are responsible."

The reporter's face returned to the screen. "As we know, there has been a good deal of resistance to the alien corporations' takeover attempts down in the slums of Snake Town. President Johnson has said he will be using our armed forces to settle this matter. Could these explosions be our forces entering West Port? We can only speculate at this time."

An hour later, more details emerged. Another reporter explained, "From information gathered from an official GD corporation representative, a massive uprising in Snake Town has been put down. Over two hundred Snake Town residents have been killed, and local hospitals are being swamped with the injured men and women. No official count is available. However, the GD official did report that in spite of their superior defense shields, twenty-five of their guards were killed by the explosions set off by the rebels. A ten-block area in central Snake Town is in ruins at this time. Security guards are now combing the rubble for additional bodies and potential survivors. More news when we have it."

Sondra commented, "I bet the rebels were behind the explosions. Look, I know how effective those personal defense shields are. I emptied twenty-eight rounds into Fernando's shield before he shot me. Looks like their shields can't stand up to major explosions." Only later did they learn the rebels were testing that theory for the armed forces, which had finally gotten organized and were about ready to launch their counterstrike.

# Chapter 15—For Those About to Rock

Shortly before Marshal Tucker conducted his raid on Rosewood Homecare, he had a long talk with President John Johnson, a lifelong friend of his. Neither liked the slow creeping takeover of Virge-C by the alien corporations. While years ago, the leaders believed the benefits of joining the Galactic Federation were more than enough to warrant allowing their corporations to purchase land, buildings, and even some companies, President Johnson's last campaign promised to set some limits upon just how far these alien corporations could go. That had more or less failed to halt or even slow them down.

"Look, I will do what you wish, if you will distribute the incriminating evidence against Dr. Decker, once I get my hands on it," Marshal promised.

A few days later materials in hand and reviewed, he sent them to President Johnson. The newscasters displayed some of the less graphical evidence, and finally Marshal's long desire to bring Dr. Decker to justice arrived. Even though the man slipped through the federal agent's net, Marshal wasn't too worried. Eventually, they'd get their hands on this evil man. Now, he had to uphold his part of the bargain.

He called the president. "Well, they've changed their tactics. They are openly taking over companies by murdering the owner's families and killing them as well, if they don't sign over their company to the corporations. What do you want me to do, John?"

"Look, I have a dozen infantry divisions under my control as commander-in-chief. But they are scattered over the world. I need time to get them together and prepared to attack these corporations. I need you to buy me time and to find out their weaknesses so we can exploit them," President Johnson replied.

Thus, for several weeks, Marshal and his band of trusted associates did just that, raising havoc here and there, with some success. A dozen of their security men were dead and more wounded. However, at this point, Diego ordered a total change in tactics. His security men now wore their personal defense shields and traded in their primitive guns for their disintegrator guns, the d-guns. Suddenly, Marshal's band was mowed down like chaff, doing no damage to the alien security men!

When he reported this, President Johnson knew he had a very serious situation developing. He couldn't order his infantry divisions to attack when their weapons would have no effect on the enemy, while the enemy's guns would wipe his men out. "Look, Marshal, we're still a week or so from being in position to attack. I need you to find a way to defeat the new defense shields of theirs. I doubt if you can find anything that will stop their d-guns, but if we're to have any chance at this, we have to be able to inflict some casualties. If our men are killed and are not able to kill the enemy, morale will evaporate and all will be lost in short order. Find me a weakness, I beg you old friend."

"I will do my best," Marshal promised.

He enlisted many Snake Town men who were fired up against the corporations' invasion of their section of West Port. In desperation, he had his company construct a dozen large bombs of the IED style. In their next battle, his men set them off, though many died from the d-gun blasts. Although the explosions destroyed many buildings, the power of the blasts finally began to harm the alien security men. While their defense shields protected them from flying shrapnel, it didn't protect them from the massive concussion waves. Several died from internal injuries while three times that many had internal damage that would take weeks to heal.

Marshall reported these results to President Johnson. "Look, it does get through their shields, but the collateral damage to buildings is severe and many of my men died just setting them off. Still, it seems to be the only way to attack them. How soon will your assault come?"

"We are moving into position even as we speak. I will give them the ultimatum tomorrow, and then we shall see. Thank you, Marshal, for all that you've done for me and for our world." He hung up, leaving Marshal deep in thought.

What was going to happen next? West Port was about to be besieged by a dozen infantry divisions, complete with their armored fighting vehicles, a remarkable sight. At least, his daughters were outside the city and would be spared, he thought. Now, he had his own preparations to make.

***

"What the hell is that?" exclaimed Ben. Dinner was on the table and everyone had just sat down when clanking, grinding, roaring noise interrupted the usual stillness of this abandoned farm. As several got up to peek out of the windows, many muffled voices drifted into the home. Sondra and the other three silently cursed their own pathetic slowness, as they too tried to rise and look, a bit annoyed that the others had rushed to see, leaving the four to manage on their own steam.

"My god! It's the whole damned army! Tanks and everything!" exclaimed Tom. "Now the aliens are gonna get it!"

"Incredible! Wow! Just look at the armored vehicles, will you?" Matt gushed.

"So much for the lawn," Ben remarked, seeing great piles of turf being chewed up by some of the heavy tank treads.

"Wow, oh wow! Look at that," Sondra finally got herself close enough to peer out of a window. Men and vehicles of all types stretched off across the fields as far as she could see in what remained of the now reddening sun, low in the west.

Just then, someone pounded on their door. Startled, Matt rushed to the front door, followed by the others, though this time Tom slipped a steadying arm around Rene, while Sandy helped Sondra, and Ben helped Adonia. Roxane decided to give Fernando some support, for he looked terribly ill at ease and was wobbling about. She didn't want him falling and hurting himself just now. Something major was about to happen.

A man in a camouflaged uniform stood domineeringly at the door. "Captain Fisk of the Third Armor Division. We are staging in this area. No one is to use their cell phones until we leave in the morning. I will be posting a guard with you to ensure that no outside communication emanates from here. Is that clear, sir?"

"Yes, sure. Go get them!" Matt declared.

"'Bout time!" Tom added, "Ya gotta show 'em who's da boss now!"

Captain Fisk glanced at Tom; recognition highlighted his face. "Tom, Tom Ferguson, is that you?"

"Fisk? I'll be darn. 'Tis you. Ya, it's me, captain."

A broad smile replaced his rather stern countenance. "You old rascal. Thought I recognized your accent. Heard you retired. You're missing all the fun. We're rocking now. Rolling tomorrow to put those aliens in their place. Sure you don't want to re-enlist? You're missing all the fun."

"Nope, we've hadda our own fun here, rescuing folks. Hey, I just gotta hitched to a fine lassie. Never guess who? Miss West Port herself, Rene Harvester. 'Course, the aliens got to her first. Murdered her parents just ta getta their small Shoe Box Company. Then, they dida this to her. Rene, this be one of my old army buddies, Captain Fisk. She's kinda hard ta understand now, but just as gorgeous though."

"Congratulations," the captain said, but his face cringed as he saw Rene. Hastily, he swore, "We'll get those damned aliens for what they did to Miss West Port, Tom. Damn shame."

Rene nodded, but didn't attempt to say anything. She knew the man probably wouldn't understand a word she might say. Plus she couldn't even smile any longer. A nod would have to do. Tom spoke for her, "Ya, they turned her into one o' their UFB women, and we hadda rescue her an' all that. Been doin' a lotta that. Got four of 'em rescued. Just blow up the whole damned GD building, will ya?"

Captain Fish laughed, "Tom, if we go that way, you got my word, I'll put a load of shells into that skyscraper! Sorry for what they did to you, misses." He looked sympathetically at the four helpless UFB women gathered around the front entrance. "I tell the others that you're here, Tom. Some of your old unit will want to see you and meet Miss West Port herself. Well, have to run. Just remember, keep quiet until we leave. We want to preserve our element of surprise, before we attack and retake control of our capital city."

"Hey, captain, how many's out there?" Tom asked, before his friend turned to leave.

"Four divisions. We got shipped in from halfway around the world, South Amton. Tomorrow's the big day. Good to see you, Tom. It's not too late to re-enlist and come join the fun tomorrow," he added.

"Gotta look after me lassie now. Sorry," Tom answered as the captain left. He explained to Rene and several others who listened in, "He was my old captain. A bunch of us gotta shipped off to flight school. I gotta trained as a navigator, but now they musta have a new navigator. Well, tomorrow those aliens are gonna learn a thing or two."

Until now, Fernando merely stood quietly at the rear, thankful Roxane was supporting him. He decided to speak up, "I wouldn't be so sure of that. They will be slaughtered. You don't know us, the aliens. Mark my word; they won't get to set foot inside the city."

"Whatta ya mean?" asked Tom. Matt listened carefully to Fernando's reply, very concerned. What did this former exec at GD know?

"Bet Diego has got the shields ready. If he has, those metal machines of yours won't be able to get into the city," Fernando answered.

"Well, we'll just see about that!" Tom retorted, leading Rene back to their dinner table.

After dinner and before the sun went down, the whole group stepped outside, gazing at the massed forces around the farmstead. Far off into the distance, armored vehicles dotted the neat rows of pup tents. Many groups of voices were heard, all talking about the coming glorious battle. Some even predicted they'd force the aliens completely off Virge-C!

Everyone rose early the next morning to watch the armada depart for the city and the big battle. The soldiers' spirits were high. The sounds of weapons being checked and rechecked echoed all around them. Repeatedly, they heard voices calling out, "We're ready to rock!" Some said, "We're ready to roll!"

Matt explained what little he knew about Virge-C's army. "There are twelve active army divisions, four are armored, but they are stationed at barracks all around our world, at strategic locations. Only one has their barracks north of West Port. So President Johnson must have had to ship some of these in from half-way around the world. Good idea making a coordinated attack, probably from all sides of West Port. The alien corporations are about to meet their match. It's about time too."

"Are we going to be safe here?" Adonia asked, watching the men eagerly marching out, heading towards the city's edge some two miles distant.

Luisa asked that same question around the same time. From atop their skyscraper, one of the taller ones in downtown West Port, she could see men and strange vehicles slowly moving towards the city, more like ants though, but they seemed to be coming from many directions.

Diego answered, "My dear, perfectly safe. I have a squad of men on the nuclear power plant near the northern edge of the city. They will guarantee we've sufficient power for the grid. Atop five key skyscrapers, we have the generators for the portable defense shields working perfectly. The force field dome covers the entire city. I have the small delta wing fighters ready to takeoff from the spaceport. We have ten thousand security guards with their PDS and d-guns ready to repel any invaders. So yes, while it looks bad, some hundred twenty thousand of their soldiers to our ten thousand, it's going to be a simple mop-up operation for us."

He chatted on, "And after today, this foolish president of theirs will be calling me, suing for peace on my terms. With even a tiny bit of luck, my dear, by tomorrow, we will begin Phase III of our takeover of Virge-C by the Federation corporations. Nothing can go wrong. I've seen to every possibility."

"Yes, but what happened to Fernando, dear? Have you found who stole him from the nurses? Won't you have to replace him? However, I can't see why anyone would really want him. I mean he looks like one of us, a UFB woman, certainly not a man," she chatted and asked what was bothering her. Just why these teachers and nurses capitulated to Diego's demands when he offered Fernando to them was beyond her grasp.

Diego growled, "No and yes and don't bother me now.

I've a war to win."

Outside the city, one hundred twenty thousand soldiers enthusiastically charged towards the city, confident of an easy victory. After all, they were told that there were only around ten thousand alien security guards. The odds were surely well stacked in their favor: 12:1. Besides, they had their armored vehicles and nearly a hundred battle tanks with their six-inch armor. Glorious victory was soon to be theirs!

The President and the generals watched the assault via live video feeds. Naturally, they were well removed from the battlefield. They watched as the lead columns reached the city. Their confidence dropped as though a bomb had fallen on them. The lead vehicles smashed into some kind of invisible force field. The vehicle's momentum crushed in their front ends. Those trailing vehicles rammed into the rear ends, causing more damage. Soon, from the pileups, they could see that this force field surrounded the city! No vehicle could pass through it!

From the spaceport, a number of small delta wing fighters took flight. Defensive planes engaged the alien delta wings. The aerial battle lasted a few minutes, before the defensive planes were shot down. After that, the alien delta wings began shooting their laser cannons at the tanks that had not yet piled into those in front of them. In short order, the hundred battle tanks were disabled, one way or another.

However, platoons of soldiers on foot soon discovered that they could pass through the force field, but only if they moved very, very slowly through it. As they did so, the defenders chose to fire their d-guns, killing the soldiers who were attempting to penetrate the force field. Sheer numbers favored the attackers this time. Yet, those who managed to safely pass through the barrier, quickly found themselves causing no damage to the aliens, who wore their PDS, while the alien d-guns quickly found their marks, for nothing could stop the beams from these alien weapons.

What was supposed to be an easy victory soon turned into a fiasco. With little other options, the generals ordered a pullback to their previous positions, some two miles from the city. High-level discussions frantically sought alternatives.

Even the last resort of dropping bombs on the city was out because of the force field.

Later that evening, President Johnson placed a secure call to his old friend, Marshal Tucker of Aerostar Engines. Marshal and his company men were still inside West Port, hold up and waiting for their forces to retake the city from the aliens. By noon, he knew that wasn't going to happen. He wasn't surprised when the President called. "Marshal, it's over. We're defeated. We can't get our planes in there; we can't even bomb them. Our men can't seem to harm the enemy who are wearing those personal defense shields you warned us about, and their damned weapons are incredibly deadly. I just don't know what to do. Do you have any idea how to shut down that invisible force field surrounding the city?"

"None at all. I've not been able to ascertain much about it, except that five portable generators are putting it up," Marshal replied. He hesitated and said, "There is one last resort. We talked about it once."

"You mean unleashing chemical weapons on them?" President Johnson asked, recalling their long conversations five weeks ago. "We haven't got any way to get them into the city, let alone inside the corporation buildings. Besides, I don't want to be known as the president who used poison gas on some of our own people, killing them, even if they are collateral damage."

Marshal chuckled. "I already worked that one out myself months ago, John. I know you'd never authorize the use of chemical weapons. So I took the liberty of coming up with an alternative. As you know, these aliens have a genetic bio agent they use to make their UFB women."

"Right. Those poor, helpless women. Yes, I've seen some of them. I feel sorry for them, but what's that got to do with the situation," he replied.

"I have a goodly supply of that very bio agent of theirs. I still have undercover men working in the various corporation buildings. It might be possible to unleash their own genetic bio agent on them. Of course, there will always be some of our people in those buildings, but at least they won't be killed by the agent," Marshal replied.

"Why you old fox! That's brilliant! Incredible foresight! Yes, by all means, I authorize its use, but can you actually pull that off?" President Johnson replied, his apathy rapidly evaporating. Here might be a way around it all.

"Let me work on it. I'll let you know how it is proceeding. Got one major problem to solve, but I think I know who might have the answer I need. Talk to you later," Marshal replied and hung up. He smiled deviously and placed another secure call.

"Hi Sondra. I need to speak with you where no one else can overhear us. Can you have Matt take care of this for us?" Marshal asked and waited for his daughter to comply, knowing that this was going to be physically difficult for her, but secrecy was paramount if he had any chance of success in this, the last possible way to avoid the alien takeover of their world.

"Okay, I'm alone. The phone is on the table. Can you understand me?" Sondra finally answered.

"Not very well. Can you say that again, dear? I'm sorry. I will have to spend time with you later and see if I can get better at figuring out what you're saying. If this doesn't work, then I'll have to trust Matt to translate for you," he replied with a very heavy heart. Still, if this worked, he'd have gotten even with the aliens for what they had done to his daughters.

"I'm having Matt translate, dad. Sure sounds strange saying that, after all these years thinking I was an orphan," she replied, and Matt translated for her.

"Thanks. What I need to know is if you know of any way that we can get some backpacks into the basements of these corporate skyscrapers." Marshal listed off a dozen, the major ones.

"The sewer systems connect to all the buildings," she began a lengthy explanation. She described how they'd gotten into some. "If you can hack into the city planning computer systems, you can bring up the entire sewer system." She gave him the names of the key documents. "If you can't get in there, let me know. I can hack from here, but I don't know how I can get those to you."

"Hang on a minute. I know little about computers. Let me bring a friend of mine in on this. You can tell him what to do," Marshal suggested. A half hour later, they hung up, mission accomplished. Marshal had his missing factor, and he busily began organizing Project Flower, as he called his secret mission, hoping it wasn't going to be a one-way mission for himself or for his agents. Still, he knew that everything depended upon somehow pulling this one off.

His engineering staff that still remained and had not evacuated some weeks ago worked on making the delivery packages, while he contacted his secret agents or those he could trust and who worked as janitors in the many skyscrapers. The aliens themselves long ago had hired local men and women to handle such mundane needs. Hence, each of their many headquarters buildings had hired a varying number of janitors whose job was to clean up the building, usually beginning around six at night. They took out the trash and vacuumed the offices and halls, though a few handled light dusting duties.

Janitorial supplies and closets were uniformly located in the basements, far from normal traffic. Each person had long ago been screened before being hired and given an ID card that allowed them into the buildings and past security, though none ever came in before six p.m. Years ago when that round of hiring began, Marshal had wisely inserted some of his own people or their wives into the work crews. Now, everything depended upon them and their loyalty to Virge-C.

Each skyscraper had a giant ventilation system, with an air intake line in the basement. These provided the necessary circulation for the building, which also included heating in the winter and air conditioning in the summer. Each month the many air filters had to be changed, again relegated to the janitors. Thus, he had the route for his attack ready. What he didn't have was any way to get the *packages* delivered inside these basements, though once there, the janitors could install them.

Thus, he needed Sondra's critical information. He smiled after the call. *My daughter is as clever as I am. Chip off the old block.* He chuckled with that thought. With his computer expert preparing precise directions for his underground couriers, he set to work making contact with his janitor agents, knowing that some may well not get out in time. One such person was Martha Wellington.

Martha took the lucrative janitor job in part to help support her four children. Her husband had been killed in an industrial accident some years back leaving her to raise their large family. Making ends meet was difficult; the death benefit settlement simply didn't cover her expenses. Hence, Marshal had helped get her this janitor job at Galactic Dynamics. "Martha, is this a good time for a serious chat?"

"Yes, Mr. Tucker. What is going on? Is our army defeated?" she inquired. Rumors to that effect had swept through West Port that afternoon, fueled by their apparent retreat. Many felt very let down, while others who supported the aliens cheered.

"Not yet. I have a vital mission for you, one that may help save Virge-C from the alien takeover. I can't tell you there isn't any danger to you. However, you have my sworn word, Martha, if anything happens to you, your children will be well provided for, including their college expenses." He knew that detail was uppermost in her mind. An education was critical to getting a well-paying job. "Do you know where the building's air intake lines are located in the basement?"

Thus, an hour passed while he lined up his secret agents. Meanwhile, his engineers got the many cylinders ready for use. Their biggest decision was on how to activate them. They could rig up a remote control detonator, but distance and building shielding presented too many problems. There was no time to test potential solutions. Instead, following Marshal's orders, they rigged them to be manually operated, though they inserted a timer device anyway, just in case.

*** 

"May I have a day to consider?" President Johnson replied. Diego called him after supper and had given the president his terms for the surrender of Virge-C.

"You will step down as president. From now on, the world will be ruled by the corporations, just as are all other Federation worlds," Diego explained. He rattled off a number of other requirements, including the dismantling of the armed forces, which he pointed out were entirely obsolete. The soldiers could apply for security guard positions with the many corporations. On it went, a rather extensive list of terms.

"Yes, of course you can take as long as you desire, ex-President Johnson," Diego sneered.

"I will need a few days to bring this to the legislature. As you know, our governing establishment is in West Brighton, five hundred miles north of here. It will take some time to work out all these arrangements," President Johnson stalled. Whether Marshal would be successful, he still had one final step he could take, though he dared not make that decision without consulting the legislature representatives. West Port could be sacrificed. It could be nuked. He highly doubted that their defense shields could withstand such a blast, though the damage would be horrific. Thus, he also ordered the go ahead preparations on that action, though he would not plead his case to the representatives until Marshal's plan failed.

Marshal only had sufficient cylinders to handle ten skyscrapers, based on rough estimates of the dosage that had been sent along with his purchase. He'd gotten the supply by persuading the supplier that the locals on Virge-C now wanted to emulate their alien corporate leaders and turn their wives into these incredibly beautiful women. Thus, he targeted the ten most powerful of the corporations, hoping the others would capitulate later on. If not, well, he'd rather not think of that just now.

He'd lost too many men during the recent Snake Town actions. He had two engineers and seven other men left. He knew from the start that he would have to enter the sewers and deliver one of the packages himself. There wasn't any other choice left to him. It was risky, but then he'd been at risk for many years, ever since Galactic Dynamics made their first buyout offer, which he'd refused, just as he had their many subsequent offers.

Thus, his other nine faithful men were not the least surprised when he stated he would deliver a package to Galactic Dynamics headquarters. Some grinned when they heard. Still, this was a very serious game, one that they knew must be won. They'd watched their world's powerful armed forces get soundly defeated. Either this succeeded or their world would become a slave world run by these alien corporations. These men would rather die than let that happen.

Marshal hadn't thought much about his dying for the last five years, not since his second wife passed away. Now, however, he had three surviving daughters to consider, and thus he had given his death considerable thought, particularly these past few weeks and had made his arrangements. What more could one do than be prepared? He didn't know, only that he didn't expect to be returning from this last mission.

He looked over his small, remaining group. Marshal didn't give them a pep talk. None was needed. Each knew this was the last possible way to save their world from the aliens and their takeover plans. Well, Marshal also knew that if they failed, President Johnson would have no alternative but to drop a nuclear bomb on West Port. Ten million Virge-C men, women, and children would be sacrificed in order to remove these alien corporations. He loved his city and its people too much to want to see that happen, though those who had already jumped ship probably deserved being atomized. Still, those were in the minority. No, this sneak attack just had to succeed.

"Everyone got their portable cutting torches?" he asked. Several "check's" echoed around the deserted lab at Aerostar Engines. "Timers set for midnight. On my mark." Again, nine others confirmed the setting. "Okay. Into the sewers. We simply must not fail. President Johnson and our world are counting on us."

"You got it boss. We will take them down," his senior engineer declared determinedly. Others nodded. Then, they headed down to the basement parking lot. Shortly, ten cars zipped off into the early evening darkness, headed for ten strategic locations, as near as they dared get to their targeted buildings.

Getting into the sewers was too easy. Pull up a manhole cover and climb down the steps. As Marshal turned on his hat light, he imagined President Johnson's commandos slipping into the waters of the Boca River. They'd determined that the alien force field did not go below the water's surface. Under the cover of darkness, a large number of soldiers were planning to slip into the river above and below the city, swim underwater bypassing the force field, and then enter the city proper. Their task was simple: find any way to eliminate the hundred or so security guards watching the edges of the city in case of a nighttime attack.

Marshal's nose soon deadened to the awful stench of the sewers. He waded along, pausing at each junction to verify his route on his map sketch. He found it slow going, primarily because the tunnels were pitch black with only his small hat light providing the illumination. Block by block, Marshal moved ever closer to the GD skyscraper. Would Martha be there waiting for him? He felt confident that he could find the air intake system if she wasn't. On he moved, imagining for a moment his other nine followers were trudging along as well. *Will this work? It has to. It simply has to.*

At last, he reached the side tunnel that led to the GD skyscraper. Ahead, he spotted the entrance grate above him. All the city's major buildings had a large sewer grate in their basement floors. Why? In case of flooding or a fire, water would have a place to go. In centuries past, fires could and did happen. The water used to extinguish them always made a huge mess. The basement sewer grates solved this. Sometimes the Boca River flooded. If a basement took on water, then when the levels receded, the water would flow down the grates, avoiding the slow and costly pumping process formerly used. This solution now gave him an easy entrance into GD headquarters.

But was the grate sealed into position? Did he have to cut his way through it or not? Up he climbed. At last, he reached the grate and pushed upwards. It gave, and he relaxed for the first time this evening, though he didn't know that Sondra had left it unlocked when she and Matt had entered GD this same way. He checked his watch. A half hour to go. Now all he could do was wait for Martha's appearance. Soon, he heard voices, the janitors returning their work carts to the basement. Good. He waited.

Martha's head appeared over the grate. "Anyone down there?" she whispered tentatively.

"It's me. All clear?" Marshal answered back, keeping his voice down.

"Sort of. They have a guard watching us tonight. I will delay a bit so I can show you the air intake system." Martha moved away and began adjusting the items on her pushcart, while one by one the other janitors finished up and headed out. Meanwhile, as quietly as he could, Marshal moved the grate up and to the side. He climbed on out and found himself in the basement. The low hum of machinery broke the stillness of the evening. The sewers had been utterly quiet.

Martha led him over to one side door. "Through there. It's well marked."

"Good. Now you get out of here," Marshal whispered back.

She nodded, whispering, "Be careful. They are on some kind of high alert tonight." She turned and left him, as he opened the door and entered, the noise of the machinery growing distinctly louder. He turned on the lights and spotted the mammoth air intake lines with their numerous filters. Quickly, he sat down his backpack and set to work, removing some filters, exposing the intake sheet metal housing.

Verifying the timer was active and working, he placed the special package of cylinders into the housing and replaced the filters. Checking his watch, five minutes remained for him to make his escape. He killed the light and carefully opened the door. Seeing no one around, he headed out and back towards the grate. *This is too easy.*

He got himself down and onto the ladder and began pulling the grate back into place. Unfortunately, the security guard chose that time to make his final inspection for the night. "You there. What do you think you are doing? Hold it right there," the guard barked.

Marshal froze, but his right hand was beneath the floor and he slowly drew his 9mm gun, while the guard walked up to him. "Just what do you think you are doing? Come out of there now." Marshal stared into the barrel of one of their d-guns.

He pretended to pull himself up a bit, just enough to get his gun above the floor. Bang! He fired, hoping against all odds that the guard wasn't wearing one of their protective shields.

He had no idea that such things could not be easily worn while inside buildings, that banging into chairs, furniture, and doors prevented their use inside.

The security guard was also well trained. The instant he spotted the gun, he too fired. Marshal's shot hit the guard close to his heart. The man slumped and died in seconds. However, Marshal felt a terrific pain in his forehead, and then a total blackness swept over his consciousness. He seemed to be floating above the floor. Vaguely, he saw his dead body partially slumped over on the floor, its lower half down the sewer hole. More importantly, he heard the telltale tiny explosion that triggered the release of the toxic genetic bio agent of the aliens. No longer could he hear well, but he found himself sort of floating through the walls and into the machinery room. A yellow gas was seeping rapidly out of the cylinders. His last thought was: *It is working*. Blackness came again. Somehow, he found himself in a hospital, along with several women in the maternity ward.

Huddled in the basement with their cars, the nine surviving members of Marshal's band waited until two in the morning before they accepted the fact that Marshal must have been caught or killed. At last, Herman, the lead engineer took control. "Okay, Ben, make a drive by of GD headquarters. See if the guards are knocked out there. "Pete you check the others. Report back whatever you see. We have to let the President know whether this is working. Already, commandos are probably inside the city awaiting orders."

A half hour later, Ben reported, "Herman, the guards just inside the main entrance are lying on the floor, as if they just collapsed. I think Marshal must have done it. Should I check further?"

"Yes, we must be sure they are really out. See if you can get their attention, but be damned careful, Ben," Herman replied, nervously. Had this worked? He could only hope that it had. Nervously, he paced the concrete of the basement, waiting for Ben's callback.

"Yes, it must be working, Herman! I can't get anyone's attention. The guards are really out. Heading back now," Ben reported in. Finally, Herman breathed a sigh of relief. It had worked. Marshal's revenge was complete. He dug out the phone and made the secure call to President Johnson.

An hour later, sporadic gunfire echoed around the perimeter of West Port. Then, the gunfire died down. The few night guards were eliminated. Sondra and her friends were awakened by the noise of the soldiers once more moving out, but it was in the middle of the night. They went back to sleep, while thousands of soldiers moved very slowly through the force field, this time meeting no resistance from the aliens in their PDS and d-guns. Even more interesting, nearly a hundred of these weapons had been confiscated from the captured guards.

Dawn brought an entirely new situation, particularly for those lesser corporation leaders, who found tens of thousands of Virge-C soldiers deployed at all major intersections of the city! President Johnson delivered a personal message via the news channels at eight in the morning.

"Citizens of West Port, alien corporation leaders, as of this morning, we have retaken control of our capital city. During the night, Special Forces raided ten of the larger alien corporation headquarters and unleashed their own genetic bio agent on them. Yes, everyone in those buildings, including Galactic Dynamics headquarters are now in comas and, if I understand this alien bio agent properly, they will revive in four days as alien UFB women, completely helpless, which is the way that these prefer their wives. Our armed forces are now in control of West Port."

"To the alien corporations which are still intact, I'm ready to meet with you to discuss our future terms. We don't want to destroy you nor do we wish to abandon our position in the Galactic Federation. However, we don't want your corporations taking over our world by extortion, blackmail, and force. We are a free people and will remain so. Have your new representative contact me at this number as soon as possible."

"I can't believe this is happening," Sondra gushed at breakfast. Everyone was listening to the news, though now the noise of the soldiers moving out so early in the morning made sense. "They unleashed that bio agent thing into ten of the biggest corporations. Do they realize that there's going to be thousands of helpless victims? What are they going to do with all them?

"Serves them right, lassie," Tom declared. "They wanta do it ta all you. Now they gatta live like they made ya all haveta live. Serves them right."

"Well, that Diego fellow isn't going to be calling the shots any longer," Matt declared.

"But how will they get all the needed shoes and clothes and lip disks that they're going to need? Don't those in the coma need medical care while all this happens to their bodies?" asked Rene.

"Yes, they do. The doctors hook them up to machines and things," Adonia answered. "But I don't know what all that does though, only that they do."

They talked a bit more, but Fernando was uncommonly silent. "So what do you think, Fernando?" Sondra asked him, noticing his pale face and that he hadn't said a word. "There should be many men they can use to take your place with the teachers and nurses."

"We have to leave here," Fernando said, remembering to speak slowly so they could understand him somewhat. Even his distorted voice sounded fearful.

"Why? Our soldiers have the city secure. Now they can work out new agreements with the aliens," Sondra replied. "Surely the corporations will realize they can't come here and just force their ways upon us, turning our world into their slave world."

"That's not the corporations' way," Fernando said slowly and softly.

Sondra began to worry. "So you think they will retaliate against us?"

"Yes. They could destroy the whole world with bombs. They don't need your people. Many Federation worlds are overpopulated. Many would love to come, colonize, and settle this world, once your people are gone. This is really bad. We have to leave soon," Fernando attempted to put his fears into terms they could understand. He knew the anger that his people would express when they learned of this attack, which, he presumed, had already happened! It was only a matter of time before the devastating counterattack came.

***

That afternoon, President Johnson received a call from Rodrigo, the CEO of the rather small Universal Mining Corporation. "President Johnson, your people have committed an unthinkable act against the Federation Corporations."

"Yes, that's true, but your corporations have committed unethical, illegal, and immoral actions against our people and companies, so I believe that is the black cat calling the black pot black. Now then, are you aliens ready to conduct yourselves in an ethical, honest manner? Virge-C does wish to remain a valuable member of the Galactic Federation, but we will not become a slave world to your unethical corporations. We should strive to work together in harmony," President Johnson replied.

"And just what is it that you are proposing to do now?" Rodrigo replied, mostly ignoring what the man said. In the end, it was irrelevant. He'd already contacted the home world's corporation leaders.

"Considering the many underhanded, illegal deals that Diego and others made, all corporations that they took over now revert back to their original Virge-C owners. Consider it recompense for their crimes against our people. We shall begin again to make equitable and fair business deals. However, considering how many of your people have been infected with your own genetic agent thing, I'm prepared to offer the assistance of our many hospitals until they have recovered from their mutation comas."

"Agreed. I'm told that by tomorrow the bio agent will have been dispersed enough for us to enter the buildings. After we see the extent of the damage, I will contact you. I suggest that we meet face to face in say a week to iron out the details," Rodrigo replied, buying needed time for home world to prepare. President Johnson agreed, and they discussed a few minor matters. Some ten thousand soldiers would remain to provide city security.

# Chapter 16—Newton's Law

Rodrigo had the tally numbers at hand. He'd organized the surviving approximately five thousand into recovery and counting parties and sent them into the ten skyscrapers. Now, he placed his desperate call. "Yes, that's right. Nine thousand nine hundred six security guards are becoming UFBMD. Twenty-five thousand six hundred ten corporation workers and executives are becoming UFB and UFBMD. How are we to handle this number? We can't handle this incredible volume of helpless individuals, let alone provide them with clothing and shoes. Yes, the disk plate version was used. Hell, they won't even be able to talk understandably when they come out of their comas. I need instructions, sir."

Mario de la Vega laughed. "My pitiful brother certainly botched this simple assignment. Well, cull the top three tiers of executives out of there. See that they and their families are being looked after. Leonardo can expect a shipment soon, hopefully in time. Cull out another hundred of the new UFBMD men, and we'll disperse them among other corporations who want a male donor. The rest, simply eliminate them. Cremation is your best bet unless there is a way to make a mass burial somewhere. Transports will arrive in three days to take the UFB and UFBMD off Virge-C. Surely, your people can handle several hundred of them for a couple of days."

"Understood. Yes, a couple hundred we can handle," Rodrigo replied, and the call ended.

"So what form should our retaliation against this upstart Virge-C take, eh?" Mario asked the assembled group of other CEOs, whose branch offices on Virge-C had been attacked and wiped out. They were in Galactic Dynamics headquarters on 9-Gamma-C in the mid-arm region of the galaxy. "This is the first time our own special bio agent has been used against us as a weapon of mass destruction."

"Could we simply nuke them?" one asked angrily.

"And make this mineral rich world radioactive for a

century? Hardly," Mario replied.

"The question really is," put in the head of Galactic Electronics, "do we want or need the people? Its population is two billion but they've only recently become a space faring world. Do we need their people or not? If we don't, we could simply drop enough chemical nerve agents on them and eliminate them all."

"Their technology is crude by our standards. Darn near every manufacturing plant is going to have to be completely modernized. Does that figure into our response," another asked.

Ramiro of General Robotics spoke up. "You know, in ancient times, whole planets were subjected to similar genetic bio agents. Robot servants were created for each and the world was somewhat productive after that, or so our history texts say. We could experiment with that approach again. It would give my corporation something more interesting to develop than manufacturing robots."

"Interesting point, Ramiro," Mario stated, amused by the idea, "but is GE ready to go with such robots? I think not. However, your idea has merit in some ways. Look, we need to keep this rebellious population under strict control. Suppose that we converted all the men on Virge-C into helpless UFBMD men. That would totally handle all possibility of any form of rebellion. Their wives and women would have to take care of them, while our resettlement program goes into full swing."

"Interesting revenge, Mario, but think this through. If we go that route, then their male children will all become super geniuses, while their female children will become UFB women. In one generation, the UFB women will replace the normal women, while the geniuses will replace the helpless UFBMD men," Ramiro pointed out the flaw.

"Point, regrettably taken," Mario replied. "Well, what about turning their women into UFB women? That would become a self-perpetuating environment. The men would of necessity be forced to spend a great deal of their time caring for their helpless women."

Ramiro nodded and said, "Except that they have a large

army right now. If we start in on that project, of necessity going door to door to find all their females, surely their army will launch a counterstrike. We're going to need to eliminate their soldiers before we dare implement the UFB woman program. Besides, we will need an enormous quantity of clothing, shoes, and lip disks to handle those kinds of numbers."

"We could hit them with a conventional attack first, eliminating their armed forces," Mario suggested. "We could then bring in an expensive Fabrication Ship to make the needed supplies until local factories can be constructed and brought online."

"Except for one detail, boss" Adriana, Mario's secretary spoke up. She knew Mario hated to be interrupted, especially by a woman. Still, she felt the need to point this detail out to these men before they acted.

Mario glared at his secretary. If she wasn't so attractive, he thought, before nodding to her to continue. She explained, "Look at this from their point of view. They attempted to use their armed forces to takeover West Point, their capital city, from us. When that failed dismally, they took other measures. I believe they feel they are in a box with few ways out. They would have to be of that mind set to have destroyed the lives of forty thousand men, women, and children of ours. While we can easily eliminate their armed forces in a few surgical strikes, they may well resort to even more extreme measures. As we all know, they possess nuclear weapons. I believe that if you push them down too hard, they will feel they have no recourse left except to use those nuclear weapons, even if it means enormous damage to their world."

Mario sighed. *Damn, she again does have a valid point.* "Yes, she's probably right. If we hit them too hard, they could well retaliate with nuclear strikes. Still, I like the UFB woman program. With all females on Virge-C turned into UFB women and all future female children also being UFB women, then that will set a very clear example for many other worlds who might be considering rebelling against corporate rule. So the question remains, how do we best implement this?"

Adriana stuck her neck out one more time. "Look, if you

go ahead with this UFB woman program, that may well trigger their ultimate response, a nuclear attack on us. While you are not talking genocide of a people, you are genetically destroying two billion people of Virge-C. Don't you think they will react badly to this? We certainly would." There, she'd done her best to defuse the situation or at least get them to rethink their retaliation.

"She has a point, Mario," Ramiro spoke up. "Look, we don't know the number or the location of their nuclear bombs. Local defense shields can't stand against nuclear attacks, only the giant planetary defense shields can. We could well lose even more of our people."

"Well, there is another approach we can use," the Galactic Electronics CEO suggested. "We hit their world with a giant EM pulse that knocks out all their electronics. That way, they can't use their nuclear bombs. Then, we systematically destroy their armed forces. Hell, turn them into UFBMD or just kill them."

"Or any other means of communications, such as their TVs and radios," put in Ramiro. "So how do we deal with them after that permanent blackout occurs?"

"We go door to door implementing our program. They will be unable to mount any kind of defense after that," Mario theorized. "Look, we must deal this upstart of a world a severe lesson or we will soon have other Scorpi-C rebellions on our hands."

Just then, Ramiro received a secure call on his cell phone. "Excuse me, I have to take this. Back momentarily." He rose hastily and left the room. "Okay, go ahead, boss." He was speaking to his sector GE CEO and immediate boss.

"This situation on Virge-C has come to our attention. What are they planning to do about it?" the man said calmly.

"Well, we're just deciding that now. The overall putdown plan is to turn all their females into UFB women. That will make their men have to take care of them and keep them out of our hair," Ramiro replied, relating their thinking so far.

"Have you mentioned the possibility of using robots?"

"Yes, but they know nothing of our advanced research

and development. I didn't tell them about that, if you are worried about that aspect," Ramiro replied.

"Good, good. We've been having a good deal of unrest on many Federation worlds. As you know, we have lost complete control over the entire Abelard Sector. Two neighboring sectors are in open rebellion now. Until Virge-C, this has been contained to relatively distant rim worlds, but now, it is striking in our backyard, the mid-arm. I've been looking at the population numbers, Ramiro. Two billion. With roughly four members per household, that amounts to around five hundred million robot assistants, along with five hundred humanitarian aid machines."

He continued, "Every one of our initial tests has proven the efficacy of our new designs and machines. We already have around five hundred thousand of these units in storage. I believe that is sufficient to cover everyone in their capital city, West Port isn't it?"

"Yes, West Port. Population is around down to around two million. Many have fled the fighting. What are you suggesting?" Ramiro asked.

"A full-scale test on a planet, but done in stages that we can manage. I would like you to make a presentation to the other CEOs and test the waters for this idea. I've not approached GD about it here, and I won't until I get positive feedback from your fellow CEOs there. Perhaps, Virge-C isn't the right planet to attempt to convert for one reason or another, so I'm leaving that decision in your hands. Keep me posted. If you give the go ahead, supplies can be there in a week for full scale implementation in this West Port."

With a wry smile, Ramiro rejoined the others. "Excuse my absence, but I've just received some rather amazing news from my boss, news that I'm allowed to share with you. There is another way we can go about this. You see, for quite some time, General Robotics has been developing a human-assistant robot, one that can dress, undress, cook, clean, and perform other menial tasks for an entire family composed only of UFB women and UFBMD men. In addition, some other mechanical devices, such as the electrostatic hair machine are also prepared. All have passed their initial field tests."

"General Robotics has enough of these on hand to handle everyone in West Port. In short order, we could turn the entire population of Virge-C into UFB women and UFBMD men. With these robots and humanitarian aid machines, these people would be able to survive, and we would not be committing genocide, just subduing the entire planet. What do you think of this proposal?"

"And what would we do with a planet filled with helpless, dependent people, unable to perform any kind of work, while consuming food and other necessities of life that others would have to provide?" asked Adriana, more than a little annoyed at this hideous suggestion, which amounted to genocide anyway. "You want our people to work to support two billion plus helpless, worthless people? That's not going to fly well at all."

Mario joined her in protesting Ramiro's notion. "She's got a point. Look, already we are facing serious protests from our average corporate worker. If we thrust the survival of two billion upon them, they will definitely rebel, and we'll have an even bigger mess on our hands. No, that's not going to fly at all. However," he said slyly, "they don't know that! How about this idea. Ramiro claims to have enough of these new robots to handle West Port. How about wiping out their army and communications first and then convert all of West Port into helpless people. Then, we go before this upstart President Johnson and tell him that unless they stop all resistance to our corporations and begin cooperating with us, we will do it to the rest of the planet. Meantime, have him come and remove the two million, resettling them elsewhere on the planet, giving us an entire city with its infrastructure intact for our resettlement project to utilize. We can bring in two million from one of our overpopulated planets."

"Hey, this is a good idea. The local force field will keep the genetic bio agent contained within the city so we can control who gets genetically modified," suggested another CEO, thinking ahead to how it could be implemented on such a large scale.

"Say, if we are clever about this, we won't need to destroy their communications systems either, and I dare say they won't be tempted to use their nuclear weapons either," Mario suddenly had a bright idea. He outlined his new plan, and it was completely accepted by all the CEOs. Ramiro then placed a secure call to his boss to inform him to send everything as soon as possible.

***

A terrified Diego awoke from his coma. Screaming in protest, he passed out numerous times until the worker finally got him to calm down some by telling him his wife was waiting for him. Like the others before him, he couldn't breathe, barely walk, and his lips throbbed. Petrified, he was taken to his wife. Someone informed him, "You are being sent back to home world, where you can spend your life in your home there." Aides helped him get out of the building, into the shuttle, and later into the deep space transport. All he could do was continuously sob. No one other than his wife and Juan's wife, Juanita, could understand a word that he said. Of course, Luisa, Juanita, and their female children were unharmed by the attack, but they too were terrified of the future. Unfortunately, their sons were now also modified and just as frightened as Diego and Juan. On the fifth day after the attack, many deep space transports departed Virge-C, carrying several hundred of the survivors. The remainder, Diego was told, were slain and buried in a giant grave south of the city.

On the sixth day, the remaining aliens also departed West Port, again loading up on several light cruisers. However, they only parked in high orbit and didn't leave the system. Shortly after the last of them left, fifty cruisers and heavy cruisers dropped out of hyperspace above Virge-C and swooped down on the unsuspecting world. The newscasts carried the story of the day: the evacuation of the aliens. Around the world, thousands cheered this welcome news, none more so than President Johnson, who believed he'd won a major war, a major victory. That was soon to be short-lived.

Even Sondra and friends cheered the news of the departure of the last of the aliens and their corporations. "See Fernando, they have all left West Port," Sondra told him.

"Left, yes, but not gone, Sondra. Now comes the retaliation. We must leave here," Fernando declared, but

260

remembered to speak slowly. He detested having to repeat everything several times, which he did when he forgot to speak slowly.

"What do you mean, Fernando?" she countered. "They have left, every last one of them."

"I see his point," Matt spoke up on Fernando's behalf. "Look, if I was the aliens and I wanted to extract revenge, I'd make sure my surviving people were evacuated before I attacked full force. I wouldn't want to undergo another bio agent attack or worse."

"You really think they will attack us now?" Sondra asked, a knot growing in her stomach. She knew that both men were right.

Fernando nodded and Matt said, "Let's keep an eye on the news."

Later that afternoon, news coverage of the jubilation of victory changed entirely. "Alien cruisers and heavy cruisers have begun bombing our armed forces," the newscaster reported. That was obvious to the group. The noise of bombs going off not too far from their farmhouse was deafening, shocking, and scary. Secondary explosions also added to the cacophony of chaos. The aliens struck back.

After an hour, the noise subsided, replaced by emergency sirens from rescue vehicles, but the group sat glued to the newscasts. When Ben and Adonia headed off to the kitchen to fix supper, it was obvious that all dozen of Virge-C's army divisions had been struck a lethal blow, destroying most all their vehicles and many personnel.

"But there's no aliens around to counterattack," Sondra pointed out the obvious. "What's going to happen now? Are they just abandoning us?"

"Hardly," Fernando again decided to speak his mind. "They are just getting started. We have to leave here." Just how, he had no idea. He couldn't walk far, but everyone knew he meant this world.

Over supper, Sondra asked, "Fernando, what will the aliens do to us next? After all, they have left our world."

"Have they? No, they have their people out of West Port so your President Johnson hasn't got any targets to attack," he pointed out.

"So what do you think will happen next?" Sondra asked in exasperation. Getting Fernando to speak his mind was difficult at best.

"This was child's play for us," he replied. "What is coming next will be really bad. We should leave here soon. Get away while we can."

"Like what? Drop a bunch of nuclear bombs on us, wiping everyone out?" Matt broke in on the conversation. Several others choked, momentarily shocked by such a thought.

Fernando sighed. For better or worse, he was stuck here with these people. "I rather expected they would have drop them already, but then I remembered this world is rich in valuable minerals. They certainly don't want to make this valuable world radioactive for the next hundred years or so. No, what they do next will be something equally terrible. You don't know the corporations as I do. They can't tolerate worlds rebelling against their total control. Mark my words; they will be taking extreme measures now that your pathetic army is gone."

"He might be right," Matt spoke up. "Their invisible force field over West Port is still up and as effective as ever, even though they have left. That can't be a good sign."

A loud roar steadily grew, as though something huge was drawing closer, sending a wave of fear through most of the group. They'd finished eating and were just spooning their coffee when this noise startled them. "What's that? Another attack?" exclaimed Rene, nearly choking on her coffee.

"Wait!" yelled Beth. "That sounds like a deep space transport landing! I'd know that sound anywhere now. Come on, everyone! It must be landing outside somewhere close to us."

"Do we want to know who is landing, though," Matt cautioned.

"Well, we certainly can't run away if it is trouble," Sondra exclaimed, carefully getting to her feet or toes rather.

"It's got to be just outside!" Beth said, getting to the door just as someone knocked on it. "I got it," she added and opened the door. She had no idea who this could be, but she wanted to see the ship, if possible. She was startled to see a middle-aged man in a black business suit and tie, carrying a small leather briefcase. "Oh, hello," she said somewhat startled by his unexpected appearance.

"Excuse me, but I'm told that Misses Sondra, Alice, and Roxane are living here. Is this correct?" he asked politely and conservatively.

"Yes, of course. I'm Beth. Come on in please," she replied. As she turned around, she saw the others making their slow way to the front door.

Roxane spoke up, "I'm Roxane. This is Alice and she's Sondra, though you probably can't understand her speech. The lip disks."

"Yes, of course. I am Mr. Able St. Johns, legal attorney for the late Mr. Marshal Tucker. Is there some place where we can sit down?" he replied softly.

He was seated at the dining room table before Sondra, Rene, and Adonia even got reseated, though he took no notice of this. Purposely, Matt ushered the three women into positions across from the man. He noticed the pangs of grief from all three, the late Mr. Tucker. Had their father been killed?

Able began, "I am sorry to bring such bad news to you, but then this has been a bad day all around. What with the bombing and such, I wasn't able to get here any sooner. Your father, Marshal Tucker, was found dead, partially in the basement sewer connecting line of Galactic Dynamics headquarters when the aliens began removing their people. He suffered a d-gun shot to his head. At this point, I'm the executor of his last will and testament. He left Aerostar Engines to his nephew, but he had made a special bequeath to his three daughters, namely Sondra, Alice, and Roxane."

"First, he has left the newly purchased Bright Star deep space commercial transport to you three women. Per his instructions, it is now parked just outside this house. Perhaps you heard it descending from the brief flight from the spaceport?" They nodded, but were shocked to hear of this incredible gift.

He continued. "In addition, it has been well stocked for a long flight and is ready for takeoff, his words. Mr. Tucker has provided each of you women with an official Federation bank account and has deposited ten million gold dollars into each account. Finally, he has entrusted me with a sealed envelope to be given directly to you three in the event of his death. I am now handing you that envelope, along with the access codes to the Bright Star. Do you have any questions of me?"

Three stunned faces stared back at him. Roxane swallowed and squeaked, "No."

"Good. If you do, here is my card. Don't hesitate to call me. Now, if one of your men would be so kind as to give the pilot and me a ride back to the edge of the city, we'd be most grateful."

"Yes, of course. Right away. Thank you, Mr. St. Johns," Matt quickly spoke up. "Dear, I'll take them. Be back shortly." With that, he escorted the attorney outside, but could not help but take a look at the huge ship now parked along the east side of the farmhouse, dwarfing the two story building!

Meanwhile, Roxane opened the envelope and laid the letter on the table so her sisters could see it too, while she read it aloud for the others.

Dearest daughters,

It is with a heavy heart that I am writing this, my last words to you three beautiful daughters. Our time together has been far too short, yet always remember I have spent most of my adult life looking for you four. I have been President Johnson's secret agent these many years, as he and I have never trusted these aliens and their corporations. I have done many covert actions on behalf of Virge-C, but with my death, that has finally ended.

Now that I have finally found you, I am no longer able to protect you, though I have already failed that with you, dearest Sondra. Thus, I please accept the last avenue I can find to keep you safe. Trouble, bad trouble is coming. My death only confirms it in my mind. I have known these alien leaders for many years. One thing I have had confirmed repeatedly is that they are never to be trusted, not ever. Their words and promises have always proven false.

I have recently purchased a new commercial grade deep space transport, the Bright Star. With it, my daughters, you will be able to flee the coming disaster that I just know is coming. I believe that one of your friends, Beth, can fly it. If not, hire a pilot and navigator. But please, dear daughters, flee Virge-C before it is too late. Oh, and do change the key-code security codes as soon as you have the ship in your possession.

Where to go? I've thought long and hard about this detail. For Sondra's sake, search the galaxy for a cure for her and the others. That should be your first and primary goal: to find her a cure. I can't imagine how impossible her life now is, so Roxane, Alice, I beg you to search for as long as it takes for that cure for your sister. Somewhere out there in the galaxy, there must be a cure. After all, these fiends invented the genetic mutation, so someone else must have invented a cure. And that is my very last request for you, to find her that cure. After that, follow your own consciences and do what you will. Be true to your own goals and mates. Raise children to be proud of their parents and their old grandfather.

Your loving father,

Marshal Tucker

Roxane noticed a few dried spots near the bottom and realized that he probably was crying when he finished writing the letter. For a time, no one spoke, stunned and overwhelmed by the inheritance and letter. Then, Beth spoke up, "Come on. We need to see the Bright Star and change the security locking codes so only we can get inside it. We don't want it stolen. Come on!"

Beth put her arm around Sondra, while Tom held onto Rene. Roxane did likewise for Fernando, and Ben kept Adoria secure while they headed outside to see this miraculous and timely ship. "Wow!" exclaimed Sondra. Most were speechless for a few minutes as they made their slow, careful way across the grass, moving all around the ship, stopping at the bay doors. It was a commercial liner. Thus, this deep space transport could carry forty passengers. Towards the front of the bay doors, ten small windows provided those sitting on the seats there with a view. The ship itself was over two hundred feet long and fifty wide, more or less oval. The cargo bay was huge, but more impressive were the cabins, all twenty of them, each capable of holding two passengers comfortably.

Each cabin held a normal sized bed, a small desk, two chairs, a small closet, and a tiny bathroom. There was a much larger bathroom further towards the rear. The galley was as large as a normal kitchen, fully equipped with all the latest gadgets, which Ben and Adonia quickly pointed out to the others. Matt joined them at this point, "Guys, this is utterly unreal!" he exclaimed. "What a ship!"

Next, they discovered three unusual machines, labeled electrostatic hair dryers. Beside each was a note describing how it was used. Quickly, the three women tried them out and were elated with the results. Then, Fernando took a turn. For the first time, his eyes lit up. Sondra was sure he must be smiling.

Shortly after that, Sondra's eyes were wet, but now that Matt was back, she allowed her tears to trickle down her face, while he dabbed them. "I miss him but this is just too much, Matt. I've been poorer than poor all my life, and now I'm a millionaire. It's just too much to take in. Sorry."

"You go ahead and cry all you want, dear. He was a great man and a father that you'll never forget," he whispered to her.

After they spent an hour looking over the interior and getting Beth's promise that she was trained to fly it and with Tom insisting that he could handle basic navigation, they headed back outside. Beth showed them how to close the bay door and then lock the ship. She entered the original codes and the doors unlocked. "Okay, what should our new code be? It should be easily remembered by us. They chose 322422 for the three surviving sisters now twenty-two years old and the fact they were originally four sisters. Beth even had Sondra punch them in with her nose just to make sure she could do it if she had to do so.

Once inside, they reread the letter, and then over coffee, Matt suggested, "Tomorrow, let's start loading our possessions into the ship, just in case we need to make a fast getaway." All accepted that idea, especially Fernando who felt incredibly vulnerable and helpless, dependent upon the good graces of Roxane and only because she carried his son. He strongly suspected most of the newly made UFBMD men were merely executed by his people. While geniuses were desirable, none of the corporate CEOs could handle or support thirty thousand of them all at one time. If he was discovered, he'd be shot too, and there wasn't a darn thing he could do about it.

Late that night as they finally wound down enough to sleep, they heard a faint explosion in the far distance, coming from West Port. A lone, barely perceptible boom was followed by silence, and they fell into a relaxed sleep.

Over breakfast, they turned on the news as usual. "Oh God, no!" shrieked Beth, when she first heard the worst news ever.

"This just in," the white-faced reported began. "The aliens have struck back with a terrible vengeance. Late last night, they exploded one of their genetic bio agent bombs inside the heart of West Port. According to the message received by President Johnson, the explosion released sufficient bio agent to infect everyone within the city, nearly two million men, women, and children! Apparently, their force field dome over the city is preventing the gas from escaping into outlying areas. Here's President Johnson with what he's learned." The reporter's image faded, replaced by a very sober man, who looked years older than he had only days before.

"Today, I bring the worst news ever. These evil aliens have unleashed their genetic bio agent on West Port. Yes, everyone there will be turned into what they call their UFB women and UFBMD men, completely helpless individuals. I am told that it will not be safe for anyone to enter the city until tomorrow. The aliens said if we don't interfere, they will land and provide each infected family with a personal robot assistant that is programmed to help them survive, and each will be given a number of mechanical machines that will help them, one being an electrostatic hair machine that handles their uncommonly long hair. After that is done, I have been told we may then begin evacuating these helpless survivors, placing them in locations of our choice, presumably relatives and friends in more distant cities."

"Further, I am told that if we offer any further resistance to the Federation corporations, then additional cities on Virge-C will also be infected, until everyone on our entire world has been genetically modified into completely helpless people. Two million people have been infected as of now. We are to also disband what remains of our armed forces."

"Under the circumstances, as your president, I am capitulating to their demands in order to save the rest of the people of our world from such an atrocity that defies all logic and humanity. These aliens are beasts, but they possess such power that we dare not resist any further. Perhaps in time, these vicious men will see reason, but until then, we must do what we can to stay alive and healthy."

"I and my staff will help organize the transference of the two million infected people to other homes when we get word that it is safe to do so. Once that move has been completed, I will submit my resignation, for I am no longer fit to be your leader. Please do not antagonize these vicious beasts any further or additional millions of us will be turned into helpless victims. Thank you. That is all."

The reporter's ashen face returned, and he began a recapitulation of the events. Beth turned the sound down. "Oh my God! We have friends in West Port. Tom, our cousins are in there, Bill and Lilly Ann!"

"So is my older brother, Jason Wade," Sandy added, "and his fiancé, Jan Engles. Please, gang, can we possibly rescue them?" she pleaded.

"Of course," Matt responded without even thinking about it. "Perhaps, though, we should wait until they are given their robot things. Then, let's get the hell out of here before more crap happens to us all!"

"I'll second that one," Alice spoke up. "Sandy, if it wasn't for Sondra here, we'd be West Port victims now too!"

Fernando commented, "I told you they would strike back hard, but this, this is something entirely new. It's never been done before, the genetic mutation of two million people. My god, what have my people become?"

Roxane answered him, "Sadistic evil bastards who do

not deserve to live, that's what. Mark my words, Fernando, their day will come. What you sew, you shall reap. What you put out eventually comes back to you. Your people are not even members of the human race!"

"No argument from me on that one, Roxane. We need to get away from here and find a safe place to raise our son. That's all that matters now, our son. I promise you, I will help teach him what's right and what's wrong," Fernando declared. She detected a passion in his tone that had not been there before. *Is he changing his viewpoint,* she wondered. *I sure hope he is, for our son's sake.*

***

Five hundred miles away in Westerbrook, elements of the First Commando Battalion licked their wounds and listened to their President capitulate to the enemy. Major Brummond fumed. "Commandos do not give up! We do not capitulate!" Several hundred cheered him.

Someone shouted, "Go underground. Hit 'em hard!"

The major smiled. "We think alike, commandos. Here's what we are going to do." He outlined a sweeping set of plans. Eagerly, his crack troops began carrying them out. Ten nuclear warheads simply vanished. Hundreds of sharpshooter rifles disappeared from the armory, along with ten trucks worth of other weapons, ammo, explosives, specialized equipment including night vision goggles, and rations. That night, dozens of trucks pulled out of what had been the barracks for the First Commando Battalion. They were on the move, a group of dedicated, determined soldiers. While the president may have given up the battle, these men and few women had not. For them, the battle had barely begun.

# Chapter 17—Chaos in the Aftermath

Matt handled the coordination of their proposed rescue of Beth, Tom, and Sandy's close relatives. True to his word, President Johnson set up a hotline for relatives of the two million victims to call and pledge to take them in and provide for their care. Still, days passed before he received the okay to head into West Port and retrieve the relatives.

"They are lucky to have you," Matt said to Tom and Sandy as they drove into the city, their first trip into West Port since that terrible attack. None knew what to expect, except terrified, helpless people. "No one else claimed them."

"Mom and dad are not doing so well," Beth explained. "Their lungs are giving out, and it's all they can do to care for themselves."

Sandy added, "My folks could care less about us, particularly when Jason blew dad off, refusing to run the farm. He went to the University instead. My God, Matt, the city looks deserted!"

The city of millions was eerily silent. Only a few cars and trucks could be seen here and there, picking up some of the survivors, though they passed by several alien checkpoints, manned by security guards carrying d-guns. Virtually no one was on the streets, which only added to the eeriness of the morning. Tom followed along behind them in a second car. Meanwhile, Alice and Roxane obeyed the aliens' order to bring Sondra, Rene, Adonia, and Fernando in for a routine checkup, based upon the corporation's records indicating that they were also UFB women and UFBMD man.

The checkup was interesting and beneficial in some ways. Sondra's lip plates were getting loose. "Ah, they have installed the wrong lip disks on all four of you," the doctor said dryly. "Idiots, the lot of them. Well, no matter, I'll have you fixed up in no time."

"What's wrong with them," Roxane inquired, fearing the worst, that something was physically wrong with them.

"They used the simple disks, not the kind that should

have been used. You see, with these simple ones, in time, the lip loops slowly are stretched, requiring larger and larger disks. Why, I've seen some women with disks eighteen inches across! Impressive but not needed. Wait, I should have asked you four if that was your desires—to have ever increasing size of lip disks?"

"No! Please no," Sondra cried out. "These are bad enough."

"Sorry, I didn't understand much of that, but I take it your answers is no and you want the correct replacement disks that you should have been given."

Sondra nodded. He showed Alice and Roxane the new, fancy ones. "You see, each of them have four holes in their gums. This small, lightweight gum bracket fits into those holes, holding the assembly firmly in place. The disks have a snap hinge here, where it joins the bracket. It just clicks in place. There are hinges allowing them to swing. Pull them all the way up and the hinges lock, holding the disks parallel to the ground so feeding them is easy and convenient. Touch the sides like this and the latches release, allowing them to drop down, where they normally reside. This way, the disks are fully supported by their gums and do not continually stretch their lip loops."

He finished up with Sondra. "There, how does that feel?"

"Much better. The constant pulling is mostly gone," she replied, and Sandy translated for her. An hour later, all four had the new disk systems and headed back out of the city to their farmhouse to await news of the rescue of the other's relatives.

Matt's first stop was at Beth and Tom's cousin's place. Bill and Lilly Ann Ferguson shared an apartment. He was twenty-three, had just finished a stint in the army, and had been job hunting, so he could marry his longtime sweetheart, Jan Engles. His sister, eighteen-year-old Lilly Ann, was planning to enter the University this fall and was giving her older brother a temporary place to stay when the disaster struck.

Beth knocked and announced their arrival, but let

herself and the others in, knowing that Jason and Lilly Ann could not possibly open a door. "We're here, Lilly Ann," she called out.

The four followed the sobbing into the small living room where both sat on her couch. Standing apart from them was a strange looking robot. It had two arms and hands, but moved around on wheels. For a moment, Matt had no idea which was Lilly Ann and which was Jason. He saw two highly attractive UFB women sitting there, massive bosoms, lip disks, malformed feet with toe shoes like those that Sondra always wore, dressed in identical tight red satin gowns. One had knee length light blonde hair, while the other had brown hair, their hair being about the only observable difference between the brother and sister. Beth pointed out that Lilly Ann was the blonde. Both were sobbing, but Bill more so. His voice was now nearly the same as Lilly Ann's soprano. Matt felt a huge surge of sympathy for Jason, a man reduced to this.

Beth introduced everyone. "Okay, let's get your things packed. We can understand you if you speak slowly. Take everything you want. We won't be coming back here, not ever."

"But we can hardly walk," Lilly Ann spoke up, knowing how embarrassed Jason was about his now feminine-like body.

"That's all right. We're used to helping you," Matt spoke up. "My wife is like you are, Lilly Ann, and Tom's married another victim named Rene."

"You are married Tom?" Lilly Ann ceased crying, looking up at her older cousin.

"Ya, married Miss West Port, Rene Harvester, only the damned aliens got ta her just like they dida ta you. No matter, we get ta along jest fine. Swell woman. Can'ta wait fer ya ta meet her. Come on, lassie, let's get ta you pack'en. You too, Bill."

Beth spoke up, "Bill, we can drop by and pick up Jan Engles for you and get you two married, if you still want to marry her. I'm sure she is in love with you, at least she was the last time I saw her."

At last, Bill had to speak up, voice or no voice. "Can we? I love her, but is it possible? To marry? As we are?"

"Ah sure, laddie," Tom encouraged him. "Nothing to it. Come on; let's get ta ya pack'en."

"Do we take this robot thing?" Sandy asked. She found a large placard with its known instructions. "Well, according to this, it understands very simple commands on this list. It might be useful, Matt."

"It got us dressed and fed," Lilly Ann tried to explain.

An hour later, they had the robot, the electrostatic hair machine, long handled silverware, six other outfits for each along with shoes, and some personal mementoes, mostly photographs, stored in one car, along with the two sitting in the backseat, a pair of erect statues in their highly restrictive corsets.

Tom now rode with Ben, making a bit more room in Matt's car. "Sandy, let' see if we can pick up your older brother," Matt suggested. He added, "Don't worry, Bill. After that, we will see about Jan for you. Sandy was very happy to do so. She wanted to say what a horrible nightmare this was turning out to be, but dare not for the sake of their passengers. Jason was probably just as terrified, helpless, and embarrassed as Bill was, if only she could somehow help him get through this, somehow, someway.

She knocked on Jason's apartment door, announced herself, and opened his door with her spare key, only to find the door was unlocked. Like the other two victims, they found Jason sitting erect in one of his chairs, an identical silly looking robot facing him. The TV was on. Jason's very light blonde hair was more than twice as thick as Sandy remembered it, but his crew cut was gone, replaced by wavy locks that reached his knees, but currently lay partly on the floor. His face was wet, and his eyes, red. Matt saw the close resemblance in their faces, but Jason's body more closely resembled Sondra's.

"We've come to rescue you, big brother, and take you away with us," Sandy explained.

"Kill me, please sis. Hell, you can't even understand me." He broke into another sobbing fit. While Sandy talked with him, calming him down some, Tom and Matt gathered up the robot, the hair machine, the new clothing and shoes, carting them out into Matt's car, pretty well filling it up. Meanwhile, Sandy helped her brother up and they set about collecting a few personal things, including his prized autographed baseball. This time, they were ready to depart in less than a half hour.

They found Bill's fiancé and her brother were now living together. Jan Engles was twenty-two with rich auburn hair. Matt could see why Bill was so taken with her, despite the genetic modifications. He hoped and prayed Jan still felt the same for Bill. Her younger brother, Peter, was nineteen with rich black hair. Like the other two men, he was an emotional wreck, while the women were in somewhat better state, and Matt understood why. He only had to look at Fernando to grasp their mental states.

While they were not registered to be taking these two, Matt simply went ahead and did so, loading their things into the second car, along with their robot and machines. Both cars were completely packed, barely enough room for Matt and Tom to drive. Following Tom's suggestion, he had Bill sitting beside his fiancé, Jan, in Tom's car, while he repositioned Peter next to Lilly Ann. Sandy insisted on sitting with her brother, chatting to everyone on their drive out of the city.

"Don't worry, Jason, my mate has come into a fantastic inheritance from her father. We're soon going to search the galaxy for a cure for them and for you too," Sandy explained to her brother and the others with her.

Sondra, Alice, Rene, Roxane, Adonia, and Fernando arrived back at their farmhouse long before they expected the others to return with the rescued relatives. However, as they pulled up to the house dwarfed by the Bright Star, concern bordering on fear swept over the five. Two military-camouflaged motorcycles were parked near their front porch! Of course, the land all around here was pretty much torn up and rutted by all the heavy vehicles that had been here when the army attacked West Port, but those soldiers were long gone. Worse, none of the men were with them; Fernando didn't count.

"What do we do?" whispered Alice nervously. "We don't

even have any guns."

"Well, if they're our soldiers, then we're probably safe," Sondra suggested, though she felt anything but safe. "Let's get inside. We can't stand up well out here." She was struggling to keep her balance, as were the other three, Rene and Fernando only just barely managing it. She added, "Alice, you help Rene. Roxane, you help Fernando. Adonia and I can make it on our own, I think."

Carefully, the five moved up towards their front door. All was utterly quiet, but then that was normal out here. Still, Sondra would have preferred to hear the chatter of the soldiers than the silence, which now seemed somehow threatening. Alice opened the door, and the five made their way inside, heading for their living room, just off the hall. Rene and Fernando needed to sit down.

Entering the room, all five came face to face with two soldiers, both heavily armed and pointing large caliber guns at them—sniper rifles, they later learned. One was a man; one, a woman. She barked authoritatively, "We are commandeering this house. . ." Her alto voice faltered mid-sentence. Her eyes stared first at Roxane, then Alice, and then Sondra.

"Oh my God!" Roxane's alto voice took up as the soldier's voice fell silent in shock.

"What the hell?" the man exclaimed.

"Another one of us?" Alice exclaimed totally awed.

"Incredible," Sondra added and took charge. "Who are you? You look just like us."

"What's she saying?" asked the man. "Their voices— sounds like you captain. Is this another trick of the aliens?"

"Who are you three? How come you look like my sister and me?" the captain finally recovered from the shock of seeing herself three times over. While Sondra wanted to explain, she quickly realized neither soldier could understand her and thus asked Roxane to explain.

"Well, can we please sit them down?" Roxane began, "and lower your guns please. We live here and pose you no threat." After getting the four seated, she explained, "We three are identical sisters, clones we have discovered. The aliens murdered our fourth sister. Sondra here rather found us and pulled us all together, before she too got genetically modified by the aliens. The rest of our group is out rescuing some others from West Port. It's a long story. She's Sondra Sofia Shelley, but has married Matt Homes, a former police detective. She's Alice Middleton, first violinist in West Port's symphony orchestra. Her mate is Sandy, who is off rescuing her brother from West Port. I'm nurse Roxane Stevens. He's one of the aliens, who did this to Sondra, but she got him back, and now I'm looking after him because he's the father of my son. I'm pregnant."

She went on as the two soldiers put their guns down and sat down as well. "Until Sondra's raid on Rosewood a few weeks ago, we all didn't know we were sisters and believed we were orphans. Different foster parents raised us four. The late Marshal Tucker, the CEO of Aerostar Engines, was our father and his first wife, our mother. Dr. Decker of Rosewood Homecare illegally and unethically somehow cloned us four from one of her fertilized eggs. We don't know how or why, really, just one of that madman's weird genetic experiments. During the raid, we retrieved his records of our birth, if that's what it should be called, and verified we four are identical clones, but we prefer sisters."

She finished up, "We thought we four were all that he made, but obviously, we missed something in those records. You look exactly like us, only your hair is much shorter. So who are you anyway? Why are you in our house? Well, it's Beth and Tom's actually. They are off rescuing the others."

"I can't believe this! It's like looking at yourself in the mirror. I've seen many things in my time, but this, well, this is beyond everything. Clones? Does that make me and my sister clones too? My God, what the hell is going on?" she gushed, very animated.

"Tell us about yourself," Roxane suggested. "Does your sister look like you and us too? Are there more of us out there? Sondra, if there are, we can't leave until we find them!"

She swallowed and tried again. "I'm Captain Lenora Cox of the First Commandos. My radioman, Sergeant Riley Mc Dougal. My identical sister, Kiesa Kay Cox, is back in Coventry Gardens. She's a dressmaker. We are orphans, raised by the

Cox family. No one ever told us who our parents were or our last name. They said no such records exist, but we did get replacement birth certificates, though they used the Cox last name on them, so we don't know how accurate they are. You said that Marshal Tucker is your father. How do you know that? He's become the most famous rebel in history, single handedly wiping out all of GD headquarters!"

Roxane said, "Hold on a second. Let me fetch all those records. If I remember something right, you might be mentioned in them." A few minutes later, she had them all spread out on the floor so everyone could look them over. "Ah, Sondra, see here? We misunderstood this later entry. We thought Case 2 meant some other people were being cloned. But look, there's Lenora and Kiesa Kay."

"Right, it says they were made three months after us. That's why we didn't think they were part of us," Sondra replied, grasping just how they'd made their error. "So Marshal actually had six daughters!"

"What she saying?" Lenora barked. "I can't understand anything she's saying."

Roxane translated for her, adding, "If you are around them long enough, you can pretty much catch what they are saying. So we goofed, Sondra. Case 2 is more of us, only they must be three months younger than us, our little sisters, sort of. If only Marshal had known this!"

"I know," Sondra replied. "He would have made provisions for them too."

"Huh?" Lenora grumbled, looking at Roxane for interpretation.

She repeated what Sondra had said. Roxane added, "Yes, I'm sure she's right. If Marshal had known about you and Kiesa Kay, I'm certain he would have included you both in his will. I don't think anything can be done about it now, but I'm willing to share part of what he left me with the both of you."

"Me too," Alice added. "I have more than I could ever spend."

"Yes, we should share our inheritance with them," Sondra added. Roxane again translated.

"What inheritance? Marshal Tucker was an incredibly

wealthy man," Captain Lenora asked.

"He left us each ten million gold dollars," Roxane said quietly. Lenora gasped, shocked. "Plus, he left us that deep space transport outside, the Bright Star. It's brand new. He left us with a huge challenge: to search the galaxy for a cure for Sondra and the others with us, but if we can find such a thing, we will also see that the others that we're rescuing also get the cure. Lenora, this is his final wish, that we find a cure for this horrific genetic mutation of the aliens. We have to do this first."

"A fricking space ship? My god," Lenora completely lost her composure.

Riley chuckled, "Well, we did try to break into it, figuring some aliens were holed up in it. We were going to kill them, you see, but we couldn't get in. Sorry, we didn't know it was yours."

"So what are you doing out here?" Sondra asked, with Roxane again repeating her question for the others.

"Simple really. While the president has capitulated, we, the First Commandos, never capitulate. We fight to the last man or woman in her case," Riley answered. "The whole First Commando Battalion is now independently armed and deployed in the field. Our job is eventually to defeat this evil enemy, the aliens, even if it takes us years to do it. The captain here is called Lone Wolf, the best damned sniper in the whole battalion! We're here to pick off any aliens who leave the outskirts of West Port. We were kind of figuring on using this farmhouse as a base. Guess that's not going to happen."

"Right," Captain Lenora added, "our main mission right now is to see if we can figure out the alien's next move for the major. We know they are beginning a major action of moving our mutated people out of West Port. Then what they will be doing with our capital isn't known."

Fernando spoke up, "They will likely be repopulating it with their own people, probably from worlds that are overpopulated." Again, Roxane had to translate what he said.

"You think they will do that? We should alert the major," Lenora advised. "If they do that, then we can blow West Port to kingdom come. That'll show these aliens we mean business."

Alice replied, "But won't they then dump their genetic bio weapon on another of our larger towns?"

Fernando added, "Well, at least they won't nuke the planet. You have valuable minerals they want or they wouldn't be here. That's something, but she's right. They'll counterattack again and again, until all of your people are dead or helpless mutants like me and the others."

"What's he saying?" Lenora asked and Roxane translated once more.

"We'd rather go down fighting than give up our freedom and become slaves to your corporations. Your Federation aliens must all be cowards," Lenora declared vehemently.

Fernando chuckled. "Perhaps we are that, captain, perhaps we are indeed. Still, I'm going to try to be the best father to my son that I can be. I think that over the centuries, we've become rather complacent, accepting what is without question or thinking. I know I certainly did. I had no real idea of what kind of life we made for our UFB wives. Now I do, and I can't condone it any longer."

After Roxane's translation caught up, he added, "I think your people took the corporation executives by complete surprise, unleashing their own bio agent on nearly all them in West Port. Still, they retaliated, but I had expected they would simply nuke the planet. Now in hindsight, I realize they do consider the mineral wealth of this planet valuable enough to try other means to take it over. Still, I would be careful or you'll bring down more corporate wrath on yourselves."

"Doesn't any world stand up to them?" Lenora asked him, finding this alien had useful insights. Besides, Fernando was the first alien she'd actually met in person, weird as he was.

"Hardly. It's suicide. Wait, some worlds out on the rim did stand up and throw off the corporate yoke there. What was it called? Oh yes, the Abelard Sector. Don't know how they did it though," he replied. "As I said, we need to get off of this world soon or we are doomed. I want Roxane to survive so my son can live. Of course, I've no idea where we can go that will be safe."

"What's going on here? What? Another one?" exclaimed Matt. He and the others just arrived and saw the army motorcycles outside. Worried, he and Tom came rushing in, guns at the ready. He stopped short, blinking at Lenora, who looked absolutely identical to the other three, except her light brown hair was perhaps only five inches long, quite short.

"Matt! Glad you are back," Sondra gushed relieved to see him safe and sound. "We have two more sisters! We misunderstood the mad doctor's records. This is Lenora Cox and her radioman, Riley. She has a twin sister Kiesa Kay, so there are five of us now. Are the others with you? Any trouble getting them?"

"Wow! Two more of you? Incredible! Pleased to meet you, Lenora. I'm Matt; this is Tom. Excuse us, but we have five more to help get inside. We could us a hand with them. All went okay, Alice. Sandy's got her brother."

Adonia spoke up, "Tell Ben to hurry up. He and I need to get started on our lunch."

It took some doing, but the many hands got Bill, Lilly Ann, Jason, Jan, and Peter safely inside, though not without a lot of wild wobbling on their part, and had them all seated in the living room. After lugging their robots, machines, clothing, and few possessions inside, everyone sat down for the lengthy introductions, after which Ben and Adonia headed off to the kitchen to fix a much larger than normal lunch.

Jason, Peter, and Bill were surprised and relieved to find that Fernando was also a man, as well as one of the aliens. Soon, he became their mentor, giving them much needed advice, tips, and moral support that the three men were sorely lacking. "You just have to get Sondra to give you her special trauma erasing help." He went on about how valuable it was, and by evening, the three men finally were brave enough to ask her about it.

At lunch, they experimented with the five's three robots. Their command structure was ridiculously small, feed, cook, dress, undress, pee, and door. The robots were able to sort of carry out these commands, and the five swore that the robots had kept them alive since they came out of their comas. Still, Sondra rightly concluded that these robot helpers were almost useless, unless the person had no one else to help them. Worse, there wasn't any way to tell the robots not to put their restrictive corsets on them. After that first afternoon and night, the group decided against making further use of them. The hair machines, on the other hand, were invaluable.

That evening at precisely 8:00, Captain Lenora made her status call to the major. She reported everything she'd heard and learned, including the warnings Fernando had given her. He asked for clarification on several points, particularly about her surprise discovery of her unknown sisters and their goal of finding a cure for the alien mutation process.

At last, the major reached a decision. "Captain Lenora, I'm changing your mission status. I want you to accompany these people on their search of the galaxy for a cure. Do whatever you must to keep them on this. You simply must bring back a cure for our two million victims. That's a direct order, captain; bring back a cure for our people."

"Yes sir, but what about my surveillance project?" she replied, hesitant about leaving the commandos behind.

"I'll send a replacement down to you. Expect him late tomorrow night. Remember, Lenora, two million helpless victims are depending upon you and those others to bring back a cure for them. Do what you have to do to keep those civies on this project. Understand, captain?" he answered firmly.

"Yes, sir. Bring back a cure."

Resolutely he added, "Don't come back until you have found that cure, captain. Over and out."

Lenora came back inside, stowing her radio. She saw everyone sitting in the living room watching the latest newscast. "Er, I just have new orders. I'm supposed to come with you and help bring back a cure for our people. So who is in charge?"

Matt replied, "Hey, the more the merrier. Welcome, Lenora. Oh, Sondra is our official leader, since she's masterminded just about all our actions. I guess I can translate for you, until you catch on to their garbled speech."

"Say, is there any chance I can bring my sister along with us? Fernando has me scared. I don't want her being mutated while I'm away. I've always more or less looked after her," Lenora asked, hoping they would say yes.

"Absolutely, she must come. Besides, we all want to meet our new sister too," Sondra replied, though Matt had to translate for Lenora. "How far away is Coventry Gardens? How are we going to get her here?"

"About five hundred miles northeast of here," Lenora replied. "I'd best take a car and fetch her, if that's okay with you. Probably need five days or so. I can leave day after tomorrow. I've a replacement coming here tomorrow night."

"Good. That will give me time to try my special therapy erasing thing on the five newcomers," Sondra replied. "Rene and I will start in on them tomorrow, but we're going to have to get them more comfortable and out of those awful corsets. We really don't need them if someone can give us a back massage when we need it."

After Matt translated again, he added, "After you are around them for a while, you can catch what they are saying. Also, after they get some practice, they will be able to get around on their own some too. Sondra isn't as helpless as you might think. We'll tell you about it when you get back."

"Okay. I'll take your word for it. One thing though, Kiesa Kay is really shy, especially around other men, so please try not to embarrass her too much," Lenora explained.

In the morning, Sondra knew that she needed to work with the men first. In addition to suffering the same disabilities as the women, they had monumental embarrassment and upset piled on top of that, for they now looked like UFB women, about as distant from masculinity as possible, at least Sondra thought so. Base on how rough a time Fernando had, she anticipated the men would require more work, and she was right. Sondra took Billy first, while Rene worked on Peter. Beth didn't want to be left out, and she tried her hand working with Jason, knowing how desperate Sandy was to help her brother.

With all the nearly nonstop sobbing and wailing, Lenora decided to have Matt give her a tour of the Bright Star, before she left the following morning. "I don't know how they can stand it—all that weeping and stuff. I know it's awful for the men, but I couldn't take it," she admitted.

"Sondra has a gift for it, I think. Besides, you are soldiers at heart," he answered.

Lenora laughed. "You got that right, Mr. Policeman." While he showed her around the vast ship, he also told her some of the things that Sondra had done and accomplished, including escaping and extracting revenge on the aliens all while being *helpless*. That put Sondra in a different light in Lenora's mind, which was Matt's purpose.

Late the second night, Beth finished helping Jason erase his emotional trauma and the hitherto fore unknown physical trauma he endured while in the mutation coma. Laughing, he commented, "Beth, I can't tell you how good I feel. Mind you, I'm still as helpless as a cat without legs, but I feel great. Thank you. Say, you are going to be the pilot. Have you got a good navigator for hyperspace travel?"

"Thanks. Yes, I have my official pilot's license now. My brother can work the nav controls, as long as we don't try to use hyperspace. He only knows a bit about it, what he learned playing soldier. Do you know anything about hyperspace navigation?" she asked. She rather liked this fellow, even if he looked like a UFB woman.

"Yes, I got my University degree in it and then this happened. I'd love to help, only I can't even push the buttons. Guess Tom can, if he can understand me."

"Sure, we all can. Just takes getting used to listening more carefully. I think we sort of substitute the missing sounds, once we get the hang of it," Beth answered. "I'll let Sondra know you're our official hyperspace navigator."

"Great. Say Beth, do you have a boyfriend? The others seem to be married," he asked hesitantly.

"Nope, not yet. I've been Sable's assistant and then Sondra's too, all while going to school. No time for it. How about you? Girlfriend?"

"Nope, same with me. School and work to pay for it chewed up all my time. I think you're gorgeous, Beth, but then I'm not much of a man now."

"Hey, I think you are, well darn keen yourself. Handsome, well that's not going to cut it anymore. You're the gorgeous one now, but it's you that I like. Together, we would make a cool pair, what with me piloting and you navigating and all that."

"I'd like that very much, Beth. Hell, I can't even hold your hand or even kiss you properly any longer."

"Oh, you can really kiss now!" She lowered her voice and told him about overheating Matt and Sondra and then later on, Roxane and Fernando. "Wanna try it tonight?" Jason pressed his body into hers. "I take that as a resounding yes!" Both laughed.

Later, Beth shared her excitement with Sondra and Roxane. "Sex with Jason is just incredible. He's the one for me, and besides, he and I want to have a genius son, just as you are, Roxane. He's the greatest," the young Beth bubbled with excitement. Ever the nurse, Roxane cautioned her that a girl was just as likely as a boy was. All three giggled.

By the next day, Bill and Peter were also doing quite well, so Sondra and Rene began working on Lilly Ann and Jan. Sondra left orders for Alice, Sandy, and Beth to *work* the fellows, drilling them on being as self-sufficient as possible, reminding them to practice, practice, practice.

With nine who needed help with most everything and only seven able bodies to assist them, certain times of the day were rather hectic. Getting everyone dressed in the morning and undressed at night took time, as did feeding everyone three times each day. Nature calls were far more easily handled. Sondra was quite thankful that Beth and Jason were hitting it off, since she took him into her bedroom with her each night. Alice and Sandy did their best to handle the other two couples, since Bill and Jan wanted to get married, as did Peter and Lilly Ann. This made sleeping arrangements simpler. Sondra looked forward to having Lenora and Kiesha Kay here, since then there would be an equal number of able bodies to help the others.

By the time Lenora and Kiesa Kay arrived almost a week later, all five were walking fairly well on their own. Some self-confidence had returned, and Matt finally was able to get someone to marry the two couples officially, though at the last minute, Beth insisted she and Jason also get married, hinting another time to do this might be a very long way off.

During this time, the others continued to track the latest news. As Tom had suggested over dinner one night, not every one of the two million victims had relatives who would take them in. In fact, the evacuation of West Port was delayed an entire week, while President Johnson desperately tried to find new living arrangements for nearly half of the city's population.

"I canna understand why," Tom pointed out, "nota everyone is a gonna wanna take care of them, nota like we do. Shame though."

Towards the end of August, the last of the victims were trucked out of West Port. In a brief ceremony, President Johnson handed over the *keys* to the city to Rodrigo, who was acting head of the corporations, at least until the many newcomers arrived. The following day, the spaceport was a hive of activity. From their vantage point some two miles to the west of it, they saw transport after transport, cruiser after cruiser, landing at the facility. Soon, there wasn't any doubt that the corporations were replacing the lost two million people with their own. Again, Fernando's suspicions were borne out. Many of the working class came from overpopulated planets.

During this arrival chaos, Lenora and Kiesa Kay arrived, the car filled with their things. Lenora had been storing much of her things with her sister, while she played soldier. Although Lenora had told her sister all about the group, Kiesa Kay was shocked to see three other women who looked precisely like her sister and herself. She was also very shy, just as Lenora had warned them.

After the many introductions were done and stories told, Kiesa Kay began observing the ill-fitting dresses that the five new victims were wearing. She volunteered to alter them to fit. "Thanks," Sondra replied to her offer. "We've just been trying to find any of our things that will sort of fit them. The aliens made them wear the very tight corsets so those fancy new gowns the aliens gave them don't fit if they don't wear the corsets. We have more freedom of motion when we aren't wearing them. Thanks for helping. We had better get your things onto the Bright Star too." Roxane had to translate for her.

Just then, Sergeant Riley came into the living room. "Captain, a word please. Urgent." Lenora stepped outside with Riley. "Captain, you best be hightailing it out of here soon. Major is going to detonate one of our nuclear bombs in the heart of West Port, just as soon as all the aliens get here. Probably, this farmhouse will soon be leveled by the blast."

"Thanks for the warning. I'll tell the others," she replied, very worried. Could Beth even fly it? How could Jason manage to navigate? He was helpless in her book.

"Shit! A nuclear bomb?" Matt exclaimed after she relayed the news.

"This place will be toast," Tom added.

"We have to leave, please," begged Fernando. "I want my son to survive." With Roxane translating for Lenora and Kiesa Kay, the group decided to depart in the morning.

They got a late start. Last minute packing and stowing their gear took the able bodied longer than expected. First, they got the nine who really couldn't help safely onto the Bright Star and strapped in for the takeoff. Beth, Tom, and Jason handled the lengthy pre-flight check out, going slowly and carefully down the checklist, picking their destination a high orbit of Virge-C for now. The others made numerous trips back and forth, stowing all the last minute items, especially since they figured the nuclear blast would level this farmhouse. "I hate to waste such a fine pot," Ben lamented, looking over the remaining items in the kitchen. Like Sondra, he was extremely frugal; until now, they had to be just to survive. Neither could truly grasp that now they had ample funds.

"Skies are clear," Tom reported. "Nothing on radar either. So we're clear for takeoff."

Jason added, "He's got the coordinates set properly. We're ready to go, Beth."

"This is Captain Beth. Buckle up. We're ready for takeoff in one minute. Here we go, gang!" She was excited and a little nervous. It was one thing to pilot a transport with her instructor sitting beside her and even to solo, but having all her friends and Jason onboard gave her the jitters. She took a deep breath and fired up the engines. Slowly, the Bright Star lifted off, while the passengers watched the farmhouse slowly shrink in size, and the city of West Port, their home, appear and diminish in size.

The control tower at the spaceport called, asking for identification. "This is the Bright Star lifting off," Beth reported. "All is well. Fine day." She didn't know what else to say. If they challenged her or ordered her to land, Tom was prepared to hit the hyperdrive button, taking them into their high orbit, which meant that the control tower would probably lose track of them, buying them more time to enter a more distant destination. The control tower merely ignored them, after confirming their identity.

An hour later, they parked in a very high orbit around Virge-C, twenty miles above the surface. "Okay, we are in orbit. Here, we are safe if they blow up West Port," Beth announced. "Now we need to figure out where we are going."

With help from Alice, Sandy manned their comm center amidships. Ben and Adonia headed to the galley to cook up some lunch. Using her computer with her feet, Sondra continued her Federation web search for a cure, while Fernando sat beside her offering some suggestions. Just then, Sandy cried out over the intercom, "They did it. They blew up West Port!" She tuned the newscaster's voice into the intercom so everyone could hear the report.

Fernando exclaimed, "We got out just in time! Now, there'll be hell to pay for that!"

"What will they do to Virge-C now?" Sondra asked him.

"I don't know, but killing a million of them will certainly bring a harsh retribution," he answered.

"And yet they think nothing of mutilating two million of our people," Sondra countered. "Beasts, all the men on both sides! We could all have lived in peace, if they only would have tried."

"That's not the corporation's way," Fernando explained. "Own everything. Exploit everything. Profit is what matters. You see, it costs billions to search out new habitable planets, to explore and map them, to establish viable colonies on them, and to populate them with all the necessities of human life. That fortune must come from somewhere; the corporations' profits pay for it. No profits, no exploration and expansion. But we best figure out where we're going to go."

# Chapter 18—Sadism

"Well, what about visiting some of the nearby Federation worlds. Couldn't they help us?" Sondra asked Fernando.

"After that attack on West Port, we're more likely to be detained for questioning at the very least. Besides, as far as I know, we don't have any cures. We only know how to make UFB women and UFBMD men, not undo it. No one wants to undo that, you see. Well, excepting us that is," he added morosely.

"Isn't there any place that will be mostly safe for us to go?" she asked. "What about that sector you told us about?"

"Oh you mean the Abelard Sector out on the rim," Fernando said. "Well, that's considered a rebel zone. The corporations are still there, but they have lost their total control over the worlds there. I suppose that's probably our safest sector."

Sondra entered that into the search engine and pulled up quite a lot of information. Apparently, this Scorpi-C world was in control of these rebel-like worlds. As she searched further, she finally found what she was desperately looking for: a possible cure. "Matt, come here and write these coordinates down and take them up to Tom and Jason. Have them enter them. Our destination is this Scorpi-C world. It looks like they have the cures that we need."

"Glory hallelujah!" he exclaimed, jotting the long series of meaningless numbers down and racing to the front of the ship.

Just as she was about to tell everyone the fabulous news, suddenly the Bright Star lurched and began moving on its own. "What's going on?" yelled Beth through the intercom. "I'm not doing it."

"Look out the window!" yelled Sandy. "What is that thing? It's gigantic!"

Fernando struggled a bit to get a view out of one of the many windows. He moaned. "What?" Sondra asked, her stomach suddenly tightening in a knot. It was a giant of a ship, that much was certain.

"One of 9Gamma-C's battleships. They've locked a tractor beam onto us and are pulling us in. We're captured and as good as dead," Fernando wailed.

Just then, the comm center acted up and a strange voice was heard throughout the ship. "This is Admiral Julio of the Battleship Elena. You are under arrest. Do not attempt to resist or you will be blown to space dust."

Sandy had the presence of mind to figure out how to reply, "Arrested for what? This is our own transport ship."

"You will be interrogated shortly," the man replied. The battleship's control over their comm system terminated, leaving them in an ominous silence.

"But we haven't done anything," Sondra protested.

Fernando whispered, "It doesn't matter to them. Someone blew up West Port so they will take it out on us. I might as well be dead."

"Oh don't talk like that. Surely, this Admiral Julio will see we're unarmed and certainly haven't had anything to do with whatever happened in West Port," Sondra replied, though she doubted her own certainty on what she'd just said.

*\*\**

On 9Gamma-C, Mario de la Vega received word of the deadly nuclear attack on West Port from a light cruiser in orbit around Virge-C. He ordered the cruiser to investigate and relay realtime video to him, while he sent an emergency summons to the other major corporation leaders on his world. Within a half hour, a dozen watched the live video in his top-floor office. Adriana was sitting quietly in the back taking notes for Mario.

"This is an unprecedented disaster," Mario declared so angrily that the veins in his neck threatened to burst. The entire city was destroyed, leveled, but more importantly, nearly a million people who had just resettled there were gone along with the entire spaceport, the only one usable by them on Virge-C.

"What do we do about that lone transport seen taking off shortly before the bombing?" asked Ramiro.

"I've ordered Admiral Julio to intercept it and arrest

them. We'll question them. If they had anything to do with it, they'll wish they hadn't!" Mario cried. "We need to teach these people a lesson they will never forget!"

"Nuke the whole planet?" another CEO suggested.

The CEO of General Electronics answered, "We damn well better not do that! We have invested a small fortune in this world. The financial loss by making it radioactive for the next century is utterly prohibitive. Fry all their communications systems with a massive EM pulse," he suggested. "Then, they can't coordinate such actions ever again."

"Yes, but how do we then get our ultimatums delivered to them?" another CEO asked. "I don't think that's the right answer. Perhaps killing them all is the best move."

"But how the hell do you get rid of two billion corpses?" Mario asked. "The decomposition stench will be overwhelming before our people can get to all the dead bodies. We need to teach them a lesson somehow. Got more of those robot things, Ramiro?"

"Nope. We used them all. But I must admit, that project has not worked out as well as we had envisioned. Of the two million victims, more or less, over a quarter died and even more were left to die by their own people. Something about being unable to find anyone to look after those who lived in that part called Snake Town. What about chemical weapons? Wipe out the larger cities, one at a time," he suggested, calming down some.

Mario finally calmed down. "Okay. Here's what we do. Make a planet-wide announcement that for every city of ours that gets bombed, we will nuke one of their cities. Pick their second largest one and have Admiral Julio take it out. Use minimal radiation bombs. Second, let's get that contaminated West Port site cleaned up. Call in the Rejuvenation Ship. Let it remove the radioactive material in that whole area and then fill it in with fresh soil, taken from elsewhere on that planet. That ought to stop their constant interfering in our business."

"What do we tell Admiral Julio to do about that fleeing transport?" Ramiro asked. "We should give him specific orders."

"Oh hell. Tell him to interrogate them and take care of them as he sees fit. I need him to orbit Virge-C, make that planet-wide announcement, find a city, and nuke it," Mario declared. "All in favor?" He finally remembered to ask for a vote from the assembled CEOs, since they had a vested interest in Virge-C as well. They backed him, and the meeting broke up.

"Adriana, send those orders to Admiral Julio now. I want confirmation from him immediately," Mario barked and watched her execute his commands.

"Yes sir. I understand. Capture this renegade transport. Nuke a large city. Wonderful. That should teach them a severe lesson," Admiral Julio replied to Adriana's message. Satisfied, Mario retired to his private office. Once out of earshot, Adriana added to the message orders, "Please notify me of the disposition of the renegades and their ship." She smiled when he confirmed her final request. All she could do now was sit at her post and wait to hear back. As soon as the city had been nuked, she had to notify Mario.

***

The group watched from the side windows as the Bright Star was pulled into the massive docking bay of the battleship, eventually magnetically grappled to one of the myriad steel walkways. A dozen heavily armed men marched down it, their boots clanking in unison on the metal, amplifying their sound. Sandy had no choice but to open their bay doors when the soldiers arrived. Like ants, the green-clad men swarmed into the Bright Star. While some searched the ship, others ushered everyone together into the main seating area.

Finally, Admiral Julio walked into the ship, a riding crop in hand. He was rather plump, though overweight would be a more accurate statement. "So what have we here, a batch of saboteurs? How many more nukes do you have? What else are you planning to blow up? How did you plant that nuclear bomb? Speak up," he barked.

Matt decided to act as spokesman. "I'm sorry. We had nothing to do with that. This is our ship, rather my wife's and her sisters. We thought we were very lucky to have escaped when we did or we'd be ashes now too."

292

Admiral Julio slapped Matt across his face with his riding crop. "Do you take me for an idiot? Obviously, you set the nuke and fired it as you left. Admit it and it will go better for you," he barked, very hostile towards the group.

One of the soldiers came up, shaking his head no, which Matt took to mean they didn't find any bombs onboard. He spoke up, "Sir, their papers are in order. Only primitive weapons, nothing more."

"Damn!" Admiral Julio replied. "Okay, keep them under guard until I decided what to do with them." He turned and left the ship, as did most of the soldiers. Two remained behind, d-guns out and ready to shoot anyone who moved.

A few minutes later, a soldier wearing a spacesuit came onboard. "Okay, you are going to be taken to Luigi's on 9Gamma-C. Sit back and enjoy the ride. Be there in a couple of hours. Try anything and I have orders to exterminate all of you, which I'd just as soon do right now. It will save me this trip."

"But what about our ship? It belongs to us?" Matt ventured.

"Oh, it'll be safe enough at Luigi's." The man kept his d-gun out, while the two other guards left. He headed up to the pilot's seat, but Matt thought it best not to try anything.

Once the ship began to move out of the docking bay, Matt whispered, "Fernando, what's Luigi's? Where is he taking us?"

"Please Matt, try something, anything! You must get him to kill us all," Fernando whined pitifully.

"Why? What's Luigi's?" Matt insisted on knowing.

"Luigi's is the most exotic whorehouse on 9Gamma-C, close to the spaceport. Spacers taking shore leave visit Luigi's. He's making us all into prostitutes for the rest of our lives. Please, you must get him angry enough to kill us all. Please," Fernando wailed.

"Hardly. We'll just have to overpower Luigi and make our escape," Matt declared.

"Absolutely!" Lenora declared vehemently. Everyone but Fernando agreed with Matt. Now they simply waited.

"What's that smell?" Sondra whispered. Noses began

sniffing. "Oh my God no! It's that genetic bio agent gas!" She finally recognized it's sickly smell. Many cursed, but soon nine slipped into comas, leaving the nine helpless ones unable to do anything at all.

"What do we do now?" whispered Rene? "We're helpless without them and they're going to be like us, helpless too. Maybe Fernando was right."

"Well, we're not dead yet," Sondra said angrily. "Besides, we can't do anything to threaten the pilot, except perhaps kick him. No, we bide our time. We'll find a way out of this and find that cure!" And then I'm going to get justice, real justice!

Hours later, they began to descend onto 9Gamma-C with its yellow sun shining brightly. "My home world. God, I never wanted to return to this den of bastards," Fernando muttered. "We're landing in Toledo at the giant spaceport. The top corporate leaders operate out of Toledo. Hey, looks like he's landing us at the long-term parking area. Wonder what that means?"

"Long-term?" asked Sondra.

"Yeh, where they park ships that are going to be planet-side for lengthy stays. Don't want to clutter up the main landing pods. Hundreds of ships come and go each day."

"So they aim to park Bright Star here for a long time? Maybe we can use that to our advantage," Sondra whispered back.

"Doesn't matter. We're as good as dead now, or you soon will wish you were," Fernando whispered back.

The man still wore his spacesuit, which Sondra thought made the pilot look just plain weird, though completely safe from the bio agent. Once he opened the bay door, he removed his suit. While she looked out at the myriad of ships parked in this lot far from the distant control tower, she saw a truck coming, though she couldn't read the writing on it. "What's that truck?" she whispered.

"Says refueling. These people always refuel any ship that lands. God knows why. Guess they want to make as much money as they can, so they routinely refill any ship that lands whether you want it or not. At least, we aren't paying for it.

See, the pilot fellow is handling it, for all the good it's going to do us," Fernando answered.

"Boy, the air here sure smells," Sondra commented.

"Yes, pretty foul around the spaceport. Always was. Pollution," he replied.

The pilot walked back inside, this time with his gun out and no space suit. Evidently, Sondra thought, the bio agent was diluted by the spaceport's air. "Okay, time to meet your new owner, Luigi. After I unfasten your seat belts, head to the bay ramp." At the same time, other men came onboard and began carrying the comatose nine out, tossing them over their shoulders like sacks of potatoes or bags of wheat. An idea formed in Sondra's mind, based on what was going on.

The pilot departed as soon as he had unfastened everyone and got them heading towards the bay area. He rushed past them and headed off, riding back on the refueling truck, which had already done its job. Apparently, only one fuel cell had to be replace, which Sondra presumed meant they hadn't traveled very far. With all the men off the ship and her nine wobbling slowly to the bay, she hung back, intentionally bringing up the rear.

Getting down the ramp in their heels was almost impossible, each discovered. Finally, Rene figured out how she could do it by stepping down sideways. Everyone else followed her lead, though each found it incredibly difficult to do, but none of those waiting on them offered to lend a supporting hand. As Sondra finally made it down, she intentionally bumped into the Close and the Lock button. The door slowly closed, sealed, and locked. Without knowing the key code, no one could enter the Bright Star, at least she presumed that was the case. If nothing else, she wanted her ship to be safe.

No one seemed to mind her action, and she joined the nine others standing before three men and two other UFB women. Two men wore security guard uniforms and held d-guns on them, which Sondra found ludicrous, as if she or the others posed them the remotest threat. The other man was immaculately dressed in an expensive, black suit with a red tie. His hair was black and oiled. A black moustache helped frame his face as one who meant business, though his eyes flickered about as though he were fearful of something. She saw their nine comatose people lying in the back of a truck-like vehicle.

The two UFB women were quite unusual looking. One woman had brilliant green eyes and flaming red hair that fell in waves to her knees. The other woman had wavy black hair and cold, black eyes. Somehow, their faces, though angelic, looked remarkably similar to each other. Each wore exotic, red latex gowns, complete with outer corsets, just as Sable had always worn. Each also had a head harness of some kind that held a black ball in their mouths, preventing them from speaking. Their fancy form-fitting gowns held their upper legs tightly together. A fancy flaring just below their knees opened out about two feet, revealing their nylon encased lower legs and requisite toe shoes, oxford style, securely tied on their feet.

"I am Luigi, your new owner. You are the most ill dressed, despicable excuses for gorgeous women that I've ever seen. But don't worry, Luigi will soon have you properly attired. I can see you'll all need to undergo a most thorough training before I can market you to my clientele. These two will be looking after your needs and training. Esmeralda and Gonzalo Sanchez. I'm told you speak a form of English. Please nod if that is correct?" Sondra nodded. "Good, good. We 9Gamma-C folks pride ourselves on being multilingual. However, we'll soon have to teach you proper Spanish. Okay, head over to the truck. My men will lift you in. Mind you, this will be the very last time anyone lifts a finger to help you. As my exotic escorts, you are required to take care of yourselves and fully satisfy your client. Failure to do so results in more drastic measures being taken and more extensive training. Now move." He pivoted and headed to the driver's door of the truck.

Sondra knew getting around wearing Sable's fetish outfits had been murder, but that was before she had been genetically modified. Her heart went out to the pair of UFB women teetering and wobbling their way towards the truck, leading the nine newcomers. *Life is about to become almost unbearable,* she thought. *Maybe Fernando was right; they should have found a way to get the pilot to shoot them. No, I have to escape and get everyone out of this mess,* Sondra resolved, no matter what.

Luigi's Exotic Escorts read a giant sign above what looked like a majestic hotel. Plush red carpeting, golden fixtures, and dozens of other UFB women dolled up in incredibly restrictive, brightly colored latex outfits stood in various locations around this main meeting room. A number of grubby men, some wearing dirty flight suits, were walking around the women, eyeing them, and discussing prices with another well-dressed man, carrying a clipboard.

"Don't worry. You're going to need to undergo extensive training before you can be put down here as a floor model. Soon you will be here providing sexual favors for the clients who pick you for their escort. Follow Esmeralda and Gonzalo. They will lead you to your new suite. Someone will get you cleaned up and into your training outfits promptly. Oh, the others will join you, as soon as they come out of their comas. After two weeks of good, solid training, I expect to see you down here as magnificent floor models too. Good day." He walked off, leaving them standing and still staring at the grandeur of this lobby.

Esmeralda nodded her head, jostling her earrings and hair about, but Sondra realized she was trying to get them to follow her. Suddenly, she heard a voice-like sound in her head. *Please, follow us.* She stared at the green-eyed woman, who nodded, a sparkle in her eyes.

At the elevators, a man took them up to the tenth floor. There, several women proceeded to undress and bathe the nine. After that, they were helped to stand by a machine, which put their inner corsets on them, tightening them down in stages. Each stage forced more and more air out of their lungs, until most fainted. When Sondra came too, she found herself wearing the strangest corset she'd ever seen. While it had dozens of unyielding steel stays and was so tight that her waist was barely fourteen inches around, unlike those that Sable had worn, this one continued down below her hips, ending near her knees, forcing her upper legs tightly together. While she had been out, they'd put nylons and black oxfords on her feet. Standing was much easier to handle now, despite the intense compression of her chest and near impossibility of breathing. She fainted again.

This time when she awoke, she was fully dressed. A shiny latex gown similar to those worn by the escort models she'd seen in the lobby covered her. Her friends were identically dressed. However, this new style corset didn't even permit her to bend at her waist nor could she even sit down! Another wave of panic swept over her, and she fainted again.

When she awoke this time, she found her mouth was forced open by a hard rubber ball, held securely in place by a head harness similar to the ones the Esmeralda and Gonzalo had worn. She was leaning against a tall stool, while a woman was waving smelling salts beneath her nose. "Now then, it's time to begin your training. If you fall down, no one will be helping you back up. As a top escort model, it is your responsibility to get yourself back up if you should disgrace your client by falling down."

"Can't breathe," Sondra tried to say, but only an unintelligible sound came out. The hard rubber ball blocked all possibility of speech. Another wave of terror swept over her, and she fainted yet again.

This time when she came around, she found herself in a strange room. At least the floor was covered with a thinner carpet, making walking easier. Her head was held in some kind of harness. In turn, it was attached to a chain that rose overhead to a heavy steel beam, a spoke attached to a central column. Her other eight companions were similarly attired and attached to other spokes. Esmeralda and Gonzalo were standing against a back wall, as a woman went from person to person waving smelling salts under their noses.

"All right. The training begins. Here's how it works. When the motor starts, each of you will begin walking in a circle. Your harnesses will prevent you from falling for now. If you don't move, lose your balance, or do anything besides walk, the machine will send a painful electrical charge into your privates until you start walking once more. The pain will also keep you from passing out. You'll walk for an hour. Then it will be time for a restroom break and lunch, before we resume the walking. After a few days of this, we'll move you into the second portion of your training, where you will do the walking without the assistance of the machine. Then, if you fall, it's your own problem to get up, which you will find incredibly difficult to do. Okay, I will leave you in Esmeralda's capable hands. Oh, I see she had no hands," the woman made a pathetic attempt at humor.

The machine began to move, and the nine had no choice but to try to take tiny, shuffling-like steps. With their upper legs held immobile by the long corset, walking was almost impossible. And yet Esmeralda and the other women in the lobby seemed to manage somehow, so Sondra figured that it must be possible.

"Try not to faint or stumble. The pain is acute," Esmeralda said encouragingly.   Sondra stumbled and would have fallen had not her head harness and chain prevented that. However, she felt a painful jolt coming from inside her privates. Now she realized they'd stuck something up there, probably while she was passed out. A long, hideous hour passed for the nine.

By the time that they were given their first break, Sondra was utterly exhausted, but was thankful the helper women handled her much needed bathroom break and then stuffed a healthy, but tiny lunch into her and her companions. No sooner had they spooned some water into her than they forced that awful ball back into her mouth. All this time, they were not sitting down, but more or less leaning against tall bar stools. With the gags back in place, they were again hooked up to the machine and forced to walk once more.

Sondra lost all track of time, all track of thoughts. All became a long blurry nightmare, filled with stabbing, shooting pains in her privates. When they finally allowed her to fall into bed that night, still wearing that strange corset and ball gag, she ached and passed out again, only this time, no pain shot through her. Sleep came almost at once.

At dawn, the nightmare continued unabated, though this time Luigi and several other men leered at them, sometimes watching them for an hour at a time. "They will make incredible additions to your selections, Luigi," one said. "Hell, I'd even pay to take that one out." He meant Rene who had to walk on her toes, unlike the others.

Just when they thought it couldn't get worse, their other nine companions joined them, their faces soaked from tears, their eyes reflecting pure terror and shock from the stark reality that faced them when they awoke from their comas. *At least, they don't have slit lips and thus no lip plates,* Sondra thought.

She watched Alice for a moment, realizing that her sister was devastated. No longer could she play her violin. Her life's goals had been taken from her by these bastards. Now more than ever, Sondra swore to get justice for Alice and all them. These aliens were nothing but a bunch of sadistic men. Women were nothing more than sex toys to be humiliated and tortured, as they desired. If eyes could kill, Sondra's would have been atomic bombs.

The only times their gags were removed was at meal times, which came around every four hours during the day, primarily because they could only eat a small amount at a time. The first time they leaned against the stools to be fed, Roxane whispered to Fernando, "They killed our son!"

"Shut up or you will not be fed!" someone yelled at her.

"You bastards!" Fernando screamed, though no one but Sondra's group understood him. They were not familiar with his garbled speech, but he received a hard slap across his face for his outburst. Sondra's own eyes watered. She couldn't help it; she knew how much those two wanted their child.

However, she also noticed a monumental change in Fernando, first from his eyes. Before, she had him pegged as a wimp, a coward, probably because he had lost his manhood and been turned into a helpless freak. Now his eyes came on fire! She didn't know psychology, but she knew people, having dealt with them all her life in Snake Town. Fernando had changed, though only later did she find out how much.

\*\*\*

Adriana, Mario's secretary, had not been idle. When she learned of the Bright Star and that Admiral Julio was to capture it, interrogate the prisoners, and then dump them off at Luigi's, she had to act. She knew what the admiral intended to do, turn them into sex dolls for the exotic prostitution trade that surrounded 9Gamma-C's spaceport, just as it did around most Federation spaceports. Actually, knowing what the admiral was planning, she took countermeasures and got him to deliver them to Luigi's care, where she had some connections.

Several days passed before she was able to get free to visit Luigi's again. "Yes, I would like my usual escort, Esmeralda, please," she explained, handing the man her ID card, which he swiped. A hundred credits were instantly transferred to Luigi's account. She sat down in one of the plush chairs in the lobby waiting for her escort to arrive. Some fifteen minutes later, Esmeralda, now dressed in an emerald green latex outfit, made her slow, cautious way from the elevator across the lobby. Adriana rose and waved, bringing a smile to Esmeralda's face.

As soon as she reached her, Adriana slipped her arm around Esmeralda's tiny waist, steadying her, and they walked out of the hotel. Once on the street, Adriana whispered, "Have the eighteen new people arrived yet?"

"Yes, I think they even aborted one of their children, too. They are having a terrible time adjusting. Nine have only just become UFB women and men," Esmeralda explained.

"Good. Okay, I believe these people are your ticket out of there. They come from Virge-C, where all hell has been happening," Adriana explained, as they slowly walked along the street.

"I think I've figured out which one is their leader. It's Sondra. She seems very much in control."

"I know they have a space ship, a new and big one, docked at the spaceport."

"I know," Esmeralda replied. "I've seen it. Sondra managed to shut and lock it when they left with Luigi and his men. Clever move. I've been watching her ever since. I've pried into her mind a little. Her goal is to find a cure for all them. I think they were headed to the Abelard Sector."

"Ah, makes sense. I've done a little checking, and they do have funds, quite a lot in fact. It's time for you to make your move. Can you get them out of the building?" Adriana asked the pivotal question. All else hinged on this detail, which was beyond her control.

"I think so. No one guards anything but the lobby after midnight. Can you handle that night watchman? If so, I think they will be able to walk well enough to get out on their own," Esmeralda answered.

"Okay, one guard, eh? All right. I'll see that he's knocked out say at one o'clock. Will that do?"

"Yes, I hope so."

"Good. They should go to Scorpi-C in the Abelard Sector. Once there, have them contact the GE Medical Research Laboratories. If cures are available, those people will know. God, I hope there's a cure for you and Gonzalo."

"Hell, no more so than we, Adriana. Okay, I'll get word to you if we're successful. How is the rebellion coming? We don't get any news in there," Esmeralda asked.

"Stalled at the moment. This mess on Virge-C is forcing many issues to the back burner here. Those Virge-C people are standing up to Mario's people. After Mario unleashed his genetic bio agent wiping out two million people, they counterattacked. Damned effectively too. They waited until Mario repopulated their evacuated city and then triggered a nuclear bomb that wiped the whole city out. Killed over a million of Mario's people and none of theirs. That's disrupted everything here on 9Gamma-C for the time being," Adriana relayed the latest news.

"Incredible! That's the best news in ages," Esmeralda replied. "What's Mario doing about that?"

"He's nuked another of their cities and promised to nuke another one if they don't capitulate in full. Time will tell on that one. So when do you want to escape?" Adriana asked.

"They need to be able to walk safely. Give them another two days. Let's make it one in the morning," Esmeralda decided, based upon her observations of the eighteen, especially the nine who were just beginning to learn to cope with their utter helplessness. "I think one is a pilot. Still, I think we can handle the ship ourselves. Autopilot and all that."

"Good. Two days. One in the morning. I'll make sure of the night watchman. Good luck, Esmeralda. Much hinges on you and Gonzalo, you know."

"I know. Wish we hadn't been captured, but that's water over the dam, isn't it? If there isn't a cure, I think I can still function," Esmeralda volunteered.

"I knew you could, dear. That's why I've not given up hope for you two. We best get you back. We don't want to arouse more suspicions," Adriana added.

***

The next morning while Esmeralda and Gonzalo watched over the struggling nine who now had to walk on their own without the support of the walking machine, she sent telepathic thoughts to Sondra. *You are their leader right? Just nod.*

Surprised to hear the ideas in her head, Sondra looked over at Esmeralda and nodded yes. *Good. I have a way for you and your friends to escape, but you have to take me and my brother, Gonzalo, with you. Okay?* Sondra nodded again. *Good. We will talk more later.*

During their lunch break, Esmeralda sent, *Two days from now, we make our escape. We have to be near the lobby doors around one in the morning. Everyone else will be asleep by then. Okay? You and your people will have to be able to walk to the lobby and then some. Okay?* Sondra nodded, wishing that she had a way to let the others know the plan.

*Don't worry about that. I will let your companions know when we are at lunch today. I don't want to cause them to fall down. Getting up is almost impossible,* she sent, sensing Sondra's great relief and surge of hope.

Two days passed rapidly, only because of the faint hope of escape, though none knew how they could possible succeed. Sondra noted they kept their heels on them at night so that they could go to the bathroom if need be. Still, with this weird corset on, if they needed to do it, they had to get out of bed on their own and push the red call button. Sondra once tried it, but had to wait nearly a half hour before a sleepy woman finally came to assist her with it. Thus, Sondra knew that they could walk, if they could somehow keep their balance. But that was one big if.

As usual, they were stripped down to their corset and

303

heels before being allowed to fall onto their beds. Sondra fell with enthusiasm tonight, for in a few hours, she hoped and prayed that they would all be out of this nightmare place. She'd seen enough of their sadism to last her a lifetime. By midnight, all the escorts were back and in their beds as well. The entire hotel was asleep, except for the lone night watchman down in the lobby. Dim night lighting did provide some illumination.

Esmeralda entered Sondra's room. "Okay, it's time. Get to your feet and make your way into the hall. We'll notify the others," she whispered, turned and moved on to the next room. Here in the living quarters, none of the rooms had any doors. They'd been removed for the convenience of everyone, especially their caretakers. Sondra knew that there wasn't anyone who could help her now. Somehow, despite the incredible restrictions of the weird corset, she had to get up to her feet alone. With a lot of struggling, lurching, and very nearly falling off the bed, she got to her feet, wobbling about wildly before she got her balance back. Nearly fainting from the effort, she paused to catch her breath. Fainting now would ruin any chance of escape. A few minutes later, she began her slow, shuffling way out into the hall, hoping and praying the others could get up and into the hall on their own. If they fell, she had no idea how she could possibly help them get back up.

Precious minutes passed before she saw all of her ball gagged companions finally standing in the hallway, along with Esmeralda and Gonzalo. The two gave them time to catch their breaths. Only when Rene stopped gasping did the two move slowly towards the elevator. Using her nose, Esmeralda pressed the button and waited. When the doors opened, she entered, nodding towards the others. Only ten could fit in it, and Gonzalo remained behind to help get the other half down when the elevator returned.

When the doors opened on the lobby, Esmeralda led the first group out onto the plush carpeting. Shit, thought Sondra. Walking was now twice as difficult on this thick carpeting, and she wiggle and wobbled far more than normal. Again, she prayed that no one would fall down. After an eternity, they reached the main doors.

Someone wearing all black and a hooded mask that completely hid their face was already there. The night watchman was lying dead on the carpet. Using a handheld device of some kind, the masked person finished cutting out a section of the doors and stepped inside. Quickly, the person removed Esmeralda's head harness and ball gag.

"So far so good," Esmeralda whispered.

A woman's voice whispered, "I'll get the others freed up."

When Sondra's gag was removed, she asked, "Can you get us out of these corsets too?"

The woman hesitated a minute and then nodded. Using that same strange device, she cut through the heavy cord bindings along Sondra's backside. Instantly, the corset popped loose and fell to the floor. "God, that's so much better. Thanks." By then, the mystery woman moved on to the next, cutting them free. By the time that this first group of ten had their gags and corsets cut free, Gonzalo brought the remaining nine up to join them. Hastily, the woman went from person to person freeing them.

"Okay, follow Gonzalo and me. We have to walk a mile to the spaceport and get to your ship," Esmeralda whispered. Turning to their masked benefactor, she whispered, "Thank you." The masked woman nodded. As Sondra passed her, she too gave the unknown woman her thanks, as did everyone else.

Now naked except for their heels, the twenty filed out onto the nighttime street of the slumbering city. Gonzalo whispered, "Keep quiet. We know this city cold. We'll take back alleys as much as possible. Keep quiet!" Off they went, only now they could breathe properly and walking was vastly easier though by no means a simple task. Shuffling like a row of penguins, the twenty moved down the street, ducking into the first alleyway they came to.

Around three in the morning, they reached the edge of the spaceport. While Esmeralda allowed them a brief rest, she and Gonzalo surveyed the situation, though Sondra and Matt soon joined them. "So how do we get inside the fence?" she asked, but had Matt translate for her. She didn't know if they could understand her or not and took no chances.

"We know of a back way in," Esmeralda whispered back. "We're just getting our bearings. We need to get to the long-term parking area without being seen. They do have patrols around the perimeter during the night, so we have to be careful. That way. We've still got a mile to go."

It was five in the morning when the exhausted group finally reached the Bright Star. The pair had led them to a section of the fence what was loose, and they merely pushed it out of the way while everyone entered. Then came the long haul across the tarmac, here very dimly illuminated. Esmeralda had a good memory and led them directly to their ship, though there must have been hundreds of ships parked here in the lot.

"Okay, my turn," Sondra whispered, moving up to the lock. Using her nose, she entered the sequence of numbers, 322422. The doors unlocked and Sondra pressed the Open button. Smiles of relief swept across many faces, as they watched the ramp lower. "Go ahead. I'll bring up the rear," Sondra whispered, watching her friends doing just that. Going up the ramp was easy. It was going down that was problematical. Sondra looked around. Seeing no one, she entered and Matt hit the Close button as soon as she was inside.

Already, Beth, Tom, Jason, and Esmeralda had reached the pilot and navigator's compartment, while Sandy and Alice sat down at the comm center. Using her nose, Sandy switched on the intercom. Esmeralda's voice came through. "Okay, here's the plan. We take off and engage the hyperdrive as fast as possible. All we need to do is enter the proper coordinates first. The destination is Scorpi-C in the Abelard Sector. We think if a cure is available, they will have it there. Use your nose, Jason. Bring up the display and let's see what is programmed into the hyperdrive now."

"But how will I fly it?" Beth asked.

"I used to be a pilot too," Gonzalo answered. "Together, we can do it using our feet, more or less. We just have to hold the ship stable until they press the Activate button. The autopilot should do the rest. How are those coordinates coming? We don't want to fire up the ship until you have them entered. The control tower will challenge us, and we sure can't respond, at least not easily."

"We need a fuel consumption check," Beth broke in. "Are we going to have to refuel to get there? I'm really a new pilot, you see. This is my first long distance flight. We can do it. We're not really all that helpless. I've seen Sondra do amazing things with her feet, so Jason, we're going to have to do it her way too. But the pre-flight checks say we need to check our fuel."

"Right, but we do that after they lay in the coordinates," Gonzalo replied, backing her up. "I've never flown with my feet before either, Beth, but we can do it. We have to."

It took them close to a half hour to find the coordinates for Scorpi-C and get them entered, pushing the numerical keypad with their noses. After more fiddling, Beth had her fuel consumption reading, opting to only travel at half speed so that they would only use about half of their fuel, just in case.

"Okay everyone, I'd say fasten seatbelts, but that's not going to happen," Beth cheerily called out. "So hunker down. This could be a rough takeoff, so don't hold that to me. We're flying by our feet, I hope. Be there in twenty-four hours if we can actually do this. Here goes nothing." She used a toe to fire up the ship.

The Bright Star pitched, yawed, and rolled, tossing the passengers about, but finally Jason managed to hit the Activate button, and the ship jumped into hyperspace, settling out as the autopilot took control, just as they were being challenged by the control tower. "We made it," Beth called out. She and the others headed down to the passenger area, joining the others, where many conversations were happening at the same time.

Roxane was sobbing. "They killed our son, Fernando; they killed him," she wailed.

"I know, dear. I know. We can have more, but I swear to you, Roxane, I will make they pay dearly for what they did to you, if it is the last thing I ever do. I will make them pay!" Fernando was livid with anger, something Sondra had never seen in the man. Something had definitely changed with him.

"Well, Jason, I guess now we aren't going to have baby

geniuses, are we?" Beth said sadly.

"I know, but still we can have children, if you still want them and me," Jason said in almost a whisper, very insecurely.

"I can never play again, Sandy," sobbed Alice. "My life is ruined utterly. There's nothing left to live for now. They've taken away my whole reason to live."

"I know honey. I know," Sandy cried, leaning into her mate, unable to think of anything remotely to say to console her.

Tom was merely crying to Rene, while Ben sobbed along with Adonia. Sondra knew the nine really needed her special therapy thing, but she also knew they had twenty-four hours before she absolutely had to have a better idea of whether anyone on this new world had a cure for them. If not, she needed to be able to give them another destination and hope. Their situation was precarious, since none of the twenty could do much for themselves, let alone operate the ship. *Thank god for the autopilot, whatever that is,* she thought.

She looked at Matt. Now that they were on their way, he too had succumbed and was crying to himself. Hence, she headed on back towards her cabin. Esmeralda saw her and decided to follow her, while Gonzalo saw the grieving party and decided to return to the pilot's seat. At least, he could monitor the instruments. *Sis got us out of that sadistic hellhole, but I'll never be a resistance fighter again, not like I was before then,* he thought sadly.

Sondra reached her cabin door and used her foot to open the latch. Inside, she sat down, carefully lowered her computer to the floor, and fired it up, just as Esmeralda entered. "What'cha doing?" she asked.

"Oh hi. Thank you for rescuing us from those sadistic people. I know. I should be helping the others over their grief, but I had better research this Scorpi-C place and see if I can find us a cure there. If not, I had damned well better find us another destination before we get there; otherwise, everyone's going to lose all hope. Hell, we'll soon starve to death," she replied, remembering to speak slowly.

"I think I got half of that. Okay if I just touch your mind a little so I can understand you better?" Esmeralda asked.

"Sure. Here we go. It's up. Now to search for Scorpi-C," she replied.

"Hey, try the GE Medical Research Laboratories. Our helper friend back on 9Gamma-C suggested we go there once we arrive," Esmeralda replied, sitting down beside her and watching her carefully. "Say, you know a bit about computers."

"Yes, my specialty back home, along with hacking into other systems and web stuff," Sondra explained, bringing up their home page to start her search. Searching on "cures" got her hundreds of links, so she tried "regrow arms." She let out a shriek, as did Esmeralda. "Look, it can be done!"

Immense relief flooded over both women. Finally, Sondra truly began to relax. There was some hope for a future now. "So you were a freedom fighter on Virge-C?" Esmeralda asked.

"Well, yes, sort of," Sondra answered. Soon, she found herself telling this green-eyed woman her life's story. When she finished, Esmeralda reciprocated.

"My brother and I are or were freedom fighters on 9Gamma-C. I am or was a hot computer hacker. You and I have a whole lot in common. Anyway, Gonzalo was into the actual fighting and sabotage thing. We did quite a lot of damage before we were caught and sent to Luigi's. What they didn't know is that we have a contact high up in the top leadership of our world. She helped rescue us. Hope she isn't caught. So what are you checking on now?" she asked, but could see that Sondra was looking at some bank accounts.

"No! My god, no! Those bastards, those sadistic, thieving bastards! They stole all of our money, all of it, millions," Sondra wailed.

"Here, let me see. Is this one yours?" Esmeralda asked. Sondra nodded. Her elation now shattered. How could they pay for these cures? Their money, gone. Then, she remembered the stash of diamonds and relaxed. They still had them to fall back on.

Esmeralda said, "When I get some time, I believe I can get your money back for you. The way really to hurt these sadistic, greedy CEOs is to hit their bank accounts. Let me think about it some."

"Please, if you can do that, it will be a miracle," Sondra replied, "but you have to show me how it's done. This could be useful back on my world too." The two chatted, and then joined the others.

"Everyone, I have two announcements to make. First, we can get our arms back. This GE Medical place can do it, and we are heading there as soon as we get to this new world. So there is hope, gang, real hope!" Sondra told everyone.

"So what's the second one?" asked Matt.

"They stole all of our money out of our bank accounts. I just checked on them and our millions are gone. But don't worry, we still have those diamonds we can use to pay for our cures," Sondra added hastily.

"Don't worry, Roxane," Fernando spoke up, "As soon as I can get my arms back, I am going to go back there and teach them a lesson they will never, ever forget. I have three scores to settle now. They aborted our son, and that is unforgivable. They stole your money, and they genetically mutated all of you. Mark my words, they will pay for this and pay more dearly than they could ever imagine! I so swear to you, my Roxane." Fernando was truly antagonistic. His eyes burned. *Something's changed with him,* Sondra thought, *really changed.*

"I think I can get your money back," Esmeralda spoke up. "Once I have my hands, like Sondra, I'm something of a computer whiz. Fernando, Gonzalo can help you settle the score. He and I have some scores to settle with Luigi and many of the top CEOs on 9Gamma-C too. We should work together."

"Well, all right, as long as he doesn't get in my way. I know a lot of inside information. I was GD's number three executive before this happened to me, though I truly deserved this, Sondra. You were right in stopping me."

"What's she mean by stopping you?" Esmeralda asked. Several chuckled. The group spent the next several hours telling the stories of their adventures on Virge-C. It helped pass the time, since everyone knew they were going to be very hungry before they got to Scorpi-C. No one could fix them anything, let alone feed those with the lip disks. However, they did get enough water to drink via the drinking fountain. Plus being naked allowed them to use the bathroom by themselves. Thus, sharing stories helped them pass the long hours, that, and a good night's sleep.

Sondra was quite on edge as the hour of landing approached. Autopilot was fine for the long flight, but could it handle something as complex as landing? Their wildly rocking takeoff was still vivid in her mind, and she'd half expected to die in a fiery crash before Beth, Gonzalo, Tom, and Jason got them into hyperspace, whatever that was. At last, she simply sat back. Whatever would happen would happen. Such things were not only beyond her control, but she knew nothing about flying space ships. Electronics, computers, and webs were her specialties, along with solving mysteries.

"Control tower to unidentified commercial transport, come in please?" Up front, the bored voice echoed into the ears of the four who had jammed themselves into the pilot and navigator's seats, preparing for the landing on Scorpi-C. Beth used a toe to flip the comm switch. "This is Captain Beth Ferguson of the Virge-C transport Bright Star. We need help landing. Please advise. Over." She repeated it twice.

"Control tower to Bright Star, what is your situation? Over." She detected slight interest in his voice now.

"We have been victims of that genetic bio agent thing. All twenty of us on board are armless now. We are trying to get to the GE Medical Research Laboratory in search of a cure, but I don't think I can land the ship using my feet. We need some help, please. Over," Beth calmly replied.

"What? No one on your ship has arms? How the devil did—never mind. Can you engage the ground control autopilot? It should be a brown switch on the far left side of most transport pilot's consoles."

"Yes, I know about it. Switching it on now. Over," Beth replied, forgetting to wait until he said over. The ship lurched a bit before ground control took over their flight.

"Ground Control to Bright Star. We have your ship under our control. We will land you at Pad 113. Please stay onboard until security arrives. Over and out."

Beth hastily relayed what was happening over the intercom. "Well, this is darn convenient."

"No kidding. I doubt we could land it ourselves," Gonzalo added. All twenty sat back and relaxed, greatly relieved. *Well, the security men are sure going to get an eye-full*, he thought. Many others had similar embarrassing thoughts, but like him, they could only endure the obvious stares and hope they would be helped.

"My god. Send for a transport. Find something to cover them with!" barked a tall, thin security guard in charge of the six men who surrounded the Bright Star, which had been landed on the emergency pad, far from any critical installations just in case of a crash. Sondra had opened the bay door and the twenty stood there waiting for help getting down the ramp.

A bustle of activity complete with a swarm of onlookers surrounded Pad 113. Awkward hands lifted each one down and helped them into a transport bus that arrived in less than a minute. "Take them to the GE Medical Research Lab pronto," the thin man ordered the driver. Turning to Matt, he asked, "I take it that you don't have your ID cards with you?"

"No, they were taken from us by the sadistic creeps who did this to us. We managed to escape and get here. Please, we need help, sir," Matt explained. "We're from Virge-C, well most of us are."

"Okay. We will quarantine your ship and await word from the medical lab. I've never seen anything like this before, though I'm told such things are becoming more commonplace," he replied.

From Sondra's point of view, things happened very rapidly after that. The city around them seemed both foreign and familiar. Skyscrapers of glass, steel, and concrete looked much like her own now destroyed West Port, and yet it was different. The medical facility was a huge, sprawling complex near the edge of the city and not too far from the spaceport itself. They arrived at an emergency entrance, where a number of attendants wearing white gowns rushed out, gasped, and carried the twenty inside, where the smell of disinfectant dominated all olfactory senses.

Shortly, two doctors appeared, sighed, and began taking down names and vital data. Ten nurses joined them and took over the record keeping. "Now then, is one of you in charge?" a doctor asked.

Sondra took charge. "I am doctor. Can you even understand me?"

"Ah, an English dialect. Yes, we have had a good deal of experience with women who wear these exotic lip ornaments. What is it that you desire?"

"Oh thank heavens," Sondra gushed, greatly relieved, though Matt was prepared to translate if needed. She hastily related what had been done to them against their wills. "Doctor, we came here hoping and praying that there is a cure that will get our arms back. If so, we all need it. I have some diamonds back on my ship we can use to pay for the procedure. Plus, back on our home world, Virge-C, they did it to two million men, women, and children—everyone in our most populous city, West Port. Is it possible for us to get cured?"

"Yes, for quite some time now, we here at GE Medical Research Labs have been doing just that. Of course, the cures available and their effectiveness is dependent upon your DNA makeup and the bio agent used on you. We will first need a DNA sample from each of you. That will be analyzed and compared to our known cures. Once that is done, we can then discuss what cures are available and their effectiveness with each of you. We will worry about payment after the cures are finished. Now then, shall we begin the process? If so, we will admit you to our medical facility and get you handled with all due speed."

"Please doctor. Yes, we all want cures," Sondra replied. For the first time since she awoke from her coma, Sondra felt genuine hope and relief. Maybe her living nightmare and that of her dear friends may soon be over, a horrible thing of the past.

With that, another flurry of action filled the emergency treatment room. Nurses took down names, photographs, and blood samples. After that, each was put into a white hospital gown and whisked off to private rooms. There, attendants gave them a bath and fed them. Then they waited and waited, which is what most patients often do in medical facilities. Two days later, the doctors began paying each one a personal visit, outlining just what could be done.

Sondra's case was similar to the others of Virge-C ancestry. "Good news. Your arms can be regrown," the doctor explained. "Now your feet, like most every other one we've worked on, can only be partially repaired. You would have to still wear six-inch heels. Now about your breasts. They can be reduced in size to about half of what they are. Unfortunately, there is just enough difference in your DNA to make the hair cure useless, so I would not be recommending that one. What about your lips? Would you like them repaired as well?"

"Yes, please. This is fantastic news, doctor. How soon can it be done?" Sondra asked. *Thank the gods for these people!*

"We can start today. We will be putting you into a four-day coma while your arms are regenerating. We do this so that we can keep your body filled with the proper nutrients to rebuild the lost bones and muscles. Of course, after that, it usually takes about six months for your arm muscles to regain their former strength." He chatted on, but Sondra stopped listening. This was almost too good to be true.

"Yes, get it done as soon as possible," she said, trying not to sound as excited as she felt. *After all, this doctor has probably seen many victims like me.*

He continued, "When you awake, you will be given a complimentary outfit from Leonardo's UFB Fashions. Usually, all UFB women and those who have had some of the possible cures obtain their apparel from this corporation, which has offices on nearly all Federation planets. Naturally, they are anticipating your future business. Now then, let's get started."

Four days later, Sondra awoke. Her face itched and without thinking, she raised her hands to itch it. As she relieved the itch, she felt her lips. They too were healed and she saw her hands. "It worked! Hands. Arms. Oh thank the gods everywhere," she gushed.

A nurse entered with a smile on her face. "Welcome back to the land of the living, Sondra. I do hope you are pleased with the results. Let's get you dressed and up and about."

"I'm so happy I could just yell!" Sondra exclaimed.

"Yes, I'm sure you are. Everyone who wakes up with their cures feels much the same way. Honestly, go ahead and yell. I won't say anything," she replied, arranging the new clothing for Sondra to put on.

"Well, I guess I don't have to yell," she giggled foolishly. "Still, I can't begin to tell you all how much this means to me and my husband and friends. You have saved our lives."

"I know. It gives us much satisfaction to be able to do so. You'll be a bit weak until we get some solid food in you. Let me help you get dressed."

Sondra looked at herself in the mirror. If she stared hard enough, she thought she could see a faint line were her lips had been slit. Her bosom was still larger than that of the average woman, a size H cup, but already she felt so much lighter. They were half the size that they had been. Her feet were still a bit malformed, and she discovered they didn't lie flat, but the new six-inch heels felt delightful compared to the toe shoes she had been wearing. Her hair was still knee-length and just as sensitive, but she adored long hair anyway.

Soon, the nurse led her to a larger room where, one by one, her other companions joined her, exuberant looks on their faces. Thank you's flew left and right. Alice exclaimed, "Now I can play my violin again, though I'll probably have to learn how all over again."

"Hey, I can sew once more," Kiesha Kay gushed. Thus flew the comments and praises.

The men were also feeling more human. While they still looked like women, they had their arms back, much smaller breasts, and with partially repaired feet. So yes, even they were quite pleased with the results. After eating a solid meal, an administrator dropped by, preparatory to their checkout procedure. He explained, "As we prepare to release you from the facility, it is my obligation to notify you that there is no charge for our services here. However, if you have the financial means, a donation would be appreciated. It cost ten thousand for each of your cures. Any amount that you can pay will help defray the cost of others who cannot afford the service."

"Can we send Matt here back to our ship and get some

of our diamonds? We'd like to pay you, if that's acceptable. You have literally saved our lives, and we must give you back a fair exchange," Sondra replied.

"That would be most gratifying. I will send someone along with him to show him the way and arrange for the diamond exchange into gold dollars for the facility," he replied formally, rather pleased they'd not done twenty cures non-grata.

While Matt was gone, Sondra watched her friends and sisters chatting gaily. So much had just changed for the better that they just had to talk about it all. Everyone was wearing black oxford style heels. The women wore similar satin gowns in complimentary colors and that hung loosely with a bit of flair below their waists, hemmed at their knees, displaying their black nylons. The men on the other hand were dressed as though they were professional women, white silk blouse with a black tie and black skirt, again hemmed at their knees. Tom mentioned he was told that most cured men preferred this look, the closest they could come to a man's appearance. He promised to *see* about that when they visited this Leonardo's UFB Fashions place.

Matt returned two hours later, having converted half of their pile of diamonds into gold dollars and donating two hundred thousand to the medical facility. The rest, he kept to cover their immediate expenses. "Look, I've a new ID card now. We are all supposed to report to the Control Tower to obtain our new ID cards as our first action. They even sent along a guard to ensure that we comply. I told them we'd by staying on our ship rather than taking a hotel in town. I hope that's okay with all of you." It was, and the group headed off to the spaceport.

After satisfying the Customs Agent and obtaining their new ID cards, they headed first to Leonardo's. Sondra gave each person a thousand gold dollars to purchase whatever they desired in footwear and clothing, though Kiesha Kay insisted that she could alter most of their older clothing. That done, Esmeralda asked for another five thousand for computer supplies, while Fernando, Matt, Tom, and Gonzalo wanted a couple thousand to purchase new Federation weapons. While most headed back to the ship to set about organizing their things and making supper, the five others headed off to see what they could buy.

Over a supper that tasted delicious, compliments of Ben and Adonia who went out of their way to create the best dinner possible to celebrate their good fortune, the men were ecstatic over their purchases. "Look at this, dear," Matt proudly showed off his new MK40 gun. "This improved model will blast a hole in anyone wearing one of those personal defense shields. Now we can't be stopped. Tons better than our 9mm guns."

"Aye, lassies, we have five of them now and four d-guns too," Tom added, not wanting to be left out of this important find. Note, the original designation of MK50 was dropped in favor of MK40 Model II, since they were that original model with additions.

"And I have some much needed computer equipment. Sondra, after supper, you and I have some scores to settle!" Esmeralda declared.

"Great everyone. Also, Rene and I will start in on giving each of you my trauma erasing thing. We all need it badly. I insist that we all have it done before we do much else," Sondra declared.

# Chapter 19—Where It Hurts

After supper, Sondra and Esmeralda set up shop in an unused cabin near the rear of the Bright Star. She had five computers running and began to give Sondra some assignments. "We're going to get our money back for starters," she explained.

"Hacking into the banks?" Sondra asked.

"Precisely. We'll need your account numbers. First, let's see where the funds went."

"I've hacked into many city systems, but never a bank. Don't they have super security?" Sondra asked.

"Indeed the best. However, there is the Blackwater Underground. We're going to use them. They will handle the transfers. We set up the transactions we desire, and they will see they are executed. Money will be transferred into accounts all over the entire Federation before making its way into our accounts. It will take several days for all of it to arrive, less the underground's cut. Now let's see where your money went," Esmeralda explained.

An hour later, the two sat back, satisfied looks on their faces. Luigi had drained their accounts and then transferred ten percent to the spaceport commander and another ten percent to Admiral Julio. "Now, we set to work," Esmeralda declared. "Payback is going to be a bitch!"

"Can we drain all of Galactic Dynamics accounts too?" Sondra asked.

"You bet we are and several other corporations that Gonzalo and I know for sure are behind the corruption of our world and yours too," she explained. "Okay, your job is to open up twenty-six new accounts in fake names. Able Zonnor, Ben Yanni, Carmela Xenos, and so on. Make up the names like that. Give me the list of names and assigned account numbers. The Underground will be using them as part of the process, before closing them and erasing all traces of those accounts."

"Coming to bed dear?" Matt asked, poking his head into their cabin, papers strewn all over the bed. Sondra was just shutting down two of the computers.

"Yes, all done, thanks to Esmeralda."

The fiery redhead chuckled, "Yes, in a few days, each of us will become billionaires, Matt. Then, you can buy all the guns your heart desires. I do hope that you will help us in the rebellion on 9Gamma-C, as well as your world."

"Sure thing. A billionaire? How's that possible?" Matt asked in disbelief.

"You don't want to know. It's complicated, but trust me. Over the next few days, millions upon millions will find their way into your account, all untraceable by the authorities and banks," Esmeralda explained. "We should have done this years ago, but I didn't think of it until you lost your money."

"With that kind of money, we could buy an army," Matt jested.

"But we don't want more bloodshed or genetic mutations or nuclear destructions," Sondra broke in. "It's already gotten out of hand. These are unethical, sadistic, greedy bastards—the men at the top, I mean. Their soldiers just do as ordered. We have to hit those who are really behind all of it," she explained.

"So how do we find those men?" Matt asked.

"I'm not sure yet. Besides, I have to first help everyone get rid of the trauma we've undergone. However, time enough for that tomorrow. I'm really tired, Matt."

The next day, Sondra and Rene began trauma handling on Alice and Lenora. Alice was in tears. She discovered the awful truth that her new arms and fingers had to be trained from scratch if she were to continue playing her violin. She was crushed again. Lenora, on the other hand, had been a commando and her loss was acute. Hence, the two began with these, the most critical as far as Sondra was concerned.

Meanwhile, Matt, Gonzalo, Tom, and Fernando took scouting trips out into the large city. The four had ideas of their own to pursue, while Esmeralda monitored the seemingly endless flow of funds into their many accounts. Sandy, the CEO assistant in her, decided on a novel approach. She began piecing together news footage of what these corporations had done on Virge-C and elsewhere. Her goal: a documentary on the crimes committed by the top corporation

CEOs. Soon, she changed its title to *How Your Corporations Spend Your Profits*, a blistering condemnation of their criminal and unethical actions, bordering on genocide.

When Esmeralda saw her finished product two weeks later, she praised Sandy and swore she had just the vehicle to get it widely distributed and viewed by millions. The computer hacker released the documentary at just the precise time there on 9Gamma-C, when it caused the most furor, aiding the rebellion in progress, but that is getting ahead of the action.

On the men's next scouting trip, they returned, looking quite different. Some of Tom's old swagger was back. "Well, lassies, how ya like our new look? Gotta hand it ta Matt. He's gotta an eye fer this." Each wore a businessman's suit, though obviously tailored to fit their grossly altered physical forms. Greys, browns, and blacks predominated, though their silk shirts were white. They still had no recourse but to wear the usual six-inch heels, though theirs were a matte black now, helping to avoid drawing attention to them.

Matt explained to Sondra, "We look more like men, though nothing can alter our voices or our long hair or our breasts. Don't worry, we're not going to cut them off," he added jovially. Esmeralda picked up his thought; at least one of them had seriously considered having his breasts removed. "We also bought jeans and shirts too. These are our fancy suits. So what do you think?"

Sondra chuckled, "Handsome as always, Matt. Good thinking." *This is hurting the fellows more than I thought. If this helps them feel more normal, then they should do it. Still, I wish there was something more that I could do to help them. Maybe if we really do end up with billions of dollars, I can use a bunch to support some scientists in finding more cures for the fellows. I think I'll talk this over with Esmeralda. She knows more about these things.*

After the pleased men finished showing off what they'd purchased, Sondra then changed the topic. "You know, we really do need to purchase a million cures and take them back to Virge-C. We can give those million victims much of their lives back."

"Aye, that we do, lassie," Tom backed her. "We gotta do

that, but it's still a war zone. Besides, the spaceport is gone."

"Well, we can land pretty much in any open space," Beth broke in, "but the real problem is fuel. Once we get back, there's no way to refuel. I'm sure the enemy isn't going to sell us fuel."

"And we need to get back to 9Gamma-C and help our resistance fighters," Gonzalo added.

Alice added her thoughts. Just now, she truly didn't want to return home to Virge-C. Her orchestra was destroyed, and she was now spending long hours each day trying to re-master her violin. Already, she'd discovered this world of Scorpi-C had nine symphony orchestras and many composers she'd never heard of. "I'd like to stay here and study their music. It's not safe for musicians back home. My whole orchestra was wiped out, though maybe if we get the cures there, a few might be able to relearn to play as I am now. So really, I'm quite happy staying here on Scorpi-C for now."

Sandy was torn between a desire to return and help form up a resistance movement to fight back, and staying here with her mate. "I'd best stay with Alice. We can coordinate your efforts from here, sending along supplies and things that you need."

Bill Ferguson spoke up, "Cousin Tom has a point. It is still a war zone. But what I don't understand is we were supposed to become an active member of the Galactic Federation. Just who runs it and where are they? Can't we take our case to them? Surely, they will listen to reason and end these wars."

Esmeralda laughed. "You still don't get it, do you? The major corporation CEOs run everything, the ones with the most money and profits, which are Galactic Dynamics, Galactic Electronics, and General Robotics, though those in food production, housing, transportation, apparel, and appliances are next in line. Look, it works like this, or at least it used to work this way until Corporate Prime got wiped out."

She explained, "Look. Take Felsing-C, a world not too far from ours. There, the CEOs of the big three run everything on that world. They make the laws, enforce them, and convict the guilty. However, they must also follow orders given to them from their superiors, their Sector Heads, which are the CEOs on our world, 9Gamma-C, who run our world and six others, including Felsing-C. In turn, our CEOs have to follow the orders they are given from the Mid-Arm Regional CEOs, who used to have to follow the orders from the CEOs of their respective companies on Corporate Prime. With the destruction of Corporate Prime, the Galactic Federation is splintered and is being run by three regional sets of CEOs, namely, the Mid-Arm Region, the Hub Region, and the Rim Region."

"These three regional groups no longer have anyone above them, and they are vying for ultimate power themselves. From what we've seen, they don't work together anymore and are going off in different directions. It looks as if these rim worlds are beginning to break free of the totalitarian corporate run. This very world, Scorpi-C is leading the way, though as I understand it, their leader is the CEO of Galactic Dynamics."

Esmeralda finished by saying, "So the original plan for your world, Bill, was for that Diego de la Vasco fellow to take over your world and run it himself, following orders from our world, 9Gamma-C and Mario de la Vega of Galactic Dynamics. None of your native people, Bill, was ever going to have any real say in your world's participation in the Federation."

Her brother added, "So that's why we in the resistance are trying to undermine Mario and his thugs. If we can bring him and his fellow CEOs down, then we free not only your world, but six others and ours as well." Gonzalo had a satisfied look on his face. *If only it was as simple as he makes it out to be,* thought Sondra.

"Hey, how come you don't have telepathy like your sister?" Bill asked.

He shrugged his shoulder. Esmeralda explained, "One of our ancestors in ancient times came from a world of telepaths. That was a half millennia ago. They brought peace to the entire galaxy, or so our ancient history says. We're descended from them, though now, no one has any idea where that world was. Hell, we only know about a small slice of the entire galaxy now. The rest out there is wholly unknown, lost in antiquity. That I ended up having telepathic skills is a

322

wonder that our family has kept secret. If the CEOs found out about me, they'd capture me and force me to be their slave, prying into the minds of their enemies and competitors. They have done that often, capturing known telepaths, and even breeding them to make more, but in that, they've failed utterly."

She went on, "Mom had it, and so did grandmother, but mom's sisters didn't have it. It's weird, and there's no predicting which children might have it. I guess I lucked out, except I've been on the run for my life ever since someone found out about it during my senior year in high school. Thank heavens Gonzalo is with me. He has saved me several times now."

Matt sighed, "So no matter what we did on Virge-C, ultimately it would be their CEO who was going to run our world as we entered the Galactic Federation. It's hopeless then—us being a part of the Federation?"

"I don't think so," Esmeralda answered thoughtfully, biting her lip slightly. "If your President Johnson could regain total control over Virge-C, he could be your ruler, and the corporations would have to recognize him in that capacity, but you are going to have to defeat the corporations first, kind of like they did here on Scorpi-C. Plus, we're going to have to do the same thing on 9Gamma-C too."

"I see. So we really do need to go on the offensive on both worlds," Matt concluded. "I say we should split up. Alice and Sandy are not soldiers. I like the idea of them staying here in the safety of Scorpi-C. Sondra, Lenora, and I at least should go back to Virge-C and see what we can do there, while you two go back to 9Gamma-C. Perhaps, there is a way our three groups can work together to bring about freedom for us all." Greatly relieved that Matt was supporting her idea, Alice grinned broadly. Sandy nodded too.

After a bit more discussion, Lilly Ann and Peter decided to stay with Alice and Sandy on Scorpi-C. They'd acquire supplies and get them sent to both other worlds as needed. Bill and Jan decided to join up with Esmeralda and Gonzalo, helping them fight back on 9Gamma-C. The rest returned to Virge-C to do what they could there, bringing back the million doses of the genetic cures as a first action.

*** 

Dr. Sam Decker, Virge-C's leading geneticist, though now a wanted man, waited patiently to hear back from 9Gamma-C. True, Rodrigo Vegas of Galactic Dynamics on Virge-C had rescued him from President John Johnson's dragnet, but Dr. Decker also knew that if he remained on Virge-C, he'd always be a wanted man, despite Rodrigo's desires to front him with a full research lab. Instead, he'd contacted some of the research geneticists on 9Gamma-C—the Federation world that oversaw the corporations on Virge-C. While he had perfected human cloning technology, these others had obviously gone in a different direction—the genetic modification of living humans, as witnessed by the many UFB women wives of the CEOs here on Virge-C. If he could combine the two technologies—well, the possibilities were boundless.

Much to the disappointment of Rodrigo, the CEO received orders from his superiors on 9Gamma-C to send Dr. Decker there immediately. Dr. Decker's transport departed from the spaceport on Virge-C a mere nine hours before the genetic bio agent attack and subsequent nuclear destruction of the entire city. Luck was truly with this doctor. Once he arrived on this new world, he spent long days in discussions with these geneticists, sharing their discoveries, though he purposely left out several critical details of his process. No way was he going to give up his hard-won technologies. If Dr. Decker did that, he knew he would lose whatever bargaining chips he had left. Still, what he did relate proved invaluable to these geneticists.

Barely a week later, Dr. Decker received a summons to report to the geneticists on the Mid-Arm Regional world of Danforth-C, whose CEOs controlled 9Gamma-C and many other mid-arm worlds. He did learn that these men were now independent. Their bosses on Corporate Prime had been destroyed. Dr. Decker smiled. At last, he and his work were going to be presented to the *top* men of the Federation, at least here in the Mid-Arm Region. These were the most powerful men in one third of the Federation, though he hadn't the faintest notion of what rim and hub regions were all about. Dr. Decker anticipated he would be given free rein to conduct all the experiments that he desired and with the very best equipment that money could buy. For the first time in his life, Dr. Sam Decker felt on top of the world!

***

Galactic Dynamics CEO Mario de la Vega placed General Vito in charge of restoring order and recovery operations back on Virge-C. The general's first action was to bring in the giant terra-former ship. What had been the largest city on this world was now a nuclear wasteland and radioactive. While he could just land at some other city and construct a new and up to Federation standards spaceport there, it was simpler to use the terra-former and start from scratch on the site of old West Port.

He watched the operation from his battleship. Literally, the contaminated earth and debris was "folded" deep underground, while the earth there rose up, replacing the contaminated land. A week later, a completely new landscape was ready for heavy construction work. The large Boca River now had a new channel, having been rerouted in a giant arc around what had been West Port, a new tall hill forced it to remain aside, while executive homes would be built on the picturesque hilltop, forming the eastern side of new West Port. Away to the west, the land was completely flat. Here the new spaceport would be built.

The general ordered hundreds of construction ships and crews to land and begin the work of erecting a standardized Federation spaceport and city to be called New West Port. At this point in time that the local *troubles* began.

The rebel commandos of Virge-C who had refused to surrender and had gone underground, continued to bide their time, wisely so when the terra-forming operations began. However, when the construction equipment and crews landed and began their work, the commandos moved back into position close to the constructions.

The sheer number of well-armed security men prevented any outright attack on the construction crews. Hence, the commandos took a different approach. They had a large quantity of explosives with them. During the daytime hours far from New West Port, they began building improvised explosive devices or IEDs. During the nighttime hours, they snuck back into the construction site and placed them in various locations, then retreated out of the zone.

Starting the second week of construction, random explosions rocked the area, as unsuspecting workers accidentally triggered the devices! True, each one only harmed a few workers and damaged their construction equipment. Nevertheless, the disruption caused the general immense trouble. With dozens of these going off each day, the workers complained, as did the security men. Slowly, the damage took its toll. Worse, they had no way actually to detect these hidden devices, at least not easily. Construction costs continued to rise, nearly doubling.

Soon, General Vito had no choice but to order a continual IR scanning of the entire area each night. When his men reported seeing the red images of men scurrying into the city laying the IEDs, he countered by sending down small fighter ships to destroy these men. The first few nights were rather successful. A dozen commandos were killed, guided by the men manning the IR scanners onboard the battleship far above the planet.

However, the commandos soon realized what was happening and took preventative measures. A simple non-reflective emergency heat wrap blanket did the trick. Holding it over their bodies, the blanket radiated their body heat back ground-ward hiding them from the IR scanners in orbit above them. Once more, they placed numerous IEDs around the construction site.

Despite the constant harassment, New West Port continued to rise from the terra-formed landscape. Emphasis was placed on getting the spaceport constructed and operational, followed by the fancy new homes for the corporate executives. Finally, General Vito reported to Mario. "Sir, despite local problems, the spaceport is now fully operational. We anticipate the CEO mansions to be ready for occupancy next week. We are ready to commence Phase II of the construction plans. A hundred skyscrapers must be built.

I'm submitting my final cost figures for Phase I now and an estimate on Phase II, based on the difficulties we've had from the locals during Phase I."

"What? These figures are double what we initially planned for!" Mario angrily barked. "What the hell is going on there?"

"IEDs sir. Random improvised explosive devices. IEDs are buried all over the site and workers accidentally trigger them during the daytime. Minor annoyance, but the results accumulate in lost men and equipment. Hence, the cost overruns. I've added that into the cost estimates for Phase II, sir," the general replied.

"All right. I'll look them over and handle the payment of funds shortly," Mario replied, hanging up on the general. "So, send them the funds," he ordered one of his aides.

"Er, boss, these figures—they are double what we expected," the nervous aide replied.

"Hell, I know that. The general just said so. Pay them," Mario barked. He hated to be countermanded by a lowly aide.

"Sir, we've only got one credit left in our corporate account," the aide finally brought the matter to Mario's attention. Until now, he'd been worried about it all, but presumed Mario knew about their precarious financial situation.

"What do you mean? One credit? Man, there's billions in our account!" Mario yelled back. The aide handed him the bank ledger. Mario stared dumbfounded at the small computer screen. "This can't be right!"

Hastily, be brought up the account ledger and stared at the bank withdrawals. One billion to this company, one and a half million to that company—so on down the lengthy list. At the very bottom, his eyes lighted on the current balance of one credit. Esmeralda's program worked very well. Like most CEOs, he didn't investigate further, since the payments seemed to be going to all the usual companies.

"This can't be right. Well, let me call Ramiro. We'll borrow some funds from General Robotics," Mario declared. A half hour later, Mario sat back in his plush chair. His face, ashen. He'd contacted a dozen of his close corporations and found that they too were broke! Somehow, the costs for conquering and subduing Virge-C had grossly exceeded all predicted figures a thousandfold or more! "This can't be happening!" he whispered to the glass walls of his top floor office suite.

*What to do? What to do?* The question refused to go away. At last, he called General Vito back. "General, due to cost overruns, I'm sorry you'll not be receiving the promised funds right away. I anticipate by next year, we will be able to send you your payment for Phase I."

General Vito's face tightened. Deep lines marred his forehead. "Sir, that is *not* the agreement you have with the military forces. Payment in *full* upon job completion. That is in the long-standing agreement we have with the corporations. I expect full payment now or we will not commence Phase II," the general replied through clenched teeth. Never before had a top CEO gone back on these payment agreements!

"It can't be helped," Mario said, unwilling to tell him that the corporations on 9Gamma-C were flat broke, and that in a year, they still might not be able to meet the payment the general demanded.

"In that case, we will be departing Virge-C today. When we receive full payment for services delivered and believable promises for payment of Phase II, we will return to this world. Over and out!" the general barked. At once, he made contact with four other 9Gamma-C generals and reported what was happening. Without fanfare, the entire alien fleet departed from Virge-C that very day.

***

"Wow! Look, this must be where West Port was at, but everything is totally different, even the river!" exclaimed Beth from her pilot's seat.

"Aye, lassie," Tom broke in from his navigator's seat. Jason was looking over his shoulder, verifying the coordinates. "This is it, but it's *so* different!" he exclaimed. "The river's a goin' ta wrong way, sort of."

"He's right. This is where West Port was or is," Jason added. "It's utterly different. I don't remember those large hills being there and the river—it didn't have that huge bend in it

328

before, did it?"

Everyone else stared out of the windows at the ground below them. They had returned with a cargo of fuel cells and the million doses of the genetic agent cure for the victims of the alien bio agent attack. However, they did not expect to see what they were seeing. Further, they'd decided to approach the West Port area and request landing instructions from the aliens. Sondra had been explicit on this point. With the aliens in total control of their world, it would be suicide to try to land just anywhere without first getting permission from the aliens, who would just as likely shoot them down as not.

She'd been manning the Comm Center as they approached Virge-C, but had not been able to raise anyone on the standard Federation frequencies. Further, she'd not yet detected a single alien spaceship anywhere, though there should have been several in high orbits around the planet. She did pick up the standard beacon locator signal coming from the new spaceport, an aid to landing craft.

"Beth, land at this new spaceport," Sondra ordered from her monitoring port. "I can't find a single alien ship, and I can't raise the control tower, so take us down there anyway. What is going on now? Why does the land look so utterly different? It should be a nuclear waste land."

"I'll man the radiation detector when we land," Matt volunteered, not trusting what he was seeing. Building over the destroyed landscape would be suicide for anyone living there. Radiation poisoning would kill them, at least for the next hundred years or so, if he recalled his high school science class right.

As the Bright Star descended to the new spaceport, they finally saw a few small figures on the ground, along with a number of large, expensive mansions further to the east, resting on these strange new hills overlooking the new river valley. Some trees had been planted there as well, though more landscaping needed to be done.

The ship landed on the sparkling clean tarmac, close to the control tower, where several soldiers milled around, watching the ship land. "I recognize some of them," called out Lenora. "They are fellow commandos. What is going on here?

Where are the aliens? Say, that's my Major Brummond there!"

Beth set the Bright Star down with a perfect landing. Lenora opened the cargo bay ramp and stepped down, followed by Matt and Sondra. "Well, I'll be!" the major barked pleasantly surprise, "Captain Lenora Cox!"

"Major, yes, we're back. We've brought a million doses of the cure for the genetic bio agent victims and many new alien weapons for us. What's going on here? Where are the aliens?" Lenora asked rapid fire, while Matt watched the dial of his hand-held radiation detector, which showed none at all.

"We don't know. The aliens pulled out of here yesterday, every last one of them," the major answered. "Where have you been? Cures? Weapons? Incredible, captain. Corporal, get on the phone, and let President Johnson know about the cures. He can coordinate that."

Turning back to the small group who had joined Lenora, he explained. "Terra-formed. The old West Port is now somewhere down there," he pointed to the ground beneath his feet. "They remade the land. It's safe—no trace of radiation. They rerouted the Baca and made those hills yonder. We figure those are mansions for their CEOs, but we've not seen any of them. We just don't know why they all left. Mind you, we've been making and laying hundreds of improvised explosive devices. It's been taking a small, but steady toll on their workers and equipment, but I swear that's not enough for them to abandon the entire world. We don't understand what's going on. Nevertheless, I moved my remaining commandos in here for now. Do you have any idea what's going on? Any other space ships up there?"

Sondra answered, "No. Not a single alien ship anywhere around our world. I suspect the corporations are having a very severe cash flow problem about now. They might be bankrupt, which would account for their sudden departure."

"Whatever the reason, I say good riddance. Now let's see these new weapons of yours. Ours are nearly useless against those personal defense shields of theirs," the major demanded.

Lenora smiled. "You'll like these. They are the latest models and will puncture their defense shields!" Eagerly, she began doling out the MK-40 Model II's to the excited commandos.

Later that day, President Johnson and his group of aides arrived at the spaceport. Although officially he had resigned as far as the aliens were concerned, Virge-C had kept him on during this crisis. Now that the aliens had mysteriously departed, he was quite worried that they'd return and destroy the entire world. However, he was very pleased to see that the rebel commandos now had far better weapons and was elated to hear that Sondra had brought a partial cure back for the many victims.

After thanking her and her group profusely, he and Sondra sat down to work out how to get the cure to the victims, since this he could handle.

While they were thus occupied, Matt placed a secure call back to Scorpi-C, telling Sandy and Alice what was happening. "I sure wish we had a way to defend Virge-C from a surprise alien attack."

"Hey, we've been doing some snooping here," Sandy replied. "They have something called a Planetary Defense Shield, which prevents all ships from getting any closer to Scorpi-C than ten miles above it. That's what we need on Virge-C."

"Wow. Yes, that's precisely what we need, Sandy! Good thinking. See if you can get us one somehow!" Matt replied.

***

A week later, the cures were being given to the victims. However, Sondra learned that by this time only around two hundred fifty thousand of the original two million victims had survived. Many had found ways to kill themselves, usually by taking a bad fall, and she understood why they did that. Still, the loss of life was staggering, but she and her group were hailed as mighty heroes for bringing them back this cure. Having their arms back meant they could live independently again and become productive in their lives, though some had begun adapting and using their feet and toes.

Two weeks later, several deep space transports arrived bringing a new Planetary Defense Shield system with them, along with the ten massive power generators needed to operate it. It took local engineers another couple of weeks to get the generators adapted to the local energy grid, but then the shields went up. As long as the shields worked, Virge-C would be immune to aerial bombardment and attacks from the aliens.

Several weeks after that, a flotilla of alien ships appeared above Virge-C, requesting landing instructions and a meeting with their local leaders. The emissary was from Danforth-C, and he met with President Johnson. "We regret the inappropriate actions our predecessors have done here on your world," the well-dressed emissary began. "Let us put that in the past. I have come from the Mid-Arm Regional Corporations to present Virge-C with its official Federation Incorporation Documents. Of course, Virge-C will remain under the control of your local officials, presumably the presidency, if I understand your political arrangement."

"Well, this is a pleasant change," President Johnson replied. "We've had nothing but trouble from the alien corporations. If I accept these documents, what are we giving up this time? You must realize our position. We don't trust the alien corporations in the slightest, not after what they've done here."

"Of course, of course," the emissary said smoothly. "Who can blame you? No, you give up nothing. According to the documents, you need to allow the corporations to conduct their businesses on your world, but they will be subject to your world's laws and regulations."

"That's all well and good, but we don't want them ever to again be allowed to own Virge-C property, land, or buildings," President Johnson countered. "That's how they began to take over our world in the first place."

Once more, the smooth talking emissary replied, "Of course, of course. No, they will only be allowed to own the buildings they construct themselves and the property that the buildings rest upon. This way, they can't take over your world as they did before. That's all in the documents, you see. No, the regional office wants to put all that behind us and move forward into a bright future of cooperation with our newest Federation member world. You have valuable minerals many corporations desire, and we have much to give you in turn, though I see that you already have somehow managed to acquire a Planetary Defense Shield."

President Johnson smiled, "Ah, you noticed that. Yes, some of our people were able to purchase one for us. Now we are able to defend our world from attacks. We should have been given one of those in the first place."

"They are terribly expensive," the emissary replied, as though that was the sole reason none had been provided before. "Now as far as we can tell, the corporations have rebuilt the spaceport here and a few mansions."

"Yes, that's true."

"The documents state that the corporations will be allowed to construct new offices and homes here in New West Port," the emissary continued. "I hope that will not be a problem."

Wisely, President Johnson replied, "As long as our own companies are allowed to rebuild their offices and homes there as well."

"Ah, that is as it should be. If you will just sign here, then it will be official. Soon, some corporations will return and begin new constructions. I'm told that they will be desirous of hiring numerous local men and women to work for them, so that will also be an economic boom to your world as well," the emissary added smoothly.

"One detail. The mansions. Those are already being occupied by our local people. We would like that to remain so, in return, I am prepared to allow your people total control over the spaceport here in New West Port. Is that satisfactory?" President Johnson bargained.

"But of course. That is most generous of you. We'll make those changes and then you can sign the documents," he replied smoothly, very much impressed that somehow he'd regained total control over the spaceport without having to bring up that remaining issue. Control over the port meant control over the trade with this world, something that the Mid-Arm Regional offices had insisted upon having. They believed these locals would take a very long time to build their own modern spaceports, if ever, because Virge-C was still in its infancy with respect to the modern space faring worlds.

Thus, President Johnson signed these new documents, making the new arrangements official. He hoped this time things would work out for the betterment of Virge-C, though he knew it had taken nearly fifty years for the corporations to make their recent power plays. What would another fifty years bring? He hoped and prayed it wouldn't be another catastrophe.

*** 

Shortly after that signing, Sondra and her group of friends moved into the mansions on the eastern edge of New West Port, as befitting their seemingly endless wealth. Quite where these men and women obtained their fortunes, none could say, except that they continued to provide for Virge-C. Not long after that, a large shipment of MK40 Model II's arrived, enough to equip a small army, along with an equivalent number of personal defense shields. No longer would those guarding Virge-C be powerless against the aliens who began to arrive once more. Additionally, Sondra's group funded a new project to construct Virge-C's new and modern spaceport, located on the other side of the world from the one at New West Port. In time, the monopoly the corporations had on space trade was mostly nullified, much to their dismay.

# Chapter 20—Rebellion

Esmeralda and Gonzalo, along with Bill and Jan, arrived back on their home world of 9Gamma-C, but without any real plan of action, except to take advantage of the now defunct coffers of the major corporations that ran their world. Esmeralda suggested, "We know they are bankrupt, but everyone else here doesn't know that. Somehow, we have to get the public aware of just how desperate these evil corporations now are."

"Aye, and get the rebellion out of hiding," added Gonzalo.

"Independence. That's what you need to fight for," Bill suggested. "It's one thing for your people to create minor disturbances around your world and quite another to have the majority of the population up in arms over the running of the world. We need a campaign to get the average man in the street up in arms over this."

"So how do we do that? We need to bring some of these CEOs to justice too," Gonzalo replied, liking the way Bill was thinking. Until now, the resistance was tiny compared to the population of the world, and the damage and disruption was little more than a minor annoyance. Often, it harmed the average worker more than the corporations.

"We can start by plastering slogans all over the place. Your corporations are bankrupt. Your corporations have squandered all their money trying to take over other worlds by force of arms. I don't know. Describe their dirty little secrets, like destroying a whole city of two million with the bio agent," Bill suggested. "With enough of these things plastered all over your cities, eventually, the press will discover them and begin to demand an investigation or an accounting."

"Good thinking, but we should let our secret agent inside Galactic Dynamics know we are back and what we're planning," Esmeralda added.

They were now staying in a rundown, disused building in heart of Toledo, 9Gamma-C, one of the pair's many secret bases. They were relatively safe here. While the others began listing out possible messages, she placed a secure call to Adriana in Galactic Dynamics, letting her know they were back and what they'd done.

"Yes, we got cures on Scorpi-C," she explained, "and Sondra is now taking a million doses of the cure back to her world. The major corporations here on 9Gamma-C are now bankrupt. We have their funds, all them, including Luigi's, But we still have a score to settle with that sadist of Luigi's Exotic Escorts," Esmeralda explained. She went on to describe their next moves. Adriana encouraged her and volunteered to keep her eyes open for developments within the corporate world.

A week later, hundreds of signs appeared around the city and in many other larger cities as well. They were spray-painted onto the sides of prominent buildings and various walls where thousands of people would be able to see them before the signs could be painted over or erased. Some told of the bankruptcy of the major corporations. Some told how the corporations had squandered their profits, hard earned by the lowly workers of those companies. Others told of the genetic bio agent attack that wiped out two million men, women, and children in West Port, turning them into helpless UFB women and men. Still others suggested the readers demand accountability from the corporations.

In the middle of this campaign, Adriana called Esmeralda on a secure line to tell her that General Vito had pulled out completely from Virge-C over non-payment for his services in the reconstruction there. The next day, these details were also plastered on many walls around the cities of 9Gamma-C as well. That their armed forces were not being paid struck a raw nerve with the average person. In their minds, their lives were being protected by their military forces, which now were doing nothing, waiting for payment that wasn't forthcoming. Anyone could land a fleet and take over their world, at least that's what the average citizen of 9Gamma-C thought.

Three weeks after the start of their campaign, word reached them that the press wanted to interview someone from the resistance movement. Wearing a mask, Gonzalo setup the clandestine meeting with the reporter, choosing a disused warehouse, one that they almost never used as a hideout. There, Esmeralda, also wearing a mask, was interviewed by the reporter.

"Yes, the major corporations of our world are nearly bankrupt. Check on the accounts of Galactic Dynamics, General Robotics, GE, and many others. They have squandered tens of billions of gold dollars and credits! They are so broke that they have not paid General Vito and his crew for the terra-forming, construction of a new spaceport, and executive mansions on Virge-C. So yes, the ordinary people of our world have every right to be terrified. Any enemy can land and take over our world without a fight, since our armed forces are not being paid. Think of the poor workers who depend on their monthly pay checks and aren't getting them," she explained.

"So where did all our funds go?" the reporter inquired.

"On ill-thought out ventures to covertly and overtly take over another independent Federation world, Virge-C. Do you realize when they failed to do that, they then unleashed the genetic bio agent onto the entire capital city of West Port? Two million innocent men, women, and children were mutated into completely helpless UFB women and UFBMD men. More than a million subsequently died. That's genocide in my book," Esmeralda answered and accused.

"Someone should demand an accounting from Mario de la Vega of Galactic Dynamics. I'm told he was the mastermind of this catastrophe." Esmeralda chatted away for nearly ten minutes, outlining all she knew, added by a few inside bits that Adriana relayed to her. Wisely, she omitted telling the reporter of Virge-C's detonation of a nuclear bomb wiping out a million workers who had just immigrated to Virge-C.

Gonzalo purposely limited the interview to ten minutes. Why? He anticipated the security guards would be tracking the reporter. He was right. However, unknown to the reporter, Esmeralda had rigged up her own recorder and taped the entire interview. When Gonzalo gave her a hand signal, she ended the interview. "Look. We best stop now. Probably Mario's thugs are coming to shut you down. We best get out of here now."

"Oh, I'm sure that's not going to happen," the reporter countered, unwilling to end this incredible interview, much of which she believed was mere propaganda put out by the rebels. Still, it was an interesting story. Hastily, Esmeralda and Gonzalo slipped out of a back door and fled the area. Two blocks away, they stopped to watch as a cadre of GD security guards swooped down on the warehouse.

"That's cutting it a bit close," Esmeralda whispered.

"Did you get it? I bet they won't let the reporter broadcast that interview," he whispered back.

"Yes, got it. As soon as we get back to our place, I'll put it up on the web for all to see."

"What? I'm a reporter. You can't interfere with the news," the reporter complained bitterly as dozens of the grey and black uniformed men of GD swarmed into the warehouse, guns drawn.

"We can. We'll take your recording now," the captain ordered. He fired his d-gun at their equipment, destroying the recorder and its interview. That done, he turned, signaled, and left the building, leaving a stunned reporter and her crew aghast.

"Well, there goes the scoop of the century!" she declared, very frustrated. "Maybe what all she said wasn't just her imaginings after all."

An hour later back at her studios, the depressed reporter was called into her boss's office. "You have to see this! Your interview is up on the Internet! How did you manage that? I thought you said they destroyed your equipment."

"They did. It must have been the rebels. They must have also taped it. Thank heavens they did. You have to listen to her claims. There must be some truth in them," she declared.

Within a few days, that ten-minute clip went viral on 9Gamma-C. After a week, nearly everyone on the world had seen it at least once, despite corporate attempts to take it down. That's the trouble with the Internet. Once something is posted, there is no taking it down. Someone will always make a copy of it and post it elsewhere. As soon as the CEOs had it down on one site, it popped up on yet another, Esmeralda's doing.

A week was all that was needed for it to reach Galactic Dynamics headquarters on Danforth-C. CEO Dansic fumed when an aide played it for him. Hastily, he ordered a full investigation, a quiet, secretive one. Within a day, he saw that the rebel was correct. The major corporations on 9Gamma-C were indeed nearly broke. The bank records clearly showed the enormous sums being spent on subduing this marginal world of Virge-C. No one bothered to dig deeper and see that these exorbitant funds were never received by the indicated companies and corporations, but had vanished, then reappearing in the secret accounts setup by Esmeralda. Further, a short chat with General Vito confirmed the payment situation.

"I have to act now," Dansic declared, fuming. "Mario's utter incompetence is costing us dearly! What is it going to cost us to take over 9Gamma-C and repair the damage these buffoons have caused?" he barked to his aides. Hastily, they began pounding away on their computers. Several hours later, his top aide showed him the final figure.

"Good God! We can't afford to pay that! That world isn't worth that much even if we terra-form the whole damned world and retrieved all its resources!"

"But boss, what else can we do? What about this Virge-C world?" the aide asked nervously. He'd never seen such an angry outburst from his boss in his entire life.

Dansic paced around his office a dozen times. *Calm. Calm, logical thought*, he said to himself repeatedly. At last, he regained control of his emotions. Thinking clearly, plans formed in his mind. No, he could not afford to bail out 9Gamma-C from this fiasco, nor could he abandon the future profits from the newly acquired, relatively primitive world of Virge-C. There was only one possible solution that would not drain his coffers and yet still provide substantial, long-term profits for the many Mid-Arm Regional corporations.

"Okay, here's what we do. Send for Mr. Le Blank. I'm appointing him my official emissary to this primitive world of Virge-C. We'll give them their independence, for now anyway. We must have their minerals. As for 9Gamma-C, we will give those rebels what they want, their independence, but we will first have to deal with those buffoons who call themselves our CEOs," Dansic replied calmly.

"Arrange for a meeting of Mario and all his aides, down through the third tier of management. Likewise for General Robotics." He listed nine other corporations as well. "We will meet with them all at the same time at the spaceport hanger bay Number Twelve. That should be large enough to house them all. Here's what we are going to do," he explained in detail, watching the snide expression that finally appeared on his top aide's face as he finally saw the whole picture.

A week later and with all preparations made in advance, Dansic stepped off his private deep space transport and walked to the hanger bay, surrounded by two dozen armed security men, who made sure that the building was secure before Dansic entered. As he walked in, he nodded to several doctors who followed him, pushing along carts loaded with equipment. One nodded back, the signal that all was prepared. He walked upright into the assemblage of CEOs and their subordinates.

Mario piped up, "All right, Dansic. We're all here. What is the meaning of this secret meeting? I can speak for all us CEOs. We have quite a lot to deal with at the moment."

"Of course you do, Mario. But it's all due to your complete incompetence," Dansic barked. "Gross incompetence. I've checked, and the reports are correct. You have bankrupted our corporations here on 9Gamma-C with your complete bungling methods on Virge-C. Now, it is time to remedy the situation. You all here have proven beyond a shadow of doubt that you are completely incapable of handling the responsibilities entrusted to you—so much so that not even the Mid-Arm Regional corporations can bail you out of this impossible mess you've made here."

"So," he went on, "I will be shortly giving in to the rebel demands for independence of 9Gamma-C. As for you men and women, who have cost your corporations tens of billions of credits, it is time that you begin repaying the corporations. Of course, you will be spending the rest of your pathetic lives paying us back."

"When I leave here, the process will begin. You few

women will be turned into UFB women and married off to worthy corporate executives. You can provide a lifetime of sexual pleasures to them. As far as you men go, payback will be a bitch. You will be turned into UFBMD men, and you will be bred to many normal women so that you may create many super-genius sons who one day can provide the necessary payback to your corporations. That is all. Enjoy the rest of your lives. May you live long and create many worthy sons."

Backed by a dozen guards, Dansic rose and left. Several men, including Mario, tried to rush him, but his guards were prepared and fired back, using stun settings. They were under strict orders not to physically harm anyone here. Mario dropped like a rock. He didn't see the doors being sealed tight and the genetic bio agent gas being released into Hanger Bay Number Twelve. Nor did he see men in bio containment suits entering later on, stripping all their clothing from them. Nor did he see them carrying some two hundred of them out of the hanger a day later.

Four days later, Mario, along with two hundred others, awoke to their own personal, never-ending nightmare. Like others before him, he couldn't breathe and fainted a number of times before he was stable enough to comprehend his newly mutated body form and apparel. At least his UFB wife was sitting beside his small hospital bed waiting for him to awaken.

"Mario, you look so utterly different, but then they said it would be so. Still, they are giving us a small home and a servant. We can still have children, but I have had to agree to let them breed you to many other normal women." She chatted on as though this was of little importance, while Mario bawled until he again passed out. Naturally, a nurse quickly revived him with smelling salts, chastising him for being such a sissy about all this.

***

Back on 9Gamma-C, Dansic went on national TV. "I want to arrange a meeting with the leaders of the local rebellion. My purpose will be explained at that time. You may choose the location for the meeting, and I will come alone and without any weapons on me. We have much to discuss. The incompetent CEOs and their underlings have been removed permanently and will never again be able to run a company, let alone their own lives. Contact me at this number." He read off a secure phone number.

Esmeralda jumped at the opportunity. "I'm here, Dansic. What's this all about?"

Dansic smiled. He'd not expected such a rapid response. "I want to meet with you personally to outline the terms of the transfer of power on 9Gamma-C to you and your people. We need to meet as soon as possible."

This time, Esmeralda used her telepathy on Dansic, not trusting him in the slightest. She saw an image of what he'd done to the CEOs and smiled. Sensing no ill will towards herself or any sign this was a trap, she agreed to a meeting, again picking the same disused warehouse where she'd given the reporter her interview. Gonzalo had the place bugged and guarded by twenty of fellow rebels, though they kept mostly hidden from view. Esmeralda waited alone in one of the two chairs in the vast, empty space, smelling of oil and filth.

"Fine place to meet," Dansic commented as he walked into the room, but curling up his nose at the foul smell of the place. Gonzalo gave her a hand signal meaning that he had come alone, though she suspected he had plenty of guards not too far away.

"Yes, safe for us both. What's this all about?" she replied, watching him sit down and noticing that he wore a PDS but had no visible weapon on him.

"As you know, the major corporations on your world are virtually bankrupt. Danforth-C can't possibly bail you out of this mess. So I have no viable choice but to grant this world its independence from Corporate Leadership. I am here to turn over control of 9Gamma-C to your people. Yes, the corporations will remain, but will be under your control, following whatever local laws you may have. Never again will their CEOs be allowed to control or run your world. Is this an acceptable solution to you rebels?" Dansic asked, knowing perfectly well that it was.

An hour later, the pair, followed by numerous guards from both sides, entered a TV studio to make the public announcement. Esmeralda wisely chose the very same reporter, whose scoop had been destroyed by Mario's thugs, to conduct this historic event. In front of the camera's and broadcasting live this time, since she didn't what to take any chance that someone would destroy this report before it was broadcast, Esmeralda and Dansic made their public announcement.

He began, "This is an historic day for 9Gamma-C. I, the Galactic Dynamics CEO on Danforth-C and the immediate boss of the corporations here on this world, am here to announce that as of this moment, 9Gamma-C is a completely independent Federation world. No longer will the corporation CEOs be permitted to run or control this world. I am turning over the entire world to you rebels."

Esmeralda spoke up. "On behalf of all us rebels, I am accepting the temporary position as President of 9Gamma-C until we can hold free and open elections. Our long battle for freedom is over. We have won. This is a day of celebration. I must thank Dansic here for having the wisdom of granting us our freedom. In time, I'm sure his corporations will once again see their profits coming in, only this time it will be coming from a free and independent world. Thank you all."

The reporter hastily asked, "And what of the CEOs who are guilty of many crimes, of which genocide may well be one?"

Dansic smiled. "The incompetent leaders have been genetically mutated into UFB women who will soon be married to other CEO men and give them pleasure and children. The men have become UFBMD men and will similarly be handled. So yes, they are paying for their *crimes*. You see, I don't feel that their deaths would be an appropriate punishment. That's the easy way out. No, they get to live the rest of their long lives, much as they condemned two million others on Virge-C to live theirs, helpless and utterly dependent upon others. Fitting, don't you think?" he sneered. Wisely, no one replied.

The two leaders chatted a bit more about how things would now be handled and then the interview ended. Once more, it went viral. Everyone saw it at some point during this very day. No one knew the reason Esmeralda stepped up to be their acting president was because of her telepathic ability, no one except Gonzalo. During the ensuing days, she used her skills to make sure those that she met, discussed actions with, and even appointed to temporary positions of power were being honest and not lying to her. In this way, she cleverly prevented ruthless others from attempting to directly gain power and a foothold in the new government. Once free elections were held, she could no longer make such a guarantee, but for now she could and did.

***

A week later, she got in touch with President John Johnson of Virge-C. Word came from Sondra of the startling developments on her world, and Esmeralda established a tight bond between the two independent worlds. Not long after that, Scorpi-C sent representatives to visit both, forming an alliance of free worlds within the Federation.

The other five corporation controlled worlds that 9Gamma-C used to control now came under the direct control of Danforth-C, though later Dansic appointed one of the five to take over control of the other four, much as 9Gamma-C had been.

***

Several weeks later, Roxane Stevens-Gabino proudly announced, "Fernando, I'm pregnant again. Yes, it's going to be another son!"

"Oh thank you, thank you, my dearest! I'm ready to be the greatest father ever, even if I don't look like one," Fernando replied.

"Well, our son will have a famous person for a father, now that you've been appointed President Johnson's Minister of Alien Affairs," she replied with a wry smile. She knew how much that appointment meant to him.

Fernando smiled broadly. While he still looked like a woman, he'd regained his own self-respect and self-worth. He still dressed like a professional woman, having given up trying to appear more masculine in an ill-fitting business suit.

Sondra and the others moved into the new mansions of New West Port. Their task was to continue to monitor the activities of the alien corporations as they soon moved in construction crews to build their new skyscrapers, companies, and homes.

However, Sandy and Alice did not return to Virge-C for another four years. It took Alice that long to get her violin playing back to the virtuoso level it had been before she had been genetically modified. Besides, when she returned, she came bearing a mountain of musical scores from Scorpi-C, greatly expanding the symphonic repertoire of Virge-C.

***

What of Luigi and his escort service? Esmeralda handled that expeditiously. With twenty well-armed rebels, she raided the service and captured the protesting Luigi. After dissolving the service and promising the UFB women their cures from Virge-C, she unleashed the same genetic bio agent onto Luigi. Four days later, he became a UFBMD man, and Esmeralda made sure that he was given the same treatment that she and her friends had endured under his control. On the off chance that male sons of his with normal women might well become super-geniuses, she bred him like a stud animal for some years. However, Luigi was never to be given the known genetic cures the others received. He lived to a ripe old age confined to the very building from which he ran his escort service, much to his own dismay.

***

As the elections for their first president ever drew close, Esmeralda reflected back on all that had happened. In a flash of insight, she realized one key fact that had actually brought all this about. The serendipity of Sondra meeting her clone twin on that dark night lay behind everything else that happened. She called up Sondra on a secure line and pointed this out to Sondra, who got a chuckle out of Esmeralda's declaration.

"And I got my sisters back," Sondra added. "That's what is truly important to me. I am not alone. I have a family."

Esmeralda replied, "True. And you are expecting, I've heard. Your family is growing."

Sondra laughed. "Yes, I'm pregnant. The doctor says it's a boy. I wonder if there is any truth to these rumors of super-

345

geniuses."

Esmeralda laughed back. "Between you and me, I think that's hokey. We are all individuals. Some are brighter than others are. I don't think genetics has anything to do with one's IQ." She had no idea just how wrong she was in dismissing the genetic breeding of UFBMD men to normal women.

# Chapter 21—Dr. Decker Rides Again

The forty-five year old Dr. Decker arrived on Danforth-C just as the breaking news of the wild events back on 9Gamma-C and Virge-C hit the newscasts. *Wow,* he thought as he watched the news, *I am incredibly lucky! I had no idea they were bankrupt on 9Gamma-C! Had I stayed there, I'd be out in the street with only my shirt on my back! Danforth-C has everything one could ever ask for.* He reflected on the tour of GD's genetics labs that he'd been given only this very morning. State of the art and unlimited funds—those had been impressed upon him by the various geneticists and doctors he'd met. They in turn were very much impressed with his cloning technology. *This could well be the very break I've waited for all my life.*

"This could well be the break we've been looking for," Dansic commented to Dr. Gleason, one of his trusted geneticists, who had just given an extensive tour of his facilities to Dr. Decker. Now he answered his boss's summons. "If we can learn all he knows about cloning, why, there's no stopping us, is there? Imagine an army of identical, top soldiers. Imagine what a group of identical super-geniuses could develop for us. Staggers the mind, my good doctor."

"Indeed. But Dr. Decker keeps the critical details close to his chest. I can understand why. After all, what use do we have with him once we know his secrets?" Dr. Gleason replied, saying what he believed Dansic wanted to hear. He guessed right.

Dansic chuckled. "Quite true. Quite. In the meantime, we need to endear ourselves to him. Every man has his weakness. We must observe him and find his. I doubt it is superb food. The man is skinny. Money? Perhaps. State of the art laboratory? Quite likely. Women? I wonder. The man isn't married. He damn well should be. He's what? In his mid-forties?" The doctor nodded, and Dansic continued, "Well, if we're to get our claws into him, we're going to have to remedy that. Surely, he's lusted after the incredible UFB women that those idiot CEOs had back on his world of Virge-C. What man in his right mind wouldn't be? Wait. You don't suppose that he's into men or boys, do you?"

The doctor chuckled. "No boss. As you know, there are quite a few UFB women around here. I caught him staring at them while we passed by them on our tour. He's anything but effeminate. I would bet anything he isn't gay. So are you suggesting that we get him a UFB wife?"

"Well, that would tie him down some and endear him to us. Yes, we should do that for sure, but I'm not certain that's going to be enough to get him to spill his secrets just yet. Still, that would make a good first step in that direction. Who have we got that's available?"

This time the doctor chuckled. "Out of my line, sir. Should we arrange for him to have a luxury suite?"

"Ah right. I'll find him the woman. Yes, a luxury suite and a fine young woman will make a good start. Continue to feel him out. I'm sure he wants to know all about our genetic mutation process and such things. Go ahead and give him full access to everything we know. He won't be a security leak. I can guarantee that. Perhaps with a luxury suite, a fine sex doll, and complete access to our genetic studies, he'll voluntarily share his cloning procedures with us," Dansic declared.

After the doctor left, he thought, *I don't dare make a mistake with this man. He's too valuable. No*, he corrected himself, *what he **knows** is too valuable. If we could clone Hans or Dexter, my God, I'd have an army of top soldiers and a bunch of geniuses working for me. No, nothing is too good for Dr. Decker right now. After we have his technology down, then—then we can do what we will with the man.* He sent an aide to compile a list of all available UFB women here in GD headquarters.

An hour later, he pulled up their images and brief bios on his computer. "I must find the perfect match for Dr. Decker," he whispered to his screen. While there were a few older women who had the misfortune to have their husbands die prematurely, he discarded these. Still, there were plenty of younger women; some were even second-generation UFB women. That is, they were the daughters of UFB women and had grown up knowing nothing else, devoid wholly of the trauma of having undergone the genetic mutation process and terror that followed.

*Yes, I must have a second-generation UFB woman, one who is wholly comfortable with her life and has no excess baggage.* He entered that criterion, reducing the pool of possible women to six. One by one, he reviewed them. Naturally, each was a stellar beauty in her own right. *Surely, there is some additional feature that would quickly endear her to Dr. Decker, but what?*

*Wait. This man is brilliant. He's going to want more than just a pretty sex doll. He could well have found one on his world. After all, he's forty-five. No, she has to have something extra, something that makes her special from his point of view.* One by one, he discarded five of remaining women. At last, his eyes focused on Breanna Clancey, a gorgeous blonde woman. He read her bio and knew he had the right choice. *It's a real shame Breanna is a helpless UFB woman. She could well have been a brilliant mathematician at the very least. Ah well, such is life. She should be perfect for him.* He sent for her and Dr. Decker.

"You wanted to see me?" Dr. Decker said upon entering this top floor office.

"Yes indeed. I've arranged for you to have one of our ninetieth floor luxury suites and a servant woman. As one of our most highly respected doctors, I'm obligated to provide you with your very own UFB woman. You are encouraged to marry her, if you find she is suitable. Mind you, all we top men in GD have such fabulous women as our wives. It would be a blot on you if you were to be seen without a UFB woman on your arm at our many social functions. Since you aren't married, I've chosen one for you. If you don't like her, then we can try another. We've plenty of unmarried UFB women who are most anxious to get married. Hell, man, raise a family. You aren't that old yet," Dansic attempted a bit of a nudge.

"Never had time for such things," Dr. Decker explained. "Mind you, I've seen some pretty incredible women on the tour today." He paused and added, "I see. I certainly don't want to become a blot on we top personnel here. I owe you so very much as it is," Dr. Decker minded his best manners, believing this was what the CEO wanted to hear. It was. He noticed Dansic relax slightly. Shortly, an aide opened the door and Brianna entered.

Dr. Decker saw a gorgeous young woman of twenty-five. She had knee-length, wavy, thick, shiny blonde hair. Her eyes were sky blue. She wore a matching strapless, satin gown that fit her curvaceous form quite tightly down to the hem just below her knees. Her bosom was gigantic, just as it was with all UFB women. Her tightly corseted tiny waist and wide hips added to her incredible silhouette. She wore black nylons and matching sky blue toe shoes. Breanna took tiny, shuffling, but confident, steps towards the two men, her large, long, dangling earrings bobbing slightly on her empty shoulders. Her eyes were bright and her smile, genuine.

"Ah, good afternoon, Breanna. Dr. Decker, this is the lovely Breanna Clancey. Breanna, this is our newest acquisition, the famous Dr. Sam Decker, who has come to our world to share in perfecting our genetic researches. Breanna, you are to accompany Dr. Decker as his UFB woman, sharing his new luxury suite, Number Six. If you two decide to marry, why just let me know. Breanna, I'll have your servant bring your things to your new suite. Now then, why don't you take Dr. Decker here to his new quarters and get acquainted?" Dansic suggested, though he knew Breanna would take that as a direct order.

"I'm pleased to meet you, Dr. Decker," Breanna said politely. This wasn't what she'd anticipated when she received her summons, but then she had long known this day would come. All UFB women eventually became some man's sex doll. That was the way it worked. Still, this wasn't what she desired, but knew she was powerless to do anything about it. With a pleasing smile on her face, she turned around gracefully and began taking her tiny steps back towards the door, knowing very well just how slowly she moved, compared to ordinary people.

Dr. Decker caught up with her as she reached the door. Once outside, she hinted, "Dr. If you will slip a steadying arm around my waist, I can walk a bit faster. It is rather challenging to walk much faster than I have been without a steadying arm. It's these heels, you see. So very little contact with the soft carpet and such a high heel. Yes, there, that's much better."

"I've never been around a UFB woman before, though I've seen them. You'll have to forgive my ignorance in such matters, Breanna. Please, just tell me what I should do. You are extremely beautiful," Dr. Decker struggled not to make a complete fool of himself. This wasn't what he had in mind, but he was wise enough to realize that when on Danforth-C, do as they do. *After all, I'm now entirely dependent on the largess of Dansic. So if he wants me to have a UFB woman around, I'll just have to make the best of it. Besides, Breanna is an extremely beautiful young woman. I could do far worse.*

"Oh sure. I understand, Dr. Decker. I was raised here in this building so I know my way around it, as they say like the back of my hand, which of course I don't have any and never did. Mom is a UFB woman, and I was born this way, so I am very used to being a UFB woman, though I do appreciate your steadying arm. I've had to depend upon myself all my life, you see, but I truly do appreciate your kindness. Keeping my balance is quite hard. Always has been. Honestly, you would laugh if you could have seen me learning to walk, though I know all babies have a hard time with that."

Dr. Decker smiled pleasantly. *She is certainly a talker.*

Breanna continued chatting as she led him on their way to the suite. "I know normal babies learn to crawl all over the place first, but I couldn't, you see, crawl that is. Eventually though, I managed to get to my knees and moved around that way for the longest time. Then, they put heels like these on my feet, only smaller of course, and started holding me up until I got the hang of walking. After that, each day, my servant girl used to walk me all around, holding on to me. A few days later, why, there was no stopping me. I walked everywhere, though closed doors are always a problem for me. Still, if you wait around long enough, someone comes by and opens it for you. I never will forget the surprised look on the CEO's face when I wandered into his top floor office all on my own. I think I was about seven at the time. He sure looked startled. So like I said, there isn't a room in GD headquarters here I haven't been inside one time or another. I know where absolutely everything is at, even your new lab, doctor."

"Oh, here, this is our floor. You must rate very, very highly with Dansic. He's giving you, well us, this luxury suite that normally is reserved for the highest-level guests when they come to visit, but now that I think about it, we haven't had such visitors, not since Corporate Prime was wiped out some years back. I overheard them talking. Dansic and several other CEOs now control this entire Mid-Arm region, and there is no one above them, so he is one of the most powerful men in the Federation now. Anyway, I've been in this suite and can tell you that it is seeping in luxury, but I do hope they have put one of the electrostatic hair machines in there for me and my hair. You do know about them?"

"Er, not really. Your hair is fabulous. So rich, lush, and long," he replied, rather taking a liking to this young woman.

"Yes, but without that machine, it's so hard to handle. Did you know I have a sense of touch with each strand? I do love to feel the wind in my hair. Such incredible waves of sensation. Anyway, I'm also very good with math. If I had been born a normal woman, I'm sure I would have been a top mathematician, but as a UFB woman, they simply won't give me a chance to do anything. Now, I can see why, well sort of. I don't have any hands or arms. Still, that doesn't affect my mind and my math skills. Long ago, I passed every online math course they have—with one hundred percent passes too, mind you. I wonder, do you ever need any math problems solved in your research? If you do, I'd love to help you with them. I work them in my head you see, since I don't have any hands to manipulate a calculator or computer. Oh, here we are. Wow, I see they've installed an automatic door opener. That's for my use mostly. Cool."

As the pair stepped into the spacious suite, Dr. Decker inhaled sharply. "Incredible! Beyond belief! I never imagined anything like this," he exclaimed, looking around the five-room suite from its main entrance.

"Oh yes, this is their most luxurious suite, as I said, for visiting top people. You must rate very highly with Dansic, but then I've already said that. Come on. I'll show you around. This is the living room with everything you could possibly want in it. The entertainment center is the best in the building. I should know, since I've seen them all. I just can't operate them, naturally. Now this is our tiny kitchen and dining area. Yes, those are real gold. If it's gold-colored in here, it's made of real gold. I'm told gold is heavy, but then I have no way of knowing that. No hands of course. This is our bathroom, which I'm really going to love. Just look at that tub. Oh great! They have a hair machine in here for me too. Good. Don't worry, Dr. Decker, I can use it by myself. All UFB women can. It was invented especially for us or so I am told."

"This is our bedroom. Plush beyond plush. I know the sheets are satin. I peeked once." Then, for the first time, Breanna fell silent. Her face, flushed.

Dr. Decker noticed her sudden silence and saw her reddish cheeks. "Something wrong, Breanna?"

"This is really embarrassing, Dr. Decker. I've never slept with a man yet," she said very softly.

Dr. Decker chuckled. "Well, don't worry about that. I'm sure we'll manage just fine. Ah, this must be the study area." He changed the topic rapidly.

"Oh yes, it is. The desk is imported. Teakwood. That's why it's black. Tropical wood, I found out. Let's check out the kitchen. I wonder if it is stocked. I'm a bit thirsty."

A few minutes later, they entered the small kitchen. By now, he realized just how slowly Breanna was forced to walk. He could have crossed the distance in seconds not minutes. "See if there is a bottle of cold water in the fridge. If so, there should be a straw in that drawer there, second one down on the right. Sorry, I can't point. No hands. So I just have to give good directions."

He found a bottle of chilled water, opened it, and found a straw for her. When he turned around, Breanna had already pushed a chair out and was just tossing her head around, jostling her long hair to one side. She sat down gracefully, an infectious smile on her face. "Just sit it where I can reach it. That cabinet contains a wide variety of liquors. Help yourself." She proceeded to sip the water, while he rummaged through the cabinet, not recognizing many of the names of the alcoholic beverages. Finally, he helped himself to a water, joining her.

"So you mentioned you are good with math," he began thinking ahead. She nodded. "Mind if I quiz you a bit? I best get some paper."

"Sure that would be great, but do give me problems similar to those you need worked out in your researches. There should be paper back in the study. Try the top right drawer, Dr. Decker."

He returned a minute later, paper and a pencil in hand. "We'll try some simple ones first," he said politely. *Obviously, she can't truly handle the differential equations that I need worked out. Hell, it takes me hours on the computer to get an approximate answer that is sufficiently accurate for my work.* He wrote out some sums, multiplications, and division problems.

"Oh those are baby problems," she replied, answering them almost as fast as he could write them out.

"Okay, I said we'll begin simple. Try this." He wrote out an algebra problem. "What are the two roots of this equation?"

Breanna answered immediately after he finished speaking the question, again startling him. So he tried even harder ones. Soon, he sighed and went for broke. *This woman knows her math. I'll stump her with one of the differential equations I last worked on.* He wrote out the rather lengthy equation.

This time, Breanna looked it over for a minute before rattling off the right answer, again shocking him. "Now that's more like it," she added.

"Amazing, Breanna. Positively amazing. It took me nearly a half hour to work that one out using my calculator. Let's try a few more I've recently had to work out, if I can remember them exactly," Dr. Decker exclaimed, genuinely surprised with the young woman's skills, to say nothing about doing it in her head.

For the next half hour, he jotted down four other equations he'd been recently working on, but Breanna had to correct him at three points where he made a mistake in writing them down. "You weren't kidding, Breanna. You have a brilliant mind for these equations. I've a mind to make you my personal assistant in my research, that is, if you don't mind working some."

"Not at all. This was the most fun I've had in months. No one around here ever gives me any problems to solve, and I've exhausted all the math courses they have. It would be fun for me. I would love to be really useful, truly useful, and not so darn helpless," Breanna replied.

Just then, her servant girl arrived, toting numerous bags on a large pushcart. "Should I put them in the bedroom closet, Dr. Decker?" she asked.

"Of course. We're sharing it, if you don't mind, Breanna," he replied, watching her move slowly after the servant girl. He listened to their light chattering, as Breanna suggested where her apparel should be stored.

"Oh do leave Dr. Decker the top drawer for his things. Tomorrow, we shall take him shopping for more clothes. I don't think he was able to bring more than one set of clothes with him," Breanna advised her servant girl.

Later, the two rejoined him in the small dining area. "They will be bringing supper by shortly, Dr. Decker," Breanna explained. "Obviously, I need to have someone help me dine. Until now, that's been one of her duties, to help me with that, but of course, the other husbands often assist their wives when they dine, but then I don't know if you want to be bothered with all that with me or not. She can stick around and help me if you prefer, doctor."

"Oh, I don't mind helping you, though I'm sure you'll have to tell me what to do," he answered her. With that decided, the servant girl said she'd be back around eight to get her ready for bed and left them alone.

Minutes later, a man brought them a dinner cart. The smell of roast duck followed the cart into the dining area, where he sat the stainless steel, covered dishes on the table, turned, and left them. "Oh, we just leave the dirty things on the cart, and someone will take them away later on," Breanna advised. "You'll need to set us a table though. I think the plates are in the left cupboard," she chatted away. Thus began Dr.

Decker's learning curve on assisting and loving a UFB woman.

Later that evening, he saw why Breanna's waist was so tiny because she wore a heavily boned, tight waist corset all the time. Plus, he was rather shocked to also discover that these women had extremely intense sexual drives. They had to find relief several times during the day, which was handled by wearing specially made dildo panties, though Breanna hinted she had heard from the married UFB women that if they had intercourse in the morning and at night, then it was barely possible for them to endure the rest of the day without receiving pleasuring. Knowing that, he made sure Breanna was fully satiated that night and again before they rose in the morning.

Her servant arrived shortly after they finished, along with their breakfast. "Oh my, Dr. Decker, you are wearing the same clothes as yesterday. You simply must have more clothing," Breanna stated the obvious.

"Yes, quite true. I've been on the run, so to speak, for weeks and simply haven't had a chance or the funds to purchase any," he replied truthfully. These past weeks had been incredibly hectic, but phenomenally lucky. "But I have so much to learn from your geneticists here. I'm to meet with Dr. Gleason this morning, so I'm afraid these will have to do for now."

"Well in that case, Dr. Decker, I can get them for you. Brenda, can you get his measurements and jot them down for me?" Breanna replied, as though this was quite an ordinary thing for a UFB woman to do. "Do you have any preferences for colors or fabrics?"

"Er. No, anything will do fine. Are you sure you can manage? What about paying for them? Like I said, I haven't any funds with me just yet."

"I'm sure GD will handle that for you. You run along and meet with Dr. Gleason; leave the rest to me. Perhaps we can meet here for lunch," she hinted.

He found his way to the seventieth floor, which housed the genetics research laboratories. One suite fully equipped was to be his or so the placard on the door said. Dr. Gleason was already in his lab waiting for him. "Ah, here you are at last, Dr. Decker. I've heard you have the lovely Breanna Clancey staying with you. So how do you like the results of our genetic experiments—our incredible ultimates in feminine beauty? Darn good, eh?" he hinted rather lecherously.

"Incredible is the appropriate word, I do believe. I'm most interested in just how these genetic modifications can be made. I take it these changes happen to every woman who is given the bio agent? Nothing is fine-tuned to her specific DNA strands?" Dr. Decker began probing for data.

"Yes, the specific genetic modifications that are engineered into the bio agent are generalized to produce the same effects on any human being. That's the beauty of these genetic alterations. Same results. That's the only acceptable method, by the way. It wouldn't be possible if we had to tailor the bio agent to fit each person's unique DNA structure. No, the real breakthrough came ages ago when these sequences were found to produce identical results on all humans," Dr. Gleason explained.

"So just how does this genetic bio agent work? Specific sequences to alter specific physical traits?" Dr. Decker asked, keenly interested in the precise details.

Dr. Gleason was very pleased to show him various slides of the splice sequences along with the specific result of that splice in human subjects. "This one produces neurons and axons in their hair, giving each hair strand a sense of touch. Of course, the hair's thickness more than doubles in diameter to accommodate the new sensory cells. And this one here lengthens the hair strands to approximately five feet in length. After that engineered length, the sensory cells die off, and the hair strand can be cut or trimmed. We don't want our UFB women walking on their hair, now do we," Dr. Gleason attempted a jest that rather failed.

"Here is the sequence that controls the production of their breasts. Notice the results are not hanging pendants but rather more like a child's soccer ball. Perky, we call them." He continued his lengthy discussion, showing the active agent splicing sequences that he *believed* were responsible for the physical effect. He didn't specifically say that no one truly knew, which sequence did what exactly.

Dr. Decker detected some confusion in Dr. Gleason's explanations or perhaps it was merely uncertainty. He probed, "And are you totally certain that this sequence here is the one that is causing the abnormal breast development?"

Dr. Gleason twisted his hands together and finally admitted, "Well, not exactly. You see, we are still studying all these sequences to find out precisely what they do and how they do it. That's why we need your help to further our studies."

"Wait a minute, Dr. Gleason. Are you telling me this genetic bio agent was just put together more or less randomly and has produced the UFB women?"

"Well, when you put it that way, yes, more or less. You see, ages ago, someone came across this formula. It works, and we've been studying just how and why it works ever since."

"Ah ha. I'm beginning to understand this much better, Dr. Gleason. Have you isolated one of these changes and applied it to a human test subject to see precisely what its effect will be?" Dr. Decker asked.

Horrified, Dr. Gleason exclaimed, "Oh no! That would be inhumane and illegal. We dare not experiment directly on humans. We study these sequences in our labs and make minor experiments on fruit flies."

"I see. Yes, that was the very problem I ran into back on my home world. Illegal experimentations. And yet, without it, how can you ever hope to advance your genetic modifications? Wouldn't it be vastly superior if your UFB women actually retained their arms so they wouldn't be so helpless?" Dr. Decker asked.

"How's it going, doctors?" inquired Dansic, who had just entered the lab to check on how Dr. Decker was faring.

"Impressive, most definitely," Dr. Decker replied politely. "However, correct me if I am wrong, but your geneticists haven't actually made any progress in making other modifications to the genetic mutations, primarily because they are prevented from making experiments on actual humans. I take it in the distant past, someone came up with this formula that works, making the UFB women, and since then, no one has made any significant modifications to it."

"Ah well, yes. That is correct. You can see why we are so interested in you and your work, Dr. Decker," Dansic answered him truthfully. *No sense trying to hide such things from the doctor,* the CEO thought, *because he will quickly discover that for himself.*

"I see. I was just asking Dr. Gleason here if it wouldn't be vastly superior if your UFB women actually retained their arms so that they wouldn't be so helpless? Personally, I could see great value in making that modification to the genetic bio agent," Dr. Decker asked.

Dansic smiled covertly. "Yes and no, doctor. You see, there are pros and cons either way on that detail. Pros are obvious, since as they are now, they are so helpless, completely dependent upon us males, their husbands, and servants. On the other hand, if they retained their arms and hands, then they would be free and independent. Combined with their other incredible beautiful traits, why, they could do and demand anything from any of us men and very likely get it." Both men chuckled, leaving Dr. Decker pondering Dansic's pronouncement.

"Still, without any proper human experimentation, how can you ever hope to make any additional genetic modifications?" Dr. Decker asked.

"Ah, we are so counting on your assistance. As it stands, you are quite right, but then our UFB women and few UFBMD men are already perfect. No additional changes are truly desired. Does not Breanna fully satisfy you, doctor?" Dansic asked wryly.

"Well, she is simply incredible. I'll give you that. Now if she still had her arms and hands, why, she would be a goddess. I would like to use her as my lab assistant. Yes, even now, she can provide a great deal of assistance to me in my researches, but I admit, she could be even more valuable to me if she had her arms and hands as well. Still, I have to admit she is truly an ultimate beauty," Dr. Decker answered honestly.

Dansic grinned. *Well, I picked the right UFB woman for him! Damn, I am good.* "Yes, Breanna is that. We have discovered second generation UFB women do vastly better than first generation women. We believe that is due in part to their having been born this way and haven't suffered the coma and trauma that the first generation UFB women have."

He continued, changing the topic, "Now your cloning process is what we truly need at this time, doctor. You see, in any society, there are key individuals who are the ones who actually make things happen. We've one super-soldier fellow—earned all sorts of medals and awards on the battlefield. We have key scientists who have developed many critical devices. Then, there's men like Leo, whose IQ is off the charts, can't be measured. True, he's only sixteen, but what that man can give to our society in just a few years will be staggering. Dr. Decker, can you see where I am heading with this?" he asked.

He went on without waiting for an answer. This was his pet project and nothing could stand in his way of achieving it. "Imagine having a hundred copies of our super-soldier, our key scientists, a dozen copies of Leo! Why, the entire galaxy would be ours for the taking. The benefits to mankind are incalculable!"

Dr. Decker chuckled, not the response that Dansic either wanted or desired. He frowned, and Dr. Decker picked up the man's annoyance. "Please, don't misunderstand my laugh sir. I wholly agree with your ideas. The trouble is from my own cloning experimentations, I don't believe that is how it will work out. Let me explain some."

"Oh please do so!" Dansic ordered. *Have I made a huge mistake in bringing this man here?*

"Yes. Well, in my first successful cloning experiments, I cloned four identical sisters. And yes, I had the same delusion you have. I presumed the four sisters would be identical in all ways, and I purposely tested that theory, cloning another two duplicates a month later. Each of the six was grown from a single fertilized egg in my special laboratory womb simulator. Once they were *born*—that is, after nine months of growth, I then placed each of the six with foster parents. One was given to a slum family. One was given to a particularly artistic family. And so on. I monitored the development of the six clones. Let me tell you first that all six turned out to be physically identical. About the only real difference between any of them is their hair—how long they keep it and how they style it. So yes, cloning makes identical physical copies of the original. Their DNA is identical. However, I was shocked to discover their personalities and skills turned out to be wholly different, as different as night and day from one to the other. One turned out to be a caring nurse, who I kept with me for many years. One turned out to be a fashion freak. One turned out to be a violin virtuoso. One turned out to be a major thorn in my side, more like a private detective."

"So you see, the upbringing of the clone became the determining factor in the final products. In no way were these six clones the same other than they looked physically identical, with identical DNA." Dr. Decker finished up and looked at the two rather stunned men.

Finally, Dansic spoke up. "So you are saying your cloning process began with cloning single cells and you had to wait twenty years for the clones to age to that of twenty years?" Dr. Decker nodded yes. "I see. So that means how they are raised made a giant impact on the final products." Again, he nodded yes.

"Well, I can see why that would be. We do have trouble sometimes with children who are physically abused as children and grow up to become societal problems. But doctor, isn't there a way to clone my super-soldier and have him come out of the process fully grown? Let me ask this a different way. Super-soldier is twenty-two. You clone him, and the final product is another twenty-two year old copy, but without waiting twenty-two years for the clone to *grow up*."

Dr. Decker chuckled. "Dansic, that was the very next avenue I wanted to explore. You see, my first cloning experiments showed me I could create physically identical copies. In the case of your UFB women, for example, we could create copies of those who are the epitome of UFB women, the prettiest of the pretty, so to speak. What is really wanted is also to copy their personalities, their skill sets, such as your super-soldier. Now if we can do that, we could achieve the ideal state you desire, Dansic."

He went on, "The key question we need answered is this: can a person's knowledge be cloned? For example, if I cloned that virtuoso violinist, then would the clone also be a virtuoso violinist? That is the key question to be answered first. I have spent the last twenty years perfecting a cloning womb that would stimulate years of body growth and development in mere months, but with the conditions on Virge-C being what they were, I was prevented from actually moving forward to answer this key question."

"You see, I was so hoping to be able to continue my work here on Danforth-C. Take the lovely Breanna. If I could clone her, would her copy also have the incredible math skills and talent that Breanna has? I would dearly love to know the answer to that one."

Dansic visibly relaxed. "Ah yes. I am beginning to understand this cloning process better now, doctor. I can see how vital this fundamental question actually is. We must have that answer. If, as you say, the clones do not inherit their host's personality and skill sets, then what's the use of the clone?"

"Well, it's not all gloom and doom, sir. You see, if you cloned a strong man, the clone would be just as physically strong. There is something valuable in just that part alone."

"Yes, I can see that. A strong soldier cloned gives us just as strong clone. Now if only we didn't subsequently have to train that clone. I can see where this is going. We simply must have these answers, but don't they all begin with this special growth womb of yours?" Dansic probed.

"Yes, that's the first step. I have designed it, but I need to build it. Then, we can set about running more controlled experiments designed to answer those key questions," Dr. Decker answered.

"Excellent. Excellent. If you will just explain all these details to my engineers, scientists, and geneticists here, why, we will work together to build this new growth womb of yours and get started on the cloning experiments," Dansic suggested precisely what he desired from Dr. Decker.

"Ah well, you see, as grateful as I am for everything you have done for me and will be doing for me," Dr. Decker replied, knowing what Dansic actually wanted from him, "if I divulge all my hard-won, hard-learned data and procedures, then you will have no further use for me. I might find myself in an early grave. No, I prefer to divulge what I know a bit at a time, enough for us all to work together on each step of the projects as they evolve. Self-preservation is a strong motivator," he declared.

Dansic bit his lip. *I suspected this doctor would be very cagey and wouldn't fully disclose everything. The man isn't a fool. He's right. Once he's told us everything, I have no further use for him, not really. Considering his record, I dare not trust him fully.* "Yes, yes, I understand, Dr. Decker. Your world is in turmoil, and what man wouldn't be looking out for his own survival. As long as we are making progress towards our common goals, you can expect we will fully support you in all ways. We should get started on the construction of your special growth womb as soon as possible."

"Indeed. Nothing would please me more than to do just that, but I also am fascinated by the genetic research and your genetic bio agents. I would also like to spend some time getting familiar with that research as well. Who knows, perhaps that will also greatly aid us all in achieving our ultimate goals? I'd like to ask one follow up question, if I may," Dr. Decker smoothed the conversation.

Dansic nodded and he continued, "You see, I've been told something rather startling. I was told that if one bred a UFBMD man to a normal woman and if she had a son by him, then that son would be a genius. And yet if she had a daughter, she'd just be a normal UFB girl with normal intelligence. Is that correct? Are there other combinations possible?"

Dansic laughed, greatly relieved. What he wanted to know was common knowledge. "Yes, there is a breeding grid with results. A normal man plus a UFB woman can have strong normal boys and UFB daughters. A UFBMD man plus a UFB woman have UFB daughters and UFBMD sons. The surprising detail is a UFBMD man plus a normal woman can have UFB daughters, but normal boys whose IQs are in the genius or higher range. So yes, you were told correctly. Leo is one of those special boys, the product of a UFBMD man and a normal woman."

He continued, "Of course, there are so few UFBMD men around. After all, what man in his right mind wants to be like that, eh? They are rare indeed. We do take good care of the three that we have. Naturally, not all the women have boys, as you well know."

"Right. Then, this is yet another reason why I need to study all your UFB genetic research. There must be a reason why these boys are special. If we can find that actual genetic cause, then we could perhaps genetically modify any man into a genius or super-genius as you call them," Dr. Decker theorized and gave Dansic a real reason to allow him to become fully briefed on the entire UFB program.

Dansic's eyes lit up. "Are you suggesting it might be possible to inject any man with a new agent that turns him into a super-genius man? Inject another with a new agent that turns his body into that of a super-strong fighter?"

"You catch on quickly, Dansic," Dr. Decker fueled the man's expectations. "That's precisely my thoughts. Mind you, I've no idea if this is possible, not without a lot of study and follow up experimentation on actual humans." *There, I've broached the hot topic! Will he reject that out of hand, as they did on Virge-C?*

"I see. Yes, we can arrange for proper experimentations. While it is illegal, corporations make the rules, and we can bend them when we need to. Let's get this going as soon as possible, Dr. Decker. Work on learning what you can from our geneticists, but also get them working on building this growth womb of yours. We need to get this cloning project going as soon as possible. Money is no object."

"Of course, sir," Dr. Decker replied. *My God, he's going to let me actually conduct human experimentations. Now we are getting somewhere at last. Twenty years of utter stagnation is gone. What a relief.*

"One other matter, doctor," Dansic inquired curiously. "How do you like Breanna? Any chance of marriage in your future?" *I need to get this man more under my control somehow. Getting him hitched to her is a small first step.*

"She's wonderful. Perfect, though I do wish she had arms and hands. In any event, I'm making her my lab assistant. I suppose I should marry her, though," Dr. Decker admitted. *I don't know their customs around here. It won't hurt to seem to be fitting in with these people.*

"Good. Good. We'll see about a wedding next week. I'm told she's been out getting you a bunch of new suits. Well, I'll leave you gentlemen to your work," Dansic replied and left. As he walked the halls and took the elevator up to his office, he reflected on his conversation. *I'm going to have to find a way to get this Dr. Decker to divulge more of what he knows faster than he intends. With the staff I have, if we knew precisely what needed to be done, we could have it all ready and in operation in no time. I refuse to be the slave of this Dr. Decker fellow. My time-line, not his! Well, where there is a will, there is a way, as I always say.*

Once seated in his office, he reflected further. *Getting him hooked with Breanna is a good first step, but I need him working flat out on this cloning business. Wait, what did he say? Arms and hands. He wants Breanna to have arms and hands. Can I use that somehow? Wait, someone brought millions of such cures to the victims on Virge-C. I should check on that detail right now.*

Dansic placed a secure call to President John Johnson on Virge-C. Pretending the call to be just a checkup making sure that all was working out to the president's wishes, he then asked about the *cure.* While the man knew very little about just what it did to the UFB women, at least their arms and hands regrew. "I say, could you possibly send ten such cures to me? I can see the great benefits in this cure." President Johnson was happy to comply.

The call finished, Dansic sat back in his large, plush chair. *I can offer Decker a cure for Breanna, giving her arms and hands, but hell, he hardly knows the woman. He can't have enough of an attachment to her to be willing to divulge all of his secrets. No, I need something more persuasive, but what would do that? What would compel this doctor to fork over all he knows in one fell swoop?* That question occupied his mind for over a week.

That night, a very happy Dr. Decker proposed to Breanna. "Look, I know you know very little about me, and I'm nearly twice your age, but I would like to marry you anyway. I've done some not so nice things in my youth, genetic experiments on humans, but those were hardened criminals who were sentenced to death anyway."

"Oh dear. Were you able to help them?" Breanna asked innocently.

"Not exactly. I admit I made many mistakes. Some experiments resulted in the test subjects losing their lungs or hearts. Of course, they died, but then they were going to be executed anyway," he justified.

"Well, then I suppose they got what they deserved, but you learned from your mistakes, didn't you?" Breanna replied, trying to put a positive spin on what he was admitting.

"Well, yes I did. I was able to help a married couple who were having a difficult time having children of their own. I was able to make six daughters from one of her eggs and his sperm. So yes, I perfected my skills and put them to good use," he again justified.

"So that was a really good thing that you did," she replied. He didn't dare tell her that he didn't give the parents their six daughters, but had given them to six foster families to raise as part of his experiment.

After more frank chatting, Breanna said, "I would love to marry you, Sam. Besides, it raises my social standing enormously to be married and not just sharing your bed at night." For the first time in his life, Dr. Decker saw and truly appreciated another's point of view. He felt a twinge of guilt for having treated her as little more than a common prostitute or social escort, even though he was sincere about making her his lab assistant.

The next day, now dressed in his new clothes, he took Breanna with him to the lab, rather surprising the other geneticists and Dr. Gleason. While he continued to study their genetic research, data, and bio agents, he had to begin to outline the construction details for his new growth womb. Worse, over half of each day was spent in such work, delaying his detailed understanding of what he truly wanted to know.

# Chapter 22—Action and Reaction

The pair was married in a simple ceremony a few days later. As far as Dr. Decker was concerned, everything was working out just perfectly. However, Dansic wasn't as pleased. The work on the new growth chamber was moving along far too slowly. He was not a man of patience, rather a man quite used to getting his own way. Worse, Dr. Decker's clone results, if indeed they were correct, had shot giant holes into his grand plan.

His plans desperately needed the results of Dr. Decker's proposed new experiments. How else was he going to get his army of super-soldiers? How else was he going to get a cadre of super-geniuses? No, somehow he had to get Dr. Decker to proceed at a drastically faster rate, drastically faster. But how?

The arm regrowth cures from Virge-C arrived. Even though the doctor married Breanna, his stated desire to have her arms regrown wasn't enough to compel this doctor to divulge his secrets quickly. Dansic knew he certainly wouldn't if he was the doctor. *Not if I was in his shoes,* he thought. As he had that thought, the image of his UFB wife's teetering heels appeared in his mind. That triggered a sudden realization of just how he could force Dr. Decker to reveal all and at one time! *Why didn't I think of this sooner? Sometimes I must be slipping.* He summoned an aide.

One of the built-in design features of this luxury guest suite was its independent air circulation system, perfect for Dansic's plans. Late that night, wearing a bio containment suit, Dr. Gleason quietly entered the suite and unleashed the proper dose of the genetic bio agent into their bedroom where the pair was sound asleep. Once he returned to the main doors, he disabled the automatic opening mechanism and sealed them inside. More importantly, the seal kept the bio agent from spreading beyond this suite. Dansic joined him. "It's done, boss. Sealed tight as a drum. I sure hope your plan works. Dr. Decker has been feeding us information a trickle at a time."

"Indeed. That will soon come to a screeching halt. We'll

have it all in just a few more days, doctor. Go get some sleep. I'll deal with Breanna in the morning." Dansic grinned at the sealed doors. *Now I have him where I want him.*

Breanna awoke and sensed something was very wrong. Dr. Decker didn't wake up, and she smelled a foreign odor. *My servant is late too. Something is very wrong. I best get some help.* Struggling and wiggling, she finally managed to get into a sitting position on the edge of the bed, no small feat for her. Panting lightly, she sat still for a while catching her breath. That done, she carefully stood up on her toes. Walking without her special heels was quite a challenge, but she had long years of practice. Wiggling and wobbling, she headed out of the bedroom and through the living room to the main doors. "What's going on?" she asked. The doors didn't open automatically. She had no other option but to yell for help and hope someone would hear her.

Eventually, Dansic arrived. Speaking through the doors, he explained, "Dr. Decker is undergoing the genetic bio agent mutation process. He wants to become a UFBMD man just for you, Breanna. In a few hours, the ventilation system will have finished removing the bio agent, and I'll send your servant to you with food at that time. Meanwhile dear, you be thinking about what gowns and colors are best suited for Dr. Decker. You always have excellent taste and style, dear."

"What? He never said anything about this to me," Breanna countered, very confused.

"I think he wanted to surprise you perhaps. Anyway, it is done. So now, we all must make the best of it."

"Well, that's true. I'll work out his new dresses. Can I get them while he is asleep?" she asked.

"Of course, but he will be in the coma for another three days plus, so there's no rush. Pick out good ones for him. Cost is no object for our good doctor," Dansic suggested, putting her more at ease.

Late that afternoon, the doors were opened, and the automatic opener was re-engaged for Breanna's sake. Although she continued to sit by his bedside during much of the day hours, there simply wasn't much anyone could do for him. As the end of the coma period arrived, Breanna oversaw a flurry of action. His body had changed rather drastically. Only now could proper measurements be taken and clothes purchased. She ordered their bed sheets cleaned and the dried husks that had been his arms and hands removed. Under her guidance, the unconscious Dr. Decker was fitted with a similar corset and tightened down to help his back support the extreme weight of his new massive bosom, the same size as hers. His hair was rich and black, falling to his knees, just as it did with Breanna. No longer would he need to shave, though she rather hated to see his black moustache vanish.

Hence, based on his hair and eyes, she ordered appropriate colorful gowns and matching heels. Believing he would look his best in cherry red, she had the servants put that satin, strapless gown on him. She stood back and looked at the sharp contrasts between his shiny black hair, black nylons, and cherry red satin gown and matching heels. Perfect, she thought, hoping that he would also like her choice.

As the waking hour approached, Dr. Gleason and Dansic arrived and explained to her what to expect. "Unless he is vastly different than everyone else, expect him to scream and panic," the doctor said calmly. "He will need your help and guidance on how everything is done by you UFB women. I'm sure you'll be a fine teacher for him. Also, expect him to deny wanting to have this done for you. He'll be in shock and doesn't know what he is saying. None do when they first come out of the coma." *I hope she believes that, at least for now,* he thought.

Dr. Decker awoke and underwent all the usual reactions, passing out from lack of breath several times. That was followed by screaming and sobbing, shocked to find his voice was now in the alto range. "It takes time to adjust to all these changes, Dr. Decker. Just be patient. Take it slow and easy. Do what Breanna says. She is a master at everything," Dr. Gleason explained when he finally was able to get Dr. Decker's attention.

"Why did you do this to me?" Dr. Decker wailed. "I was helping you, sharing what I know."

Dansic answered, "But Dr. Decker, Breanna believes you wanted this done to please her. We will discuss this all later after you've become adjusted to your new life as a UFBMD man. She's gone to a lot of trouble to pick out the proper gowns and colors for you. She has superb taste in clothing. Now servants are coming with your supper. Enjoy. We will talk later. Just relax and get accustomed to everything." *There, I defused that for the moment.* He rose and left them, while two young servant women entered with their supper.

"But I can't breathe," Dr. Decker protested. "I can't stand up without falling, let alone walk!"

Breanna giggled. "Silly man. Yes, you can. In a few days, you will be quite comfortable with the corset. It takes a lot of practice to master walking well, but we'll do it. Look what they brought for our supper. Wow." Sam wasn't much interested in the expensive cuisine, but after one servant put a bite in his mouth, he felt ravenously hungry. Soon, however, he felt stuffed, and Breanna giggled again. "I know. We can only eat smaller portions at one time. Once we finish eating, she should put her arm around you and help you practice walking. You'll feel lots better once you are able to master that," she added encouragingly.

For him, it seemed one long nightmare before he finally found himself sitting on the edge of his bed wearing only the overly tight and restrictive corset, his black hair draped over his left shoulder, the ends resting on the floor. Breanna now sat beside him. "That will be all for tonight. I can take it from here," she explained to the servants who bowed and departed for the night.

"I do so love you, Sam," she whispered. "Can you feel with your hair too?"

"Yes, it's the weirdest thing. So indescribable and about the only good thing about all this," he managed to reply, trying hard not to upset her. She leaned over and gave him a passionate kiss. New emotions and feelings suddenly swelled up in him.

She giggled. "Now I can pleasure you much as we UFB women do each other. Look, your nipples are getting hard too." Already, his passions had exploded, and the pair managed to indulge themselves in a round of what Sam later called the most intense pleasure and gratification he'd ever experienced. As the days passed, that became commonplace. He now understood what Breanna had meant by needing pleasuring so frequently throughout the day.

The next morning after the pair finished another bedroom romp, were dressed, and fed, one servant girl put her arm around him and ushered him off to pay a visit with Dansic, per his orders. Had she not been holding him, he knew he would have fallen down at least ten times! By the time they reached Dansic's office on the top floor, he was gasping for breath.

*Just as good. He can't talk while he's recovering.* Dansic began, "Dr. Decker, you have been going far too slow on giving us the knowledge you have on cloning. So you see, I had to speed it up."

Dr. Decker managed to gasp, "How? Why?"

"Because you are giving us only a minuscule bit at a time. Now then, here's our new deal. You will relay absolutely everything, every detail, to my personnel. All there is about the construction and operation of the growth womb. Everything. Plus, we want to know every detail concerning your cloning process. We want it as fast as my men can duplicate it. You are to divulge absolutely everything you know."

"I'm a fair man. I have here the arm regrowth cure. Once you have done that, I will see that it is administered to you and to Breanna. After all, you did say you wished she had arms and hands. Once that is done, you may continue to work in my research labs, as we put your cloning discoveries into operation. We have many experiments that must be conducted as soon as possible. I must have those answers and have them soon. Far too much depends upon the outcomes. Do you understand me? Don't try to fool us or lie to us. If you don't comply, you'll remain a helpless UFBMD man, and I'll see you're bred to many normal women, if only to begat lots of super-genius sons. This isn't an idle threat."

"How? How can I trust you?" Dr. Decker gasped.

"Obviously, you can't. However, as I said, I'm a fair man. If you comply fully with this request, I'll see you and Breanna get your arms and hands restored. After that, you can continue your research. We both want that to happen. If you refuse, then I will move you both to simple housing, and let you get by, as you can, which isn't well at all, not as helpless as you both are. Do I make myself clear, doctor?"

"Yes," he gasped. While many thoughts raced through his mind, he knew Dansic had him in a vice grip tighter than if he had pointed a gun to his head, for he might have found a way to dislodge the gun, but not as a helpless woman-like person. *These CEOs cannot ever be trusted.*

"Good. Then before I return you to Breanna, remember, she was told that you wanted this done to please her. It would not be wise to tell her otherwise." He signaled, and the servant girl entered, helping Dr. Decker get up and leave the office.

"You need more walking practice, but let's go slow," she advised.

"I nearly fainted before. Slow, please," he gasped, but found he had mostly recovered from the long walk to the man's office.

"So what did the boss man want?" Breanna asked once Sam was back in their suite and sitting down.

Although still gasping for breath, he replied, "He made me a promise. After I tell him all I know about my researches, he'll give us both the arm regrowth cure. Then, we can be independent again, and you can really help me in the lab."

"Oh, that's wonderful," she replied, but then her face fell. She added, "But then I won't be an official UFB woman for you."

"That's fine with me, Breanna. I want your help, and I want you to be as independent as you and I can be, dear. You don't need to be helpless for me to love you."

"Oh, then I guess that's fine with me. With arms and hands, I can do so much more to help you with your work. I promise to do all that I can. Come on; let's get you into the hair machine. Your hair is now a mess. Don't you just love how it feels?"

"But she's not here to hold onto me," Sam protested, his stomach knotting in fear.

"Sure, you can do it. Up you go. I'll try to help you somehow."

Thus began the most frightening two weeks Dr. Decker had ever experienced. There was almost nothing that he could directly control. He was completely dependent upon everyone for nearly every action of life. Even during his flight from Rosewood, he felt in control of the situation, however tenuous it was. However, he did as he was ordered to do. That is, he spent long hours each day explaining in detail all the he had learned and discovered in his researches.

"There, that's the last of it," Dr. Decker declared. "Now hold up your end of the bargain, Dansic. Give us the cure."

"Not so fast. We need to get the device made and verify that it works as you claim," Dansic countered. "For now, you can spend your days in your suite with Breanna. We will come get you if we need some advice. You're going to have to be patient a while longer for your cures."

For another three long weeks, Dr. Decker was confined to his luxury suite. Almost at once, he went along with Breanna's suggestion that they wear only their nylons and heels, because all they needed to do to arouse the other was to rub their massive bosoms against the other's. Once their nipples touched, emotions swelled, almost uncontrollably.

After several days of enjoying sex four times during the day, Sam commented, "You know, before this happened to me, I would get aroused many times during the day, but such moods passed easily. Now, why, I can't seem to control myself. I want you all the time. What's happened to me?"

"Our sex drives, dear," Breanna replied, "are now very strong, far stronger than normal, at least as far as I can tell. We UFB women are barely able to keep them under control during the day, but only if we have it when we wake up and before we sleep at night. Still, it's hard. Without that, honestly, we UFB women spend many hours during the day pleasuring each other. So yes, it is part of what we are now, dear, so let's just enjoy it. I certainly do." To solidify her statement, she maneuvered her bosom against his, rubbing hers against his with the expected results. Passions exploded once more.

Six weeks passed. Still Dansic not suggested it was time for their arm regrowth cures. Dr. Decker, frustrated by his utter helplessness, fumed. "Damn that man! He promised me he'd give us the cure if I helped him, and I've done that and then waited forever. Somehow, I have to get him to live up to his part of the bargain. Breanna, we must have our arms back."

She didn't say anything but looked a bit downcast. "Don't you want to have arms and hands, dear?" he asked, seeing her mood.

"Well, I've never had them. What if I don't know how to use them? What if I can't do anything with them?" she admitted her greatest fears about this whole idea of a cure. "What if I let you down completely? They could be useless for me, since I never had them to lose in the first place."

"Oh Breanna, I hadn't thought of that. You're right. I bet you'll have to learn how to use them, just as I'm struggling to learn to stand and walk on these mutated feet and how to deal with this long hair. Still, I know you can master it. Compared to what we are enduring now, learning to use hands and arms will be easy for you. Trust me on that. No, the problem to solve is how to get that despicable man to live up to his side of the bargain, assuming he even has that promised cure. I'd sure like to give him a taste of his own medicine. Let's see how he likes being as we are, eh Breanna? I bet he would sing a different tune then."

Hesitantly, Breanna spoke up, "But maybe that's why he isn't giving you the cure. He suspects you would then turn him into a UFBMD man."

"Hum, you have a point there, my dear, a really good one. I need to think about this a bit. There must be a way out of this mess. Luck has always been on my side. It's about time I get a bit more luck." He fell silent, thinking over what she'd said. *There is so much truth in what she said. If I get a chance, I sure wouldn't hesitate to reciprocate. I wonder if that cure actually exists. If it does, where is it kept? If I could find out, maybe I could somehow inject it into us.* Thus, six weeks after the mutation, Dr. Decker had a new set of goals to pursue—ones that would have been simple to carry out if he wasn't a helpless mutant. Now they seemed out of his reach.

Thinking of being out of his reach, Dr. Decker had a flash of insight. *That's it. That's what is really happening here to me and even to Breanna, though she doesn't even know it.*

*It's our reach. Our reach has been very nearly wiped out. Arms and hands allow us to reach out several feet in many directions. As we are now, about all we can reach is with our mouths, sort of. He's cut our physical reach down to nearly nothing, especially since we can hardly bend with these infernal corsets on. So I need to figure out how to extend our reach and not by using others to reach for us, like our servants who feed and dress us. I'm sure I'm on to something here, just not what.*

"Come on, Breanna. It's time I saw everything in this building. You once told me you went everywhere around here. I need you to take me everywhere too," he said with a renewed vigor that brought a light into her eyes.

"Yes, yes I have been everywhere in the building. I see. It will give you lots of practice walking. That's a good thing, dear. You won't feel so badly if you can walk well and have confidence that you can do it. Where do you want to start?"

"Well, for starters, let's visit all the labs, shall we? That shouldn't attract too much attention to us," he suggested. Dr. Decker didn't know precisely what he was looking for, only that he would know it when he saw it. The two set off, side by side, taking their tiny shuffling steps. While she was a master at it, her heart ached to see the awful time Sam was having. Still, she knew in time and with practice, he would get as good at it as she was, if only that time would hurry up and come.

As they headed out of their suite, several other UFB women were making their way along the hall. Several greeted Breanna with cheery hello's. In spite of everything, Dr. Decker found their cheerful greetings a welcome relief and shared their greetings along with Breanna, who whispered their names and marital status to him. Further on down the hall, several more appeared, greeting the pair warmly. One said, "Oh, Breanna dear, and Sam, we are all taking tea in Sofia's suite. You are both most welcome to come join us. Oh please do come. Everyone is just dying to congratulate you on your marriage and to meet Dr. Decker here. I must say, doctor, you look fabulous yourself. I bet you are giving Breanna here a run for her money."

"Oh can we?" whispered Breanna, who longed for their

company having been more or less deprived of it for the last six weeks.

"Sure, why not?" Sam replied. These women were all quite beautiful, highly attractive as was any UFB woman. Somehow, he felt a kinship with these women. At least he looked like one of them and was just as helpless as they were. Company in misery, perhaps, he thought, though he had no solid idea of why he went along with their suggestion to take tea, just trusting to his luck. As they turned and joined the ever-growing group of UFB women, he also realized for some reason he didn't feel embarrassed by his looking and dressing like these women. He had noticed he always felt embarrassed when around other men, but not these UFB women and didn't quite know why. Perhaps, that was why he changed plans and joined their tea.

The tea was held in Mrs. Gleason's suite, the UFB wife of the doctor. Some twenty-three women of varying ages arrived and took various seats around their large living room, sitting on sofas, love couches, and chairs that three servant girls hastily arranged. While Breanna introduced him to each of the women in turn, Sam realized several were in their fifties and yet looked much like Breanna, in their mid-twenties. Mrs. Gleason commented, "We age remarkably well, don't you think, doctor? For we women, this is a great benefit, since beauty is one of our prime attributes. I don't look a day over Breanna, and yet I'm old enough to be her mother and then some."

"And bearing children," put in another older woman. "I'm a grandmother now. My Roberta gave birth to twin girls last week. They are doing just fine—third generation UFB women now. Oh doctor, I'm sixty, just so you know."

"Incredible, ma'am. You don't look a day older than Breanna. Incredible. Oh, congratulations on becoming a grandmother." *Now why did I say that? Being polite? I've never cared about having children or a family before. What's coming over me?*

"Why thank you, doctor. Yes, as she says, we age well. Honestly, it's more like hardly at all. I say, do you have children back on the world you came from? It must have been hard on you to have left them behind," she asked politely.

Sam chuckled. "No, I've never been married before, until I met Breanna here. Rather smitten with her. Actually, you could say I was married to my work, my researches, but now—well, that's all changed."

"Just like my husband, Dr. Gleason," his wife commented. "I keep telling him to stop working so hard and enjoy life. Deaf ears, you know. I swear. Now Breanna, have you taken Sam over to General Robotics to meet your parents?"

"No not yet. We haven't had the time, but I really should. I know mom would love to meet him," Breanna replied.

Until now, Dr. Decker hadn't thought about Breanna having living parents. She'd not really said anything about them, but obviously, she had parents. *General Robotics? How interesting. I wonder,* he thought. "Is it possible for us to visit them, Breanna? I should have insisted they attend our wedding. I'm sorry I didn't even think about that."

Breanna laughed. "I didn't mention it. There's been some friction between us. Dad didn't approve of my learning all the math I could, but Dansic heard about me and swapped another UFB woman with GR for me. I'm very glad he did, since I was able to take every online course there is. I suppose we can get permission to visit them. I haven't seen them for a couple of years now."

"And right he was to fetch you over here," put in another young woman, also a second-generation UFB woman. "We're not as helpless as most men think, are we Breanna?" She giggled and added demurely, "I'm learning how to pilot a transport ship. I use my feet, you see. They say I have a knack for it. At least, GD gives us UFB women a chance to learn to do things, not like some of the other corporations.

"She's Carlin Cody," Breanna whispered to Sam. "She's Fiona Cody, her younger sister."

Fiona spoke up, "And I'm a navigator in training. I enter the codes and run the transport's nav system using my toes. Only GD gives us UFB women a chance to do useful things. You see, Dr. Decker, we UFB women aren't as helpless as one might think. We just need a chance."

"Well, and a lot of assistance too," Mrs. Gleason amended their declarations. "You see, doctor, while we're all sex dolls, gorgeous ones at that, some of us have other skills, just like ordinary people. Now myself, I have no such illusions. I'm quite content to be a loving wife and mother to my six children, as some others here are. And yet, Carlin, Fiona, and Breanna, for example, have additional gifts or skills. Thank heavens we are here at GD where Dansic allows them to perfect their gifts somewhat. Other corporations generally don't. But at the formal balls, you'll see what we mean. Ah, here comes the tea. I'm so glad you and Breanna could join us this morning." The three servant girls entered carrying trays filled with teapots, cups, and straws. Hastily, they set about serving the gathering of women.

"Yes, quite," Carlin Cody added, "but what I want to know, Dr. Decker, is do you think we actually *are* the true ultimate in feminine beauties? I mean are we just what you would treasure in a woman?" Her voice had an overtone suggesting there was more behind her seemingly suggestive questions.

"Well, me personally, Carlin, not exactly. I mean Breanna is the finest woman I've ever met, but really, you should have your arms and hands. I think it's an incredible waste for you to be so utterly dependent."

"Really? Is that all?" Fiona asked, joining in with her sister. All the women covertly glanced at Dr. Decker. Some were in obvious agreement with his statement, while others were aghast at his suggestion.

"Well, not really. Your breasts—well they are a bit much, don't you think? And it would be so much nicer if your feet were not so, well malformed. Don't get me wrong," he hastily added, "women in heels are quite the thing, but these, well they are a bit too much, don't you think?" *There, I've turned it around on those two*, he thought.

"Well, I like the way you see it," Carlin replied stoically. "See, not every man sees us as the perfect women."

"Yes, but," protested Mrs. Bartel, Dansic's wife, "the top men have created us to be what *they* desire in perfect women.

What Dr. Decker is suggesting would ruin all of us, if our bodies had those changes. No other women in the world are treated as superbly as we are—lives of utter luxury and sex. My goodness ladies, don't forget about that! Of course, you second generation women have no idea about sex, but let Mrs. Gleason and me tell you, we UFB women experience sex at least a hundred times better than normal women experience it. I'd never want to give that up, not ever."

Mrs. Gleason echoed her, "She's right. Arms, hands, small boobs, regular feet—why, next, he'll be saying we shouldn't have such impressive waists too. If we give up all that, we'll be not much better than a normal woman is. No way do I want to change anything about the way I am! You second generation women simply have no idea how awful life is for the normal women of our world. You've no idea how wonderful you really have it."

Mrs. Bartel added, "She's right, ladies. All this talk of piloting space ships—that's not something that any UFB woman should be doing. You're probably just bored and protesting because Dansic hasn't found you suitable husbands yet. Well, he just did for Breanna here. I will speak with him about hurrying it up. I know once you've had sex with a real man, then you'll soon forget such silly notions as piloting ships. We women are supposed to look fabulous all the time, give our men the best sex possible, and as many children as he desires. That's our true purpose, ladies, not such silly things as having arms and doing the mundane things normal women do. God help us if we get arms. No way am I going to dust, vacuum, and wash dishes. Bah. You would do well to simply forget such silly notions."

"But honestly, Mrs. Bartel, don't you sometimes wish you could do all the things a normal woman can do? Hold your babies, change their diapers, and hug your husbands?" Carlin countered, not the least bit annoyed with Mrs. Bartel's outburst.

Dr. Decker saw an instant flinch from both older women. "Well, I'm thankful I don't have to change their diapers," Mrs. Bartel hastily pointed out the only counter she had to the younger woman's protest. That brought several chuckles from the older women who, Sam guessed, had had a baby.

"Look," Fiona spoke up, "we're not saying we want to be normal women. What we are saying is we don't want to be so helpless, so dependent on others for everything. Besides, our boobs are just too darn big and heavy. Don't forget, we all heard you both complaining about them when they swelled up when you had your babies. This isn't much of a life just sitting around sipping tea all day. We want to contribute to our world too and not just by looking pretty and having babies. Anyone can do that."

Carlin added, "I don't think Dr. Decker is saying we should be normal women. He's saying we shouldn't be so helpless, that we should be able to contribute and help our world survive better, not just sit around being sex dolls."

Dr. Decker nodded. "She's right. Our hair is fantastic. Our sex, well, it is almost indescribable. Each of you looks stunning, gorgeous, and highly attractive, far, far above the norm. I'm not saying you should give that up. Good lord no, but with a few small changes, each of you could be so very much more, contribute so much more than you can now. What I was suggesting is that you keep the very best of yourselves, that which sets each and every one of you apart from all other women, and add more onto that by being able to do so many more things in life and not have to have others do them for you."

He went on, "You see, I have made my dear Breanna my lab assistant. She has skills I do not. Her help in the lab will greatly enhance and further my research. Yet, if she also had her arms and hands, then she could be so much more. That's all I'm saying. Look, back on my world, I used to have a nurse assistant to help me. She kept all my records and assisted me with all my operations. If she didn't have hands, then I could not have used her and would have had to hire a woman who could do those things."

Breanna spoke up, "He's got a point. I've thought long and hard about this. I think everyone wants to be helpful, to aid and assist others. It's part of being a human being, to want to help others. And just look at us, we can hardly do anything at all, except use our minds and satisfy men in bed. It makes me feel awful at times—when I can't help someone I want to help. Surely, you've felt this way before too, haven't you?"

"I know you did, Mrs. Bartel," Carlin barked. "I saw you crying while standing over your daughter when she was just learning to walk. She fell down and couldn't get up. Remember, several of us were there, and none of us could do anything to help her get back up. We had to wait around until some man came by and had him do it."

With a red face, Mrs. Bartel conceded that point. "Well, perhaps you have a point there, Carlin, but that's a small sacrifice to make to ensure our husbands desire us above all other women."

"Yes, we all want to be wanted," Mrs. Gleason added, "especially by the best men on our world."

Carlin snickered, "You mean the wealthiest, most powerful men on our world, don't you?"

Mrs. Gleason flushed, "Of course, dear. Why would I want to be married to a miner and live in a dirty apartment all my life, wearing rags for clothes?"

Fiona laughed, "It isn't that bad, is it?" Several others chuckled.

Another woman, who had been mostly silent all this time, chose to add her thoughts. "Another point. I don't think the CEOs would ever allow us to have arms and hands, though maybe they would allow us to have better feet and smaller boobs."

"Why?" asked Carlin.

"Because as we are, we are dependent on them for everything. Look, we can't possibly live on our own. Now, if we had arms and hands, why, we could darn well do anything we desired. If we didn't like the man, we could divorce him, move out, and find some other man to marry, or live our own lives. I know Dansic. He'd never let you have arms, Mrs. Bartel. If he did, he'd have a very hard time controlling you. You are a very spirited woman. Some of the decisions Dansic has recently made have really bothered you. Remember, you and I talked about them at length. If you weren't so completely dependent on Dansic, we both know you would have taken strong actions against him."

"Well, you have a point," Mrs. Bartel replied quietly, knowing she was dead on the point. "Honestly, ladies, discussing this is pointless. Dansic will never allow UFB women to have arms and hands. So why waste our energies even talking about it? We should agree on what fashions we want made for us for the summertime. That's something we can get done. We can plan the Midsummer Ball too."

Dr. Decker grimaced. Dansic had reneged on his promise to give him the cure to regrow his arms. It was going on seven weeks without his fulfilling the bargain. From what was said at the tea, he realized they were probably quite right. Dansic would never give him or Breanna the promised cure. No, he needed to find another way to get it. However, the morning wasn't wasted. Several UFB women were on his side. Plus, he'd learned Breanna's parents weren't here at GD headquarters. Another idea formed in his mind.

The tea broke up at lunchtime. The many women shuffled off to their own suites, as did Sam and Breanna. Over lunch, he suggested, "Breanna, I've done you a horrible disservice. I should have met your parents long ago, perhaps even asking your father for his permission to marry you." He knew he never had such a thought, that such things were irrelevant. He'd marry whoever he desired, but this was just to set her up.

"Well, dad's head of General Robotics. He and Dansic don't get along too well, but by swapping me with one of Dansic's daughters, he hoped to gain a better relationship with Dansic. It didn't happen though. Still, Dansic did allow me to study all the math I desired, so it is better over here for me, I think. You really want to meet them?"

"Sure, my dear. We should pay them a visit and soon, if that's allowed," he replied. Later that afternoon, Breanna led Sam out the front doors of GD headquarters. Walking along the street on their own, Dr. Decker felt very ill at ease and somewhat frightened. His utter helplessness very nearly swamped him. If he lost his balance and fell, Breanna couldn't possibly help him regain his feet. Plus, the streets were packed with many other people going about their afternoon business.

Many stared at the pair as they took their slow, shuffling steps, while others moved past them, unwilling to be forced to walk so slowly. If one of them bumped into him, Sam knew he'd fall and there wasn't anything he could do about it.

"Feel the wind with your hair? I do so love this, don't you?" Breanna whispered. She sensed his fright and tried to get him thinking about something pleasureful. They had to walk three blocks, but it seemed an eternity before they walked into the foyer and beneath the giant sign, General Robotics. They made their way up to the reception desk.

"Breanna Clansey to see my mom and dad, please," she said calmly.

"Why, it is you. You are looking even prettier than when I last saw you, Breanna," the mild-mannered middle-aged woman declared. "One minute while I notify them and slip your visitor's cards on your dresses. And just who is your beautiful companion, dear?"

"My husband, Dr. Sam Decker. Thanks," she answered. Both watched her eyebrows rise. She stared long and hard at Sam, before fastening the card to her strapless gown.

"Okay, you know the way, Breanna. Top floor, main office. Your mother is on her way there now." The pair turned, and Breanna led him to the elevator bank of six, some twenty feet behind reception. She squatted down and pressed the Up button with her nose. Minutes passed before they stepped out of the elevator on the hundredth floor. Sam couldn't see much difference between this skyscraper and GD's. The layouts were remarkably the same, probably due to standardized Federation construction.

Rene Clansey was a splitting image of her daughter, though obviously she must be in her mid-forties, Sam estimated. UFB women did not show their age, but her father definitely appeared to be middle-aged. He had a black moustache and short hair. His roundish face and dark brows gave him a look that reminded Sam of a childhood bully that had tormented him. Both Rene and Helmet stared at Sam, while the pair walked slowly into the room and bobbed their heads about to get their hair to one side so they could sit down on the plush couch, facing her parents, who sat on leather chairs, off to one side of the office suite.

"Well, this is a pleasant surprise, Breanna," Helmet said.

"It's so wonderful to see you again, dear," Rene added. "We heard you were married. So this is the fine young man? Or is he a she?" Rene was definitely confused.

"Dansic turned him into a UFBMD man, mom, in order to force him to divulge all his research secrets. He promised him that he would give him the cure to regrow his arms and mine too, but you know Dansic, he's not done it, and it's been seven weeks now, and he'll probably never do it," Breanna answered her.

"So you are the famous doctor who has developed the cloning process?" Helmet asked.

"Yes sir. I'm very pleased to meet you and your wife. When I married your beautiful daughter, I didn't know she still had parents or I would have invited you to our wedding. Forgive me, sir," Dr. Decker replied, attempting to be as polite as he thought the situation warranted.

"Well, no matter. Dansic wouldn't have allowed us to come anyway. There's ill will between us, more so of late, if I'm not mistaken, particularly where you fit in, Dr. Decker," Helmet began. "So tell me about your research and just what Dansic is doing with it."

"But Helmet, they've come to meet us, not talk shop," Rene protested.

"I would love to tell you all about it," Dr. Decker replied, seeing just the opportunity he had hoped for. He spent a half hour outlining in detail all that had occurred and what little he knew of Dansic's plans. He ended by saying, "So I've lived up to my part of the bargain, but for seven weeks now, Dansic has failed to live up to his and give me and Breanna the promised cure so our arms and hands can be regrown. And yes, your daughter is extremely good at the math that I need in my research, which is why I have made her my lab assistant."

"But Breanna dear," Rene spoke up, "surely, you don't want to have arms and hands, do you? You wouldn't then be a true UFB woman."

"I do mom, because then I can help Dr. Decker so very

much more in his research," Breanna countered.

"Rene, why don't you take Breanna with you and see to preparing a feast for us. Tonight, they will be our dinner guests. I insist. Besides, Dr. Decker and I would like a private chat," Helmet declared. It was obviously an order for the two women to take their leave, and with head tosses to get their hair out of the way, both women rose and made their slow way out of the office.

"Now then, Dr. Decker, you and I can have a private chat. Dansic has gone too far, making a rapid growth-cloning womb of your design. We can speculate just what people he wants to clone, but that's not going to do either of us any good," Helmet began.

"No it isn't. I rather wish Dansic didn't have a monopoly on my cloning technology," Dr. Decker hinted. He relaxed. Helmet agreed wholeheartedly with him.

"Let me make you a far better counteroffer," he began. "You see, for many years now, GR has been inventing better and better personal servant robots, all designed to replace the expensive servant girls our UFB wives and daughters need. Such a waste of human resources you see to have to have them constantly attending to their needs and yours too, now as well. My research teams have pretty well gotten these robot assistants working as best as can be hoped for. I want to establish an experimental colony of them to see if they are able to live and be productive on their own."

He continued, "I can't provide you with that promised cure. Lord knows where Dansic obtained it or if it is even a real cure. Mind you, he probably just made it all up. Everyone knows our geneticists have never been able to regrow arms. Lord knows that would be a great leap forward for those who have lost a limb or two in the all too common industrial accidents. So here's what I *can* offer you."

"I'm about to establish a remote, self-sufficient colony of UFB women and men. If you will join the colony, I can put you in as their leader and give you a state of the art laboratory including one of your cloning womb devices. There, you will be free to conduct any research your heart desires in complete isolation from interruptions and in total freedom. No one will be watching over you, insisting you develop this or that. You can have free rein to research whatever you desire in one of our state of the art labs. The new personal assistant robots are good enough to act as your hands for now, until you can develop such a cure. If Dansic actually has found such a cure, I will find out and get it to you, one way, or another."

Dr. Decker was amazed and shocked to hear this offer. "You are serious about this, aren't you? Well, that would be ideal for me. But how can you do all this? Dansic isn't about to let go of me."

"Look, Dr. Decker. Through no fault of your own, you've been forced to give Dansic a monopoly on some extremely critical technology and developments. This alone has totally upset the proper balance among the various top corporations here on Danforth-C. We CEOs simply can't allow Dansic to have this monopoly. So I can guarantee you that we will rectify this unfortunate situation at once. All I need is your agreement to share your knowledge with all the rest of the corporations. You promise to do that, and I'll see the situation is rectified at once. But it would be in your best interests and my daughter's as well to become a part of this special new colony. That way, you would be beyond the reach of Dansic and his crew. What say you, Dr. Decker?"

"Your offer is most welcome indeed. How soon can we make it happen?" Dr. Decker replied. *Luck is once more on my side! My own private state of the art lab and with no strings attached. Remote. Beyond Dansic's reach? Incredibly good luck indeed.*

"I'll call Dansic and tell him that you are spending the night, chatting with Rene, who has longed to visit with her oldest daughter. I'll make preparations this evening and tomorrow morning, why, we'll put it into action. Mind you, I'm going to have to trust you will later on uphold your side of the bargain and tell our scientists all that you know," he replied solemnly.

"You have my word, which is about all that I can do," Dr. Decker answered with a light tease.

Both men chuckled. "True, quite true, but once you get used to our new robot assistants, then that may well change.

Come on; let me show you around GR's labs. Do you need a steadying arm?"

"If you don't mind, yes, I really do," Dr. Decker answered.

Later, they joined Rene and Breanna for supper, after which Helmet excused himself and left the three alone. "Oh I do hope that you and Breanna will be having children of your own soon," Rene declared.

"Me too, mom, just as soon as Sam wishes it."

"I knowyour daughters will be as we are, dear child, but what will your sons be like?" Rene asked. "I've heard that with a UFBMD, sons might well look like their fathers."

Breanna giggled. "I know mom. That doesn't bother me. I'm sure that we'll love them all." The three chatted for quite some time.

Sam mostly tuned their chatter out, focusing on just what the future might well be. *A special colony? My own lab, free from all interference? My God, this is almost too good to believe. Best, I don't have to do anything up front and be betrayed yet again, not like with Dansic.*

\*\*\*

"What is the meaning of this special meeting?" Dansic growled. It was nine o'clock the following morning. Twenty-five CEOs from as many corporations here on Danforth-C assembled in his personal meeting room—a special Planetary Council had been invoked and called for. He had no choice, but to allow the men to assemble.

"We all know about what you are doing with Dr. Decker's research and special growth womb. Cloning. We simply will not tolerate GD having a sole monopoly on this new vital technology and knowledge," Helmet began. "So as of this moment, GD must share everything you've gotten out of Dr. Decker. Also, he is now under the protection of GR and out of your hands permanently."

Dansic argued for a while. Even though he was the top leader here on Danforth-C, he could not and was not prepared to take on all the other major corporations, particularly over this unproven technology. After arguing against this for a half hour, Dansic finally conceded the issue. Around ten, the many

CEOs called in their own geneticists, doctors, scientists, and engineers to meet with and duplicate what Dansic's crew had gotten from Dr. Decker.

Amazingly, his people had fully documented everything Dr. Decker had said. Thus, it was trivial for them to get copies made, though they would have to construct their own grown womb devices. Given this fortunate situation, the CEOs then met once more in Dansic's meeting room.

"So what now? Where will Dr. Decker be staying?" Dansic probed, having seriously regretted ever allowing Breanna to take him to see her parents.

"As you know, GR has been building a special colony where our newest robot assistants will provide all the help that hired servant girls now do. We are setting up this experimental colony for many UFB women to see how it progresses. If all works out, then we will be making these robot assistants available to everyone who has a UFB woman. That alone will save all of us a small fortune," Helmet replied.

"Plus, I'm willing to accept any of your own UFB women into this colony. Perhaps, some of you have some who are, shall we say, a bit rebellious? Here's your chance to divest yourselves of these hard to handle UFB women," Helmet suggested, knowing many of these CEOs faced such problems, particularly among second and third generation UFB women.

"Well now, Helmet, this is indeed good news," Dansic declared, seeing a way to divest himself of quite a number of these UFB women who were causing friction among the others. "No limit on the numbers?"

Helmet laughed, "None at all. As many as you care to divest yourself of. Need them at the spaceport by noon on Saturday. Mind you, the colony will have its own fabrication machine so that you will not need to send along volumes of clothing and such." The men discussed this a bit further and then the meeting broke up.

# Chapter 23—Serendipity

Dr. Decker spotted Carlin, Fiona, and several other younger UFB women he'd meet at the tea. They, along with many other UFB women, were at the spaceport, going with him to this new colony. In a flash, Dr. Decker realized Dansic had taken this opportunity to divest himself of *undesirable* UFB women, that is, those who wanted more from their lives than to be a simple sex doll, like his wife and Dr. Gleason's wife.

"Glad that you could come with us, Carlin, Fiona," he said, while trying to keep his balance on the windy tarmac.

"Well, we didn't have any choice," Carlin protested slightly, but added, "but once we heard what this is all about, why, we jumped at the chance. Do you think we can really do this? Live independent of all the help we must have?"

"I hope so. Plus, I have an advanced lab, and I fully intend to one day get us the cures we need," Dr. Decker declared.

Breanna looked around at the assembling women. "They are all fairly young, Sam. Probably second and third-generation UFB women. Some are barely ten years old or my eyes are deceiving me."

Sam laughed, "No, I can see that much myself. However, once they mature, there's no telling any UFB woman's age." Breanna and several others close to them laughed loudly.

One added, "But that is one of the points about being a UFB woman. We don't lose our beauty as we age, not like normal woman." More chuckled at that.

A light cruiser provided their transportation, and an hour passed before the hundred ten were helped onboard and strapped in for the trip. Once the ship departed, a prerecorded video played. Helmet's image appeared, and he outlined the situation.

"Some time ago, we came across an unknown, but habitable planet. It is uninhabited. The corporations decided against migrating large populations there and developing it, for its natural resources are barely average. Instead, GR has built a small town there and installed everything a human could want or need to live a productive life. We are testing our latest robot personal assistants that are designed to provide all the help that your normal servant girls have done in the past. They are voice-activated. At the end of the video, a list of the commands will be displayed. The crew will give you some robot instruction training as well."

"Your new town hasn't got a name, so you may choose any name you desire. The world is designated 192Scorpi-C. You may elect your own leaders, however, for the beginning, Dr. Sam Decker has been appointed your temporary leader. Initially, there are six onsite technicians to make sure the robots work as intended. Plus, there are two medical nurses who will be able to handle any medical issues that arise. Once all is working well, they will depart, leaving you to your own lives without any interference at all. Here, you can become all that you desire to be."

"There is a fabrication machine in the town so you can have all the gowns, heels, and other items you need and in any quantity you desire. An advanced medical machine is able to handle any medical emergency that might arise. All the doors are fully automatic, and there is a small nuclear reactor to supply your energy needs for a century or more. The food dispenser is automated with a wide variety of meals. In addition, a normal colonization supply container is on site, in case you wish to indulge in all manner of other activities. Based on our initial studies, we recommend that four of you live together in the same home, though this isn't a requirement."

This was followed by an extensive list of robot commands, along with video showing some of those who were already living there demonstrating them. "It seems simple enough," Breanna whispered to Sam. "Do you think we'll be able to do your research with their help?"

"I certainly hope so, my love. I hope so. I'm counting on it."

"Excuse us," Carlin broke in on their conversation, "but could Fiona and I live with you two? It says four of us should live in the same house. We are willing to share whatever duties we can."

"Sure, if that's okay with Breanna," Sam replied.

"That would be really nice. Thanks!" Breanna replied, relieved to have two close friends living with her and not two strangers.

***

Serendipity. That was the name Breanna suggested and won the most votes from among the two hundred sixty-three members of their new town. It was located in a temperate zone where the annual range of temperatures was quite mild, never too hot or cold. With almost no axis tilt, this planet didn't have wild swings in seasons. The town consisted of two hundred single story homes, all nearly identical, except for ten, which were warehouses or laboratories. Dr. Decker was quite pleased to see that this time he got what he'd bargained for. His lab was all that was promised and located next door to his new home. The medical center lay on the other side of his house.

All the streets were paved, but there were no grass yards per se, but then Sam hadn't expected any. They had no way to take care of a lawn, though just beyond the edge of the small town grasslands rolled off as far as the eye could see. Myriads of wild flowers also grew with abandon just north of the town, while a small deciduous forest lay to the south.

One central building served as the community center, while the tiny spaceport lay at the edge of the town. Their first stop was the center where those who were already here met with the newcomers, the two nurses, and the six technicians.

One of the young normal human nurses, Lucretia Simonee, twenty-five, led the discussion and welcoming party. Then, she introduced Dr. Decker. "Now, it is my pleasure to introduce the only man who will be living here with you, Dr. Sam Decker and his new bride, Breanna. Doctor, would you please rise and let everyone get a good look at you. Officially, he will be your leader until you work out how you wish to be governed. Dr. Decker."

Startled by the vital fact he was the only male here, Sam carefully rose and looked out on the sea of long haired beautiful women. Browns, blacks, and blondes predominated.

391

Lucretia's flaming, shoulder length, red hair stood out sharply. "Our first actions must be to get everyone teamed up in groups of four or so and find a home for each. Then, we must all learn to work these robots. That is our top priority today," he suggested.

He sat down, and Lucretia took over. "He's right. We'll get everyone divided up into house groups and get you to your new homes. We have numerous placards in each home with all the robot instructions on them. We two nurses and the six technicians will now get you paired up and into available homes. We will meet here again tomorrow after lunch and go over any difficulties anyone is having. There is a red emergency button in each home. When you press it, an alarm sounds in the medical center where we're staying. We'll respond as rapidly as possible. Good luck ladies and gentleman."

As Breanna and Sam walked towards their new home with Carlin and Fiona following along behind them, she whispered, "Now Sam, we can begin our family, but what about everyone else? How will they be able to have children?"

"I don't know. I neglected to ask about that detail. First, we best see if these robot things are going to work."

Their home was Number 42, Main Street. Although it looked exactly like all the other dwellings, to the pair, this was home. The doors opened automatically, sliding off to either side. Once inside, they saw the robot assistants. They looked anything but human. True, they had arms and hands, sort of, but they were cylindrical in shape, resting upon motorized wheels. Their *heads* were domes filled with various electronic sensing circuitries and could rotate three hundred sixty degrees, a bit unnerving when the women first discovered this. Still, with their mechanical arms, they were able to assist them with their needs, primarily dressing, undressing, bathroom needs, and handling their eating requirements. Fortunately, each home had four electrostatic hair machines, which pleased everyone.

Clothing and shoes had already been provided, based upon the styles and colors the women had back home on Danforth-C. The kitchen had a food dispenser with disposable tableware. Each dispenser had a menu selection, which could be operated via nose presses. As they soon discovered, the robots carried the items to the tables and fed them, though rather awkwardly. Still, after the first few days of adjustment, the group was satisfied they could survive with these robot assistants, though many had secret fears that they wouldn't.

Dr. Decker's next order the following afternoon was to have everyone here go around the entire facility and learn just where absolutely everything was located, particularly the medical center and the communications center. A few days later, the six technicians departed, along with one of the two nurses. Lucretia stayed behind and met privately with Dr. Decker.

"So how come you aren't leaving too?" he asked.

"Well, I was supposed to, since everything is mostly automated. If there is a medical emergency, the medical robots are supposed to be able to handle it. Still, seeing all of you here, why, I just didn't feel like I could truly leave. What if something goes wrong? I'm the only able-bodied person here now. I just couldn't leave you all alone. I know they wanted this to be an experiment, but still, you are human beings, and things can go wrong. I hope you don't mind my staying."

"Not at all, Lucretia. Actually, I'm very grateful you stayed behind. I too am more than a little concerned about everyone's welfare. But I have one question. I'm the only man. What about the others? Are they never to have their own children?"

Lucretia flushed. "Well, there isn't any reason they can't, except that you are the only man present, and you are married. So I just don't know. Perhaps you should bring that up at the next meeting."

Interestingly enough, at the next community meeting, Carlin brought up that very topic. "Dr. Decker. Some of us were hoping to begin our families. You know, have children of our own. How are we going to be able to do that?"

Carefully, he rose, wobbling slightly. He still wasn't totally used to his new life limitations. "How many of you want to have families soon? Er, I suppose you should stand up so we can get some idea."

Nearly forty women stood up, somewhat overwhelming both Lucretia and Dr. Decker. Breanna spoke up, "Sam, it is okay with me if you sleep with them when it is their fertile time. If you don't, we can't have much of a future, can we? I mean children are our future. I think GR kind of forgot about that detail." Sam flushed, but he had no choice in the matter. He could not deny these women a chance to have their own children, especially so since Breanna was already pregnant with their first child.

Sensing his deep embarrassment, Lucretia rose. "Okay ladies. Those of you who want to have a child soon, come by the medical center, and I'll help you monitor your fertility cycle, and let Dr. Decker know when it is time."

Later that day, Lucretia took Dr. Decker aside. "Doctor, is it true that a son from a UFBMD man and a normal woman may well be a genius? I've heard all sorts of wild rumors about that."

"Yes, I've heard that as well, but to be honest, I simply don't know. Why?"

Now it was Lucretia's turn to flush. "Well, I'd like to try to have a son by you as well, if that's okay with you?"

Dr. Decker laughed. "Sure. The more the merrier. I'm just worried about our small gene pool, what with me being the only possible father. Still, I can't deny these women a chance to have their own children, or you, not with all you're giving up just to be here with us and help out."

She laughed. "Thank you, doctor, thank you." She paused and teased him, "This must be male heaven for you, what with two hundred absolutely stunning women and you being the only man for them."

Sam laughed. "You know, I was never much interested in being either married or a father before. My research was my life. Now I can't even tell myself apart from these women."

Lucretia laughed. "Not that's an understatement, doctor. If I didn't know you, I'd say you were just another of these fabulously beautiful women."

"They'd be even better if they had their arms and hands. I intend to invent such a cure."

Both smiled. Lucretia whispered, "Best of luck on that. I

wholly agree with you. I think this whole UFB woman thing is just a sadistic plot by the top CEOs."

That night as the two lay beside each other, Breanna said, "Sam, this is wonderful of you—sleeping with these other women. You, like us, have a very powerful sexual drive. Now that I'm pregnant, it isn't healthy for our child for us to keep on having sex. This way, my being pregnant isn't going to frustrate you."

"I know what you mean. This body's sex drive sometimes drives me nuts, as it does for all you women as well. I'll do my best to relieve you each night with my caresses. No sex until you say it is okay once more. Agreed?" She gave him a loving kiss.

***

A month later, forty-one of the other women were pregnant, including Lucretia, who was elated to discover she would be having a son. Likewise, Breanna was also having a boy. As expected, the ratio of boys to girls among the pregnant women was evenly divided. Many others also wanted children, but wisely decided to wait and see how this all worked out for the others. Secretly, many hoped it would work out, for they too wanted children of their own.

At this time, elections for city mayor were held. Dr. Decker refused to allow himself to be nominated or voted for, explaining he wanted to spend all his time trying to find cures for them. "Look, getting our arms and hands back takes priority over everything for me," he explained. Not too surprisingly, Carlin was elected to be their mayor, though she had Dr. Decker's promise that she could come to him for advice anytime she desired.

After the brief ceremony swearing her in, Mayor Carlin met in private with Dr. Decker. "Okay, now what do we do? I should explain. Fiona and I were trying our best to be something more than helpless sex dolls, as you know. I'm almost a pilot and she's almost a navigator. Not any call for either of these skills here, as I see it. But doctor, I think we or I speak for all of us who came here to Serendipity. We want to learn how to be independent women, to live real lives. You are giving us a chance by helping us have children, but that's only the start. We don't want to be dependent upon these robots forever. It's not wise. What if there is a power failure or the robots break down or there is some kind of emergency or something? We have to learn to be able to survive on our own. So where do we start? What should we focus on doing first?"

"Without arms? Lord, Carlin, I surely don't know. I'm trying to get started in my lab on finding a way to regrow arms, but I'm almost completely helpless to do any of it. These robots only carry out the simplest of commands. It's incredibly frustrating," he admitted for the first time.

"Well, Fiona and I have made some use of our feet and toes, but these fancy nylons interfere. True, the exotic polymers of the stockings don't tear or run and are mostly indestructible, but they also don't let us use our toes much. While these gowns are really sexy, and we look very good wearing them, they also hinder us," she explained.

"And these corsets are even worse," Dr. Decker added. "I wonder, has anyone tried to get by without wearing them?"

"Backaches doctor, really bad ones. I tried when I was younger. I think we are stuck with them."

"Well, the only other idea I have is something I've been considering for some days now. By accident or clever design, they put four of us in one home together. I think that if we four work together, kind of as one unit, we may be able to get something done, Carlin. That's the best idea I have. Lose the gown and nylons and try to work together with three others. Maybe the team can accomplish what one of us cannot do," Dr. Decker suggested.

"I like that. Builds teamwork and spirit. I'll so order it. But what should we focus on doing or learning how to do first, doctor?" Carlin asked.

Dr. Decker sat back in thought for a moment. "Well, we're dependent upon those automatic food dispensers for our food. If they run out or breakdown, we're going to starve. There's a small stream nearby, so if the water tower fails, we can get water from there. So it's food that is our Achilles heel right now."

"I agree. So you are saying we need to grow our own crops. What about meat and milk?" she asked.

Dr. Decker laughed. "One thing at a time. Let's see if we can possibly grow crops and make edible meals from what we grow."

"Great. But where are we going to get the seeds to plant in the first place?"

"You're forgetting Lucretia said there's a complete colonization container in storage. There's bound to be what we need in there."

"Thanks doc. You always are a step ahead of the rest of us." She leaned into him, her best attempt for a hug and left to announce her first project. To his amazement, every one of the women was behind Carlin's idea of learning to grow their own crops. Later that day, robots began delivering pants and blouses to every home.

"I guess I still look darn good even in pants," Breanna teased him the next morning. She'd ordered a robot to get her into the new pants and blouse combination, but to remove the nylons.

"Dear, you look good in anything or nothing," Sam commented wryly.

"Bet you say that to all the girls," she retorted playfully.

"Around here, that's quite true," he bantered back, lightly pressing his body into hers and giving her a kiss. "You know, I never knew what I was missing. I'm the luckiest man in the world to have married you, Breanna."

Later that evening, Carlin reported, "Well, at least when we fall down, we can more easily get back up. These pants make it a whole lot easier, just not very attractive."

***

Three months passed in Serendipity. Pregnancies were beginning to show as was their first crops of greens. While the plot was small, fresh vegetables were a welcome addition to their diet. Some of the women worked in the fields, while others began inventing ways and means of handling the cooking process. Over two hundred women put their hearts and souls into these projects, which were now seen as paying off. More elaborate survival projects hit the design stages.

Amid all this, Dr. Decker received a call to report to the comm center. There, he found Dansic was waiting to talk to him, about the last person he wanted to speak to. Still, Dr. Decker tossed his hair about until it was in front of him and sat down before the microphone and video camera.

"Ah Dr. Decker. I wanted to call you to relay the results of our cloning experiments. Yes, your growth womb works very well. The clones appear to be twenty-one and only after three months in the device. Marvelous contraption of yours. Over."

"Yes, well I lived up to my promises, unlike some man I know. Over," he retorted.

"The results. Yes, it was as you suggested. The bodies we made were precise duplicates of the original," Dansic explained.

Dr. Decker interrupted him, "But the personalities were totally different?"

"Well yes. It seems if the clone doesn't think about it and just does it, they retain some physical training, such as knowing how to fly a transport. The second that they stop and think about it, they get confused, complaining they've no idea how to fly. One super-soldier has declared himself to be a pacifist, if you can believe that."

Dr. Decker again interrupted him, "Told you so."

"But it isn't all doom and gloom, doctor. The clones are very easily re-taught their soldiering skills. So we're on our way to make an invincible army of clone super-soldiers. Just thought you would like to know that. Over."

"What about my promised cures? Over," Dr. Decker took one last stab at getting it, assuming a cure even existed.

"Well, I'm told that with all those GR robots, you have no need for arms and hands. Anyway, I have to go now. Over and out." The video screen filled with static and he stood up carefully and flipped the off the swtich.

"What did Dansic want?" asked a curious Breanna when he returned to the lab.

"To tell me what I already knew about the clones and to gloat over his continued betrayal. He's still not going to give me our promised cures, Breanna, so it is up to us to find it, if we ever can. Working with these stupid robots is making this process a billion times harder than it should be."

That was the last official word Serendipity ever had from their home world of Danforth-C, though they followed the local news there for many months. It was as though everyone back home more or less forgot about them, a fact not lost on any of the over two hundred UFB women. However, based upon the news that they did hear, Dr. Decker was able to make a reasonable guess about what happened to Danforth-C.

GD created thousands of their super-soldier clones, retraining and arming them. Not to be out-done, GR and other corporations followed suit and within a year, a devastating civil war broke out. Dr. Decker's best guess was that since GD was losing the war, they launched nuclear attacks and the others countered, turning the heart of the mid-arm corporations' control planet into a radioactive slag heap. Probably the killing blows were delivered by their various battleships, which subsequently went on to destroy each other. In the end, a profound silence fell. The comm center on Serendipity went silent. They were unable to raise anyone anywhere after that point in time.

Once again, Dr. Decker's fantastic luck held. He, the two hundred sixty-two UFB women, and one normal woman survived. When the shock of the news of the self-destruction of Danforth-C finally wore off, Mayor Carlin Cody held another community meeting, though several women sat in the rear watching over the forty-two infants who had been born without any medical problems, an equal number of boys and girls, though much to everyone's great surprise, Lucretia's son, Hermes, had arms.

"Well, as everyone knows, our world of Danforth-C is no more. Thanks to Dr. Decker, we few have survived the holocaust. Following his advice and with his foresight, we are managing to survive on our own. We are able to raise good crops and prepare them without the assistance of the robots. How long will these robots continue to function no one can honestly say. Thus, it is imperative we continue to learn to take care of our own needs, as independent of these machines as much as possible. Think over your needs and come up with bright ideas of how we can proceed. Tomorrow, we will meet again, and I hope each of you will have something to contribute."

Carlin continued, "As of this year, our population has grown by forty-two boys and girls, almost a sixteen percent growth. We must look to the future. If we are to survive, we must continue to add to our numbers. I hate to ask this of our doctor, but all of us who are of childbearing age must have more children as soon as possible. He is now working on a way for us women to breed each other. If he's successful, then we really can have a future for ourselves and our children. If we continue to work together, we can and we must survive."

Her last pronouncement brought a round of cheering, primarily by her verification of the rumor circulating Serendipity that Dr. Decker was working on a way for two women to be able to impregnate each other. Many women had formed close bonds with each other and greatly desired such an ability. Those more in the know, such as Nurse Lucretia, also realized their gene pool was incredibly shallow. With only one man among them, genetically speaking the future didn't look very bright or hopeful, a fact pointed out by Breanna and her math results. However, if he could somehow be successful by using the women-women combinations, they just might truly have a future, gene-wise that is.

Lucretia thought, *There are now two of us with arms and hands. If I can only have more sons.* She also allowed her own flaming red hair to grow as long as it could. In this way, she felt more like the others and not so entirely different. Lucretia did have one last resort available to her. There was a single fully fueled deep space transport parked in their spaceport. While it would only carry twenty, if she had no other choice, she could attempt to fly it to some other world and try to bring back some able-bodied men. She was very reluctant to do that, since the women here would likely find themselves at the mercy of the men. She'd seen enough of that on Danforth-C. Dr. Decker also knew this and had agreed with her conclusion: to use the transport as a very last resort.

Thus, Dr. Decker's main research thrust for his first two years was finding a safe way to extract two viable eggs from ovulating women, join them together, and implant the resulting fertilized egg back into one of the women. While it took him a frustrating two years, he was finally successful. Carlin and Breanna became the first two women to bear each other's child, both girls of course.

After that, Dr. Decker was swamped with breeding requests and was more than happy to work flat out on the project. Having his own private harem of some two hundred sixty-two women greatly exceeded even his genetically enhanced sex drive, although he continued to need *relief* at least four times a day.

As expected, their babies inherited the genetic traits of their parents. Each would become a "super model" in their own right when they reached adulthood. Lucretia's daughters were UFB women as well, but her sons were quite brilliant, had arms, and were rather handsome men, again as Dr. Decker anticipated.

By the third year, Dr. Decker was finally able to devote much of his research time to finding cures. His breakthrough came when comparing DNA sequences of himself, Breanna, Lucretia, and his son by Lucretia, Hermes. With Breanna's aid, he was able to isolate the genetic changes that ordered their bodies to discard their arms. Emboldened, he worked out a genetic splicing sequence to add them back into their DNA. That took a hundred times longer than it ordinarily would have if he'd only had his hands available.

When it was time to test the genetic modification, he listened to Lucretia and Breanna. Both were adamant that he not use it on himself, but rather on Breanna first. If something went wrong, they couldn't afford to lose their only breeding male. Thus, Breanna became his first test subject and the first of them to have arms regrown.

She was in a coma for four days, while her body responded to the genetic engineering. However, by the second day, everyone in Serendipity dropped by to see for themselves. New arms and hands were already developing, as was sweeping hope for over two hundred others. She awoke to the new experience of learning how to use her arms and hands.

It took Dr. Decker another year to get everyone and their babies handled, but almost a year later, everyone had arms and hands. The morale of Serendipity skyrocketed, as did their will to survive, flourishing as never before. In subsequent years, Dr. Decker managed to get breast sizes reduced by half. While they were still huge, at least they no longer had to wear the restrictive corsets to help their backs support the weight of the overly large bosoms.

That task accomplished, he worked on their feet. Like many others before him, although unknown to him, he was only partially able to reconstruct the genetic blueprint for normal feet. Still, everyone was thankful for the partial repair of their feet, which made getting around far less precarious. Although he continued his research in later years, he was unsuccessful in developing further cures. His attention shifted over to providing top quality medical services for the rapidly growing town.

He and Breanna learned to write records using their toes. They kept accurate records, particularly birthing records and the physical shape of the newborns. Ten years from the colonization of Serendipity, Breanna and Dr. Decker were able to show conclusively that the new children continued to carry forth the special physical traits of the UFB women, as modified by Dr. Decker. At this point, everyone relaxed, knowing that their children would continue to be like themselves, physically. Perhaps it was vanity in these women, perhaps not. Still, Dr. Decker continued to observe none of the UFB women or himself seemed to age. At sixty, he still looked like a ravishing woman of twenty-five. At seventy-five, he finally detected some traces of aging in his physical appearance, though his bones ached. He documented this phenomenon, but had no explanation for its cause. Similarly, he had no explanation for why clones did not have the same personality and knowledge of their host, but of this he didn't care in the slightest. He had found true happiness with Breanna and his many children, something that had been entirely lacking in his first forty-five years of life.

Lucretia's three sons, Hermes, Aries, and Theos, were quite brilliant. Though Dr. Decker had no real way to test their IQs, as children, they were observably brighter than the other children. Thus, Dr. Decker placed great hopes that their combined intellects would one day help raise the living standards of all Serendipity.

However, unknown to Dr. Sam Decker, his cloning experiments and inventions had spread from Danforth-C before that world died. He could never have predicted the outcome and fallout from that. Had he known, he may well not have shared any of his research and results with Dansic or anyone else.

The End.

# A Favor to Other Readers

How about helping other readers? Many readers rely on reviews to make the decision whether to buy a book. You can help them make their decision by leaving your opinions and viewpoint in a short review of the positive things of this book. Writing the review and expressing your opinion only takes a few minutes, and other readers will appreciate your efforts.

Click this link: Slow Comes the Dark Volume 2 Serendipity
            http://www.amazon.com/dp/B00NRD8R5W
scroll down to Customer Reviews; click on Write a Review, and enter your review. Thank you.

# Author Information

## Visit My Amazon.com Author Page
Vic Broquard Author Page
http://amazon.com/author/vic-broquard

## Follow My Blog:
http://www.broquard-ebooks.com/blog/

## Follow Me on Social Media
Facebook
http://www.facebook.com/vic.broquard/

Google+
http://plus.google.com/102242823668960002176/

LinkedIn
http://www.linkedin.com/profile/view?id=297732151

YouTube
http://www.youtube.com/channel/UCQWcs-
WAX2YqViIiafUqJuw

# Other Books by Vic Broquard

Without Warning (fantasy)

The Trident Series: (fantasy)
    Volume 1 The Trident and the Book
    Volume 2 The Trident and the Scepter
    Volume 3 The Trident and the Resurrection

The Adventures of Elizabeth Stanton Series: (science fiction)
    Volume 1 The Evolution of the Path
    Volume 2 The Great Messiah
    Volume 3 Of Kings and Queens and Troubadours
    Volume 4 Chaos in the Aftermath
    Volume 5 Power Plays
    Volume 6 Age of Exploration
    Volume 7 Abducted
    Volume 8 The Emperor and Empress
    Volume 9 A Job Worth Doing
    Volume 10 Degradation
    Volume 11 The Second Crusade
    Volume 12 When Worlds Collide
    Volume 13 Dark Ages

The Lindsey Barron Series: (fantasy)
    Volume 1 The Rod of the Apocalypse
    Volume 2 The Board of Governors
    Volume 3 The Crown of Moses
    Volume 4 Dominus for President
    Volume 5 The National Health Care Program
    Volume 6 States Justice
    Volume 7 Cross and Double-cross

Zoran Chronicles Series: (fantasy)
    Volume 1 A Dragon in Our Town
    Volume 2 Dragons, Power, Courts, and War

Planet of the Orange-red Sun Series: (science fiction)
    Volume 1 When Kingdoms Fall

The Return of the Wizards: Twelve Companions – The Making of Wizards (fantasy)

**Slow Comes the Dark Series: (science fiction)**

www.ingramcontent.com/pod-product-compliance
Lightning Source LLC
Chambersburg PA
CBHW070903260626
47162CB00007B/2544